Praise for the novels of Diane Whiteside

"A very interesting story related in prose so steamy that it fogs one's reading glasses." —*Booklist*

"*The Irish Devil*'s erotically thrilling and suspenseful story line keeps the reader riveted to the book. Diane Whiteside has created fascinating characters that turn an ordinary story into a work of sensual art . . . I highly recommend *The Irish Devil*, but be advised . . . it's a scorcher." —*The Road to Romance*

" A warm, exciting, passionate story." —*In the Library Reviews*

"A devilishly erotic story set in the Old West, full of vivid imagery that sets your heart aflutter . . . a hero who will melt your heart and make your blood pressure rise all at the same time." —*Affaire de Coeur*

"Hot and gritty, seething with passion and the aura of the Wild West, Whiteside's debut presents readers with a solid western as well as a highly erotic romance, and the combination is sizzling. Erotic romance fans have a tale to savor and an author to watch. SPICY." —*Romantic Times*

"A beautifully researched novel with believable characters who will linger in the memory long after you close the book . . . If you like your love scenes tender and a tad kinky, you'll love this book . . . This is a keeper." —*Sensual Romance Reviews*

"A very sensual, romantic love story. It is very well written and leads you on a journey of sexual exploration sure to leave you tingling . . . Snatch this one off the shelf, it is a definite keeper." —*The Romance Reader's Connection*

BOND of BLOOD

DIANE WHITESIDE

BERKLEY SENSATION, NEW YORK

THE BERKLEY PUBLISHING GROUP
Published by the Penguin Group
Penguin Group (USA) Inc.
375 Hudson Street, New York, New York 10014, USA
Penguin Group (Canada), 90 Eglinton Avenue East, Suite 700, Toronto, Ontario M4P 2Y3, Canada
(a division of Pearson Penguin Canada Inc.)
Penguin Books Ltd., 80 Strand, London WC2R 0RL, England
Penguin Group Ireland, 25 St. Stephen's Green, Dublin 2, Ireland (a division of Penguin Books Ltd.)
Penguin Group (Australia), 250 Camberwell Road, Camberwell, Victoria 3124, Australia
(a division of Pearson Australia Group Pty. Ltd.)
Penguin Books India Pvt. Ltd., 11 Community Centre, Panchsheel Park, New Delhi—110 017, India
Penguin Group (NZ), Cnr. Airborne and Rosedale Roads, Albany, Auckland 1310, New Zealand
(a division of Pearson New Zealand Ltd.)
Penguin Books (South Africa) (Pty.) Ltd., 24 Sturdee Avenue, Rosebank, Johannesburg 2196, South Africa

Penguin Books Ltd., Registered Offices: 80 Strand, London WC2R 0RL, England

This is a work of fiction. Names, characters, places, and incidents either are the product of the author's imagination or are used fictitiously, and any resemblance to actual persons, living or dead, business establishments, events, or locales is entirely coincidental. The publisher does not have any control over and does not assume any responsibility for author or third-party websites or their content.

First edition: October 2006

Library of Congress Cataloging-in-Publication Data

Whiteside, Diane.
    Bond of blood / Diane Whiteside. — 1st ed.
        p. cm.
    ISBN 0-425-20774-9 (trade pbk.)
    1. Vampires—Fiction. 2. Texas—Fiction. I. Title.

PS3623.H5848B66 2006
813'.6—dc22

                                                                                    2006020602

PRINTED IN THE UNITED STATES OF AMERICA

10 9 8 7 6 5 4 3 2 1

To Daio, who helped make *vampiro* science solid

PROLOGUE

Cinco.

Five orgasms for her but Rodrigo still hadn't climaxed. Blanche forced herself to count in Castilian, not her native French, the difficulty just enough to keep her mind on this moment. She had to remember every minute. It could be her last night with her beloved husband.

Rodrigo growled softly. Anticipation stirred again, deep within her, at the sound. He tossed his head back, biting his lip until the blood flowed.

Nom de Dieu, she wanted him to enjoy this last night as much as she did, not calculate every move. Carefulness be damned, she wanted her passionate, young caballero, the finest knight at the king's court. She pushed back her delicious lassitude, fighting to concentrate on him. "Rodrigo, mon amour, fill me. Ride me hard, leave us both sweating and sated. Now, s'il vous plaît!"

"Easy, mi corazón," he muttered. "We have time for you to soften and take me fully into you." He knelt above her, braced on his strong arms, breathing harshly as he brought his hunger under control.

She stroked his shoulders, pleasuring herself with his heat. He dwarfed her—and he held her heart, as her first husband never had. When his breathing was steadier, he lightly caressed her rounded belly and smiled, his white teeth gleaming in a stray beam of moonlight. "Mi amor, tienes mi alma en tus manos."

Blanche's heart turned over. How could she carry his soul in her hands? She tried to find words but Rodrigo spoke again.

"You and our children, you are my life. If anything should happen to you—"

"Relax, mon amour," she murmured and tenderly pushed a lock off his forehead. "Our little angel is well. You know how he likes to sleep through our lovemaking."

"Daughter," Rodrigo retorted with a kiss on her forehead. "Only a niña would be lulled to sleep by lovemaking, after a storm of kicking at any other time. Sweet-tempered in the bedroom, like her madre."

Blanche snorted at his compliment, glad she'd distracted him from too much thinking about the future. Rodrigo frequently prayed for an easy pregnancy, like her first, which had yielded the twins. And she knew perfectly well that he hoped for a daughter with blue eyes, like hers. But all of that was God's doing, not a man's wish. Just as whether or not he'd come home alive from fighting the Saracen invaders was God's will, not a woman's prayer.

His callused finger swirled through her creamy folds, triggering a groan and wriggle from her. She moaned and happily accepted a little more of his cock. It always took so much coaxing and love play for her petite body to welcome his shaft. Her adoring husband was so very careful of her comfort and pleasure. Five years younger than she was, he treated her like a precious gem.

He stroked her again and cream rushed to embrace his cock, as she trembled. Her channel rippled and her hips rolled involuntarily, remembering the delight he always brought. He circled her pearl cautiously, first at a distance then closer, like a scout surveying a castle. "Ah, mais oui, exactement, mon amour," she sighed.

He fondled her gently and she arched, moaning his name.

He rubbed very lightly. She rocked against him, the mindless rhythm of love and lust burning away thought. She was so sensitive now that even a little touch could send her over the brink. And then he touched her favorite spot.

Seis!

Blanche shrieked her satisfaction, barely remembering to continue counting in Castilian. Waves pounded through her and seized his cock like a conquering army. Tightened and released, tightened and . . .

His loins jerked, fighting her body's demand that he finish. His finger pressed down on her pearl again and she sobbed. The pulses began to build once more and leaped into him through their intimate connection. Her body pushed up against him insistently and her cavern tightened like a glove.

His hips thrust, settling his cock into that secret place deep inside her. His control snapped. He pounded into her again and again, growling like a wild beast. He stiffened as pleasure launched him into flight.

"Rodrigo!" she screamed as the deepest climax of all raced through her.

Siete!

He roared his satisfaction as he poured his essence into her womb. He collapsed afterward, barely able to roll onto his side and hold her close. His body softened.

Bien, now he'd at least have some sleep before he went off to fight.

Dark as it was in their small bedchamber, she could only catch occasional glimpses of him. But she could feel him and she could smell him. Traces of horses, certainement. Leather and the oil used to keep his armor rust-free and moving smoothly. Another oil, the one used to clean and protect his sword, a beautiful Toledo steel blade the king had given Rodrigo, in gratitude for his loyal service during the civil war. Under that—and the musk of his hunger—was a faint whiff of sandalwood, an exotic spice from the East that his Moorish cousins had given him. All the scents spoke to her of beautiful man, superb lover, and devoted husband.

Blanche smiled, eyelids heavy, content at having finally eased him.

Her sated husband was warm against her, a strong bulwark against enemies. His arms tightened possessively around her as he snored, just a little. She whispered her love to him softly, as she slipped into sleep.

"Para siempre, te llevo en mi alma." *I will carry you in my soul forever.*

A door slammed. Someone, wearing very heavy boots, staggered across the floor and fell onto the bed next door, sending it slamming into the wall.

Grania woke with a start, instinctively reaching for her absent gun. A snore came through the thin walls, then another, and another.

She relaxed slowly, as she remembered where she was. A cheap motel, deep in the Texas Hill Country outside Austin. Not Colombia, where she'd spent last summer studying owls—and keeping her weapons close at hand for protection against rebels and thugs. She was here to interview for a job at the Texas Hill Country Raptor Center, where she could be both scientist and veterinarian.

The ancient clock radio flickered and announced the time, two a.m. She flopped onto her back and stared at the water-stained ceiling.

A dream of Rodrigo—she'd been doing that all her life. But a sexual fantasy, especially one so incredibly detailed? Now that was a first. Probably because she was so nervous about getting this job.

Soothed by the explanation, Grania stretched, then settled herself again, wrapping her arms around the pillow.

And another dream claimed her, like a hammer blow between the eyes.

Blanche sat beside her Princesse, *the French king's daughter who'd come south to marry the Castilian heir, and tried to keep watch over the* Princesse's *two young sons, the* Infantes de la Cerda. *Her baby gave a last thunderous kick to her ribs, then settled down as if respecting the solemn occasion. Her own son and daughter were safe at the palace, where their high spirits and quest to master the art of walking wouldn't cause a disturbance.*

Toledo's great cathedral was filled to overflowing with the host of knights and men-at-arms. The Lion and Castle blazed on surcoat after surcoat, emblem of the kingdom who'd fight first and strongest against the Moroccan invaders. A few women had crowded in as well—the Princesse and her ladies foremost. But this ceremony was for the men, the fighters who'd save them all. Time for strengthening their hearts and souls, and stiffening the spines of their loved ones who must helplessly wait and pray.

The great military orders were also present, but in smaller numbers. The gray mantles of Calatrava, the white habits of Alcántara, and the red cross—the espada *with its long downstroke, like a sword blow to the heart—of Santiago, the largest and most ferocious order. Rodrigo was honored to be one of them, a novice in the only knightly order with the amazing wisdom and flexibility to accept married men.*

But, as a novice, he was not obliged to pray with them today. Instead, he knelt beside Infante Don Fernando de la Cerda, *the Castilian heir and governor of the realm in the King's absence, whose confidant he was—and whom he easily outshone in his wife's eyes.*

In Rodrigo, the height and strength of his father's Celtic and Visigoth ancestors blended perfectly with the warm skin and raven hair of his mother's Moorish blood. If she could see his eyes more clearly, she knew they'd be the darkest brown—almost black when angry, but softening to a warm glow when playing with children. He had a hawk's beak of a nose, a little crooked from some boyhood fight with one of his brothers. There were scars on his torso, of course, as befitted a gallant knight, but none on his face. Head and shoulders taller than most men at the Castilian court, he was as passionate about singing and playing the lute as he was about swordplay and horses—as his heavy muscles could attest.

Rodrigo would go to war with the mesnaderos, *the royal household guard, together with his best friend, Fearghus of Inverness,*

who'd come from Scotland to fight infidels. And eighteen-year-old
Diego Sanchez, Rodrigo's escudero.

Blanche gritted her teeth. She'd never trusted Diego, despite his
being an orphan the king had commended to Rodrigo's service. Diego
was too aware of his pretty face and too willing to give the easy answer to any difficult question. More than once, she'd caught a look of
sheer, blazing hatred in his eyes, when he stared after his master.

She'd warned Rodrigo, of course. But he'd shrugged her caution
off, reminding her of his sworn duty to obey the king and honor his
oath to train Diego. She had never convinced him his escudero was
dangerous.

Chanting in Latin, the archbishop lifted the cross to bless the as-
sembled warriors. A shaft of light set the great golden cross ablaze
until it seemed to belong to a different realm. Crossing herself re-
flexively, Blanche's gaze slipped back to Rodrigo, standing head and
shoulders above the crowd of armed men. His face was transfigured,
rapt, as he stared at the symbol of his faith. His lips moved, silently
from this distance, as he gave himself up to the service of God and
King. He seemed in no way to be a creature of this earth.

A shudder seized her. Mon dieu, what if he was injured? Or captured? No, if that happened, his Moorish cousins would see that he
was ransomed. Surely she'd know if he was wounded; after all, she'd
sensed it when he broke his arm. But what if he never returned?

The royal lion on Rodrigo's chest shifted in the golden light, its
paws reaching for his heart.

The Princesse hissed something terrified and clutched her two
young sons close. But, for once, Rodrigo's wife paid her longtime pa-
troness no heed. Instead, she bent her head and began to pray desperately to San Rafael Arcángel, patron saint of healers and travelers.

ONE

Rafael Perez accelerated down the last icy hill, whipped the wheel around, braked hard, and cut the engine with a flourish. The armored Toyota Land Cruiser skidded through a one-eighty into a stop precisely where he'd planned, throwing up a fine cloud of powdery snow over the boardwalk.

Moonlight reflected from clouds and snow-covered mountains, making the former ghost town bright as day to his *vampiro* eyes. FALLEN ANGEL screamed the red light on the saloon's false front, while a neon bronc rider endlessly strove to outlast his twisting steed. Storefronts urged expensive diversions, from the latest high-tech snowboards to jewelry and electronics. One displayed extravagant lingerie on realistic mannequins, including a long, frothy concoction of silk and lace, trimmed with sable, and complete with matching sable slippers. His wife would have loved it.

Rafael's face hardened at the reminder of a loss never quite forgotten, despite the passing of seven hundred years. Turning away, he scanned his surroundings for watchers. The streets were empty, except for the sole traffic light blinking yellow in the distance.

After all, when a predator like Rafael visited another one, he expected to risk an ambush. Which was why he'd brought his best weapons: two of his oldest—and therefore strongest—*hijos*, the *vampiros* he'd sired.

Ethan Templeton cast one last, long look around the otherwise darkened buildings, then set the safety on his rifle. "No snipers so far."

"You astound me with your suspicions, *mi hijo*," Rafael observed sarcastically, as he unbuckled his seat belt. "Jennings promised to return my hospitality back in 1859, should he ever gain an *esfera* of his own. We have been invited for a night of good whisky and skiing. Have you no trust in his goodwill?"

"No," Ethan said simply, unlocking his door. "Better men than he have hungered for Texas."

"Which is why you're here and Gray Wolf is back there," Jean-Marie, Rafael's best spy and eldest *hijo*, retorted from the backseat, above the unmistakable click of semiautomatics being double-checked. "So you can go into danger, while the heir stays safe."

Rafael's mouth curved as he opened his door. Ethan was so good at looking for trouble, even when the chances were slim.

Poorly set ambush, Ethan commented mind to mind when they all stood on the boardwalk. *Not a* prosaico *in sight, when it's midnight in a top Colorado resort?*

Rafael snorted silently. *It's midnight on a Sunday, Ethan, with a blizzard coming in. There shouldn't be any* prosaicos *around. It had better be peaceful here, with or without an ambush.*

After all, assassinations were the usual method for a *vampiro* to take over an *esfera* and become a *patrón*. Just like Chicago mobsters during the 1920s, *vampiros* fought bitterly for every scrap of advantage, resulting in a rapid turnover of *patróns* and *esferas* whose boundaries were fluid, to say the least. The average *patrón* only survived for thirty years or so before being killed by a younger, smarter, or faster challenger.

But Rafael had received Texas and Oklahoma from a Spanish king and held them ever since—despite frequent attacks from greedy *vampiros*, many of which had once called themselves his friend.

The best attacks involved *prosaicos*, ordinary mortals who'd never drunk vampiro blood or tasted it so seldom that their everyday lives hadn't been affected. In other words, their scent hadn't been changed by frequent contact with *vampiro* blood. Since the vast majority of mortals had no idea that *vampiros* really existed, it was very easy for those allied with *vampiros* to hide among their *prosaico* brethren— becoming invisible to keen *vampiro* senses. Given the opportunity, a hidden *prosaico* would make the perfect assassin. A paranoid *patrón* therefore allowed no strange *prosaicos* near him.

But this was Jennings's town in Jennings's *esfera* of Colorado. It could easily be full of watchers, especially *prosaicos*—who could be assassins, if Jennings had ambitions to take over part or all of Texas. As a guest, Rafael would be well within his rights to refuse to leave his armored SUV if he saw any *prosaicos*, or even kill them if he felt particularly threatened and *prosaico* law enforcement members weren't around.

But none of that applied in this case, since there were no *prosaicos* and no silent watchers on the rooftops. There might be an ambush waiting inside but that would be dealt with in its own time.

Jennings has been running Colorado with a heavy hand. Tortured or killed most of the old vampiros, *then replaced them with his own* hijos, Ethan pointed out, settling his black parka over the extra ammunition at the back of his waist.

Jean-Marie's shrug was as blatant as his parka's blue and silver. *All new* patrones *do that. He's only held Denver for twenty years, so it's still recent history.*

Verdaderamente, Rafael agreed. *Relax a little, Ethan—Luis is just behind us with a dozen* vampiros. He waited for Ethan to push the saloon's doors open.

The Fallen Angel's interior was an almost perfect recreation of an 1880s Rocky Mountain saloon. Carved wood, etched crystal, flocked red wallpaper, and sawdust-covered floors greeted Rafael's appreciative eyes. An ornate bar covered one wall, while a staircase led to a balcony that swept around the other three sides. The lighting was soft and intimate, mimicking the effect of old-fashioned oil lamps and chandeliers. A stage let beautiful women strut their charms, while small tables invited men to join games of chance. Upholstered booths recessed into the wall invited more intimate encounters.

Poker players, all *vampiros*, occupied most tables, with pretty girls leaning over their shoulders or sitting on their knees. A pair of bartenders polished glasses, one of them chatting with the cowboys drinking there. A jazz trio played ragtime variations on cowboy standards, providing a comfortable backdrop.

The temperature inside was closer to September than January, with the occupants dressed accordingly. The men wore long-sleeved shirts and jeans, not sweaters and turtlenecks, while the women's dresses left very little to the imagination.

The three Texans crossed to the bar and leaned against it, taking in the scene.

Sure would've appreciated fine clothing like that, first time I rode into Abilene in '66, Ethan drawled, eyeing the closest poker player. *Especially these ladies' silks. They're* prosaicas, *of course, not* vampiras. *But they're still lovely.*

The half-dozen females he gave El Abrazo *to didn't even see their first dawn,* Jean-Marie remarked. *Bad record, but I've heard of worse. Gorshkov actually managed to keep two alive for several days by—*

Just because one patrón *torments females with* El Abrazo *doesn't mean that gentlemen need discuss it,* Rafael cut in, baring his fangs slightly.

His *hijos* wisely fell silent as he turned to the closest bartender. "Glass of rye, please. Pikesville Rye, if you have it. And for you, gentlemen?"

A few minutes later, civilized behavior was restored with the arrival of excellent whiskies. Ethan drank his Jim Beam Black bourbon with evident satisfaction, his hazel eyes lazily scanning the room.

Rafael, who'd finished his own survey minutes earlier, drank rye, pleased to find this much civilization in Jennings's domain. Jean-Marie hummed an old tune as he sniffed his Glendronach scotch, a song he'd once whistled before garroting French sentries during the Peninsular War.

Jennings strolled through a side door a moment later, a stocky man, tough and level-eyed, who'd sailed with Drake. Three beautiful young women accompanied him, who smiled curiously at the Texans.

"Don Rafael! What a pleasure to finally welcome you to my *esfera*."

Rafael embraced him. "Jennings, amigo! You remember Jean-Marie, of course. And this is Ethan Templeton, my *alferez mayor*."

The two nodded to each other. Rafael smiled to himself, to see them so apparently friendly on the outside, but measuring each other so thoroughly.

"Gentlemen, may I introduce you to my friends, Amber Townsend, Serena McAlpin, and Anya Martinez?"

"*Estoy encantada, señoritas.*" Genuinely delighted, Rafael bowed. All three women were extremely attractive to his *vampiro* senses, glowing with sensuality and emotion eager to be brought to a carnal boil—and tapped. They were also healthy and athletic, well capable of multiple orgasms to feed him and his *hijos* many times.

Behind them, other unattached women gathered to watch hopefully, their eyes caressing the three Texans' bodies. Ah *sí*, truly Jennings had prepared a garden of delights to accompany the promised fine skiing and whisky.

Jennings rumbled wordless approval. "Would you care to sit down for a few minutes, Don Rafael? Share some whisky with the ladies? After all, you and I don't need to try the slopes at night."

Rafael smiled down into Amber's glowing brown eyes. "Yes, indeed I would enjoy that." And just where will I take the very first nibble on that long neck of yours, *querida*?

They settled into one of the upholstered booths, Jennings bringing both Serena and Anya. Ethan and Jean-Marie took a table close by, where Ethan would have a clear line of fire if necessary. More of Jennings's lovelies joined them there, to be readily appreciated by the younger Texans.

"What do you do back in Denver?" Rafael's keen *vampiro* senses heard Ethan croon to the blonde cuddled against him.

"I'm a kindergarten teacher." She smiled back up at him, batting her long eyelashes innocently. Rafael shook his head and turned his attention back to Jennings. Ethan might enjoy himself now but he'd be bored within hours.

Amber snuggled closer to Rafael. "Where do you come from in Texas? I've been to Dallas."

"Outside Austin, on a ranch in the Hill Country."

"A genuine cowboy?" Her eyes were huge.

He grinned, thinking of just how long he'd been a *vaquero*. "Yes, ma'am."

Her hand began to stroke his knee tentatively. "Wow. That's not much like Connecticut, where I was born."

Jennings smiled from the other side of the table, very well pleased. *Too* well pleased by a minor flirtation.

Rafael's senses came alert. Surely Jennings wouldn't be stupid enough to try anything, especially with so many *prosaicas* around? Even if the room was full of his *mesnaderos*?

A shot rang out. The bullet creased Ethan's head, drawing blood.

Time slowed to a crawl.

The gun sounded like an AK-47—single shot or full automatic?

Rafael's eyes snapped back to Jennings. Knowledge lay there— that Jennings's man had fired as planned, but earlier than expected. Then Jennings shrugged and reached for his gun, mouth curving as he anticipated success.

Ambush. The saloon's air was about to fill with lead.

Rage heated Rafael's blood. The fools knew they'd kill every female in the room, yet they'd started this anyway.

Rafael pulled Amber's head onto his lap, palmed his Beretta, and blew a hole in Jennings's head. If he died here, he'd at least do so while saving the women.

He shoved her down his legs and yanked the girl next to Amber onto the floor as well. Jennings's body started to dissolve into dust, as Rafael managed to pull the third girl under the table. A long minute later, they began to wail.

He lunged out of the booth, a Beretta in each hand, killing any of

Jennings's *vampiros* that survived Ethan and Jean-Marie. The room was full of flying lead and women's howls.

The fight was over in less than two minutes, leaving behind dust as *vampiros'* bodies and blood quickly disappeared. The women remained, sobbing hysterically.

Rafael holstered his guns. *How's your head, Ethan?*

Already healing, sir. The prosaicas *are all alive, although a few will need some stitches.*

Good fight, Jean-Marie commented. *Plus, thanks to it, we'll have more friends in Colorado now and other places.*

They'd have been more dangerous if we were facing Madame Celeste and Devol, her enforcer. Now that'd be a real fight, against a worthy opponent, Ethan commented, as he hunted for first-aid supplies. *We'd have to use all our men, close the borders . . .*

Or that Russian assassin, Jean-Marie agreed, heading for an unconscious *prosaica. He's a devil to be truly feared. Only Don Rafael can smell him, since they're both* vampiros mayores.

Rafael froze briefly as he bent to the terrified girls, still cowering under the table. *Madame Celeste would never leave New Orleans to visit Texas, the home of "cows and snakes." As for that Russian assassin, he's not even on this continent, so why worry about him either?*

There'd been no word of Diego since Communism fell. After two centuries of torture at his hands, Rafael knew that *pendejo* too well to think a *prosaico* mob could destroy him. But if he ever showed his face in Texas, revenge would be very sweet.

Grania O'Malley swirled the last of the no-name, nonalcoholic beer in her glass. It was as weak as Tiffani's arguments, here at the graduation party. Her advisor's customary bash was a roaring success, as could be expected given the quantity of food and drinks produced by his wife's cooking class. Families bragged loud and long to anyone who'd listen about their member's astounding accomplishments. Students and alumni chattered and argued anything from UC Davis campus politics to the best way to count those elusive ferruginous pygmy owls in Arizona. This was UC Davis's liveliest graduation party, where conversation and music blared from almost every corner.

"Okay, Dr. O'Malley. I'll be going now and you can fix my grades with the registrar." Tiffani, who reeked of perfume and other chemicals, started to turn.

Grania fixed her best glare on the blond freshman. The slender girl froze.

"Final grades for the quarter, and the school year, were due this afternoon at two. Why should I change yours?"

Enormous brown eyes stared at her over a martini glass. "Because I need you to, that's why. Because Toby O'Brien got an A from you. Because . . ."

"Toby attended *all* the classes and completed *all* the homework *and* the labwork," Grania pointed out.

"But I took all the tests!"

Grania raised an eyebrow. "Is that how you got through high school?"

"Of course. I had all the requirements covered and still had time for parties."

What had her high school really been trying to teach her? Social passing, where a student shows up for class and gets a good grade, whether or not he learned anything? Heck, by those standards, Tiffani was quite accomplished. She at least tested well.

Grania's jaw set. But it wasn't good enough to work with her owls. "Here at the university, you've got to do a lot more than just the minimum in order to earn top grades."

The chit had the honesty to blush slightly before she charged on stubbornly. "So? I need an A to make up for my other grades, so I can come back next year. I want to be a wildlife vet, just like you. It's why I signed up for your section."

Heaven protect me from idiots. "But a good grade in one class won't help you with all the selection boards you'll face in the future. You need to work hard and long."

She lowered her martini, staring. "What do you mean?"

Give her a chance. She does have occasional flashes of brilliance.

If she'd just string them together into a consistent string, she could be something special. "You missed four labs and five take-home quizzes. If you give me some of those by tomorrow . . ."

"Tomorrow? Tomorrow?!" Total horror was written on her face. "I can't do that! There's Brad's party and Andy's. Then we're all driving down to San Francisco afterward. I can't possibly be back here before Sunday night. No way I'm doing more work on a Saturday, especially when school's out."

"In that case, I really don't see how I can change your grade."

"You're supposed to just give it to me for attending the lectures! Isn't that how you made it through?"

"No, sister, it isn't."

Tiffani shook her head, unwilling comprehension starting to dawn.

Grania began to hammer some lessons home. "Try hard work and paying attention to your advisors. No social life either, and no plagiarizing."

"No *parties*?"

"The odds are fifty to one—hell, a hundred to one against getting a good job as a wildlife vet. You still want that job?"

Tiffani nodded silently. Tears glistened but she blinked them back fiercely.

"Then start working your ass off for it right now, like I have. And watch your back. Because you won't see the knives coming until they're sticking out of you."

"Knives? Ohmygawd, you're not kidding. Maybe not literally true but not a joke either." She swallowed hard and offered her hand solemnly. "Dr. O'Malley, I'll work on those lab write-ups tonight."

"Good." They shook hands silently.

Tiffani stumbled off toward the gate, shaking her head and mumbling, "Knives?"

Grania shook her head, hoping the child pulled it together, and turned for the bar. Her sudden movement made the ornate gold cross fleury slip free from behind her dress. It swung wildly on its heavy gold chain, an echo of a barbaric past that suited her medieval velvet robes. Its style seemed extremely familiar to her, although it had been made in Texas, just before she bought it.

She started to tuck it back against her skin then smiled. She could afford a little time to dream about dating somebody in Texas.

Grania ran her fingers over the heavy metal curves as an expert tracker would. She slowed her breathing, until the party faded and only the jewelry was real against a haze of light.

Three months after his trip to Colorado, Rafael wished he'd never challenged fate by saying Madame Celeste wouldn't visit Texas. Now he found himself dressed in his finest garb, meeting Ethan and Jean-Marie outside the great hall at Compostela Ranch, his home. He'd originally built it as an indoor riding arena, then converted it later to an exercise yard where the *cachorros*, the immature *vampiros*, could master their *vampiro* strength and speed. The massive limestone walls also made an excellent backdrop for the scented vines and plants of his herb garden.

Tonight, he was wearing a Charro suit, formal attire that emphasized his Spanish origins. The short, tailored jacket, brilliant white shirt, wide leather belt, and narrow necktie all reminded him of his *caballero* past—except for his entirely modern gun. He was the only one who would openly carry a weapon tonight, the revolver traditionally worn with a Charro suit and the symbol of his authority as host. Given these guests, he wore a Super Redhawk, lethal and accurate, rather than the more sentimental pearl-handled Colt Ulysses Grant had given him.

Jean-Marie was as relaxed as any modern man could be when clad in a fine Gucci blue silk suit. Ethan, on the other hand, wore a black, western-cut tuxedo with embroidered red flames flashing from the shoulders, collars and cuffs, and beautifully tailored to conceal the revolvers holstered underneath. As the host's *alferez mayor*, he could stretch custom far enough to carry weapons but only if they were hidden.

Gray Wolf and Luis Alvarez, Rafael's *siniscal* and oldest *compañero*, met them at the great hall. After almost two hundred years, Luis appeared barely forty and was as strong and fast as most *cachorros*. Born a Galician peasant, on the northwest coast of Spain, his eyes still carried shadows from when Napoleon's men had destroyed his family—then been gutted by Rafael.

A *compañero* was a *prosaico* who drank *vampiro* blood frequently, developing a craving for—an addiction to—his *vampiro primero*. Traditionally, *vampiros* were leery of creating *compañeros*, because it was impossible to predict how long it would take for a *compañero* to develop his craving for a single vampiro. So *vampiros* only created *concubinos compañeros*—sex slaves and blood sources.

But despite the stigma attached to *compañeros*, Rafael had proudly fought beside them, using their strength and their ability to fight in daylight like a *vampiro mayor*. Later, he'd made all of his recruits serve a novitiate as *compañeros*, thus allowing him to judge their fitness to become *vampiros*.

The agony was that it was also impossible to predict how long a *compañero* would live. During most of his life, he'd appear the same age he'd been when he first began to drink *vampiro* blood frequently. But when the *vampiro* elixir began to attack him, he would suddenly show signs of aging and die within weeks or even days.

Normally a *compañero* could hope to live for a century, or a century and a half. For a *compañero* to attain two centuries was astounding. Death would come fastest, the longer he had lived.

Rafael had fought more battles with Luis at his side than with anyone else, a history that Luis occasionally took ruthless advantage of—such as his absolute refusal to yield his post beside Rafael during daylight battles. At least, not until there was a *vampiro* who could pick up some of the burden.

Rafael had once thought he could persuade Luis to change his mind. He'd never force him to become a *vampiro*, since he never forced anyone even when they'd already agreed to do so. Luis, like everyone else, would only become a *vampiro* when his eyes were open to the consequences and fearlessly accepted them. But, *maldito sea*, if Luis withered and died of old age before that happened, it would break his heart!

Any day now, Jean-Marie would be able to walk in twilight and Luis would become a *vampiro*. Until then . . .

Rafael automatically searched Luis's face for signs of aging—and found none. He relaxed slightly. Luis would be the next *compañero* to become a *vampiro*—and no one would be happier than Rafael when that happened.

Luis bore his inspection with his typical slightly paternal forbearance. When Rafael relaxed, he bowed, holding back a smile, before disappearing into the great hall. He, after all, had duties to perform, as he'd reminded Rafael so many times before.

"Ready, Gray Wolf?"

"Yes, sir." Gray Wolf's smile at his *creador* was quiet but genuine. A Native American and Rafael's second oldest *hijo*, he was elegantly dressed in a simple black silk shirt and black pants, with his long black hair neatly tied at the nape of his neck. For a man who owned more than one eagle feather headdress, it was a notably inconspicuous appearance. On the other hand, it was probably best to encourage Madame Celeste to overlook him, thereby continuing her usual treatment for men she couldn't seduce.

Ready, Luis, Rafael ordered telepathically when he entered the great hall with his three eldest *hijos*. Fine tapestries and antique carpets glowed like jewels under the immense wrought-iron chandeliers, forming a brilliant background for seven score men in all their finery.

"*Vampiros y compañeros*, please welcome *nuestro Señor*, Don Rafael Perez!" Luis boomed. The big room erupted in cheers as the assembly stood up. Even the snipers in the balconies shouted greetings, adding to the clamor that literally shook the massive rafters.

Rafael lifted his arms in response from the front of the dais, his heart swelling. Who could want more than this, to be accepted as leader by the finest men in North America?

The bright haze solidified into a big man standing in front of a crowded room. Taller than any other man there, black haired and dark eyed, he wasn't handsome, certainly not when compared to any of the four men behind him. Yet he held her attention as he raised his hands in greeting, evoking a flood of love and respect from the assembly.

Damn, he was stunning, more impressive than the Kodiak bear she'd seen standing tall and free in Alaska.

Her breath caught as a frisson of sexual awareness tightened her chest. What would such a man be like in private? Domineering, arrogant, overwhelming . . .

Beautiful man. Heat came to life deep inside her. Well worth dating.

Familiarity teased her, as if she'd seen him before somewhere, touched him somehow. She tried to breathe but she was caught in stasis.

Suddenly her cell phone rang, the modern metallic ring yanking Grania back to the raucous party. She automatically reached for the phone, cursing silently as his visage faded.

"Hello?" He'd been tall, maybe two meters? But what color eyes did he have? Shit.

Beth's voice snapped across the line. "Got a situation here, Grania."

Sometimes Beth sounded entirely too much like her policeman husband. Grania's brain reluctantly snapped back into full awareness. "Hmmm, let me see. Larry's gone to Tahoe with the family and you've got two, maybe three, animals coming in."

"Two. Are you psychic or something?"

"Doesn't take a psychic to know that one vet wouldn't call another during a party if things were boring. What're the cases?"

Beth snorted. "Told Andy you'd figure it out, without me saying a word. Now he owes me a double mocha latte. Barn owl found by the road, ETA twenty minutes. Coyote hit by a pickup, ETA one hour."

Grania was already heading for the door. "Give me fifteen minutes. I'll take the owl, of course."

She caught her hostess's eye, pointed significantly at the cell phone, made an apologetic face. Nodded sad agreement with the other woman's instant understanding, then waved good-bye. She'd stop by tomorrow for a more private farewell to the couple who'd helped her, ever since she'd come from Colorado as a kid too young for the bachelor's degree in her backpack.

Beth sighed. "Thanks. I knew I was asking a lot, since you're leaving California in two days, but I hoped you'd help. You're the best with owls there is."

Grania shrugged, uncomfortable with the praise, even from an old friend. "Yeah, right. Just make sure the coffee's hot and there's lots of it."

"Gotcha. One extra-large espresso coming right up."

Grania snapped shut her cell phone and swung herself into her old pickup. If nothing else, she'd be with friends, both human and feathered, on her next-to-last night in California.

Rafael's earlier joy had changed to cool wariness by the time he watched his helicopter land on his private helipad. The raven-haired Madame Celeste emerged first, bedecked in an emperor's ransom of rubies and diamonds blazing above gold brocade that blatantly displayed her full breasts. Georges Devol followed her closely in funereal black, nervous as a sinner in a room full of priests.

Rafael's eyes narrowed. Both Madame Celeste and Devol were so gorged with blood and emotion they were almost sluggish. It was the surest guarantee of good conduct any *vampiro* could provide. His mouth tightened at what must have happened, during the airplane flight from New Orleans to Austin, in order to satisfy that pair's horrific tastes before they took the helicopter here.

Rafael's head came up as a *vampiro mayor* lightly touched his mind. A younger *vampiro* wouldn't have noticed the probe but Rafael recognized it immediately.

Diego. *Madre de Dios.* And close enough that he could kill the bastard at last.

Rafael's mental shields held of course, as they always had against Diego. Two centuries of every imaginable torture had taught him much, including how to protect his mind from everyone except The Syrian who'd raped him and forced *El Abrazo* on him. In contrast,

The Syrian had pampered Diego and never forced him to learn complex skills, like how to shred a man's mind as easily as his body.

A memory welled up unbidden: Diego's face the last time they'd met, roaring with triumph as he raised his sword high above him lying broken at his feet. His soul long since commended to God, Rafael had growled defiance as he waited for Diego to finally send him through death's door.

Then The Syrian's voice had snapped across the arena. "Do not kill the unbeliever. We have not broken him yet."

Now Diego Sanchez, dressed in the gaudy attire of a boy toy, looked up at Rafael. He deliberately bit his lip and licked the drop away: He was even more sated with blood than Madame Celeste or Devol.

"Who did you bring with you?" Rafael's voice was harsh and cold, hardly hospitable. *Por Dios*, he would not have that snake on his land, where he might study his defenses—and prey on his people.

His men stiffened, weapons rustling.

Diego dripped acid across their mind link, the one shared by all *hijos* of the same *creador*. Rafael ignored him, locking down his old shields.

Madame Celeste drew herself up, playing the affronted empress to the hilt. "My enforcer, Georges Devol, whom you know."

Rafael didn't favor Devol with so much as a glance. "The terms of the meeting, madame, were that you could bring Devol with you and no one else. The other man must leave my land immediately."

"What!" she shrieked. "This is outrageous! You cannot expect me—"

"Otherwise, the entire meeting ends here and now. Your *juguete* has no place in this. Your choice, madame."

Diego's thoughts battered at him angrily but he ignored them with an effort.

She considered him, while his snipers kept their rifles at the ready.

Desire me, she thought at him, using her greatest weapon.

Seven centuries as a *vampiro*, including two centuries of brutal training, allowed him to withstand the carnal hungers she poured over him. A younger *vampiro*, certainly any *compañero* or *prosaico*, would have crawled to her feet begging to serve her in any way.

"Madame?" he prodded, careful not to show his gritted teeth.

"Oh, very well." She gave in with a Gallic shrug. "I had hoped for a little extra amusement. Perhaps the three of us together . . ." She let her voice trail off.

He regarded her stonily.

"Back on the helicopter, *mon cher* Beau. Next time will be better, I promise you."

Is that his new name?

She kissed Beau on the cheek, sending him back to the helicopter with a pat. He lingered in the door for a moment, glaring at Rafael.

You're living on borrowed time. The words hung in the air like a cloud of acid on the ancient channel used by The Syrian and his *hijos*. *I swore I'd take my revenge five hundred years ago.*

I'm surprised your form of evil still breathes, Rafael responded with all his old venom.

I was biding my time, letting you build a good esfera *for me.*

Like hell!

Besides, it's been a plush life, Diego went on. *First Russia, now screwing this bitch.*

Whoring and killing. You killed for money in Russia and broke every law of chivalry, both Christian and Muslim.

And it felt good too. All that emotion to feed on . . . Until the damn Wall fell and the new government kicked me out. It was time to hunt you down, even if it meant sleeping with sluts like this one.

And now you will die.

The helicopter's blades speeded up, forcing Beau to enter. But he still managed to laugh when the door slammed behind him. *Didn't two centuries of trying teach you anything? I beat you in every fight we ever had, so all you know is how to lose to me. The next time we fight, I'm going to take your magnificent* esfera.

Nunca!

But I won't take it yet. Not until I find out how to break you.

Rafael snarled. *You tried for two centuries and never did,* hijo de la gran puta!

I'll see you crawl, yaa Himaar. *You'll beg me for death by the time I'm done with you.*

No, because this time, it is I who will grind you under my heel, like the cockroach you are! Rafael snapped his fingers.

As if sensing their argument, the helicopter rapidly lifted off and headed east, flying too fast like a hare frightened by a hawk's presence in the sky above.

Rafael glared after it. This time, he was not a young *vampiro*, trained by two hundred years of agony to crawl and bleed. He'd spent five hundred years preparing to kill that *pendejo*—and he'd do whatever it took to crush him into dust.

Madame Celeste slipped her arm through his, rubbing herself against him, as if he was standing still for her convenience.

"*Mon chéri,* I am delighted to finally visit your home," Madame Celeste purred as she reached up to Rafael. It was a full kiss, of course, with all of her usual aggressiveness. She sighed into his mouth as she pressed herself against him. Her scent was full of lust, surprising for a *vampira* who'd fed so recently.

Rafael freed himself as soon as he politely could, following her lead and ignoring Beau's departure. Unfortunately, a gentleman could not wipe his mouth after a woman kissed it. "Allow me to present my men," he began.

"Ah, *chéri,* forget the formalities for an instant," Madame Celeste interrupted as she dragged a scarlet-tipped nail up his arm. "Let's visit alone first, as *patrón* to *patrón,* before we involve anyone else in our games."

"Certainly, madame. The guest house then," Rafael agreed politely and offered her his arm. Not his office, of course. It would take weeks to remove her stench from his sanctum.

Rafael took a last breath of clean air and joined Madame Celeste inside the guest house. It was a small, simple dwelling place, normally used for the few cattlemen or scientists permitted to stay overnight at Compostela.

Madame Celeste cast a swift, all-encompassing look around the room, her lip curling at the longhorn steer head over the mantel and the Texas flag on the wall. Then she planted herself in the middle of the leather sofa, patted the seat beside her invitingly, and batted her eyes at him. Her gold brocade dress was cut so low he could see her nipples, a calculated frame for the great crimson ruby that dipped between her breasts.

Rafael briefly wished he could courteously decline her invitation and sit in the rocking chair. Instead, he inclined his head graciously and sat down on the sofa, as far away from her as possible.

There were no watchers present, of course. He was, after all, more than five hundred years older than Madame Celeste in the only measure that counted, when two *vampiros* were granted *El Abrazo*. He was more than capable of destroying the woman in one-on-one combat, should she be foolish enough to try it.

"Mon petit chou," she cooed and scooted next to him, her skintight skirt sliding up her thighs.

He gritted his teeth at the endearment. Little cabbage, indeed. "Champagne, madame?" he offered. He retrieved a bottle from the ice bucket Luis had thoughtfully left on the table, behind the Remington bronze. Krug's Clos du Mesnil, a Cuvée Prestige—the highest level of quality—and one of the most expensive in his vast wine cellars.

She pouted as he carefully popped the cork. "I'd rather talk about us, *mon amour*. Remember the Mardi Gras we spent together?"

"Certainement, madame." That had been more than seventy years ago. Why did she remember that interlude?

"The best Mardi Gras I've ever enjoyed," she mused. "You were *magnifique*, a stallion beyond compare, a god among men." She toyed with the ruby, running her fingers over it and her breasts, as if tempting him with her wealth and desirability.

"Surely others have inspired you since then." He handed her a crystal flute filled with the fine champagne.

"Non, you brought me pleasure like no other can," she insisted and tossed back her wine. She must have drunk so much blood for so long that she'd forgotten the pleasure of other tastes.

Rafael hooded his eyes as he sipped his wine. He'd learned how to survive as a sexual slave once before, including how to read his partner's every fancy and divert them whenever necessary. He'd done so cold-bloodedly with Madame Celeste during that Mardi Gras, but his gut recoiled at the thought of doing so again.

"*Merci*, madame, you flatter me immensely," he murmured. "But enlighten me please. I thought we met tonight to discuss an alliance."

"*Exactement*, Don Rafael!" She turned to straddle him.

A hand on her waist stopped her. "Remain seated, madame, *s'il vous plaît*. Your couturier would never forgive me if anything happened to your magnificent dress." Would she care more for her clothing than the superb champagne?

She harrumphed her disappointment but settled back against the cushions. "It's so simple, *mon amour*. We unite our two *esferas* . . ."

What? He set down his glass. She wasn't here to discuss joining their armies against the greedy *vampiros* of northern Mexico, who'd overthrown their longtime *patrón* a decade ago? They were too young to realize their reckless pursuit of drug profits would bring down a horde of *prosaicos*, destroying them and any other *vampiro* close by.

"And seal the compact with our bodies, *tu comprendes*? We'd be gods, ruling the largest *esfera* in the world. We could conquer every other American *esfera* in an instant and rule the continent inside a year!" she finished with a snap of her fingers and eyes glowing.

No way in hell would he start a war of aggression. His mouth set hard but the bloodthirsty bitch was too caught up in her fantasies to notice.

"And the nights, ah, the hours of passion we'd share. *Quelle extase!*" She turned his face and leaned to kiss him. He blocked her by lifting his glass in a toast. He had seven score of *vampiros* and *compañeros*. But she had ten score, a force to reckon with, even if almost all were younger, and therefore weaker, than his *vampiros*. He tried turning her aside with honeyed words first.

"You flatter me, madame. Men flock to you like bees flying toward the perfect rose, drunk on your beauty. To be your consort is a heady drink, far too much for a simple man like myself."

"Ah, *mon amour*, don't you see? That's why we'd be so magnificent together! We'd rule everything from the Atlantic to the Rockies, from the Gulf to the Ohio River. And in a year or two, we'd have all of the United States and Canada. Who could stop us?" She ran her tongue over her lips, her nipples pointed and hard against the brocade. A crimson-tipped finger ran up his thigh. "And the fucking, *mon étalon*. To have you between my legs again, filling my cunt with your magnificent cock . . ."

"*Non*, madame." Rafael gripped her wrist hard enough to catch her attention.

"What do you mean? We would rule North America together!" She leaned forward again.

"No." He put her aside very firmly, praying none of his men would die because of his decision. "I am honored by your high opinion, but I already have more than I ever dreamed of. I regret I must decline your generous offer; uniting Texas with any other territory is impossible."

She stared at him, her brain finally starting to work. Her black eyes were enormous with lust. "*Mais*, Don Rafael, don't you desire me?"

"Madame, please remember that immense territories have never lasted long among our kind. Content yourself with what you have."

"But I know you want me; every man always has. Why do you keep refusing me?"

"Madame, the answer is no. Neither your great estates nor your beautiful body will take me away from Texas."

Understanding slowly dawned in her eyes, and the birth of her notoriously foul temper. She threw her champagne in his face and sprang at him, her fingers slashing at his eyes. "*Nique ta mère!*"

Rafael grabbed her wrists, wishing he could break them for the insult to his mother.

She spat curses at him, hissing and scratching, slipping from his grip like an asp, as she tried to make contact with his loins. "*Raclure de bidet!*"

He wrestled her to the floor, barely dodging the table. A twist, a roll and they were in front of the fireplace. He finally brought her under control by lying on top of her, straddling her legs, with her wrists gripped in one of his hands. Her carnality surged against him, seeking an entry.

"*Soyez tranquille*, madame," he insisted, enforcing the command telepathically as well as vocally. "Remember you are the *patrón* of New Orleans."

She stretched against him, rubbing her breasts against his jacket. He lifted an eyebrow but didn't move.

She circled her hips against him, making the sexual offering of herself more emphatic. She slammed her gift at him, demanding that he lust for her.

His cock stayed relaxed, an emphatic declaration of disinterest.

"*Dardillon!* You should be hard as a rock for me!" She spat at him but he dodged easily, his face calm.

He seared tranquility into her brain, wishing *vampiro* custom allowed him to do so permanently. But no, she'd be a worse enemy if he did so, and she'd still be unfettered once she returned to Louisiana.

"You truly don't want me," she hissed as she stilled under him.

He watched her warily until her breathing evened out, before releasing her. *Madre de Dios*, he'd rarely seen a woman so angry. But when had anyone ever refused a carnal invitation from her?

She straightened her dress with angry jerks. Rafael poured her a fresh glass of champagne, which she accepted with a sneer. She downed it in rapid gulps before she started talking again. "Haven't you ever wondered why I took over New Orleans only after that Mardi Gras we shared?"

Ay, mierda, *she can't have taken over New Orleans and the South-east because of something I did.* Rafael inclined his head neutrally and let her speak.

"I needed that territory so you'd stick around me. Me, *La Patróna d'Esfera de Nouvelle Orléans*! Not just another chick good for only a few weeks," she snarled at him. "And if I can't have you, then by God, I'll dance on your grave."

"You can try, madame. But you'll fail."

"And I'll succeed. My assassins have killed more than one *esfera*'s *patrón*." She rose impatiently and began to pace.

Rafael raised an eyebrow, genuinely unworried. He took up a pose leaning against the mantel, where he could watch her. "Their tricks are well known to the least discerning *vampiro*. They will not succeed here."

"Even the best *vampiro* assassin in the world and a *vampiro mayor* at that? The little golden toy who enlivens my bed in gratitude for a place to stay? He'd kill you and a hundred others, just to please me."

A chill ran down Rafael's spine for the first time. Diego was famous as an assassin for the Russians, legendary for sowing terror wherever they wanted. If there was chaos in Texas, the oldest and most stable *esfera* in North America . . .

He made sure none of those concerns showed on his face, of course, as he countered Madame Celeste's challenge. "Texas is not like other territories, madame. Even if I die, Gray Wolf will lead the armies of Texas against you. You will regret the day you caused a painted savage to go to war."

She paled slightly. Good; she still remembered some of her childhood's horror stories. Then she bared her fangs at him in a travesty of a smile, the ritual start to a *vampiro* duel. He went on full alert, ready to shapeshift in an instant.

"Or I'll send in my darling Georges to frighten the locals. He would make Texas so hot that *los prosaicos* would destroy you and all your precious *vampiros* and *compañeros*."

Madre de Dios, she couldn't be that reckless. A horde of terrified mortals was the only thing every *vampiro* feared. What they lacked in individual strength, *prosaicos* more than made up in numbers and determination. But if she harmed the people of Texas, he would utterly destroy her.

"Madame, do not try to alarm me with your talk of assassins and mobs. Texas is too strong for you to take down," Rafael snapped. "Save your strength for where it can be put to better use, such as stopping the river rats that bring drugs and weapons into your great city."

"Don't bother me with your pretty speeches, Don Rafael. We

understand each other well enough without them," she snarled and turned for the door. She stopped when Rafael clamped his hand over her wrist.

"Do not start a war you cannot win, madame, lest you be destroyed by it," Rafael warned, his voice hard as his revolver's steel. "You are my guest tonight, protected by the laws of hospitality. But if you attack me, then I and my Texans will bury you."

"Damn you, let me go!" She yanked but his grip was immovable. Her language turned as foul as New Orleans's sewers.

"You and your entourage are leaving now, madame. If you ever step foot on Texan soil again uninvited, you will die." He forced her to meet his eyes, fury boiling inside him. "Do you understand me, madame?"

"*Oui, je comprends,*" she muttered sullenly.

He released her slowly, wishing for the first time in his life that he could break the laws of hospitality and kill his guest.

She nearly spat at him but changed it into an offended snort. She stormed out, striding down the hill toward the helipad and Devol.

TWO

The last Galician bagpiper played gallantly on, as if his music alone could stave off defeat. Blood and corpses choked the Genil River and covered the field. The locals called Ecija "The Frying Pan," a name that seemed bitterly appropriate to the thousands of men dying there.

Infante Don Fernando had died months ago of disease, taking the army's hopes with him. His second-in-command had foolishly accepted battle here, on ground that favored only the enemy. Rodrigo and Fearghus's private estimate of the odds against them seemed confirmed when their squires vanished early in the battle: Fearghus's squire was killed by a Moorish arrow through his throat, while Diego was swept away in the enemy's first charge.

Rodrigo had once hoped to be granted a vision of how he'd fare on this battlefield, the visions that were his family's gift. But they came least often to those most deeply affected by the vision. Now he was bitterly glad he didn't know his fate in advance.

Surprisingly, the infidels had chosen to butcher the Christians rather than capture them in hopes of gaining fat ransoms later. Rodrigo and Fearghus were two of the few knights still standing as they expertly, grimly took advantage of every bit of terrain to kill one more enemy. To stay alive just one more minute.

Blood and guts dripped from their swords, while their muscles burned with exhaustion. His helmet long since gone, sweat burned in Rodrigo's eyes and under his armor. Blanche and his children were a distant thought, consigned to God's care. He'd been shriven of his sins that morning so his soul was safe. Only his God and his country remained to be fought for.

Then Fearghus slipped on a patch of blood, involuntarily dropping his guard. A Moor immediately took advantage of him, sending him to the ground.

Rodrigo swung his sword like Death's scythe and beheaded the fellow. He had no time to step astride Fearghus's prostrate body and guard him before another man sliced the back of his leg. He fell backward and saw the clear blue sky overhead, filling his world with a sudden purity like the Virgin's mantle or Blanche's eyes.

A sword came down, like a hawk dropping out of the sun on a rabbit, dazzling his eyes. He flung up his arm but the blow smashed through.

All went black.

"Hello, Andy." Grania stepped inside the clinic, pulling her lab coat around her. Beth would return her rented academic robes on Monday. Her long lab coat was much more familiar and more comfortable. You never knew exactly where, or how, wildlife might try to greet their so-called rescuers.

"Espresso's on the table, doc." The big tech smiled his big gap-toothed grin at Grania. A retired rice farmer and Vietnam veteran, he should be sleeping in his bed right now. Instead, he'd chosen to follow his wife, one of the top animal rehabbers in California, and become a licensed vet tech. So here he was, well after midnight, standing guard over an animal carrier in the antiseptic maze of stainless steel and tile known as a wildlife rescue center.

"Blessings upon you, O procurer of the nectar of the gods!" Grania made a deep bow and headed for the table. Her long, red hair was still neatly pinned up in a chignon, legacy of the graduation ceremony's formality. Normally, she'd wear it braided around her head, emphasizing efficiency and simplicity.

He chuckled at her latest sally in their ongoing game of complimenting each other's coffee, then began to describe the patient. "Owl's in the carrier over there." He nodded at a blanket-covered lump in a quiet corner of the lab, then went on. "Adult barn owl, maybe a male. Found beside a hiking trail near Redding. Debilitated but showing only a superficial wound on one leg."

Grania froze, her coffee cup halfway to her lips. Shit, shit, shit. Probably goddamn rat poison or brodifacoum, to name the poison itself. Her eyes met Andy's. His were just as enraged.

"Rat poison," she growled.

"Could be wrong," he offered but with little apparent hope.

"It's the most frequent cause for barn owls being brought in here. Those birds are the best killers of rats and mice that God put on this planet." She slammed her coffee cup down, barely managing not to splash it. "But when people get impatient and start poisoning mice, barn owls clean up the leftovers . . ."

"And die from the same thing that killed the mice. Their blood won't clot."

Her stomach heaved, thinking of all the raptors she'd lost. "So even a little wound on the leg will kill a fabulous bird like an owl."

"Police did say that this guy is still somewhat alert. He may have reached us in time," Andy offered.

"Damn, I hope so." She stared at the carrier, willing strength into her feathered patient.

"That's what I always say." His tone shifted, gaining echoes of the top-notch Marine sergeant he'd once been. "Got the north operating room ready for you. Dr. Driver and my missus are already prepping the south for the coyote."

Grania smiled reluctantly; he'd come a long way from the farmer who'd wanted to exterminate every varmint who could possibly kill one of his chickens. She finished buttoning her lab coat, grateful she'd at least worn trousers under her academic robes instead of the dress she'd originally considered. They weren't jeans but they were better than a miniskirt.

She surveyed the equipment laid out; yup, everything she'd need for an intake exam. Then she sorted through the clinic's gloves bin, found the pair she wanted, and began to pull them on.

"Sure you don't want the black ones, doc?" Andy asked, narrowing his eyes at her reprovingly.

"Nope. If he's that debilitated, I want to be as gentle as possible with him."

"You're the only vet who doesn't use them for owls."

Grania shrugged. "Maybe I'm reckless."

"Yeah—and vampires fly every full moon. Ready for the patient?"

"Sure I am."

He gave her a long, considering look, which she met with a raised eyebrow. Yielding to her certainty, Andy produced the animal carrier and set it on the table. He produced the clipboard and stood ready to record the exam.

Grania took a deep breath, centering herself in preparation to deal with the owl, and started the best job in the world.

She peeled back the heavy layers of blanket covering the carrier's front and the pale, heart-shaped face of a barn owl stared out at her. He considered her for a moment, then hissed at her faintly, as if in greeting.

Grania ignored him. He was completely a creature of the wild. Her job was to heal him and return him there. She wasn't about to encourage him to stay by talking to him directly, which might make him think humans were creatures he wanted to be around.

She unlatched the carrier and reached for the big bird; to her great joy, he snapped at her. A practiced grab saw his feet, with those razor-sharp talons, wrapped in one of her gloved hands.

Another twist of her shoulder lifted the owl up and out of the carrier, with her arm sliding up his back, as if he was Kermit the Frog and she was Jim Henson.

She held him out at arm's length to look him over.

Dark brown eyes stared straight back at her. Then the barn owl shrieked, like a querulous old man clearing its throat. *Greetings, ancient one*, he announced.

Grania's heart stopped and she nearly dropped him. He was talking to her? Impossible!

She'd heard a great many owl calls, more than one in the middle of the night. She understood perfectly well why most haunted house stories were thought to come from barn owls hooting at humans. She'd looked owls in the eye before and known that they were considering her every bit as much as she was studying them. But she'd never before thought that one was talking directly to her. Owls simply did not do that.

She barely managed to regain her grip. Her breath whistled out, as if to say, *Who?*

The barn owl stiffened, as if disgusted by her incomprehension. He cleared his throat again, like a soft cougar call. *You. You are the ancient one, who has been guarded by the wise one.*

A conversation? She was having a conversation with a barn owl?

This time, Grania held on to him and even managed to grab the back of his skull with her forefingers. Held this way, he wouldn't be able to sink that deadly beak into her through her glove.

"You got a problem with the owl, doc? Should I call Dr. Driver to help?"

"No, no *problemo*, Andy." Grania smiled at Andy. It felt like a grimace to her, but it seemed to reassure him. "Just making sure he's got no big neurological problems." *Like talking to me.*

She studied the feathered beast warily. He watched her silently and blinked once again, like a professor waiting for a student's slow response. Maybe the rodenticide was having an unusual neurological effect? No, hissing that sounded like human speech wasn't anywhere in the avian medical literature. Heaven knows, she'd treated enough rat poisoning cases to know that body of literature.

Folk legends began to run through her brain, such as hearing a barn owl at night meant something weird was about to happen. Poltergeists, people called barn owls.

She kicked herself mentally. Just do a standard examination, Grania. Pretend everything's normal and soon it really will be. Gross examination first, for things like head tilt, wing damage, eyes. You've done this a thousand times before; you can do it now.

She cleared her throat, somehow still holding the owl, and began the first step in a blessedly familiar examination ritual.

A glance at the mirror over the lab sink showed the barn owl's reflection. Dammit, why did he look quizzical, as if she was disappointing him?

He hissed at her again, almost sweetly. It sounded nothing at all like a typical barn owl call, which was usually compared to a mountain lion's howl.

He was the best-behaved barn owl she'd met, since she fell in love with that great horned owl at the age of three. That enormous owl had been her very first friend other than her godfather. He had talked to her every night at sunset, as he sat on a tree before starting the night's hunt. She'd taken a lot of flak for her obsession from the other kids in the orphanage. So she'd studied him and his brethren harder, hoping to explain him better. Hoping maybe the other kids would understand her, and her passions, a little better. And accept her a little bit. Like that had ever happened.

She lined the barn owl up straight and true, to see if any part of his body was leaning. While considering him, she absentmindedly hooted back at him, in a great horned's call.

The barn owl hissed again, emphatically repeating his original call. *Greetings, ancient one.*

Andy dropped his pen.

She choked, her fingers slipping off the back of the owl's head.

He glared at her. For an instant, he could have bitten her through her glove.

Then she recovered her grip.

Why the hell was the owl repeating the same call? About an ancient one, as if he was talking about reincarnation?

Utter nonsense in more than one way.

He hissed again, a commonplace barn owl call.

She hissed back at him, trying to mimic his call. *Greetings, brother of the night.*

Somehow he gave the impression of settling ruffled feathers and relaxed against her palm.

Grania forced her mind back to her job. If she didn't, this owl would die. She cursed her own selfishness and laid him down to palpate him, the next step in the formal examination. She had to save his life.

Resting her fingertips lightly on his belly, she closed her eyes and focused hard on the barn owl. The ancient fan whirred overhead then faded into obscurity.

Slowly his abdomen came into focus before her mind's eye. Blood was hemorrhaging into his stomach, where a mouse's last fragments rested. Not too much blood though.

Thank God he showed so much spirit. They'd reached him early enough to save him. With vitamin K, a lot of TLC, and some luck, he'd be flying again soon.

Rafael stood on the porch, drumming his fingers on the column as the helicopter circled overhead. Small chance there were any New Orleans *vampiros* left in Texas and, yet, it was better not to take the chance. Behind him, the night shift of *vampiros* and day shift of *compañeros* gathered, watching him silently. He and Donal O'Malley were the only *patrones* to have *compañeros* serve as novice *vampiros*, not just sex slaves and food sources when present at all.

The eastern sky lightened beyond the distant hills, shifting from black to indigo. The warning sign sent a chill through Rafael, although it no longer meant danger to him personally. His *vampiros* were safe now in the deep shade, but it would be better to send them all the way indoors.

The radio crackled to life. "Don Rafael?" Caleb's voice asked politely. "May I speak to you, please?"

"Certainly, amigo. What is it?"

"We have a limousine here, at the ranch road east out of San Leandro. The driver has an invitation in your name for Miss Shelby Durant, a student at Yale. He keeps apologizing for being late, saying he became lost on the ranch roads."

Rafael nodded, every sense on full alert. What the hell was Señorita Durant doing here now? The Oscar-winning, eighteen-year-old star would hardly invite herself a day early simply to discuss fund-raising for the Special Olympics. "And?" he prompted Caleb.

"I haven't seen Miss Durant but her scent is, ah, unlike anything I've smelled before, sir. It's not *prosaica*. But it's not *vampira* or *compañera*, either."

Rafael growled, baring his fangs completely. His men's heads snapped up and they stared at him. Ethan drew his gun.

"Who else is with her?"

"Lucien Saint-Gerard is the driver, sir."

¡Ay, mierda! "Send them up but don't let them out of your sight."

"Yes, sir."

Rafael met the long, black limousine in front of the main house, where the drive made a great circular sweep before a spectacular view of the eastern valleys. Ethan, Jean-Marie, and Gray Wolf stood in the house's shadows with the rest of his *vampiros*. *Compañero* snipers lined the roofline, displaying the extent of his power. The sky was still dark, with only Venus to give any illumination, although the sun would soon change that.

The grassy sweep between the house and the drive was in full shadow, as was the house and the porch, shielded from the rising sun by the eastern hills. The sun's rays would only shine down on Compostela when it rose high enough to be seen over those hills.

The sleek limousine slid to a stop on the macadam drive's east side, with Caleb's armored Suburban pulling in to block him from behind. The limo's driver stepped out promptly and turned to face the house. Lucien Saint-Gerard, of course, once an ornament of Marie-Antoinette's court, before he'd become a pimp and whore in New Orleans. Now he was an errand boy for Madame Celeste and still the worst sort of procurer. He wore a silk Italian suit, disheveled and bloodstained.

Rafael's nostrils flared slightly at the scent but he kept his expression haughty and bored. Luis flanked him, in his role as *siniscal*, while Caleb moved to block Lucien from returning to the limo. His two oldest *compañeros* were a deadly force in their own right, especially since they could act in daylight, unlike a *vampiro* such as Lucien.

"Don Rafael?" Lucien bowed as formally as at Versailles—one leg forward and flourishing his arm. Rafael gave the appropriate response of a head of state greeting a traveling diplomat—a perfunctory nod.

Lucien glanced suggestively at the stairs into the house. Rafael made no response but Luis took a single step sideways, completely blocking the steps from Lucien. The visiting *vampiro* was now trapped in the open, watched by Rafael and his men.

He cast his eyes down, more like a snake than a courtier studying how to mend fences. They flickered sideways, measuring escape routes from the rising sun. "Forgive me for being late but I was overwhelmed by the magnificence of your mountain scenery."

Rafael waved his fingers for the newcomer to continue. The longtime city dweller had probably been thoroughly lost.

"I have brought your gift as Madame Celeste ordered." Lucien turned and pulled the limo's door open with a flourish. A stench rolled out, worse than the foulest of sewers. Then he yanked Shelby Durant, the most promising actress of her generation, out of the black conveyance.

The previous Christmas, the world had celebrated her as Joan of Arc, the warrior maiden who'd freed a nation. She'd been fêted and showered with awards, including an Oscar. But today, a sewer rat would have been more attractive.

She was covered in blood, vomit, and excrement. Her dress had been clawed to shreds, as had her underthings. A few drops of blood welled sullenly, slowly, from long scratch marks on her breasts and belly. Two great, purple bite marks gleamed at the base of her neck. Other than those, she was ashen white, as if she could fade into a mist. Her eyes were squeezed shut and her face was contorted into a grimace, while her tongue darted out over her lips. One hand plucked at her nipple, while the other rubbed continuously at her mound.

"What the fuck—" Caleb muttered.

Her once-golden head of hair came up in a heartrending parody of its former alertness. "Fuck? Yes. Now. All of you. We fuck." She stumbled across the grass toward the men, fumbling at the remains of her clothing.

Rafael clenched his fists. Lucien had forced Shelby, famous for her strong views on premarital chastity, into *El Abrazo*. To see her deep in *La Lujuria*, an infant *cachorra*'s mindless demand for sexual congress, was an abomination to both God and man.

Could any of her sanity remain? *El Abrazo* was notorious for scouring a woman's wits to dust, more so than a man's. *Dios* alone knew how Madame Celeste had survived her passage. He'd always wondered how much of her sanity had been permanently scoured away.

Lucien sauntered after Shelby, beaming like a proud father as she staggered forward. "You see, Don Rafael, the perfect fuck and the perfect meal, to seal the bargain with Madame Celeste. Durant will do anything and everything, just to get a little blood and sex from you, even when you kill her. Nothing like feeding on a dying *vampira*, while you're fucking her. We'll finish her off in the main house, then share a bottle of champagne."

Rafael's fangs stabbed against his jaw as a stream of curses spun through his brain. But he had to rescue the young lady before he could kill Lucien, that spawn of Satan.

He started toward her, speaking soothingly as one would to a very small child. "*Dulce* Shelby—"

Suddenly the first bright shaft of daylight lanced across the hilltop. It caught Shelby in the back, the shock arching her slender body like a medieval saint in the grips of the final passion. For a moment, sanity—or something close to it—glinted in her blue eyes.

Santísima Virgen . . . Rafael blurred into motion, hoping to pull her into the shade. But he knew, even as he leapt, that all his speed couldn't save her now.

Shelby blazed—incandescent as a magnesium flare, brighter than the sun itself, brilliant as the love so many people held for her. Within two seconds, her flame consumed her and became a pillar of ash that quickly crumpled upon itself. A little breeze ruffled the grass but all signs of her were gone.

"*Merde,*" the murderer muttered.

Rafael crossed himself.

"Don Rafael, she was only a female, nobody to fuss over," cooed Lucien, fingers twitching nervously below his bloodstained cuffs.

Ethan growled an order. Behind Rafael, soft clicks told of safeties being set on sniper rifles, soft thuds as boot heels snapped into place. Another order and the *compañeros* began to march.

Lucien's eyes darted from side to side, his head swiveling, his tongue darting over his lips like a nervous cobra.

Rafael's lip curled. He didn't need to look to know that his men had now taken their place as an honor guard, their weapons at rest before them. His *compañeros* lined up around the drive, circling him and Lucien, while his *vampiros* stood deep within the house's shadows. And *compañero* snipers stood erect on the roofline like gargoyles ready to hurl evil away.

"What is the first law of *La Esfera de Texas*?" Rafael asked, his deep voice carrying effortlessly across the hushed space.

"Only *El Patrón de Texas* may create a *vampiro* in Texas," the assembly growled behind him.

Lucien muttered something profane under his breath.

"What is the penalty for breaking this law?" Rafael continued.

"Death."

"Give me an hour and I could get you another girl. Eighteen— no, call it twelve—hours after that, she'd rise and be desperate to be fucked. You could fuck and feed on her easily," Lucien suggested desperately. "Or maybe you'd prefer a boy?"

Rafael looked Lucien straight in the eye. "Last night, I refused Madame Celeste's offer. She left an hour later with the rest of her entourage."

The slime turned pale and shot a glance at the limo, checking the distance. Too far, compared to the speed advantage Rafael's greater age gave him, even if he managed to get past the *compañeros*.

"You broke Texas's first law when you gave *El Abrazo* to Señorita

Durant," Rafael continued implacably, "and are hereby sentenced to death. However, because you have been a diplomat for Madame Celeste, I will offer you a choice. You can fight a judicial duel against me, to earn the right to return to New Orleans. Or you can be executed here and now, under Texas's law."

Lucien's jaw dropped. "Duel against you?" He shook his head. "I won't give you the opportunity to drink my blood. I'll die when and how I want."

He snarled at Rafael like a cornered rat. "But I've seen someone who's faster than you are and will drink your blood on the dueling field one day: Beau, Madame Celeste's little toy. When she tells him to kill you, she'll grind Texas into dust."

He bowed mockingly to Rafael, sweeping his hand high over his head as if he doffed a plumed hat. Sunlight caught his fingers. His fist became a torch, then his arm and head . . .

Rafael crossed himself. *El hombre propone y Dios dispone.* Man proposes and God disposes.

Even so, I will never create a vampira. It is the only way to guarantee protection of the innocents, the women who cannot survive *El Abrazo* and stay sane.

The sun rose up over the horizon, all golden magnificence—as if it was laughing at his determination.

Someone waved a cup of coffee under Grania's nose. She was in the vets' lounge at the clinic, sleeping on the sofa as usual. "What time is it?" she answered, without opening her eyes.

"Dawn in Texas where you're going," Beth answered quietly. "Your owl's doing great, my coyote's vitals are stable, and the techs will be here soon to start feeding the rest of the animals. Time for you to wake up so we can spend the day at the spa."

Grania opened one eye and reached for the coffee. "If I can pay you for it."

"You can repay me by getting your nails done the first time you go out with a guy in Austin."

Grania snickered and sat up. "Pink or blood-red?" She sipped the perfectly made brew.

Beth sat down facing her and took a sip of her own coffee, her exquisite manicure very much in evidence. "Hmmm, not blood-red. Maybe lipstick red?"

"Or blue?"

"We're talking both fingers and toes," Beth pointed out. "How about pink—and I won't demand you get a bikini wax."

Grania laughed. "Deal."

Beth nodded, satisfied. "Have the dating services found you any interesting guys yet?"

Grania shrugged.

"Were they that bad or didn't you look?"

"Truly dreadful," Grania admitted. "But I just want to try my hand at dating. Not jump right away into love and marriage and the baby carriage."

"Try your hand?"

"I've only had sex with three guys in my life. Seems to me I should practice, so I know what I'm doing, before I start seriously hunting for Mr. Right. Otherwise, things could go seriously wrong."

Like they did for my mother when she met my father. If she'd known more about men, she might not have fallen for such a slimeball.

Beth shot her an incredulous look and started to laugh. Grania's color mounted but she kept her chin up. Dating services seemed so trivial anyway, after those dreams of the love Blanche and her knight had shared.

"Only you—" Beth gulped. "Only you, dear friend, would think of dating that way." She fumbled for a paper towel and wiped away the tears of laughter. "Have you ever been on a date?"

"Not really."

"Not really?" Beth's voice rose a little. She cast a quick glance around but there were no sounds of anyone else around. "How can you never have been on a date and not be a virgin?"

"There's lots of guys around while you're out in the field, surveying owls. But there's not many places to go on a date out there."

"True. Plus, who the hell has the time when you're working sixty to ninety hours a week just to get your degree and keep a roof over your head?"

"Amen. Back at school, dating was impossible. Sleep becomes a luxury, let alone hunting a man."

"If Steve hadn't been a cop who understood long hours, I don't think we would have made it." Beth's voice became gentler, as her face softened with memories. "So you're thinking of taking a lover for some advanced education, before you start husband hunting?"

Grania met her friend's eyes steadily. "Why not? Good study habits worked in school. They should do just as well in preparing for a stable family."

Beth giggled suddenly. "Wonder if you'll meet a real cowboy, if you're not looking for someone who wants marriage right away. Hope you'll find somebody really sexy anyway."

She raised her coffee cup in a toast, which Grania matched. "To cowboys!"

"To cowboys!" Grania echoed.

THREE

Rodrigo took the cold compress off his forehead and forced his eyes open. "When you searched the battlefield, then prevented us from being beheaded . . ."

"Bah! We are cousins, Hamza, born of the same grandfather. Of course I would help you in every way I could." A warrior's strong hands gently replaced the compress.

Rodrigo briefly gripped his cousin's hand. "I am grateful, Achmed. Every day, I give thanks to God and pray He will bless you and your children for generations to come."

"We are united in blood, as we could be united in the same faith. Do you remember how we learned the Quran together as children?"

Rodrigo smiled reminiscently at lost pleasures from a simpler time. "When we recited its beautiful Surahs for my mother, reminding her that in the eyes of Allah, as the Prophet said—peace be upon him—Muslims, Christians, and Jews are all children of the Book."

" 'We make no distinction between any of them and unto Him we have surrendered.' "

"Surah Al-Baqara, ayah 36," Rodrigo agreed.

"Have you thought of taking the next step and embracing Islam fully?" Achmed asked quietly.

Rodrigo stiffened, unready to disappoint his cousin, no matter how long he'd expected this question.

A low growl echoed through the room. Rodrigo knew, without opening his eyes, that Fearghus's fine Scots temper had been roused. He lightly touched Fearghus's hand and his friend relaxed somewhat.

"I have the greatest respect and admiration for Islam, as you know, my beloved cousin. The Five Pillars on which it is constructed are foundations every man of faith can admire. Shahādak, the open testimony; Salāt, ritual daily prayer; Zakat, poor-tax; Sawm, the fast, and Haj, the pilgrimage to Mecca."

"Then you are agreed! You will be known as Hamza all the time, not only when you visit us. It is a most praiseworthy name, since it belonged to the Prophet's uncle."

"No, Achmed. We can argue the merits of the two faiths for hours, as we have done so many times before. My heart belongs to Jesucristo and always will, no matter what comes. And I venerate the Santísima Virgen, without whose feminine purity, wisdom, and grace none of us would obtain the reward of Heaven."

Achmed stormed to his feet, knocking over a stool. *"Conversation will save your life, especially when that eastern fanatic preaches of killing all infidels. Be reasonable for once."*

"I am being reasonable," Rodrigo answered calmly. *"I am deeply honored that you consider me worthy of celebrating Islam. But I will walk in the footsteps of my fathers."*

"Our grandfather was born a child of Islam," his cousin retorted.

Rodrigo opened his aching eyes and speared Achmed with a steady look. *"True, but that was before he was shown the light, like St. Paul on the road to Damascus, and converted to the Christian faith. I am a child of that path and am sworn to follow it, no matter what comes after."*

"Are you certain? You would find safety as a Muslim. These new

men, who come out of Morocco or further east, think only of killing infidels. They do not even try to take captives and ransom them later. If we had not found and claimed you, you too would have been executed at Ecija."

"I am as certain of this decision as I am of my mother's name." *Rodrigo shifted against the pillows, catching and almost tearing one of his half-healed wounds. He choked on the pain but forced his voice to remain calm. "I will follow the way of the True Cross as long as there is breath in my body to worship* Jesucristo *and the* Santísima Virgen.*"*

Achmed sighed. "Very well, you stubborn fool. I will keep your sword in a safe place until you can return to your wife. It's too fine to leave where idle eyes might see it and catch the wrong idea."

"True," Fearghus rumbled. "The Castilian king might be better at poetry than politics but he gave Rodrigo one of the best swords in Toledo."

"I'll also send another message to your wife, Rodrigo, since there was no answer to the last. Allah forbid another missive goes astray."

June first and the start of her first full month in Texas. No more classes, no more exams, no more papers to grade. She was finally free to live her own life.

Grania grinned at herself in the small bedroom mirror, as she finished braiding her hair and pinning it up. Her movements were totally automatic, learned before she could write her name. She'd practiced them on other girls at the orphanage under the watchful eyes of nuns who'd never wasted anything, especially a girl disciplined enough to help with the younger children. Now the easy fluidity of long experience allowed Grania to pay more attention to her adorable small cottage than her hair.

It was a tiny bungalow in the Mexican style, all plaster walls, soft curves, brilliant color, and quixotic works of art. Its warmth was nothing like the orphanages and group homes she'd grown up in, with bunk beds stuffed into every available bedroom. This wasn't even similar to where she'd lived while in college. Not a dormitory, an apartment, nor a cabin miles from the nearest road and shared with a group of noisy fellow students.

No, this home was a cottage and an acre of land only ten minutes from work, all for her. A small workroom just off the laundry room even provided private storage for her guns.

The little house was completely furnished, thankfully, since she owned no furniture of her own. And if she ever brought a man home for the night, they'd have to make love on the living room floor: It was the only space big enough for two people to come together. Unless, of course, they lay on top of each other in the single bed.

Grania snorted at the thought as she pushed the last pin into place. Her five-feet-ten length was barely comfortable on that narrow bed. Any man taller than she was—such as her knight from the dreams she'd had all her life—would have a hard time lying down on it, let alone making love.

She touched the cross at her throat, remembering how he'd looked in his sick bed—all pale and wan, with a great, white cloth bandage wound around his head and almost covering his eyes. Holy shit, that wound could have killed him. She shook off her automatic medical speculation about coma, concussion, blood clots on the brain . . . After all, he was only a dream.

Soon she was standing in her usual uniform of polo shirt—emblazoned with the raptor center's logo—and neatly pressed khaki pants. Her cowboy boots were impeccably clean, although not polished. Her watch did an excellent job of telling the time or acting as a stopwatch, no matter how often Beth urged her to replace it with something more feminine. She was neat, clean, and a wildlife veterinarian tonight. After all, the raptor center's open house was hardly the place to go man hunting.

Grania tossed a smiling apology to Beth's picture. So far, the dating services' offerings had been uninspiring, to say the least. But she'd keep trying. She was now putting down roots in one place for the first time in her life. She could afford to take time to learn how to date, before getting serious about any particular fellow.

In the meantime, she had a lot of unpacking to do. All her books, of course, and at least some of her posters, like the one showing a sabre-toothed tiger's muscles and skeleton.

Her late godfather Tom McLean's official portrait hung in pride of place on the mantel, in the full glory of his deputy sheriff's uniform. She had other pictures of Tom too, but her favorite was the one she'd taken herself, from when he was totally focused on finding a lost child in the Arizona desert. He'd learned tracking from his father, who'd been taught by his uncle, one of Geronimo's last surviving braves.

Folks said Tom McLean could follow a pocket mouse across solid rock. She was just glad he'd found her in the abandoned commune, then become her godfather. No closer kinship was possible between them since Arizona state law didn't permit an abandoned baby, like her, to be adopted. Tom had done as much for her as he could, especially teaching her everything he knew about wildlife and how to watch them. Someday she'd pass the same skills on to her children. She'd clean his guns on his birthday next week the way other women lit candles in remembrance.

She blew a kiss to his picture and headed for her old pickup. After a week's duty as the new wildlife vet at Hill Country Raptor Center, now she'd attend the regular monthly open house and do her best to charm the sponsors whose money kept the center open. It would probably be much like trying to coax money out of alumni at college.

Grania parked her truck in the side lot at the raptor center, with all the other employees' vehicles. The center occupied the side of a steep hill, with its main parking lot next to the narrow rural highway below. Its main building was rectangular, built of adobe with a tiled roof. It was starkly modern, efficient, and full of windows.

Large cages for convalescing and resident birds clustered among the trees in back. A huge flight cage, suitable for exercising the largest raptors prior to release, stood slightly isolated just below a knoll. Smaller flight cages were scattered along the path to it.

Even after a week's employment there, the center still looked like heaven on earth to Grania. Its unofficial overseer, a slender older woman with improbably red hair, glanced up from the reception desk as she approached. "Hi, Linda."

" 'Evening, doc." Linda smiled at Grania. "Go look at your door. There's a surprise there for you."

"Oh, yeah? Thanks!"

On her door? It was too soon for her nameplate, wasn't it? Grania hastened off with a quick wave, Linda's chuckle burning in her ears.

The raptor center's interior was laid out in two parallel rows. The front row, facing the road and the main parking lot, contained the public spaces, such as the lobby, the conference room, the director's office, and so on. The back column, facing the birds' pens, contained the working spaces: the library, the lab, the operating rooms, the ICU, and the kitchen, with the door opening to the hillside beyond. The indoor ward, or ICU, was actually a soundproofed closet with a locked door, lined floor to ceiling with cages. Its silence and darkness were vital for calming and healing distressed birds and completely off-limits to casual visitors.

A dogleg built into the hill, on the lower level below the kitchen, held the rodent room, where mice, rats, rabbits, and chicks were raised to feed the birds.

Grania's office, in the back column, was smaller than Beth's walk-in closet, with its bare white walls and clean, albeit battered, metal furniture. But it had a door with a nameplate: Grania O'Malley, M.S., D.V.M., Ph.D.

She grinned as she traced the letters. It was the first time she'd seen all her degrees spelled out, where she could touch them. "Cool!"

Tom would be so damn proud of her for pulling it off. Or Sister Mary Catherine, who'd named her for the Irish pirate queen. The old nun would be so thrilled to see that one of her chicks had made it all the way through school and earned a doctorate.

A soft cough interrupted her reverie and Grania looked around. "Hello, Bob." She held out her hand and the lean Texan took it with a smile. He was slightly taller than Grania with a hawk nose, strong jaw, and weather-beaten face, above the Texas uniform of starched white cowboy shirt, jeans, and boots.

"Ready for the crowd?"

Grania shrugged. "Of course. Though I've got to admit, sometimes I'd rather watch over the convalescents in ICU than deal with a fund-raising event."

Bob threw back his head and laughed. "Wouldn't we all, darlin', wouldn't we all!"

Bob proudly introduced Grania as the new vet to the first arrival. From then on, the open house was a whirlwind of people and conversations as dozens of guests and staff toured the center or strolled the paths outside, under the guidance of trained educators. A very placid merlin or a burrowing owl, and their favorite educators, taught enthralled children about raptors in the library.

Most of the guests were former, or current, volunteers at the center. Others were local animal wardens or cops who'd brought patients, plus scientists from nearby colleges and universities eager to talk shop at the world-renowned raptor center. A handful of guests were local leaders strutting with pride over the center's success. All were eager to talk to the latest addition to the staff, while hordes of children asked endless questions in between mouthfuls of soda and cake. All in all, it was very similar to receptions for donors at the group homes Grania had grown up in, except for the intense interest in her personally.

Twilight was softening the hills' outline when she finally had a chance to take a deep breath and finish her watery lemonade. The children were gone, while a few adults chatted with some of the most experienced rehabilitators in the kitchen.

Satisfied that everything was in order, Grania returned to the library to refill her glass. Rounding a corner too quickly, she ran into a man stirring his lemonade to dissolve the sugar. Liquid erupted but he deftly managed not to spill on anything.

"Oh, I'm so sorry," she apologized. "Did I spill any on you?"

"No, ma'am," he drawled, blue eyes alert under hair as bright as any carrot. "Everything's fine with me. But you sure look like you could use some more lemonade." He smoothly plucked the glass out of her hand and filled it.

"Thank you. I'm Grania O'Malley, the new vet here."

"Caleb Jones, geologist working for the Santiago Trust."

Was Santiago Oil & Gas a subsidiary of the enigmatic Santiago Trust? When she'd researched the center and its neighborhood—standard practice when a scientist hoped to spend the rest of their life at a job—she'd heard rumors that the trust was older than Texas, richer than Fort Knox, harder to figure out than the Pentagon, and more dangerous to its enemies than a nuclear bomb.

"Glad to meet you." Shrugging off her clumsiness, Grania started to satisfy her curiosity. "Where'd you go to school?"

"Yale."

An Ivy League boy with that Texas drawl? Grania promptly began to ask him questions about Yale's program, comparing it to her experiences at the University of California.

They chatted for a few minutes about their degrees, their specialties, and their observations of the local ecosystem. He had some interesting theories on how the underlying geology affected the local plants and thus, the animal life, and hoped to do some research to support his ideas.

He pointed out a rock formation on the hill, his denim jacket stretching across his shoulder and outlining a shoulder rig with two guns. Why on earth was he armed?

Grania topped off her lemonade again to give herself some time to think. He wouldn't need guns to rob this place, even if there was anything easily stolen. Maybe a policeman, given how his eyes constantly surveyed the room. But why would a geologist become a cop?

She sipped the sweet, watery drink, while watching him. A puzzle like Caleb was far more interesting than lemonade.

When Grania looked up to continue the conversation, her breath stopped at the reflection in the window. Dear God in heaven, Bob was talking to the big man from her dreams at the other end of the library.

Impossible. How the hell could he be here, in the flesh?

Their eyes met in the reflection on the window pane, hers wide with surprise, his eyes turning hungry.

Grania flushed, her gold cross's chain chafing her throat. Her sensible cotton bra suddenly seemed coarse and tight. Her gut clenched and she coughed, trying to get some air into her lungs.

"You okay, ma'am?" Caleb questioned. "Would you like a cup of water?"

"No, thank you. I'm fine." *Or I will be, as soon as I stop looking at that man.* She saw Linda speak softly to Bob, who excused himself and stepped away. The stranger glanced around the nearly empty space and strolled over to the coffee urn. Two other men followed him, both wearing denim jackets identical to Caleb's. One had almost a familial likeness to the stranger, with similar hawk-like features in an ageless, tanned face.

If Grania'd had a breathing problem before, it was ten times worse now.

The stranger was taller than she'd imagined, two meters, making him six feet six in comparison to her five feet ten. Thick black hair that reached his collar, with a heavy wave in it. Dark, dark eyes—not black, maybe chocolate brown, and very old eyes in that young face. Olive skin. His hawk nose was a little crooked from an old break. A deep, almost brutal scar cut across his forehead. White shirt and dark jeans outlined the magnificent muscles of a very strong, fit man.

Lucchese boots, alligator skin no less, and well broken in. Damn, he must be stinking rich.

The tall stranger didn't walk like ordinary men: No, he glided across the floor, as elegant and powerful as a Utah mountain lion she'd once studied for hours. *Predator and dangerous*, insisted her instincts, but her feet didn't move. Her knees were too weak to carry her away, especially when heat spiraled down her spine and into her core. She knew, with the inarguable clarity of shock, that she was hot and bothered and wet between her legs.

"Caleb?" a deep rumble questioned. He exuded competence and the quiet aura of danger, a man who didn't give a damn what the world thought of him because he could remake it to suit himself.

Hell and damnation, she only came up to the man's shoulders. She wouldn't even have the usual confidence builder of looking him in the eyes.

"Don Rafael, may I introduce you to Grania O'Malley, the center's new vet?" Caleb offered.

Grania held out her hand helplessly. The only phrase that ran through her head was, "Want a ride, cowboy?" Somehow she managed not to say it, by saying nothing at all.

First talking owls and now this.

"Grania, this is Don Rafael Perez, the Santiago Trust's administrator," Caleb finished.

"Your servant, señorita." Don Rafael bent and kissed her hand, his lips warm and intimate against her skin. Did he linger a bit longer than necessary? No, that was impossible.

"Señor Perez," Grania stammered. Dammit, now she even sounded like an adolescent girl.

"San Leandro is honored to have a doctor of your skill join us. If there is anything I, or the Santiago Trust, can do for you, you have only to ask."

"Thank you for the offer. I'll remember that," she managed, startled at his generosity. He'd just pledged the Santiago Trust to help her?

Oh hell, she'd been making small talk with donors since she was five years old. Why couldn't she say something interesting now, when it mattered?

"Please excuse us, *doctora*, but Caleb and I must return to the ranch. *Buenas noches*." Don Rafael bowed politely, lifting his hand in a brief salute.

Grania nodded formally, cursing her inability to get past clichés. She drifted to the front window so she could catch a last glimpse of him.

Two identical, big, new Mercedes sedans waited for him, not pickups or SUVs; classy and expensive, to match those well-worn Lucchese alligator boots he was wearing.

Three men, all with the thick chests denoting Kevlar vests hidden under their cowboy shirts, were lounging beside the cars. As deceptively innocent as a pride of lions by a water hole—and as ready to spring into action. They looked as if they could stop an armed attack in a matter of seconds, without turning a hair.

They came to attention when Caleb left the center and quickly pulled one big sedan up to the entrance. Rafael got into the backseat, Caleb took the wheel, while the previous driver—a particularly deadly-looking fellow—moved to the other car. And as the two cars turned down the long driveway to the highway, both vehicles displayed the slightly too solid handling of armored vehicles.

Why on earth was he being protected so heavily? Were the rumors about the Santiago Trust true? A chill ran down her spine.

Grania barely refrained from pressing her nose to the glass when the two sedans pulled out onto the highway. She told herself firmly to walk away while she still could. He might look like the man of her dreams, but how many people had she ever been able to trust?

Bob called her from the lobby. "The open house is over now, Grania. Did you still want to come for barbecue with us?"

She plastered a smile on her face. "Yes, of course. Just give me a minute to grab my purse."

It'd be good to join the others for barbecue and shop talk, do some bonding with the raptor center's team. And if she hadn't calmed down enough to sleep after that, maybe she'd do a little birding tonight before turning in.

And with any luck at all, she wouldn't dream of Don Rafael.

The armored Mercedes Guard sedan headed west on the narrow dirt road, its luxury and Caleb's skill making a comfortable retreat for Rafael on the journey home. The chase car followed closely, keeping watch even here within Compostela Ranch.

Rafael stretched out his legs and considered the evening's events, idly humming an old Castilian *cantiga*.

He'd known Caleb for almost seven decades, first as an excellent oil exploration geologist and later as Gray Wolf's beloved *compañero*. When Caleb had suggested this reception, he'd promptly accepted, glad for a change of scenery after weeks of constant protection at Compostela. It had been days since Ethan's men had last disposed of an enemy *vampiro*, or one of Madame Celeste's few *compañeros*, and the ranch's charms had grown thin.

The excursion had been quite pleasant. He'd enjoyed spending the time in the modern recreation of a falconer's mews and being around the great hawks. Hell, Rafael had even enjoyed fencing with the director, Bob Harrison, about the possibility of conducting ecological surveys of neighboring Santiago Trust lands.

Then he'd seen the new vet, Grania O'Malley, and a relaxing evening had turned into a frustrating one.

She reminded him of someone but he couldn't think of whom. Certainly not his late wife, who'd been short of frame with dark hair, creamy skin, and rich curves. Grania was entirely different, with her long legs and hair the deep rich red of an autumn forest. She had blue eyes like the Bay of Biscay, skin touched with gold from the sun, and teeth white as pearls. Fearghus had always praised that coloring above all others.

Por Dios, she was lovely with her oval face, straight nose, high cheekbones, and mobile mouth made to welcome a man. He was suddenly hungry to see her blue eyes dark and dazed with passion, her mouth swollen from his kisses, her hair tumbled from his caresses. And once she was his lover, he'd see her clothed in silks as soft as her skin. Then he could explore her ripe breasts and narrow waist, crooning endearments before he drifted lower to learn her woman's secrets. Would she moan softly or cry out when rapture shook her from a man's intimate kiss?

Grania. He said the name out loud in the Gaelic fashion, as Donal O'Malley had taught him two centuries ago. Graw-nya. The name suited her, especially its English translation as Grace. She was strong and elegant, well made for hours of delight in bed.

He'd studied her like a hunting cat at the reception, watching for signs of her current relationships, since he never seduced someone who was committed elsewhere.

But he couldn't read her thoughts. He hadn't probed, of course; that would be discourteous—and a boring practice, when one lived as long as he had. But every other *prosaico* he'd ever met all but shouted their thoughts aloud. It always became so easy to insinuate oneself into their life or their bed.

But not *la doctora*. She was a pool of silence, except for the movements of her lithe body and the glances from her beautiful eyes. The only hints she gave of friendship to any man were to Caleb—Caleb, who had never had a carnal thought about a woman! True, Rafael had scented her musk but her smiles had only been for Caleb.

Rafael ground his teeth in jealous frustration yet again.

There were hundreds, even thousands, of other women who would welcome him to their beds. A snap of his finger, a quirk of his eyebrow, or a word on the telephone—and they would run to him.

But it was this woman, this highly educated *doctora*, who uttered inelegant words like "Cretaceous" and "Pleistocene" to Caleb, who locked his mind in carnal paths. How her red lips would open under his mouth, how her sweet channel would pulse around him as she moaned her pleasure. Or how her white neck would arch for his bite as they flew together into ecstasy . . .

How could he seduce her and see his fantasies come to life? Should he whisper sweet words about rocks born millions of years ago, while offering roses? Bring Caleb along on a date to assist him? Assist *him*!

He thumped the leather seat angrily. No, he had no need of assistance. He had seduced women before and he would find a path to this one, even if her thoughts were locked behind a wall as stout as a Santiaguista fortress. Tonight, he would enjoy himself and plot her conquest tomorrow.

Rafael keyed the intercom, satisfied with his decision. He ignored the nervous side of himself, the stomach that hadn't knotted so strongly over meeting a girl since he was sixteen. "Emilio? Do you approve of the new Mercedes?"

"*Sí*, Don Rafael," Emilio answered promptly. As leader of Rafael's daylight guards during this crisis, he wore body armor which thickened his appearance, plus a small headset to talk to the other companions in the chase car. A CAR-15, duplicate of the assault rifle he used as a Navy SEAL, rested on his lap while his head continuously swiveled to scan their surroundings. "The car's armor is barely noticeable, even close up, and both cars are still remarkably fast."

Caleb took a corner neatly and accelerated gently into the setting sun. He enjoyed driving and took as many classes as possible, including stunt driving. Less than fifteen minutes remained until darkness when Rafael's *vampiros* would take over patrol duties from the *compañeros*.

"Should we buy more?" Rafael asked, idly rubbing the rich chestnut wood trim. Mercedes had done a remarkable job of concealing the gun locker in the passenger compartment.

"No, two should be fine," Emilio answered. "Your biggest protection is how you continuously vary your schedule. You don't need caravans of identical Mercedes to play shell games with, as Saddam did."

"More armored Suburbans then?"

"No, sir. Eight should be enough. But you might want to consider another helicopter."

"You've been talking to Ethan." A few longhorns lifted their heads as the cars approached, only to go back to drinking from the spring-fed pond. The landscape was quiet, settling into a summer night's lassitude.

"Of course, sir. The skies are your biggest vulnerability."

Rafael grunted his agreement and clicked the intercom off, not particularly worried this close to home. Riding in an armored sedan, his strategy was that of the turtle and the fox: Unless the fox can figure out how to get the turtle out of its shell, the fox is out of luck.

His Mercedes was almost impossible to break into—and protected its occupants with almost no loss of performance. So his enemies' tactics would be to force it to stop then somehow break into the sedan itself. After that, there'd be hand-to-hand combat involving Rafael, a *vampiro* mayor, and his arsenal. He almost pitied Madame Celeste's assassins.

The road narrowed to a single lane as they climbed toward the pass. He'd have to go out again tonight to feed. No one at the ranch would be able to distract him from the red-haired scholar. He drummed his fingers, irritated at his obsession.

"Madame Celeste has never mounted an airborne attack," Rafael objected, forcing himself to stay in a martial train of thought.

"There's always a first time. Sir."

Rafael chuckled at the polite reproof from a man he'd first seen in diapers. "We'll talk about it more back at the ranch. I'm sure you already have a recommendation."

"Yes, sir."

Rafael keyed the intercom off. Ethan and Emilio could talk high technology together for hours.

Did Grania enjoy such mechanical marvels? Or did she pay so much attention to her patients that the surrounding world faded? Did she focus on her lovers as fiercely as her patients?

"Excuse me, sir," Emilio's voice came clearly through the intercom, backed by rushing wind from the window he'd just cracked open. "Do you know if Johnson sold his helicopter? The old police chopper he uses for crop dusting?"

"Not to my knowledge. In fact, he spoke of overhauling its engine." Rafael listened to the steady beat of the helicopter's blades. Definitely Johnson's toy. He frowned, considering possible explanations as the hair on his neck prickled.

"Any idea why it's so far inside your ranch?"

"No, not this late in the day. Might be picking up alfalfa." The road was very narrow here, squeezed between a steep hillside and a cliff dropping to the San Leandro River below.

Emilio started to turn but before he could look out the rear window, Caleb shouted and hit the gas.

"Ambush!"

Then the hillside exploded into a rocky geyser as the Mercedes swerved. A boulder caught the car's rear and sent it sliding perilously close to the cliff edge. Emilio closed his window quickly and brought his rifle up to the gun port in the windshield, ready for action. Rafael snatched the two Colt .45s from the hidden locker, ready to fight if the car was forced to stop. He looked back for the chase car and found only a cloud of dust and rocks.

Madre de Dios, let his men be safe.

The wheels gripped the road again, sending up a plume of dust. Caleb pushed the car, sending it forward like a knight's charger hearing the sweet horn call to action. The big engine snarled as it fought for speed.

"Incoming! Get down, sir!" Emilio yelled.

Light and noise burst just behind them. A shockwave pummeled the heavy sedan and jolted it forward. The Mercedes reached a rock-free stretch of road and raced forward as another explosion rattled the car. Rafael sent up a quick prayer to Santiago.

"RPG, sir, firing from the hilltop," Emilio reported. Bullets pinged against the windows. "Shit, they've got two shooters in their chopper, too."

Don Rafael, we're starting one of our helicopters now. ETA five minutes. Jean-Marie's voice was icily calm.

Maldito sea, no, Rafael snapped back. *There's still too much light for you to be outside.*

I've been a vampiro *for almost two centuries, enough to walk in twilight. You need another* vampiro *to fight beside you.*

Mierda. Rafael cursed but didn't argue further. If Jean-Marie was killed, he'd destroy every *vampiro* in New Orleans and sweep their ashes into the Mississippi.

The Mercedes was running hard now, faster than Rafael would have thought possible on the poor road. Bullets thudded against its windows and sides. The helicopter followed directly behind them, avoiding the hillside while spitting fury from its open doors.

"All of our men are out of the chase car and have taken cover, sir. Nobody was hurt."

Gracias a Dios. Rafael crossed himself and tucked some extra magazines into his pockets from the locker's supplies. He'd donate a new roof to the Catholic church in thanks for his men's lives, and perhaps a new air conditioner for the Baptist church's Sunday school.

"They're heading toward the son of a bitch with the RPG and wish us luck with the chopper," Emilio added.

Despite their peril, Caleb whistled a slightly off-key version of "Minnie the Moocher" as he brought the Mercedes sliding around a corner. He accelerated quickly and hard as the road turned south before the final run to the pass, marked by power lines. Bullets splatted against the windows like sleet, while still more lead pinged off the Mercedes's armored flanks.

Rafael joined in the song's nonsensical chorus. A good steed and good comrades; what knight could ask for better companions in a fight?

Caleb swerved into the pass, setting up for the sharp turn that followed. The setting sun burst into their eyes as they passed under the power lines, which crossed the road here. Instead of squinting, Caleb hit the gas harder and the Mercedes's engine responded with a powerful roar.

The chopper came through the pass high and turned into the sun. Suddenly another, larger chopper dived at it from the west, guns blazing. Rafael's hand tightened on his gun as he watched intently. *Mierda*, he hated to be an observer.

The little one dived to escape but its blades caught a power line, snapping the metal like twigs. Sparks flew, lighting the sky like fireworks.

The blades' remains kept beating, once, twice, but they couldn't keep the bird in the air. It hung in the sky for an endless moment. Then the nose dropped and it dived into the hill below the road. The resulting explosion was brief but intense.

Stay here until Ethan can take over, then report to me, Jean-Marie.

Très bien, Don Rafael.

Caleb didn't stop until he reached Compostela's ranch house. That was where Jean-Marie found Rafael an hour later, drinking a mint julep on the porch. Barely visible from the ranch, headlights and flashlights marked where the local sheriff and his men studied the crash, under Ethan's scrutiny.

Rafael sprang up and hugged him, scrutinizing him for any injury. Satisfied, he clapped his *hijo* on the back. Jean-Marie simply grinned the entire time, clearly ecstatic at having crossed this threshold in a *vampiro*'s life.

"An occasion like this deserves a celebration. Champagne or mint julep, *mi hijo*?"

Jean-Marie tossed his heavy Kevlar vest onto another chair. "We always celebrate fights in Texas with a mint julep. So a mint julep, s'il vous plaît."

Rafael punched him lightly in the arm and poured him one. "Report, *por favor*."

They began to walk together, instinctively heading for the shooting range.

"They were humans, not *compañeros* or *vampiros*. Probably mercenaries; certainly they had some military training."

Rafael grunted. "Not surprising since Madame Celeste's current offering for my head is fifty million dollars."

"And likely to go up, so you'll need to stay here at Compostela."

"No. I will not spend my days pacing like a caged bear."

"You cannot risk your life by going where we can't protect you," Jean-Marie retorted.

"I will go and do what I please. If necessary, I can take more guards with me." He relented at the sight of a seething Jean-Marie, biting his tongue. "Content yourself, *mi hijo*. I survived today because my protection was good and will remain so. There is nothing to worry about."

"You should be more careful," Jean-Marie insisted stubbornly.

"I must also live my own life, not cower in fear of Madame Celeste's next attack. Remember the *vampiros* of Texas have fangs too. Lars is in New Orleans, with permission to kill her given the chance."

His eldest *hijo* smiled, with a flash of fangs. "I hope he succeeds soon. He has the looks to get close enough to behead her."

"Perhaps, perhaps not. But I also told him to do everything possible to unsettle her."

"It's past time she faced a true master of dirty tricks, someone who could shut down her nightclub and its casino. It's the source of most of her money—and her pretty boys."

"A fair payback, indeed. I'm not sure what she'll do when she hears that this attempt failed. Will you stand watch in the comms center tonight? You'll know how to interpret any rumors coming out of New Orleans."

"*Certainement, mon père,*" his *hijo* agreed promptly. "We can dine here together first."

"I go out to feed, no matter what happens," Rafael said briskly but softened when Jean-Marie opened his mouth to start arguing again. "Relax, Jean-Marie, the arrangements are so new that no ambusher can have anticipated them. Ethan and his men will accompany me, as well."

Grania parked her truck close to the marina, less than two miles from the raptor center. She'd eaten barbecue and talked shop with the other vets, a very relaxed and happy gathering. She'd admired pictures of their children and said the right things, all the while wondering if Rafael Perez was married. Foolish, foolish thought. Silly of her to keep thinking about a man, just because he looked so much like someone in her dreams.

So she'd gone back to her little house and looked at other guys at the online dating services. That was a really stupid thing to do; all of them looked totally boring, after seeing Rafael Perez. Cursing herself for a fool, she'd finally logged out and decided to go owling.

Tonight she needed those birds' wildness, their ability to appear when and where they chose—which was always when and where they were least expected, and most likely to startle their searcher the most. They had the ability to blend into their surroundings whenever they chose, or to speak in a series of calls that sounded like voices from beyond, that could be understood if you just tried hard enough. They were the symbol of all that was truly wild and unknowable and she'd always needed them as much as she needed air to breath. Tonight she wanted to be with them, in the simplicity of their world—not the world of crowds, where Rafael Perez walked.

The raptor center was located on the western edge of a state park, mostly oak, mesquite, and rocks crossed by a few hiking trails. On the eastern edge was a large lake, where a popular resort was very busy on this Memorial Day holiday. Santiago Trust property bordered the raptor center on the north.

Grania parked on the boundary between the raptor center and the park. She walked into the forest slowly and quietly, taking her bearings from regular observations of the stars, as Tom had taught her. She spotted an eastern screech owl, and a barred owl, and noted them both carefully in her logbook, just to reassure herself she could still behave calmly and scientifically—no matter how jangled her nerves were.

She followed proper owling etiquette, of course: She had full permission to owl at both the raptor center and the public park. She didn't use tapes of owl calls, since she preferred not to, whether or not it was breeding season. She was always extremely still and quiet, doing everything in slow motion—as much or more so than Tom had taught her. When she found an owl, she sank to the ground, until the owl relaxed from its elongated alarm posture into the plump relaxed posture. The eastern screech owl was so certain of its superb camouflage that it almost seemed to sneer at her puny attempts to find it. She'd rarely revisit the sites where she spotted the owls, certainly no sooner than three to four weeks, in order not to upset them. And she was definitely not going to tell anyone about them—she would not let anyone disturb these, or any other, owls for any reason whatsoever.

She also carefully used her military prototype night-vision goggles to watch the owls from the greatest distance possible, thereby reducing their stress. Her night vision goggles and matching image intensifier were a gift from some American Special Forces troops she'd helped in Colombia. The heavy gear was a duplicate of what the troops used and far too expensive for even a wildlife researcher's dreams. They'd refused to let her give it back to them. Now she wondered if a bird would perch on one of its loops and whorls, the ultimate compliment for anyone trying to be inconspicuous in the woods.

But even owling couldn't hold her full attention now. She still found her thoughts straying to a certain tall man who glided like a cougar.

Eventually she found herself on the edge of a mesquite thicket, high above the lake below. The stars were bright, the air hot and humid with a lightning storm sparking the sky to the south. The mesquite's pungent scent soothed her, with its reminders of childhood trips with Tom and her college days in California.

Grania took a deep breath and exhaled slowly, letting all the evening's frustrations go with it. She inhaled again, savoring the mix of familiar and unfamiliar scents. Texas air.

She settled deeper into the thicket, intent on learning more of her new home. Yoga breathing came easily as she centered herself then let her consciousness relax and welcome the world around. The night's small animals gradually crept back as she became part of the thicket's world.

Grania smiled at the great horned owl watching her from a branch high above. "*Bienvenido*, amigo," she murmured under her breath and was content.

At least until more two-legged visitors arrived.

Rafael cast a quick glance around and was satisfied. He'd found a good patch of grass, blessedly well free of fire ants. He swirled a blanket across the ground then kissed Brynda again, long and deep. She moaned into his mouth and arched as he squeezed her plump behind. She was a dear friend, a widow who worked for his longtime attorneys. She was also a willing lover who'd never objected to sharing her blood with him. She only balked at copulation, thanks to some odd need for professional distance between them. But her blood tasted sweet, if not fiery hot, and should soothe his frustration over that red-haired *doctora*.

His tongue probed the recesses of Brynda's mouth, enticing her. She shuddered and rolled her hips against him. She gasped for breath, her blond hair tumbling over her shoulders. He kissed her cheek and slid his hand inside her waistband.

"Damn, Don Rafael, that's it. Rub my ass! Lower, stud. Get your hand down where I can really feel it. Oh, yeah, that's it." She reached up for another kiss.

Well, you couldn't say that Brynda didn't know exactly what she wanted. Rafael smiled to himself as he obeyed. "*Dulce* Brynda," he purred.

Or that she didn't communicate those wants to her lover, even if her language usually reflected her late husband's naval career more than her staid life as a paralegal. Her shorts were too tight to provide much room for play, even if they did ride so low on her hips that his fingers easily dived between her buttocks. One finger circled her anus, as his other hand unzipped her shorts.

She broke away from his kiss, gasping, and yanked off her shorts. "Goddamn, Don Rafael, you could make a nun leave the convent! Where the hell did you learn that move? Never mind, just do it again one more time before your hand goes where it really belongs."

Rafael kissed her again as his hand delved lower, moving more freely now. She quivered and stretched, rubbing her breasts against his chest. He allowed himself to forget his surroundings in the mesquite thicket. Or that Ethan and two of his men were only paces away.

No, this was the time to build his partner's passion to its peak so it would infuse her blood with the largest possible amount of emotion for him to feed on. And maybe, just maybe, he could lose himself in this moment long enough to have a climax of his own.

Perhaps. A *vampiro* didn't need to have an orgasm when he drank. The bite enhanced the other's emotion, whatever that was, so his lovers always had a very strong orgasm when he fed, thanks to his insistence on sexual pleasure. But often enough, he'd simply be relaxed afterwards, similar to the comfortable pleasure brought by his own hand.

Tonight he wanted more. He wanted the mindless release of the *petit mort*, the small death that sexual rapture could bring. He needed to forget the red-haired vet and live only in the world of his *vampiro's* body, where he'd dwelt for seven and a half centuries.

So he sucked Brynda's ear, matching the rhythm to his fondling of her clit. She shrieked and her language promptly descended into Anglo-Saxon. He licked her neck, easily finding her most sensitive spot, nipped it lightly and licked it again. She all but collapsed against him at that, groaning his name.

His fingers stroked her folds, evoking a rush of cream that dampened her thong. He tugged up her short top and laved her nipples until they gleamed, tight and berry red, in the moonlight.

She sobbed his name in response, pulling his head closer. He suckled her, scraping his teeth over the rich buds to make them as sensitive as possible. He'd enjoyed bringing Brynda to orgasm more than once from attentions only to her breasts.

Rafael eased her down to the ground. She grunted in relief as her thong came off. "Goddamn, that feels better! That thing was getting in the way."

He ran his hands slowly up her thighs, enjoying the slickness of her arousal. She writhed, shamelessly encouraging him. He paused, smiling as her desperation increased and his cock swelled slightly for the first time.

She grumbled and yanked at his hands.

Rafael chuckled and lightly bit one of her superb nipples. She screamed and arched as her first orgasm took her. Before it finished, his fingers brought her to a second climax, then a third with his mouth over hers. The fourth came from focused attention by his hand to her clit. Sweet, very sweet.

He bit down hard on her jugular when the fifth climax swamped her. He'd enjoy a drink and hopefully forget the redhead, even if his cock hadn't hardened enough for an orgasm.

A woman choked from somewhere close by.

Rafael froze, *vampiro* senses coming to full alert.

What the hell? Ethan cursed. *Don Rafael, there's a woman in the thicket just north of you. Tall, brown hair or maybe red.*

Downwind of us, of course, so we couldn't smell her, Rafael muttered. *Whoever she is, she's as stealthy as a* vampiro. He withdrew his fangs from Brynda but continued to rub her clit gently. She moaned softly, easing down slightly from her sexual peak. Slight rustles marked Ethan moving into position near the other woman.

Rafael shifted too, testing the air until he caught the watcher's scent.

¡Coño! The lady vet was spying on him, she of the red hair and the

even more incredible long legs. And she was unmistakably aroused, her sweet musk tickling his nose. His cock immediately came to full alert, filling his jeans with the white-hot pressure of intense hunger.

Should I kill her? Ethan asked, his tone as dispassionate as if they discussed the best color for a new truck.

No! Rafael snapped. The little lady was poised to fight. He'd never seen a human deliberately attack a *vampiro*. Such courage to protect someone she didn't know! She did not deserve to die, unless of course she did actual harm. *No, she has made no move against any of us. I will order her to leave and forget what she's seen tonight.*

He focused his attention on Grania and reached out to her mind. He'd done this a million times before to thousands of other people. Just a simple suggestion followed by a painless bit of forgetfulness, the fundamental skill of *vampiro* survival among unpredictable *prosaicos*.

His probe met a blank wall. He knew it was Grania, could feel the peculiar mental texture that made it uniquely her. But he couldn't find a way to speak to her.

He searched her mind's façade for an opening. Every human had a portal for telepathic suggestions, whether they were an ancient *vampiro* or a *prosaico*.

Nothing. He couldn't find so much as a crack.

Abandoning subtlety, he tried force. *Go away,* pequeña. *Go away!*

Her shields remained in place. Not a muscle of that gorgeous body moved.

GO AWAY!!! Rafael shouted as strongly as he could on every channel. Ethan and his two men flinched.

A faint quiver ran through Grania. Her scent hinted of pain but not panic. She stayed where she was, inside the thicket.

Shielded by her satiation, Brynda sighed and stretched, an aftershock rippling through her.

Rafael closed his eyes for a moment. He had to admire Grania's steadfast courage, her refusal to run although she must know she watched a *vampiro*. What now? Trust her not to kill him or to speak of him? His *vampiro* instincts stayed calm so it might work.

Don Rafael, I've got her in my sights, Ethan offered.

No, we will let her watch, Rafael decided, following his instincts. His cock promptly throbbed eagerly. He smiled wryly. Obviously being an exhibitionist appealed to a side of himself he hadn't seen in centuries. Or perhaps it was the audience that appealed.

Afterward, you will watch and kidnap her if she starts to speak of this. ¿Comprendes?

Yes, sir.

Rafael ran his hand through his hair as he pondered how to provide the best show for *la doctora.* Then he brought Brynda across his chest, her expression open for Grania to see, and shifted her legs. The silent watcher would know what went on but not all the details.

He glided his tongue over Brynda's lips, teasing her back into awareness.

"More?" she muttered. "You want me to come again?"

"But of course, señora. You are so beautiful under passion's spell."

"Flatterer." She chuckled and opened for another kiss. "Oh yes," she murmured a moment later when he fondled her breast. "Oh yes."

Rafael stroked her breasts, plumping them until she shuddered and groaned. He twisted her nipples lightly, then tugged them, as her hips rocked against him.

The rich spice of Grania's musk teased him. He smiled in pure masculine triumph as his cock grew harder still. The red-haired vixen was interested and aroused by what he did.

Rafael teased and tormented Brynda's superb breasts in all the ways she liked best. She sobbed and pleaded with him for a climax. Then she gasped that he was doing exactly the right thing when he outlined her intimate folds and played with her clit.

He slipped two fingers, then three, into her, setting her hips rocking. She pumped hard against his hand, following his lead, and arched back against him. "Damn you, finish me!"

Grania's scent built around Rafael, hungry and excited. His cock throbbed against the denim's bondage.

The first pulse of climax swelled deep inside Brynda. Rafael's forefinger found her G-spot just as his fangs sank into her neck. She bucked and screamed as the powerful shock pummeled her, sending wave after orgasmic wave through her. "Oh yes! God, yes!"

Grania groaned. The unmistakable scent of her climax slid into his nostrils.

Rafael sucked hard, the sharp, bright taste of Brynda's carnal pleasure flowing into his mouth through her blood. A storm built from his spine through his balls and burst like a geyser from his cock. He fought to retain consciousness as stars burst behind his eyes.

He recovered quickly, soon enough to feel Brynda shift away from his hand. He eased it free and kissed the top of her head, shuddering.

Where had such a strong orgasm come from? And, *Dios mio*, what was he going to do with Grania?

Grania straightened cautiously and slowly steadied her breathing. An orgasm. She'd had an orgasm without touching herself in any way, just by watching That Man with another woman. A scene that had felt—impossibly!—like reliving her own memory. She'd read of such orgasms in sexuality textbooks but never experienced one before.

And yet it had undeniably happened.

She closed her eyes for a moment.

She had to think about something else, like a man who drank a woman's blood. But she'd seen Don Rafael do exactly that.

She'd seen his teeth. Functional fangs, apparently razor sharp, comparable to those on a vampire bat. But those pests required their prey be asleep, not at an orgasmic climax.

She'd seen him sucking on the woman. She'd seen drops of blood appear on the woman's skin afterward, and on his chin. The only conclusion was that he'd been drinking her blood.

So what was he? A vampire? But vampires were creatures of myth and legend, studied by social scientists. No veterinarian, or other trained biologist, had ever observed one.

What did the scientific method say to do when an observation didn't match accepted theory? Research, analyze, repeat the observation. Formulate a hypothesis only if absolutely necessary.

She needed to see more of him before she could decide on an explanation. And she had to stop wondering what he'd look like without any clothes on.

FOUR

Rodrigo awoke with a start, a sword at his throat. He'd been dreaming of his return to Toledo and Blanche, now that his strength was returning, and was hopeful his ransom would follow quickly.

His eyes flashed open and met Diego's viciously satisfied ones. Rodrigo began to sit up but the sword pressed deeper, drawing blood, and he desisted with a growl. Beside him, Fearghus cursed softly. The only other sounds were the normal ones of his cousin's men sleeping nearby, at his estate deep in Granada.

"Madre de Dios, Diego, what mean you by this?" Rodrigo demanded. "I mourned you as dead."

"I am—to you and all other infidels. Now I am Jamil and a true believer."

"How could you renounce Christianity so easily? When you were supposed to have been knighted by the king this fall? Apóstata!" He spat in Diego's face.

Diego's expression contorted with rage and he lifted his sword for the killing stroke. Rodrigo poised himself to spring.

Suddenly a leaden weight fell upon his limbs and he couldn't move. What devil's magic was this? Why didn't the noise of his argument with Diego wake his cousin's men?

A figure took shape out of the shadows next to Diego. Wrapped in a black cloak, it barely reached Diego's shoulder. "Are these the infidels you spoke of, yaa ibni l-'aziiz?" the man asked in the pure Arabic of the Mediterranean's eastern edge.

My dear son? Had Diego been adopted?

Diego's hands clenched his sword in the moonlight then relaxed slowly. He lowered the curved blade carefully. "Yes, yaa 'abi l-'aziiz. They are the only Christian knights still held captive."

Dark eyes, like pits under the cloak's hood, scrutinized Rodrigo, until his skin tried to crawl off his bones. Rodrigo fought to free himself but could not. How was The Syrian binding him? He longed to kill the cochino *and purify himself afterward by a good fast with his fellow Santiaguistas.*

"Filthy pig? You dare to befoul me, a true Muslim, by that name?" the newcomer snarled. He backhanded Rodrigo, sending him crashing off the cot and onto the floor. Stars danced before his eyes as blood's copper-sweet taste rushed over his tongue.

Fearghus murmured a nearly inaudible encouragement as Rodrigo slowly hauled himself upright. He gathered himself to attack—but the same heaviness suddenly caught him.

The Syrian surveyed him, as grudgingly as any farmer studying a balky donkey, before turning to Diego. "They certainly look strong enough to survive days of torture, as the others did not. Let's take them and go."

Torture? Days of torture?

"What of the others?" Diego asked humbly. "There are many other men here who could provide you with similar enjoyment."

The Syrian slapped Diego, sending him staggering. Ay, mierda, how Rodrigo enjoyed that sight, despite his anger at his own helplessness.

"Every other man here is a Muslim, a follower of Islam," The Syrian snapped. "No Muslim preys upon another Muslim. Unless you

*wish me to doubt your conversion, you will not mention this to me
again."*

"*Forgive me, yaa 'abi l-'aziiz. I did not mean what I said.*" Diego's
voice and attitude were utterly humble as he prostrated himself to
The Syrian. *His eyes briefly promised vengeance to Rodrigo for having witnessed this humiliation before he kissed The Syrian's feet.*

"*You are forgiven, yaa ibni l-'aziiz. All of us make mistakes and
you will learn from this.*" *He hoisted the now-bound Rodrigo effortlessly over his shoulder and turned for the entrance.*

"*Our hosts will be furious that you have kidnapped us,*" Rodrigo
growled, *even as the air was jolted out of him.* Furious is a very mild
description of how Achmed and my cousins will feel. And they are a
very proud and powerful family. *Hope flickered in his heart.*

The Syrian laughed. "*Let them be insulted and come after us.
Even if they come with Abu Yusuf, who defeated those heathen dogs
at Ecija, I can destroy them all.*"

"*Since you can read their minds and make their limbs turn to water,*" Diego agreed, *as he dragged Fearghus out like a trussed goose,*
"*you will pour their blood upon the ground like water or drink it like
wine.*"

*Rodrigo's stomach knotted. Still he swore to Santiago that, no
matter what it took or how long, one day he would come home to
Blanche and his children.*

Grania told herself one more time, very firmly, that she couldn't possibly have seen a vampire. She'd seen a very handsome man—admit-
tedly, a man so sexy she'd like to have an affair with him—masturbate
a woman and bite her neck. But that was all.

Okay, so he had long teeth, really long teeth. The female he'd been
with had a few drops of blood on her neck, just above her jugular—a
spot analogous to where the Mongols had routinely, and repeatedly,
taken blood from their horses. Certainly, the female didn't seem to
have been harmed, judging by how she was fondling his head as he
licked her neck.

But even if vampires existed, the only observations of them came from historians and anthropologists. Were those descriptions accurate enough to be reliable? But if anything like those vampires did walk the earth and did have evil intentions toward humans, she would not like to meet one. Nor fight one, even if they had only half the powers attributed to them.

She'd thought of trying to stop Don Rafael from harming the woman. She'd even started to get up. But there didn't seem to be any doubt that—Brynda, was it?—was having one hell of a good time, the way the lucky woman was carrying on.

"Oh, Don Rafael, as ever, you're so damn good for a girl," Brynda cooed eventually and kissed him on the mouth. Grania gritted her teeth, all too conscious of her pounding headache, the wetness between her own thighs, and her nagging jealousy of the other female. She might have had an orgasm but she'd have preferred to enjoy it in a man's arms, as the other had.

Don Rafael kissed her gently and said something so softly, Grania couldn't quite catch it. Brynda blushed, looking almost like a teenager for a moment, before getting dressed as he gathered up their belongings. They walked back toward the lake together, arm in arm.

Grania followed them cautiously, using all her years of training and experience in stalking wild animals and grateful for having walked this terrain a few times before. It was still nerve-wracking to plan her route as carefully as possible, keeping her quarry always in sight while staying downwind of them.

They sauntered, dammit, with him supporting Brynda a bit in the beginning, while she told him he was better than shopping or chocolate.

Grania used the upright crouch her godfather had taught her to follow them—placing her weight very precisely on her feet, outside first then rolling the foot on and off the ground, ever ready to withdraw it at the slightest hint that a twig underneath might snap.

The humid air weighed heavily on her skin, while sweat beaded and rolled down her back under her shirt. Mesquite twigs slid into her hair and attached themselves to her jacket. She ignored them.

She wished to God she had her shotgun. It would make even a vampire pay attention, should Don Rafael turn hostile toward Brynda or herself.

Finally, Don Rafael and Brynda reached the lakeshore a mile from the resort. The road here was lined with great palm trees, tall but fat and round at their base, as if ready to hide Ali Baba's thieves. Beyond the public park's mesquite thickets lay a series of tiered gardens with sparkling fountains and finally, the marina and resort itself, like a vision of paradise against the hills beyond.

The marina's bright lights danced across the water, illuminating small sailboats and powerboats. Above it rose the Arabian Nights fantasy of the resort's main buildings. Grania could distantly hear a band playing a country-western tune, while a DJ's voice exhorted dancers to come learn a new line dance.

Grania promptly took cover behind a palm tree, where she could see but not be seen.

Brynda kissed Don Rafael on the cheek, looking the very picture of smug femininity, and sauntered toward the marina.

After she'd passed a turn in the road and was out of sight, Don Rafael stretched his arms and legs, then his back, in a manner similar to a large raptor—such as a condor—preening on its nest. His big, muscular body was incredibly graceful—and Grania's mouth went abruptly, embarrassingly, dry with lust.

He shimmered in the moonlight and Grania blinked in surprise. When she focused again, a very large great horned owl was taking flight from where he'd been standing.

Dear God in heaven, where had that great horned come from? And where had Don Rafael gone?

She stepped out from behind the palm tree, determined to investigate. Suddenly a man's arm slammed around her neck and dragged her back against him, using a choke hold. Startled and angry, Grania fought hard, using every dirty trick she'd ever learned, but to no avail. She kicked, she jabbed him with her elbows, she tried to throw him.

The fellow was simply much stronger than she was; he never even grunted when she kicked him. He wasn't Don Rafael, being only a few inches taller than her and more slender than Don Rafael. At least he was professional enough not to have a hard-on.

Finally she forced herself to relax, trying not to curse him or visibly seethe, and waited for an opportunity to escape.

Then Don Rafael walked onto the road, clad only in his shirt and jeans, and faced her.

What the hell? Had he really turned into an owl? Were her eyes deceiving her? Where were the rest of his clothes?

A lifetime of training as an observer was suddenly useless when faced with so many contradictions and impossibilities. She fought to remain calm.

"*Buenas noches, doctora.*"

"*Buenas noches, señor,*" she managed to answer, after only a slight hesitation.

"Did you enjoy your observations, *doctora*?"

She could have killed him for that quip. After all, he was the one who'd been behaving outrageously by drinking blood.

She forced herself back to calmness, deliberately relaxing every muscle in her body one by one. She'd talked her way past murderous ruffians in Colombian swamps, while counting owls, and survived. Surely she could deal with a pair of Texans.

The man behind her eased slightly, as her body became supple, but was still implacable.

"They were somewhat . . . unusual, señor." She shrugged, striving for a light atmosphere, and wished her headache would disappear.

His dark eyes fixed on hers, as if he wished to rip her thoughts out of her. "Do you intend to share them with others?"

"What's to share? A man and woman did some necking in the woods. Would anyone in authority believe the man bit the woman for a nefarious reason, especially when he's such an important member of the community?"

"Do you mock me, *doctora*?" His voice was deadly soft. The forearm against her windpipe tightened.

She swallowed, hard, and reminded herself they had power here, not her. "No, I'm just telling the truth."

He studied her then nodded. The forearm left her throat but her attacker didn't release her. Grania managed not to wipe her brow.

"How discreet are you, *doctora*?"

Grania gave him the simple truth. "If the lady is unharmed, I will be completely discreet."

"So very much the medical practitioner. If I hear you have been indiscreet about tonight's activities, you will immediately regret it. Greatly."

"If I learn that the lady has been harmed in any way, you, sir, will immediately regret it. Greatly." She silently challenged him to contradict her.

"Upon my honor, I would never harm a lady." He bowed to her, as formally as if at the royal court in Madrid. Oddly enough, she believed him completely.

"*¿Con el permiso?* May I remove this impertinent twig from your jacket, *doctora*?"

She stared at him in shock. He wanted to help her clean up? Here and now? His expression was completely sincere. The arm across her throat relaxed, a light weight like a heavy collar, rather than the hard bar of imminent death. Don Rafael's minion was no longer threatening her. Don Rafael was giving her a free choice.

Grania considered him suspiciously before inclining her head. "Certainly."

"You may depart, Ethan."

Ethan hesitated. If anything, his grip tightened on her. "She could be the bait for another assassination attempt, Don Rafael."

Assassination?

"There is no threat to me here and now." Don Rafael's voice was deadly calm—and it sliced the night air like her best scalpel.

"As you wish, sir." Her jailer reluctantly released her and was gone—without a sound.

Don Rafael removed the twig from a pocket flap on her sleeve. A moment later, another twig dropped to the ground as he methodically removed the signs of her passage through the thicket. He was also quite possibly checking for recording equipment, weapons, or any other means of causing trouble.

Grania kept her mouth shut and submitted, all too conscious of the big hands moving so expertly over her. Without the fellow holding her, she had nothing to think about except Don Rafael's deft touch and how his breath stirred her hair. How the night's soft air wrapped them like a cloak.

She was a wildlife biologist. She knew perfectly well, from years of study and observation, that grooming rituals, like this one, both cleaned the recipient and soothed her. Don Rafael was gentling her to his touch—and she had very little say in the matter.

The light sandalwood scent of his body was reassuring, even when underlain by sweat and musk. His breath stirred her hair and his hands were callused. He worked steadily, with an even rhythm that seduced her into relaxing.

Somehow her eyes drifted shut, as her breathing matched the pattern of his movements. Something deep inside her, beyond her mind's control, whispered agreement and pleasure in his touch, as if he were the most welcome of lovers. Her muscles slowly unclenched and her pulse slowed to a more normal beat. The night's tensions started to drift away, as Don Rafael behaved like a gentleman. Thought slowed to a crawl. A deep throbbing ache awoke inside her, tightening her breasts as if they longed to be fondled by him.

"Will you give me the kiss of peace, as a token of your pledge?"

Grania's eyes drifted open and she found Don Rafael standing very close to her. She considered his oddly medieval phrasing warily. If he hadn't harmed her by now, what was the risk in a kiss? "If you wish."

She reached out to take Don Rafael's hands but he was so close, she touched his arms instead. Warm, strong muscle, vibrant with health and life, welcomed her. She shivered and instinctively caressed him a little.

His eyes flickered briefly but she was too absorbed in controlling herself to try to read his expression.

She bit her lip at her sentimental lapse and deliberately took a more formal stance, her hands resting lightly on his shoulders in an ancient folk dance hold, learned during childhood. She planted her feet and turned her face up to him. "Whenever you're ready," she announced, deliberately trying not to be enticing.

"Ah, *doctora*," he murmured and bent his head. He brushed his lips against her temple, gentle and undemanding. She relaxed and started to move away, hoping her contact with him was over.

His hands slid down her arms to her elbows as his mouth drifted lower. She froze, startled, her mouth half open on a good-bye. His lips covered hers, gently sipping the breath from her. She murmured as their lips and tongues stroked each other, angled to fit together, glided, tangled, wove a web of magic. She pressed up against him and trembled. He groaned something and kissed her harder.

Her hands slid down from his shoulders, over his arms, exploring the iron heat of his biceps. She murmured her approval and tilted her head back to smile at him, everything in her seeming to slowly swirl into a lava pool of lust.

"Ah, *doctora*, your kisses are more heated than your hair," Don Rafael purred, stroking her back until she stretched against him like a cat begging for more. She rubbed her leg along the outside of his, the roughness of their jeans heating the fire in her core still further. She sighed and slid her hand into his hair, unconscionably eager for more kisses.

"*Querida.*" He bent his head toward her again.

Just then a car's headlights swept over them briefly, as it twisted and turned along the lakeshore road, no more than two miles away.

Don Rafael broke the kiss and listened, his attitude alert and almost feral.

Grania jerked away from Don Rafael and tried to recover her sanity. Good God, what had come over her? She might not be the world's most experienced female but she wasn't a virgin either.

"Satisfied now?" she asked, managing just enough bravado to meet his eyes. Her headache was almost entirely gone.

He glanced down at her. A ghost of a smile teased his mouth before vanishing quickly. "*Sí*, we have an understanding. *Buenas noches, doctora.*"

"*Buenas noches*, señor."

He strolled down the road, humming a medieval *cantiga*, and disappeared from sight at the first turn, where the road curved around a promontory. Grania stood quite still until he was gone—and her knees had stopped shaking.

Then she ran to where she'd last seen him fully dressed—and first seen the owl. She searched the spot as thoroughly as possible but could find no sign of his missing boots or other gear.

Where the hell had they gone? Had Ethan taken his gear or did he have more men around?

A headlong run around the bluff took her to an overlook above the marina. From there she could see Brynda sharing a drink with friends on a big houseboat. She showed no signs of weakness or injury and was protected by others. Grania shook her head at her own concern for someone who didn't seem to need it and headed back to her truck.

It was a relief when she was finally driving home, after a very long hike, without any trace of her sick headache. She'd never felt anything like it before so perhaps it was an allergic reaction to some vegetation. Hopefully, she'd never have anything like it again.

And the next step? Tell the police? As she'd promised Rafael, not unless Brynda was hurt. So tomorrow, she'd go back to the lake and check up on her.

And at some point, as she was unhappily aware, her scientific curiosity would insist she understand exactly what happened when Don Rafael drank Brynda's blood.

Don Rafael turned away from Grania's cottage after the last light turned off and headed back to his Mercedes. "Keep a very close eye on her, Ethan. We want to be very sure she doesn't talk."

"Yes, sir." Ethan was wise enough not to ask why the woman was still alive.

After all, Rafael had killed (when mind control wouldn't resolve the situation) people who knew far less about *vampiros* than Grania did and were, therefore, less of a threat than she was. But his gut knotted fast and hard at any thought of injury to her—and raced to turn itself inside out at the prospect of killing her. He simply could not do it. Obviously, the reason must be that he needed to learn where she'd gained those impregnable mental shields. In seven centuries, he had never encountered such barriers nor heard of any so strong.

Since a frontal attack had been so thoroughly rebuffed, a more subtle approach was called for. He'd seduce her—and see just how quickly she'd stop paying attention to Caleb and start focusing all of her passion on a man like himself.

Rafael quickened his step, ignoring the voices that hinted this lady would not be so amenable to his plans. He'd survived by playing sexual games all of his life as a *vampiro*. He'd bet a thousand of his finest longhorns that the redheaded *doctora* would be whispering her secrets into his ear within a week.

In New Orleans, Beau strolled back into Madame Celeste's headquarters in the Warehouse District, ready to start some action after taking more than a liter of blood from a silly coed a few miles away. He'd bled her until she'd passed out, and all the while she'd thought she was going to die, making for a meal of almost incomparable richness. Then he'd ordered her unconscious mind to forget the experience so that she could heal—and he could feed upon her again in a few months. It was the way his *creador* had taught him to prey upon *prosaicas*, providing almost as much energy as death throes while keeping the stupid cows alive for another round.

Madame Celeste's headquarters was a two-hundred-year-old, four-story building. An enormous, gaudy casino lured in hordes of tourists on the first floor, with its King Bacchus theme, while the nightclub occupied the second floor. The world's beautiful people fought for invitations to the private club on the third floor. Madame's private quarters took up the entire fourth floor, with a helipad on the roof.

Irritatingly, Madame Celeste's private elevator was off-limits to all *vampiros* tonight. So he took the public elevator to the private club on the third floor, then worked his way through the crowd.

Tonight, the fashionable club was a hive of activity, with many of New Orleans' junior *vampiros* actively hunting *prosaicos*. There was a brilliant dance floor in the center where beautiful, half-naked *pro-saicos* sweated and danced under ever-changing lights. A bar covered one wall, above which shadow dancers, both men and women, gyrated ever more lewdly. The private booths were immense and circular, their circular beds screened by floor-to-ceiling shimmering curtains. The walls were covered with pale golden woods, on which flashed an ever-changing montage of past Mardi Gras celebrations.

To his more senior eyes, it was a tawdry place where no illusions held. *Vampiro* senses could easily see past the flashing lights and darkened corners to the frayed wires and duct tape—not necessarily in the same place—the chipped paint, the uneven floors, and the remains of last year's or last decade's hot décor.

Worse, he could smell the alcohol and drugs used by tonight's crowd and last night's, and so on back in time since Madame Celeste had opened this trap for fools and lazy predators. Chemicals that dulled *prosaico* senses and spoiled the taste of a good meal for a *vampiro*.

He pasted an insincere smile on his face and glided across the crowded dance floor, his Armani wardrobe and angelic looks winning him immediate acceptance and come-hither glances. He sneered privately. Give him genuinely terrified prey anytime, not drunks. A *vampiro* needed the rich flood of emotion to live on, not prey who'd blame the experience on something that came out of a glass. Any *vampiro* who made a steady diet of drunks became as sluggish and stupid as his prey, making himself very vulnerable in a duel.

Which was probably why Madame Celeste encouraged her *ca-chorros* to feed in places like this. And why so few of her *vampiros* had survived to full maturity, let alone twenty or thirty years.

He headed for the old-fashioned private stairs. The *vampiro* guard silently let him pass and Beau went up, allowing none of his disdain to show.

Madame Celeste was a fool to let her *vampiros*, however young, feed so publicly. The last Soviet *vampiros* had thought themselves equally invulnerable to public opinion and allowed their *hijos* to do as they pleased. He himself had been trapped in Moscow by generations of Russian rulers who'd used his skills for their own ends.

But it had been a good life in its way. Ah, the delights of those long winter nights and the torture chambers with the endless supply of victims' pain to drink!

But they'd been too blatant for too long and even the stolid Russian cows had finally revolted. He'd needed all the bitter lessons learned in seven centuries as a *vampiro* to survive the fall of the Kremlin and eventually make his way here.

Here to New Orleans, one step away from Texas—and finally killing Rafael.

Madame Celeste's private quarters were quieter than he'd expected, with no covey of young male *vampiros* singing her praises. Shockingly overdecorated, even to one who'd known Catherine the Great's love of homages to herself, the rooms were full of pieces acquired from conquered *esferas* or sent as tribute. Neither logic nor comfort was apparent, just a jumble of expensive furniture and artwork leaving very little room to move.

Beau automatically schooled his features into adoring anticipation and hunted for her, careful to make sure she thought she was always first on his mind—no matter what he really thought of her. He found her in a small sitting room, with a PC open before her. Probably financial records; she trusted no one with her complete portfolio.

He sniffed lightly; it was good he'd fed so deeply. She was very hungry and would probably want to drink from him.

"Madame." He bowed with a flourish, shifting slightly to see some of her spreadsheets.

Madame Celeste glanced up and spotted him. "*Mon cher* Beau." She smiled lasciviously and began to quickly shut down the computer, her long nails clicking over the keys.

"*Ma belle,*" he sighed suggestively, shifting into a pose that displayed his male assets.

"Does my darling boy need more money?" She chuckled and rose, gliding over to him and stroking his face.

"Money, pshaw." He kissed her fingers, keeping a schoolboy's pout on his face. "I was merely thinking how soon we could be together."

"Together? Ooh, sounds good," she purred, sliding her arms up around his neck.

He wrapped his around her waist and pulled her closer. She was soft and scented, well-curved, a very delectable, feminine armful—if you enjoyed women who would kill you as easily as they'd fuck you. "Very good," he agreed. She was exactly the sort of woman who was best handled by keeping her always in sight, so you knew exactly what she was up to. He bent his head toward her, offering himself like a hopeful gigolo.

She nipped his lip, drawing blood. He pursed his mouth in a mock pout, as crimson welled and dripped slowly down his chin.

She touched her finger to it, smelled it, tasted it—her eyes closing as she savored the incomparable richness of a *vampiro mayor*'s blood. She moaned softly, her other hand slipping down to fondle her breast.

He was too skilled in the hunt to let his satisfaction at her eagerness show. He had a great deal of blood to offer, after drinking so much tonight. A *vampiro*'s hunger for blood diminished with age, unless under great stress. At his age, Beau could readily survive on only a mouthful or two. But Madame Celeste needed far more and he'd made sure he had enough to be her sole provider. Just one more link in the chain to bind her to him. He didn't want her to throw him out until he'd killed Rafael.

She ran her fingers down his silk shirt until she reached his belt. He arched his back slightly, offering his chest for whatever handling she chose to give. It was unlikely she'd want to arouse him, since she rarely paid attention to anyone else's sexual needs for long.

Her hand delved into his trousers and he grunted in surprise. She squeezed him boldly, measuring him. "You're not wearing a thong."

He raised an eyebrow. "Do you want me to start doing so?"

She freed him from the cloth and began to fondle him. Why was she working him like this tonight? His hips began to rock, matching her tempo.

"No. Undergarments for men are a waste of time. Take your jacket and shirt off too. They'll mess up my hair."

He obeyed, tossing the expensive silk across the table, and looked back to enjoy his cock hardening rapidly under her expert touch. She was watching him very closely so he closed his eyes and drew an expression of increasing lust over his face.

He had no idea what she planned and he was enjoying both the danger and the unexpected hand job. He also knew exactly how to rip her head off with a single blow, should she try to attack him. He kneaded her shoulders, careful not to disturb her makeup or her coiffure, and groaned her name appreciatively.

"I want to drink from your thigh when you come," she murmured.

"Under my balls?"

"*Oui.*"

A very dangerous spot for a male; one false move and he could be castrated by a quick bite. He'd often seen that done, especially when torturing *vampiros*, since their horror made for an incredibly delicious meal. Still, a *vampiro* could heal any wound, even that one—and Beau would kill her if she tried it.

"Of course, my dear, whatever you like," he cooed.

"Silly boy. I don't need your permission. I can just bite you wherever I want."

"Sorry, darling," he muttered, becoming more and more absorbed in her expert handling of his cock. He took one of his hands away from her shoulders to tease his chest.

She assessed his condition rapidly and smirked, then dropped to her knees and pulled his trousers down. He eagerly angled his hips forward slightly, to give her a better angle.

A harsh cough interrupted. Madame Celeste sighed. "This had better be good, Devol."

Beau's head came up in pleasure at the sight of one of Madame Celeste's and his favorite sex partners. He always gave Devol the same wary caution a *prosaico* would give a rabid dog—and he respected Madame Celeste because she was the one person who'd managed to bring the brute to heel. Devol could spend an entire night killing or screwing, whichever his mistress commanded.

"You ordered me to report immediately how well the Eastern pros did in Texas." Devol was dressed very simply in jeans and a T-shirt, displaying the hard muscles that were part of the reason for his nickname, the "Bayou Butcher." He had brown hair and eyes, with average features, average height, and average build. There was little to distinguish him from any other man in a crowd except the expression in his eyes, which was usually pure concentrated hate.

But not tonight. Devol's voice was neutral but his eyes burned with carnal flames as they took in every detail of Beau and Madame Celeste's position. He shifted his stance slightly, allowing more room for the erection in his jeans.

"Yes, I did, didn't I." Madame Celeste turned and sat at Beau's feet. She reached behind her head and undid her dress's fastening, pulling it down to expose her magnificent breasts. She pulled on both nipples until they stood brilliant red, prominent on the rich curves. Then she leaned back against Beau's leg and stretched, sending her short skirt slithering up her legs. Her hand swept the length of his cock, gliding her blood-red nails over his engorged flesh.

The enforcer swallowed hard but made no move to touch himself.

"Report, Devol." She teased her breasts, her eyes half shut. Beau dropped to the floor behind her and cupped her breasts. She arched back against him, displaying herself completely, as Devol continued to talk.

"The attack was completely unsuccessful. Neither Don Rafael nor any of his men were injured, while all of the Eastern pros died in a helicopter crash."

"Amateurs," Madame Celeste growled and went on at considerable length in gutter French. Her hips began to move faster and faster, as she became more and more flushed. Beau smiled to himself; she always became aroused when she was angry.

His hand delved between her legs and worked her dripping folds. He rubbed her clit hard and she arched back against his shoulder, groaning incoherently. He pressed firmly and she stiffened, the shock-waves of orgasm pulsing through her.

Finally, she sighed and sank down against him bonelessly, her cream having thoroughly wet, and quite possibly ruined, his extremely expensive silk suit. He held her silently and waited, his cock still unrelieved. As was Devol's. As Madame Celeste certainly knew.

It was undoubtedly what she had enjoyed the most, the fact that she'd had her release but her two men had not. Power was her aphrodisiac, just as the scent of death aroused Devol.

A long, sharp fingernail teased his throat and he obediently slanted a look down at Madame. "Yes?"

"You must go to Texas and destroy Don Rafael for me."

"If you insist," he demurred, trying to sound reluctant.

"You'll leave tonight, after we dine together," she purred and leaned up to plant a crimson kiss on his mouth. "Devol is going to Texas, too, and can back you up, if you need help."

Help from Devol? The man could be very useful and he could be very deadly. Beau would have to wait and see.

Madame Celeste smiled into Beau's eyes, very sure of herself. He smiled back at her, well pleased to be finally free to destroy Rafael.

Madame Celeste rubbed herself over Beau's chest, her eyes slitting with pleasure like a cat's. "What are you doing over there, Devol? Strip and get your ass down here."

"*Oui*, madame," Devol responded immediately and peeled his T-shirt off.

Beau smiled and turned his attention to enjoying himself.

FIVE

Rodrigo flexed his fingers, fighting to reach the cuffs that clamped him to the rack. His arms and shoulders screamed with pain at even that slight movement, forcing him to desist. He'd fought so long and hard on previous occasions that this time, the servants had wound the rack so tightly he could barely breathe before they fled. He knew, without needing to look, that Fearghus was in similar straits beside him, here in The Syrian's mountain sanctuary on the far side of the Mediterranean from Castile.

Two months since they'd last been strapped into the racks. Two months of healing their bodies, while praying for the poor devils who took their places in it. And who they'd been forced to clean up after, scrubbing every inch of this hellhole thoroughly—and puking their guts out over what they found.

He'd been gone so long from Toledo, his beloved wife must have given birth months ago. The new baby—surely a daughter—must be walking by now, under the protection of her older brother and sister.

"Lassies with eyes as blue as the North Sea," Fearghus announced *loudly. A loud groan of straining machinery announced the Scotsman's struggle against the other rack. "That's another sight worth living for. Especially when their hair is as red as a fire's heart and their skin as smooth and fair as cream."*

"Can such a paragon exist?" Rafael queried, wondering if the North Sea was the same color as the ocean near his birthplace in Galicia.

"Of course. We have only to find her," Fearghus answered simply. Suddenly he sucked in his breath, the familiar sound of someone ripped by an incautious move. "Your turn to name something new."

Rodrigo ignored the iron collar scraping his chin raw and holding his head immobile. The trickle of blood down his throat and over his chest meant The Syrian and Diego, who'd eagerly embraced the promise of eternal life as a vampiro, *would soon come to drink his and Fearghus's blood. The Syrian preferred to do so after torturing his victims. The first time, he'd whipped Rodrigo and Fearghus into near unconsciousness before he'd bitten them. He'd shown other tricks after that but had always been careful that Rodrigo and Fearghus could heal.*

"A white owl flying silently across the snow, under a brilliant moon, free and fast," Rodrigo answered, playing his part in the game they'd devised to lift their spirits, always fighting not to succumb to hatred and despair.

In a far corner of his mind, Rodrigo could almost understand The Syrian's hatred of Christians. If his wife and children had been slaughtered while on pilgrimage to a holy city, as The Syrian's family had been massacred on the road to Mecca by Renaud de Châtillon a century ago, he too might have sworn vengeance on all Christians. But The Syrian's enjoyment of torture? Diego's vast delight in his victim's terror, as if he'd finally found what he most loved? Those were evil deeds, that both the Quran and the Bible fulminated against.

Madre de Dios, how he continually prayed for deliverance for himself and Fearghus. Especially after Achmed had tried and failed to rescue them, at the beginning of their captivity back in Spain. The Syrian had triumphantly paraded his cousin's broken, bloody body before him and warned them not to look for help anywhere on this earth. Still, Achmed's family had evidently raised enough of a furor to force The Syrian to return to his own territory, hundreds of leagues from Castile.

"Hear anything?" Fearghus asked.

"No. Do you?"

"Nothing. I'd like to hear birdsong again one day, though. Living at night, as those demons do, is—" He fumbled for a word.

"Tedious?" Rodrigo asked wryly.

Fearghus chuckled at the black humor. "Of course. Very tedious. But at least, I'm closer now to Jerusalem than I ever hoped to be when I left Inverness and Scotland. I've given thanks to the Almighty for that."

"And I." Rodrigo fell silent, counting the other small things he'd said thanks for. That his wife and children were still alive, Dios mediante. Every day he was still alive. The glimpses of daylight. The chance for revenge one day.

He gritted his teeth and stared straight up at the stone ceiling, lost somewhere in the darkness overhead.

The vision smashed into him then, clear and completely real, just as if he was standing in front of it at that moment, but with a shimmer of light around the edges. It was exactly the way the vision of the great northern storm had come to him when he was ten, as his grandfather had taught him to recognize the family's gift.

He saw himself facing The Syrian in the blazing red-tinted light of sunset, with his sword in his hand, ready to kill. Every detail was as distinct and solid as if he could touch it.

The vision stamped itself into every fiber of his being, then vanished from his waking sight.

The dungeon's door closed with a loud bang. Silken robes whispered across the stone as the two vampiros approached.

"Yaa kaafir, are you finally ready to convert?" The Syrian asked Rodrigo genially, strolling into view by his head. He spat a stream of dark coffee onto the floor and tested the ropes' tension with a long, bloody fingernail.

"No," Rodrigo gritted, saving his curses for later.

The Syrian shook his head. "Pity. You could save yourself so much pain if you'd accept that you will never return to Toledo." He ambled over to the Scotsman, whose blond coloring always fascinated him.

Diego snickered as he leaned over Rodrigo. "How does it feel to be helpless, you who were once so big and important? No large family now to help you with all their connections. No royal family—no king or infante—to favor you and shower you with rich gifts, like fine armor or a magnificent sword. Are you finally ready to start begging for your life?"

He ran a finger down Rodrigo's throat, nail digging deep enough to draw a thread of blood.

"But I still have my honor and my faith, which is all that matters to a knight," Rodrigo snapped back. "I will never beg."

Diego flushed angrily and turned toward his master, probably for permission to begin the night's tortures. The perfumed beast was still examining the other knight's muscles.

"Very pretty, don't you think, yaa ibnii?" The Syrian purred, pinching Fearghus's thigh.

"Damn you, keep your hands off me, you stinking great goat," the big Scotsman roared and was ignored.

Diego sneered. "The other is bigger, especially his male equipment. There's much more there to torture."

What were they planning now?

"True," The Syrian agreed, turning to consider Rodrigo, his beady eyes as intent as any rat's.

"He also speaks Arabic so you can curse him more easily, instead of having to use clumsy Castilian," Diego urged.

What was that devil leading up to now?

"Or I could loan the smaller one out as a slave to the vampiros in the mountains west of Constantinople," The Syrian countered, returning to Fearghus. "They have a liking for golden ones there. With two centuries before a young vampiro can tolerate even twilight, there'd be many long nights for him to glow like a pearl. This one would fetch us great sums of gold."

"*But if you sent the bigger one to the eastern courts—*" Diego gestured at Rodrigo, *his tone implying far more than the simple words.*

"*They'd know exactly how to use him.*" The Syrian *finished the sentence with a licentious smile at Rodrigo's naked body.*

Rodrigo's *skin crawled.* "*We are no slaves! We are knights—*"

The Syrian *slapped him, the blow's force nearly breaking Rodrigo's neck against the unyielding collar. Rodrigo's teeth cut his tongue.*

"*You are whatever I deem you to be,*" The Syrian *said coldly.* "*At the moment, I wish a Christian* vampiro *to torture,* prosaicos *having proven far too fragile. So one of you will become a* vampiro *tonight and the other will become his first meal.*"

"*And the first emotion you taste,*" Diego *added, watching Rodrigo closely,* "*will be the emotion you hunger for throughout the rest of your miserable life. Horror. Terror. You shall become a demon, who your church will demand immediate death for.*"

"*Never!*" Rodrigo *and* Fearghus *shouted in near unison.*

"*I will never yield to you,*" Rodrigo *snarled, in Arabic.* "*This I swear by all that I hold holy.*"

Diego *laughed at him.* "*You can't stop us.*"

Rodrigo's *vision blazed before his eyes again,* The Syrian *at the point of his sword in daylight.*

Utter certainty imbued his riposte. "*If you force me to become this, then I will take such a revenge on you as the world will remember forever.*"

The Syrian *and* Diego *fell uneasily silent for a moment before* The Syrian *raised an arrogant eyebrow.* "*Yaa ghabi, you have no power to stop me. Because you're being so foolish, you're the one who'll be a* vampiro.*"

Casually, he leaned down and sliced open Rodrigo's neck. Blood spouted in a great fountain.

"*Damn you to hell, take me instead,*" Fearghus *roared and was ignored.*

Too angry to be careful, Rodrigo *shouted an Arabic curse that made even the elder* vampiro *hesitate for a moment.*

"*May I give him* El Abrazo, yaa 'abi l-'aziiz?" *Diego asked far too eagerly.*

The Syrian's eyes flashed. "No," *he snapped and bent to drink.*

Rodrigo flinched when the fangs' sharp bite and The Syrian's loathsome smell sank into him. He cursed again, promising vengeance no matter how long it took. Vowed that The Syrian and Diego would be utterly destroyed.

But all the while, it seemed his throat and all of his blood was vanishing into the voracious whirlpool, the bottomless abyss of hell that was The Syrian's mouth.

The Syrian sucked harder and faster, ripping open Rodrigo's jugular until blood poured from him like wine out of a goatskin.

Dizziness crept into Rodrigo, then blackness at the edges of his vision. He was losing consciousness. Madre de Dios, *give me strength to survive, he prayed.*

His vision reappeared, more distant and haloed in light than before but still recognizable, of The Syrian at his sword's point.

"Drink," *The Syrian ordered, holding his dripping wrist in front of Rodrigo's face.*

He was so very weak. Still, he stubbornly locked his jaws.

"Drink!"

He shook his head.

For the first time, Rodrigo heard a vampiro's *telepathic order.* Yaa ghabi, *drink!*

The mental compulsion to obey was almost unbearably strong but somehow he found the strength to fight it. He shook his head again, his eyesight very gray now.

Diego screamed in frustrated rage. Fearghus was openly praying, his voice choked with tears.

A hammer smashed through the side of his face, sending his teeth flying. Holding Rodrigo's head in a grip of iron, The Syrian poured his tainted blood into Rodrigo's mouth.

Rodrigo tried to spit. But Diego grabbed his jaw and held it still, as The Syrian forced a torrent of bitter crimson down his throat.

Violated and befouled, forced into El Abrazo, *Rodrigo fell into a well of nightmares, as the* vampiro *elixir began to remake his body.*

Grania kept her head up and her pace steady, determinedly ignoring the men behind her. Four miles down, one mile left before she'd be home an hour after dawn. She'd run track in high school and college. She still liked to run fast, burning the road away with the tensions of her job. She sure as hell wasn't fleeing from her shadows—but she was testing those men's limits.

A lot of people couldn't keep up with her, or had to work hard to do so. But these guys kept the same steady distance from her the entire time. They'd never tried to catch her, just watched her. It was almost as if she was in the middle of a bad spy novel, where the FBI waited to see who the double agent was working for, no matter where the double agent went or what he was doing.

Thankfully, her little house stood on the edge of what had once been a small agricultural village. Five houses remained, separated by pastures and peach orchards, none of them with a good view of her bungalow. The narrow roads, as they wound and dipped through the hills, were almost as private as the houses, giving her occasional opportunities to observe her followers.

One of her shadows resembled the hawk-like fellow who'd been guarding Rafael at the open house. Which meant Rafael still thought she might be part of an assassination threat. The paranoid asshole.

And if Rafael wasn't neurotic, then he lived in a world as violent and vicious as what she'd seen in Colombia.

Hell. Her shoulders and back remembered how easily his highly competent bodyguard had subdued her. She cursed again under her breath and kept running. She wasn't part of any conspiracy, as any investigation would prove.

Dammit, she was not going to put up with this.

The road made a sudden turn at this point, cutting close to an ancient, unused barn. Making an immediate decision, Grania stepped off the pavement and waited behind the barn.

Sure enough, not a minute later, her two shadows came past. They quickly pulled up when they saw the road ahead was empty.

"Looking for me, gentlemen?" Grania asked, stepping out into the morning sun.

They whirled to face her, hands instinctively reaching for guns.

She harrumphed silently; it figured they'd be armed. She waited, her own palms flagrantly empty.

They relaxed slowly, looking a little embarrassed. One of them was definitely the fellow who'd been with Rafael at the open house, identified by the same ageless, hawk-like look to his face. He tried out a charming smile on her. "Good morning, ma'am."

She lifted a quelling eyebrow. She'd had too many younger children in the orphanage try to charm her out of treats for her to be impressed by empty words. Later experiences with university students had only broadened her list of silly excuses to be ignored.

He, at least, had the wits to immediately drop his nonsense and adopt a businesslike mien. He straightened up and nodded to her, watching a bit more warily. Good.

"Your ID?"

"Ma'am, who carries ID on a morning jog?"

"Anyone who doesn't live locally and has to drive there."

"True." He considered her thoughtfully. The other man, slightly older and definitely more battered around the edges, shot a quick look at him.

Grania's voice sharpened, as her temper shortened. "Don't push me, when you've been following me for four miles. The rancher who lives on this place is a deputy sheriff. You can either show me your ID or I start screaming."

"Wouldn't want that to happen, ma'am."

She gave him a very suspicious glare but his expression was entirely innocent. He reached into his back pocket and pulled out a small wallet, flipped it open and held it out to her. "Lieutenant junior grade Emilio Alvarez, US Navy," Grania read out loud. She thumbed through the rest of the wallet rapidly, considering the contents. "Coronado, California, is it?"

"Yes, ma'am." Alvarez was standing at parade rest, facing her. His companion was a few paces away, clearly ready to jump her if anything went wrong.

"A Navy SEAL?"

"Yes, ma'am, I'm with the Teams."

"Here on leave."

He nodded.

Grania turned over the implications in her mind. A Navy SEAL as bodyguard to an executive of the Santiago Trust? Whatever Rafael was, he was damn important—and the threat to him was huge.

Her stomach tried to turn itself inside out.

She handed Alvarez back his ID. "Are you going to follow me for the entire day?"

He shrugged. "Those are my orders, ma'am."

Wasn't this going to be fun? "Great. Well, let's get going again, guys."

She began to stretch, preparing herself to finish her morning jog.

Showered and fed an hour later, she sat down at her computer. After all, her real problem was how to cope with last night's events and her own reactions to them. She wasn't required to think about bodyguards; just how not to fall apart whenever she saw Rafael.

Her physiological reactions to him were extraordinary. To have an orgasm without any direct physical stimulation? And afterward, while taking a shower at home, she'd masturbated and climaxed so strongly she'd passed out. That was the first time she'd ever lost consciousness from an orgasm. And to do so from masturbating, while fantasizing about Rafael with another woman?

Almost as unusual was the dream last night, of Rodrigo being forced—raped, actually—into becoming a vampire. That vision, unlike her earlier dream about owls, felt like a memory, rather than a fantasy. But so many of her dreams about Rodrigo had always felt real. She'd dreamed about Rodrigo all her life, even before she could write her name or his. Those dreams had been one of her few child-hood refuges, in a world of solitude and torment.

She blinked rapidly, refusing to admit she was crying. In this situa-tion, as in almost every other trial throughout her life, she was on her own. Her intellect would bring her through, as it had all the others. Dreams were vaporous follies and not to be relied on.

The first step was to come up with a valid theory explaining how Rafael and Brynda had behaved in the woods. The scientific method gave a standard set of steps for developing such a theory. After the years of working for her Ph.D., she could plan rigorous research in her sleep. Surely explaining a man and woman necking in the woods, with a little biting and bloodsucking, would be easy.

Half an hour later, she sat back, furious. How many millions of references could a single topic generate on the Internet? Too damn many to be useful, at any rate. She'd have to look at books and ar-ticles. Hopefully, they'd have some useful analysis of vampires.

At least it was finally late enough in the morning that she could go check on Brynda, to see if Rafael had hurt her.

Grania settled into a chair outside the coffee shop and slid her sun-glasses on top of her head, ignoring her omnipresent male shadows across the street. Her table gave her a superb view of the lake, marina, and Brynda reading a letter on pink stationery. It was also the most comfortable place she'd ever set up watch in, with the graceful chair, the delicious iced coffee, even a free newspaper waiting for her, as contrast for the daily paper she'd bought.

She flipped a page, trying not to watch the other woman too open-ly. Sales of jewelry, shoes, lingerie—all at prices that made her head spin. New shipments just in from Mexico sounded more interesting. She sipped her coffee, enjoying the extravagance of splurging on ha-zelnut liqueur and cream.

Smaller ads for smaller shops and restaurants. A consignment store in Austin's historic district advertised its supply of stylish wom-en's wear . . .

"Excuse me?"

Grania's head snapped up at that all-too-familiar Brooklyn accent. Her eyes swept over Brynda. "Yes?"

"Are you looking at today's *Austin American-Statesman*?" Blond hair pulled back into a ponytail, tank top cut low, capris, sandals. Good color, with no sign of any serious injury. If summarizing her condition for a medical chart, the only items Grania might note would be the two small red papules directly above her jugular. But they were so small and insignificant that even an acne specialist might not mention them.

"No, I'm not." Grania put down the free newspaper, leaving it open at the current page, and pulled out the respectable daily. "Here you go."

A long, superbly manicured nail tapped the consignment store's ad in the free newspaper. "Great place. I picked up a barely worn Richard Tyler cocktail dress there. Normally twelve hundred dollars but I bought it for twenty-four ninety-five. That's ninety-eight percent off."

Grania was impressed. Anyone who could do that kind of math, this early in the morning, was definitely of sound mind. "Extraordinary."

"You should check them out. It'd be a sin not to make the most of your height and coloring. Classic look for you, I'd say—very Jackie O or Catherine Zeta-Jones."

Grania gaped, barely managing not to glance down at her brilliant purple T-shirt with its ten-K-race logo. "You think so?"

"Oh, yeah. You'd have to brush your hair out, of course, or maybe wear a high ponytail. A little makeup too, nothing very heavy. But the guys would follow you around like puppies with their tongues hanging out. Well, thanks for the paper." Brynda picked it up, nodded in a friendly fashion, and returned to her seat.

Grania carefully ripped out the store's ad before she left.

She was frustrated and irritable by the time she grabbed lunch at a burrito restaurant in a heavily painted, hole-in-the-wall storefront. An exhaustive search of Austin's public libraries, including the University of Texas's superb collections, had uncovered no impartial, third-person accounts of vampires. Oh, she'd found some speculations by sociologists and anthropologists, but nothing useful to a biologist. Let alone a veterinarian trying to explain a man sucking blood from a woman's neck, while she was in the heights of orgasmic ecstasy.

Surely somebody else must have seen something like this before now. She could not be the only person who wanted to describe a vampire incident.

She cursed, considered her bank balance, and cursed again. This time in Spanish, which triggered awed looks from the teenage Hispanic males at the next table. She raised an eyebrow. They applauded. She laughed reluctantly.

Then she departed to search the local bookstores, starting with the ones most likely to carry speculative literature. If there were no fact-based observations recorded, then she'd have to look at the accounts commonly dismissed as pure fantasy.

She reached the final bookstore on her list just before dark. A fifty-year-old business in an eighty-year-old store, it advertised itself as providing old-fashioned service and books for all tastes. More to the point, its website had prominently mentioned vampire literature.

It was located on a street corner in an upscale western suburb, once a placid farm town. The businesses nearby were prosperous and friendly—a bank, a twenty-four-hour drugstore, restaurants and coffee shops, an ice cream parlor where teenagers giggled. There was even a park with green grass and a bandstand, designed to entertain both children and parents. But no families played there tonight.

The sunset's normal blaze of gold and red was framed by scudding black clouds, edged in eerie green. Lightning sparked and flashed in the western skies as Grania whipped into a parking place in front of the bookstore. Her truck's radio blared a nearly continuous litany of counties watching for severe thunderstorms. Driving home into that storm could be tricky, especially if it decided to spawn a tornado. But this was the last bookstore on her list and the only one carrying those European academic studies on vampires and Dracula.

She drummed her fingers on the steering wheel, considering the risks. Bags of vampire books on the floorboard seemed to mock her hesitation. Finally, she shrugged and went in, determined to find the books and leave as quickly as possible.

The revolving door delivered her into a shadowy world, with bookcases rising up on three sides. Placards advertised books, both recent and far older. Lining the walls above the bookcases were pictures of famous gunfighters, every one prominently displaying his firearms. Hanging from the rafters above were the flags that had once flown over Texas, their faded colors shimmering in the last glow through the skylights. Half of them were Confederate battle flags, companions to the wall of books dedicated to the American Civil War.

A battle flag twitched and swayed in a faint breath of air. It settled sullenly, sending dust swirling down.

The hair rose on the back of her neck. In another time and place, she'd have double-checked her guns.

"Can I help you, ma'am?" a man asked politely from beside her.

Grania spun, startled. He was young, perhaps twenty, and probably a college student. Objectively speaking, she'd describe him as her height, blond, and quite muscular for his age, with regular features. Given the way he was smiling at her, he knew exactly how attractive he was—and expected her to fall at his feet. Why hadn't she heard him approach? And why did he seem so familiar?

"I'm looking for some vampire books," she answered equally politely, quickly masking her expression and making herself unreadable. The worst situations—at the orphanage, boarding schools, boardrooms, examination halls, anywhere—had never broken her composure. Something told her that she needed to be on guard here.

The bookstore's two clerks ignored the byplay. They were far too busy checking out a stream of customers desperate to return home before the storm.

The blond's eyes narrowed and a frown flickered over his face before he smiled sweetly. "Which ones in particular? As you can see, the staff is occupied at the moment."

Well, it was a public building so what harm could he really do?

And she really did need to leave as soon as possible so help finding the books would be useful. "Thank you. I'm looking for some vampire nonfiction."

His smile broadened. "A very popular topic. Most of those books are over here." He led her toward the back wall, his arm reaching out to wrap around her waist. "And please, call me Beau," he crooned.

Grania sidestepped his hand. "I'm specifically looking for the *Proceedings of the Fifth Ravenna Conference on European Folklore Traditions*," she announced briskly, deliberately not sharing her name.

She hadn't given it to him by the time she left either, thirty minutes later, with all the books she wanted.

Masking his irritation, Beau waved good-bye to the tall redhead as she sped off. She'd definitely been the best prospect he'd seen for dining since arriving in this rough-edged town; someone who depended on logic always fell so much harder and tasted so much better when forced into terror. But surely the next time they met, he'd be able to seduce her into meeting him alone. And then . . .

He smiled, testing his fangs' tips with his tongue.

He wasn't worried about not being able to reach past her shields. They'd been in a public place so he hadn't tried very hard. Next time, he'd succeed.

When he did, he'd plant the compulsion for her to return, so he could feed on her again and again. As his *creador* had taught him, there was no need to kill a good meal immediately. Not when you could train it to return to your hand, thus saving you the trouble of hunting.

Even if one of his victims accidentally died, it wouldn't look like a *vampiro* had killed him or her. After all, he didn't want Rafael to know he and Devol were nearby too soon. That *alferez mayor* of his was too damn good at hunting down foreign *vampiros*. He was the leader of all of Rafael's troops, both the *mesnaderos* at Compostela Ranch and *vampiros* and *compañeros* from the commanderies in all of Texas's important cities. Not a *vampiro* touched Texas soil but

Rafael's *alferez mayor* didn't hear of it, sooner or later, and demand an explanation. If their reasons were weak, they were either exiled or killed—usually the latter. He was brutally effective, whether he did so alone or with dozens of his men.

Still, if truth be told, Beau was more concerned about what Devol might do, since that cutthroat had never been taught discretion by Madame Celeste. But surely even Devol wasn't vicious enough to kill Texas *prosaicos* in such a way that they'd look like Hollywood's idea of *vampiros*—and bring the mob howling down upon every *vampiro* in North America.

Besides, if Devol started anything like that, Beau would rip off his head immediately, no matter what Madame Celeste might say. He'd seen the Russian mob in action and he had no desire to repeat the experience on another continent.

Plans made, Beau's eyes crinkled happily as he strolled down the street, all the while considering various ways to break the tall red-head. Pain? Visions? Telepathy? Combinations of any or all?

He spotted a girl fumbling with a cell phone, in the alley beside the ice cream parlor. "Can I help you, honey?" Honey. What a perfect description of her usefulness.

"My battery's dead and I need to call my folks." Desperate brown eyes looked up at him, filled with the innocence of someone who'd never encountered anyone who'd harm her. He catalogued her quickly. Five and a half feet tall, with an athletic build, wearing a T-shirt shouting "synchronized swimmers do it together," brown hair, tanned skin. Even better, she was at least twenty years old so she'd be able to provide him a very long drink. Excellent.

His body tensed, as heat started to build in his groin. Beau quickly slouched and fumbled for his cell phone like a graceless American boy. "Would you like to borrow mine?"

"Oh, thank you!" She took the proffered phone and flipped it open.

Call the weather, Beau ordered, mind-to-mind, *and step behind the parlor.*

She obeyed promptly.

Good to know that Texas *prosaicas* were as easy as all the other *prosaicas* to command.

Except for that damn redhead.

His chest was tight, his breathing fast, as he followed the brunette, anticipating the feast to come. His cock filled with blood and semen built in his balls.

The phone filled the alley with reports of possible tornado sightings. The little athlete tucked it against her shoulder, listening as he'd ordered. Arching her neck perfectly for his bite.

His fangs came to full extension, sharp as daggers.

He touched her mind and located her worst nightmare.

Then he took her by the shoulders and washed her mind in pure terror, knowing that no matter how greatly her nightmare frightened her, her fear would deepen tenfold—or more—as soon as he began to drink . . .

SIX

Blanche paced under the colonnade by the herb garden, staying in the shade lest a stray beam of light strengthen the misery inside her skull. She'd awoken last night with stabbing pains, similar to but greater than what she'd felt the day of the great battle at Ecija. Rodrigo's pain echoed in her flesh now, as it had then. As a knight's wife, she would keep vigil with him, even though she was physically separated from him.

The children played happily by a stand of rosemary, next to a shallow pool of water watered by a statue of a lion. As usual, Fernando and Beatriz, the five-year-old twins, had their hands full keeping two-year-old Inez out of mischief. All happy, healthy, lively children. Rodrigo would be so proud if he could see them.

Blanche fingered her rosary, reassuring herself that all would soon be well. It would be, as soon as she was released from waiting for the Princesse. Then she could pray for Rodrigo in a chapel, while Fernando took the other children off to Maria. She'd been selfish, keeping the children here with her, as a reminder of their father, while she waited for her mistress.

As for the Princesse, *all she thought about was her sons,* los Infantes de la Cerda, *and their grievances.*

Sancho, Alfonso X's younger son, had recently prevailed upon his father to follow this frontier kingdom's ancient customs—and make him the heir to the throne. In one stroke, the Princesse's *two sons were disinherited, against her marriage contract and the customs she'd grown up with. Ever since, the* Princesse's *temper had fulminated like water drops sizzling on an overheated stove. She'd even spoken wildly of fleeing the Castilian court.*

Blanche's hand tightened around the gold cross Rodrigo had given her, its heavy carvings digging into her skin. If she left with her mistress, how could she obtain news of her husband?

The stout wooden gate slammed open, banging against the door. Blanche quickly slipped the precious cross down her camisa's neck, next to her skin. The Princesse was always encouraging her to forget all traces of Rodrigo.

Then she gritted her teeth, opened her eyes, and stepped into the light. "Your Highness." She managed a steady curtsey.

The Princesse stood in the center of the small garden, chest heaving like a warhorse ready to charge. Her eyes circled the plants sightlessly, her hands clenching and unclenching. Fernando and Beatriz clustered together, gathering Inez between them, as far away from the Princesse as possible, which wasn't enough, given her past behavior.

Blanche swallowed hard, praying to Notre Dame that the Princesse would not become more difficult than usual. She was usually sweet-tempered in public, but in private, with those who'd accompanied her from France . . . "Fernando, please take your sisters to Maria. Their new shoes should be ready."

Fernando nodded, his eyes alive with understanding and worry. "New shoes" meant that all three children were to stay with her maid until Blanche came for them. It also meant that he must go immediately and ask no questions. "Oui, maman."

He was always careful to use French around the Princesse. A diplomat, just like his father.

The gate's closing triggered a flood of French invective from the

Princesse. *Blanche handed her mistress a goblet of French wine when the calumnies eased. A short laugh was her only thanks but at least the* Princesse *spoke more softly.*

"Ce sale bête—"

"*The* Infante *Sancho?" Blanche asked dryly.*

"Oui." *They shared a brief smile before the* Princesse *sank down on a bench, swirling her embroidered skirts around her knees. "I cannot speak of it. Even his mother, the Queen, agrees that he has gone too far this time."*

Blanche perched on a low wall. "I grieve for all of your family, Your Highness."

The Princesse *drank most of the goblet before she spoke again. "One thing at least is going well: We've now found a way to escape."*

Blanche gaped at her. Flee Castile for Aragon, the kingdom's principal Christian rival on the Iberian peninsula? The Princesse *nodded impatiently.*

"Mais oui, *where else? Of a certainty,* mon frère Philipe *will recognize them as heirs to Castile. And with the kings of France and Aragon behind them, my sons will be restored to their rightful place." Her eyes shone with a madwoman's intensity as she imperiously held out the goblet.*

"Their kinsmen can bring great force on their behalf," *Blanche agreed politely as she refilled the goblet. Her head was aching as if a blacksmith's hammer was pounding on it. What had happened to Rodrigo?*

"Bien, *you understand perfectly." The* Princesse *tapped a long finger against her cheek, as she did when planning a trip to the market. "Don Salvador Lopez will smuggle us out as soon as you marry him."*

Blanche stiffened in outrage.

Oblivious, the Princesse *continued talking, still steadily tapping her cheek.* "Père Bernard *will perform the ceremony tonight at—"*

"No, Your Highness."

The Princesse *gaped at her but quickly recovered. She set down the goblet and rose to her full height, towering over her lady-in-waiting. "What did you say?"*

Blanche stood up too and looked her in the eye, refusing to be cowed. Her duty as a wife, a vow made during a holy sacrament, came before any oath to a worldly overlord. "I am the wife of Don Rodrigo Perez and I will not marry another."

"He has been dead these two years and more!"

"No body was found."

"The infidels made a pyramid of their heads!"

Blanche tilted her chin higher. The agony in her skull threatened to split it apart. But now the pain reassured her that Rodrigo was alive. "Others have come back alive since then. Until a body is found or someone swears a holy oath they saw him dead, I am still married."

The Princesse glared at her. "Do you understand how difficult it was to find anyone who could smuggle us out of here? The only thing Don Salvador asks for is you. He is willing to marry you, you stupid fool."

"I am afraid what you ask is impossible, Your Highness."

The Princesse visibly fought to control herself. "He's far richer than Don Rodrigo could ever have hoped to be," she coaxed.

Blanche shuddered and crossed herself, as appalled as if Satan himself had tried to tempt her. What did money have to do with adultery?

The Princesse's control snapped and she slapped her, sending Blanche staggering. She came after her again, her hand raised for another blow.

Blanche saw red then. She was a married woman and would defend her honor against anyone who sought to besmirch it. She shoved the Princesse hard, sending her over backward into the pool with a mighty splash. The lion imperturbably poured water over the Princesse's head.

"Do not speak to me again of adultery, Your Highness," Blanche warned, glaring at her erstwhile mistress.

The Princesse screeched in rage, her hands clenching and unclenching as if she wanted to rip out Blanche's eyes. She erupted out of the pool, water streaming from her ruined dress. "Salope! Queen Violante will force you to obey me!"

An instant after she left, Blanche ran in the opposite direction. Betrayal had walked through this small courtyard, ripping her away from any ties to her birthplace. Tears burned in her eyes but there was no time to weep.

She couldn't go to the King. A blind fool about his womenfolk on the best of days, he wouldn't believe her and would simply return her to the Princesse *and the Queen for discipline.*

She had to escape with her children to the Santiaguistas. As the wife of a Santiaguista novice and the mother of his children, Blanche had the right to claim protection and shelter from them. Besides their stout fortresses and hundreds of knights, they had numerous convents and priories. Surely in one of them, she and her children would be safe. There she could pray to San Rafael Arcángel for Rodrigo's health and safe travel.

Grania's eyes snapped open, assessed the scene, and shut again. Her own bed, the very narrow cot set diagonally across the tiny, brilliantly painted bedroom. The white curtains swaying, as the rain pounded against the windows. Definitely her house, late at night after a thunderstorm.

So where the hell had another dream about Blanche come from? She'd only once before dreamed about that medieval woman, hoping to dream about Rodrigo. She'd thought that first dream was a wet dream, finally arrived after years of daydreaming about her knight. But this hardly fell into that category. Worse, it was about the same woman—and her children had the same names.

Better to forget those dreams.

She hadn't seen Emilio and the other guy since before the thunderstorm, which might be why she was so damn uneasy. Was there so much of a threat to Rafael that he needed every available man on guard duty?

She punched the pillow, rolled over, and tried to go back to sleep. Long, fruitless minutes later, she gave up. She'd done much of her Ph.D. thesis before dawn, after eighty-hour weeks as a vet and student. Analyzing data on vampires at night would be a cinch after that. For one thing, she'd gathered a whole lot less scientific data on vampires than she had for her thesis.

At the Commandery in Austin, the rain was coming down almost loudly enough to deafen a *vampiro*. Inside the great hall, Ethan was holding the morning muster of *compañeros*. This hall had once been a barn and it retained the honest simplicity of those origins, with stone walls and floors, wooden beams, and steel shutters, despite its high-tech equipment. The furniture was comfortable, old enough that a man didn't need to worry about being polite, yet young enough that he didn't fear to break it.

Two dozen *compañeros*, dressed in a variety of clothing, from the roughest work clothes to the most impressive office attire, occupied the chairs and the benches.

The Commandery's great hall had been impossible to break into when Ethan first entered in 1860. Now it was both impossible to break into or break out of, if you were impure of heart, as Don Rafael liked to say.

For this muster, as all others, every door was bolted from the outside except two, one which Gray Wolf guarded, substituting for Ethan's top lieutenant, who was at the Dallas Commandery tonight with Hennessy.

Gray Wolf stood at the back of the hall, apparently casual, his black eyes sweeping the room. Jean-Marie leaned against the side door, turning a coin over across the back of his hand as he watched.

"Any more questions?" Ethan asked.

The men shook their heads.

Gray Wolf straightened up. *The muster is wrong tonight*, he said softly, his words whispering across their link. Keeping the conversation soft so that only the three of them, Don Rafael's eldest three *hijos*, could hear.

Shit. Implications and contingency plans raced through Ethan's head. *Are you sure? Do you know who or how many?*

I'm sure of it but I don't yet know how many men. Gray Wolf's tone was grim.

Jean-Marie came erect, the coin stilling between his fingers like a knife blade. *Beau must have managed to capture and take over at least one of our men.*

He'd need a blood exchange to do that. Damn. *The roll call will tell us who it is.*

Or flush out the mole before Ethan reaches him, Jean-Marie remarked.

Agreed. Ethan raised his voice. "Line up for inspection, boys, so we can have you out of here and on the job."

Chatting to each other, the men followed the same ritual they did every morning before going on patrol, moving into a single, long line that stretched the hall's length.

The inspection looked like that performed in any police station at the start of a shift. The biggest difference was invisible to the naked eye: Ethan, as the leader of this muster, also sniffed each man, looking for traces of hostile foreign *vampiros*.

Inspecting the first few *compañeros* went quickly and quietly. Focused on the men in front of him, Ethan had little attention to spare for the others further away.

There's trouble building toward the rear, Gray Wolf warned. *A half dozen are jostling each other like horseplay. But they're getting closer to the side door by Jean-Marie.*

The Frenchman laughed. *If they try to rush me, I'll stop them.*

Warn me when it's about to start. Ethan continued the inspection, repeatedly encouraging his men to carry more firepower and wear their body armor.

His ears caught Jean-Marie's footsteps moving away from the door. *What the hell?*

Jean-Marie's voice was very relaxed, almost placid. *It's almost time,* mon frère. *You will need room for the dance.* The *heraldo's* damn intuition had kicked in again.

There's only one, Gray Wolf announced. *But I'm still not sure exactly who . . .*

Now! He's making a run now! Jean-Marie shouted.

Every *compañero* spun but only the *vampiros* and the traitor knew what to look for.

Teixeira, who'd been a *compañero* for less than five years, bolted for the side door an instant after Jean-Marie's shout—and a second after Ethan leaped into motion. He caught the young *compañero* from behind within two strides and held him brutally tight, ignoring the other's struggles.

Interrogating him was next. If Teixeira survived that, then Ethan could either execute him himself (the more merciful death, no matter how he chose to do it) or take him to Don Rafael.

Gray Wolf and Jean-Marie paced around them, watching Teixeira's every move. The other *compañeros* formed another circle, growling, anger growing in their eyes.

Ethan got a single whiff of Teixeira's scent and nearly gagged. "Christ, you reek of Beau and Devol. What did you do, roll in New Orleans filth?"

Teixeira spat at Gray Wolf.

"Asshole." Ethan tightened his grip, breaking his captive's shoulder.

The other screamed and sagged, but his eyes still flashed defiance.

"The penalty for treason is death. But before then, his memories will be stripped. Ready, men?"

"They'll grind you into dust, Templeton. The rest of you, Madame Celeste will pay you a fortune—"

Ethan cut Teixeira off ruthlessly as he probed deep and fast, projecting the answers to everyone else present. Not many people, even *vampiros*, let alone a *compañero*, could survive telepathy done this forcefully. But it was the only way to discover what had happened before any suicide compulsion could kick in.

Images flashed: Teixeira making a phone call to Madame Celeste's New Orleans casino, Teixeira meeting Beau and Devol in a Houston hotel room, Teixeira handing over a map showing the old smuggling routes from Mexico, Teixeira dropping to his knees and drinking blood from Devol and Beau . . .

Teixeira screamed like a lost soul and sagged against Ethan. He released him immediately and stepped back.

An instant later, Teixeira crumpled to the floor, his windpipe locked and his heart stopped, his sightless eyes staring at the ceiling. The scent of death spilled across the room.

The other *compañeros* snarled, aggrieved at being denied a share in killing him.

Ethan propped his fists on his hips and glared at his recalcitrant *compañeros*. When they were finally quiet again, he spoke. "Remember this, men. If you're tainted unwillingly, which could be done damned easily, then Don Rafael is willing to forgive and cleanse you. But if you're willing—as Teixeira was—then death to all traitors!"

"Death!" they howled, like wolves baying at the moon. "Death to all traitors!"

Hours later, Grania was willing to shoot everyone who'd ever written a so-called rigorous study of vampires. None of them seemed to agree on even the fundamentals, such as what a vampire was or did. She paced her cottage, ignoring the litter of papers on the kitchen on the table.

Snarling curses, she settled down again with a fresh cup of coffee and pulled over a new lab notebook. Computers were all well and good, but sometimes it was best to use the old standbys. She'd describe a vampire herself, by listing the most distinctive characteristics.

Apex predator at the top of the food chain.

Feeds primarily or solely on blood.

Hunting technique emphasizes sexual attraction.

May, or may not, kill prey.

May, or may not, be seen in daylight.

May, or may not, be capable of sexual acts, specifically orgasm and/or ejaculation.

The last characteristic really left a lot of activities open for further questions. Had Rafael climaxed while he was feeding on Brynda?

Could he climax when he wasn't feeding? Could he climax when he was alone?

Grania crossed out that list of questions, which had nothing to do with distinctive characteristics. Better to concentrate on the details of a vampire's attack, such as where the vulnerabilities were. All the sources at least agreed that vampires were too strong and fast for standard escape and evasion tactics.

Outrun? Not unless you were another vampire.

Shoot? You'd need a first-shot kill, given their speed, which meant accuracy and stopping power. Semiautomatic weapons weren't accurate enough for that, if vampires were as fast as these accounts indicated. An excellent revolver would provide the accuracy if it had the stopping power, or maybe a heavily loaded shotgun at close range.

Gory prospect. She'd be better off unpacking her books and thinking about animals she could do something with.

But it was more fun thinking about Rafael. His beautiful, graceful body—just like her knight. His fangs—so much like every description of a vampire.

Cursing her unruly libido, she took another shower, using lukewarm water. Her body promptly remembered what it had enjoyed the last time she had stood in the small, green tiled enclosure and her fingers started playing with herself again.

Strumming her nipples, squeezing her breasts, and lifting them to the water's caress, as to a lover's. Stroking down over her belly to her hips.

She wondered if Rafael ever did something like this. Did he truly enjoy women like that loudmouthed blonde? Or did he sometimes pleasure himself, if only for some quiet?

Her hips rocked, as her hand slipped between her legs and began to play with her folds.

Wasn't this how he'd teased Brynda's clit in the woods?

She moaned, her hand working harder, deeper. Cream slid down her thigh in answer, as her body heated and tightened.

She called herself names and tried to think of other things, like grant applications for research money or examining an eagle.

But the image of Rafael kept coming back. What would he look like if he fondled himself? Would he look ecstatic or pained? Or both?

Her hand moved faster and faster, her hips thrusting hard against it. Her head fell back, her body arching into the water as she sought more.

Would Rafael move with style, like the way he'd handled that woman? Or would he be direct?

Would he prefer to touch just the shaft of his cock or someplace else?

She climaxed, crying out as the orgasm raced up her spine, as if running up a man's shaft. Her body bowed, face freezing in a rictus of pleasure too great to be expressed. Her feet and legs unable to hold any more, she collapsed slowly against the wall as consciousness slipped away.

She woke up to a cold-water shower. Again. Just as the sun started to rise.

SEVEN

Pain, so intense that nothing else existed. Light bursting into his eyes. He cowered back, shaking. Tried to curl himself into a ball. The thudding inside his body. The rush and whoosh of a mighty river, noises so loud as to crush all else.

He was hungry, ached with it. Could not have formed words to say what he needed.

Someone jerked his head back, tightening his skin over his skull. He screamed as his eyes opened to a whirling display of lights. He retched, voided himself, fought to escape from the light and the sound of his own voice.

"Filthy brute!"

A snort of laughter. "You were worse."

"Impossible!"

He cowered away from their voices, pounding like spikes into his brain.

Rough hands lifted and cleaned him, uncaring when skin tore. He howled, fighting. They restrained him easily.

"Few remember their awakening," the older voice mused above him, continuing to turn and scrape him contemptuously. "It is a time of insanity that destroys most."

"You said before it always kills children."

"And pregnant women."

The words were sounds only, with no meaning behind them yet. But bone-deep instinct told him these beings were enemies to be avoided as much as possible.

Vertigo swept him when they lifted him, carried him to another platform. He bucked against their hands and screamed. Fought again to escape. He jackknifed away, almost breaking the fetters binding him.

Close at hand, someone cursed them. But they laughed.

He fought on, heedless of the bonds they laid over him. Eyes dry and burning. Skin tight and aching. So very, very thirsty.

Someone spat. "Will he never stop fighting?" The young one's voice.

"It is said that those who are forced into El Abrazo, *struggle the hardest when they rise for* La Lujuria. *But you were very willing to become my adopted son, so matters went much easier for you."*

He was hungry, so very hungry. Every cell of his body was starving. But for what? Something to fill his throat and something else.

"Bring the blond over. This one's ready for his first meal." Great satisfaction in the older man's voice now. "And deepen the cuts in the blond's belly."

A breeze touched his face, redolent with sweet perfumes. Ah, sí, that was what he longed for. He turned his head from side to side, seeking the source. There!

They tied a warm body down next to him. He cringed from its heat but the coppery smell was too attractive to keep his distance. His nostrils flared and he purred.

"Unfasten him and step back."

The younger voice was uncertain. "Are you certain, yaa 'abi? He might turn on us, even with the other half gutted."

"While vampiro *blood is far tastier than* prosaico, *neither of us have a thousand cuts in our skin. No, he'll tear the unbeliever's throat*

with his bare hands, plunge his hands into the heart, and gorge himself on the blood."

"And rape him as well." The younger voice sounded eager.

"It is how the first meal is always taken. The way you, as all other
cachorros do, took your first taste of emotion—the emotion that you
will crave as an immortal vampiro."

"And after that critical first meal, there are the months and years
of thoughtless lust that so very few cachorros survive." The younger
one happily smacked his lips.

"Yes, La Lujuria, the mindless hunger for blood and carnal satisfaction. Only two years for you, but as many as ten for others."

Loud sounds as bolts turned. Disorienting feelings as air played
over him, when the chains loosened then disappeared. He flinched but
didn't completely curl into a ball. The smell lured him closer.

Thuds echoing through his bones as the two speakers withdrew.
Clinks of glass on glass as they poured refreshments for themselves.
He tried to gather his body together so he could feed. But his muscles
wouldn't answer.

A very soft voice touched him. Friendly and kind, unlike the others. But laden with great pain. "Rodrigo," it groaned.

He stilled. The word meant something. It sank into him, claimed
him. It belonged to him.

But he was starving for the blood. He could hear it rushing through
that body, so close, a delicious river he could pour over himself for
fulfillment. He started to curl his fingers, one by one, so he could drive
them deep. Drink deep.

The smell was greatest in the man's belly. He could start there.

"No, laddie!"

The voice, which had been kind, rebuked. He flinched away.

"Easy now, easy. They said you'd be crazy but I didna expect
this."

Pause. He relaxed slowly but didn't approach the man's middle
again, fearing rejection.

"I dinna want to die." The voice was bitter. "Still, you'll have to
kill me."

He fought the chaos inside his skull and found a word. "No."

"Yes."

"No!"

"Only one of us can live and that's you, Rodrigo. I've prayed and prayed but it's a bitter draught to swallow."

The others stirred behind them. He twitched, senses coming alert. But their conversation returned to changing their clothing and he relaxed.

"No," he muttered, still unyielding.

His friend's voice hardened. "They'll na stay away for verra long, Rodrigo. I give you my strength willingly. In return, I ask that you kill both of those murdering, torturing bastards, should God ever grant you the chance."

Enemies. Kill. Yes! howled his instincts.

"Use your teeth on my neck." His friend swallowed hard before going on, still barely loud enough to hear. "You can drink all my blood that way. You'll need it all, lad."

He shook his head. "No kill."

"You must. It's the fastest way to die." Complete certainty cut past the pain in his friend's voice. "Or they will spin my death out over days and weeks."

"No!" Instinct told him his friend was correct. He gulped. Wished for another choice. Wished he could kill the enemies now. Instinct said hurry.

"You remember how, Rodrigo. You saw them do it to me and they did it often enough on you. Teeth, laddie, teeth. The sharp, pointed bones in your mouth, Rodrigo," the man coaxed.

Teeth. Is that what they were?

He ran his tongue over his teeth, exploring. Didn't the two on the front corners need to be longer . . .

They suddenly extended, dropping down to touch his lower lip. Razor sharp and deadly.

A swift, indrawn breath from the other. "Blessed Virgin," the man whispered, "you extended your fangs."

Fangs. Something done right in this chaos.

He needed to see.

He opened his eyes a crack. Squinted against the blinding light. Blinked rapidly until the blurs focused.

Rodrigo bent over the other man, heavy iron chains clanking around his arms and legs. Big, golden haired, burly.

"I have prayed all day. God forgives you and so do I, Rodrigo."

He touched his tongue to the blood flowing down the other's forehead. Sweet, a physical echo of the caring in this man's voice. Emotion was in the blood itself, sí! Tasting of trust and resignation. Confidence in Rodrigo.

The other sighed, relaxing a bit. "That's it, laddie. You've the knack of it now. But I wish I could have seen the sea just once more. The bright blue and the sea birds flying . . ."

Rodrigo's tongue moved faster, gathering the coppery nectar. His hands began to knead the hard muscles, offering comfort. His friend sighed, a sound touched with relaxation and physical pleasure.

The blood suddenly tasted richer and darker, like red wine. The pain in his head slipped back, clearing his thoughts somewhat.

"Fearghus," he murmured, eagerly finding every drop of blood on the other's face and neck.

"Praise God, Rodrigo, you've regained that much of your senses. Yes, I'm Fearghus."

"He's being very slow, isn't he, to kill the big blond?" The hateful younger voice.

"Yes. Sometimes young *cachorros* have no idea how to feed. We may have to disembowel the blond, just to get him started."

Fearghus flinched. Rodrigo bared his fangs, instinctively possessive. "Kill!"

"No, you can't fight them, not yet!" Fearghus was frightened and his blood suddenly tasted sour.

Disgusted, Rodrigo spat the offending drops onto the great table. "Kill," he repeated, more softly.

"Not yet," Fearghus groaned, tears running down his face. "When you're stronger, laddie."

Rodrigo stroked Fearghus's forehead. "¡Sí!"

*Fearghus smiled at that, his eyes blazing with a warrior's confi-
dence. "Grind them into the ground for me, Rodrigo. It's all I ask in
return."*

*Revenge. Rodrigo smiled. The blood's taste strengthened, rich and
complex like a fortified wine and so very satisfying.*

*He stroked his friend's cheek, silently assuring him that all his
wishes would be carried out.*

*"He's playing now!" the younger voice roared. "I want to see him
kill the infidel."*

*A grunt of disgust. "Fetch my knife, yaa ibni l-'aziiz, and I'll gut
the blond."*

*"Bite me now," Fearghus whispered. "Give me a fast death, Ro-
drigo. And drink deep."*

*"No, not that one!" the older voice roared. "He's not worth dull-
ing my best Damascus steel blade on."*

*Rodrigo rose high over his friend, extending his needle-sharp
fangs. Tears rolled down his cheek, burning like fire against his skin.
His body remembered clearly now how it had felt, when those two
fiends had bitten him.*

*Fearghus's eyes met his. "Always remember: revenge for both of
us." Then he turned his head to one side, baring his neck where the
great vein beat so temptingly just below the skin. He closed his eyes,
his lips moving silently.*

*Rodrigo bit down hard and fast, easily reaching the jugular. He
tugged a bit, widening the holes, until the blood gushed into his
mouth. Strong, rich, complex, satisfying. Someday he'd understand
all the emotions he'd tasted this day.*

*"He's biting him on the neck! Can't you stop him? The blond will
die too fast and the show will be over too soon."*

*"Alas, no. Once a vampiro—even a cachorro—has his teeth set
in his prey, there's no breaking him loose." The older man spat in
disgust. "Come, yaa ibnii, we'll have to play with those new slaves
after all."*

*Rodrigo drank deep and long, as he'd seen his captors do to help-
less prey they meant to kill. Quickly driving Fearghus into uncon-*

sciousness where those fiends could no longer harm him. Giving him
the grace of the fastest possible death, as he'd asked, where he'd be
free from the demons here.

   Fearghus's eyes closed, his face at peace. The same expression he'd
worn when speaking of the ocean.

   Dios mediante, *one day he would be able to take revenge and es-*
cape these devils.

Revenge.

   Rafael's fingers twitched as he stared out the window, affecting a
calm he was far from feeling. *Dios mio,* how he hungered to fulfill his
promise to Fearghus and kill that treacherous rat. He was free to do
so, now that he wasn't bound by the laws of hospitality.

   He ignored the voice of bitter memory, which wanted to remind
him of all the times he'd tried to kill that *pendejo*—and paid dearly
for failing.

   He glanced around the boardroom, notable even in Texas for its
size, opulence, and spectacular view of the Dallas skyline. He owned
the whole damn skyscraper as well, to tell the truth. The entire de-
velopment was a miracle of the most modern security precautions,
backed up by a dozen—or more—of his best *compañeros.* Only two
of them were in sight at the moment, in deference to his current guest's
"delicate" sensibilities.

   Three men and one woman, the top corporate raiders of North
America, all multimillionaires in their own right, had visited this room,
one after another. They'd been appalled to learn that they were expected to forego the comfort of their own bodyguards. However, once
they heard how much they stood to gain if they stayed, they'd reconsidered their objections. Now the last one, a petite Chinese-American
lady, with the face of Kwan-Yin and the appetites of a great white
shark, sat before her computer, studying the detailed analyses Jean-
Marie's spies had prepared, intent and quivering with greed. Another
hound about to be set loose on Madame Celeste's foreign assets.

   He gave them two months, perhaps as little as one, to impoverish her, in revenge for her fumbling attempts on his fortune. His lip curled, remembering how Gray Wolf had dealt with the most recent corporate raider who'd tried to nip the Santiago Trust's fringes.

The Santiago Trust was protected by layers of corporations and trusts, built up over the centuries he'd lived in Texas. A web of relationships created by the finest and most devious minds, both legal and criminal, it was older than any software who'd tried to track it and guarded by programmers who'd built the languages and tools used by hackers. Whenever any of those walls failed to keep out importunate fools, Ethan's men dealt bloody death.

He glanced at the clock and strolled back to the head of the long table. "Your fifteen minutes are up, señora," he announced. "Are you satisfied with the reports' veracity? Any questions? No?"

The lady turned off her small, elegant computer with a polite smile and nod.

"A thousand thanks to you for joining me today," Rafael continued. "Señor Alvarez will escort you out."

He shook hands politely, kissed the señora's fingers—which fluttered her Chinese-American heart for the second time that day—and escaped to the helipad. Two minutes later, he and his bodyguards were flying toward the airport and his Gulfstream jet. He'd be home well before dark, surrounded by *compañeros* ready to kill at the slightest disturbance.

Yesterday afternoon, his sentries had scented traces of a young *vampiro*, possibly eighty years old, on a cargo jet in Austin. It was undoubtedly Devol, Madame Celeste's enforcer. That bayou slime was arrogant but not a fool, which meant that his blatant announcement of his arrival was a distraction, rather than a mistake.

And the only asset Madame Celeste had, who was greater than her Bayou Butcher, was Beau with his five centuries of experience as an assassin in Russia.

When he'd learned of Devol's arrival, Rafael had immediately pulled Grania's watchers, overriding Ethan's objections with the logic that they needed every available man to search for Devol. It wasn't his only reason.

The searchers had found no furthers traces of Beau or Devol, while he'd been left with far too much time to think about the red-haired *doctora*. She was a stranger possibly involved with his bitterest enemy, given that he couldn't read her true motives. Yet every instinct he had demanded that he make Grania his lover as soon as possible. As often as possible.

He growled a curse at his own folly, as he strapped himself into his seat. His men eyed him warily and kept their distance, silently allowing him time to think. The pilot understood his urgency perfectly and took off within minutes after they boarded, shooting the powerful jet toward the south and home.

Grania. Rafael considered, staring sightlessly at the prairies below. She of the courageous heart and the rich passions and the truly formidable mental shields.

She was certainly brave. *Madre de Dios*, none of his *vampiros* would have challenged him as she had last night. If she were a man, he'd have recruited her in a moment to join his band of *compañeros*. He'd have expected her to quickly earn the right to become a *vampiro* in Texas, after which he'd have years to enjoy her company.

But she was not a man so that could never happen. Instead she'd remain a *prosaica*, grow old, and die in the traditional way. She'd be dead in fifty years, perhaps sixty—no matter how much his heart cried out that that was only the start of the time they could have spent together.

But he could still enjoy her company in the time they had, as he'd enjoyed other beautiful *prosaicas*. It should be enough to satisfy his clamoring instincts, which even now threw up demands to explore her surprisingly delicate wrists or her long legs or . . . He'd control how and when they came together, of course.

Such a relationship would certainly present great difficulties. But overcoming hurdles to gain such sweet rewards were the challenges that still delighted after so many centuries. Although she'd responded when he'd kissed her, Grania was rightfully skittish after seeing him with Brynda. Surprisingly, he hadn't been able to touch her mind to soothe her.

Her mental shields were the greatest shock of all. He'd always been able to touch the mind of anyone he wanted to, except for his *maldito creador*, of course. But not hers, no matter how hard he'd tried. But that would just make seduction all the sweeter for having to work on it the harder.

But to make her conquest more certain, he'd need an ally. The best choice was Bob Harrison, the raptor center's director, who wanted to explore the land that Gray Wolf had kept undisturbed for the last century and a half. Now Gray Wolf was willing to allow a few scientists to explore it as well, if they were closely watched by Caleb. And the entire survey was blessed by Rafael, of course.

If he were given permission to explore, Bob should feel very friendly toward Rafael. Hopefully, he'd create opportunities for Rafael to be near *Doctora* O'Malley at the raptor center. With any luck at all, Bob would see himself as a *casamentero* and start throwing them together.

Rafael silently laughed at himself. He hadn't plotted so hard to be near a girl since he was fifteen and greatly enamored of Maria Sanchez, she of the laughing eyes. Still, he'd call Bob from the plane.

To Rafael's complete lack of surprise, Bob was more than happy to stay late at the raptor center, in order to nail down the deal. Half an hour after they started talking, an ecstatic Bob was ticking off possible scientists to assist in the survey, when a noise from the driveway beyond made Rafael straighten to full attention.

Grania's truck had just driven up and parked. Here, tonight, he'd see her. *Gracias a Dios*, he'd given Ethan strict orders that she was not to see the men or the vehicles. If there was trouble, Rafael would call them. He knew damn well they'd listen to everything that went on inside the building.

He marked her trip inside the center by the strong, confident sound of her boot heels ringing on the stairs and down the hall. But she stopped in her tracks at the sight of Rafael, shocked and wide-eyed, with a lab notebook in her hand. Adorable too, hair escaping from that long braid and a faint tang of sweat, as if she'd spent the day working at some form of hard labor. ¡Ay, so many other enjoyable ways to make her flushed and sweaty!

He bit his lip at her wariness. She was even more skittish than two nights ago, more than a woman's affront at a stranger's kiss would account for. If all those windbags who'd stretched the truth and told lies about *vampiros* had been nearby, he'd have gladly drawn and quartered them for frightening her.

Bob, an ever-gracious host, performed introductions. "Grania, have you met Don Rafael Perez, one of our local landowners? Don Rafael, may I introduce you to Dr. Grania O'Malley, our new vet?"

"*Encantado, doctora.*" Rafael bowed low over her hand.

"Señor Perez." Her tone couldn't have been colder as she removed her fingers from his grip.

Bob, no fool, glanced between the other two in the room before he started to grin. He controlled himself quickly but not before Rafael felt himself begin a slow, almost adolescent flush.

"Did you know that Don Rafael manages the land bordering us, Grania?"

"Really?" She shifted from foot to foot, her eyes darting toward then away from Rafael.

His eyebrows drew together at her unusual fidgeting.

Grania stared at a window, as if trying to frame a sentence. But she could also see Rafael's reflection there, so terror wasn't her only emotion. Curiosity as well? If so, was it academic or sexual?

"Well, now, I really must be getting home, so Betsy and I can eat dinner before choir practice," Bob announced, his West Texas twang very pronounced. "Will you give Don Rafael a tour of the center?"

Grania's head snapped around, sending the dark copper braid thudding against her arm. "What?"

"Thanks, honey. I knew you could handle it for me." Bob was gone within minutes, whistling softly, as he took the stairs to the parking lot two at a time. Grania seemed torn between outrage and indecision at her predicament, clutching her notebook like a shield.

Rafael smiled privately. It seemed he'd acquired a *casamentero*.

La doctora glanced out the window at her truck and visibly decided against running. *Pobrecita*. Rafael took pity on her and started an unexceptionable conversation, something she should be able to carry on in her sleep. "What did you do your dissertation on, *doctora*?"

She stiffened, drawing herself up like an affronted nun. Much better; at least she wasn't skittish. "You're really not interested in my research, señor. Let's just talk about the center."

"Ah, but I am interested, *doctora*. It will add so much to my understanding of the center's capabilities."

She eyed him suspiciously, keeping her distance from him. Finally she made up her mind and turned for the hallway without waiting to see if he followed. "Population studies of owls, primarily in wilderness areas. I was interested in projecting the results, based on prey populations and reproduction rates." She glanced at him over her shoulder, then as quickly looked away. "The kitchen's in here. As you can see, we're very careful to keep everything organized so it can be measured out for each individual bird."

"Most impressive, *doctora*." He gave a perfunctory glance at a very cramped, clean space. "*Por favor*, tell me more about your research. What effects did you find the numbers of prey had upon owls?"

He kept up the flow of polite conversation as she showed him through the center.

A pair of stout doors intrigued him briefly, named "ICU 1" and "ICU 2," each guarded by an electronic lock. "What are those?"

"Intensive care units. Soundproofed rooms, steel doors, windowless. The birds have to be kept absolutely quiet when they're very ill."

"*Por supuesto*," Rafael murmured, with a reminiscent smile. His father's falconer had blistered his ears—and other portions of his anatomy—with the same lecture.

He stayed very quiet in the convalescent wards, moving as delicately as if walking on eggshells. A red-tailed hawk with a splinted wing surveyed him with a single eye then shut it, reducing his arrival to the category of trivial interruption. A barn owl blinked sleepily at him, clearly dozing. The room was peaceful and soothing, capable of healing both man and beast.

Grania started becoming calmer the longer she saw the birds' comfort with him.

"Tell me more about your work in Colombia," Rafael urged after they left the ward. "Washed down perhaps by a drink for dry throats?"

"Water and soda are all we have," Grania said dubiously.

"Soda would be delicious," he accepted politely and followed her to the staff lounge. Soda. He shuddered to himself and continued to talk about subjects that cheered her. "The swamps there must have been very different from the deserts you were accustomed to . . ."

That topic kept them going all the way to the staff lounge and more talk of her research until Grania began eyeing the clock just before midnight.

She jumped when he started a different topic. "Do you have any questions for me, *querida*?"

Her eyes narrowed suspiciously.

Mierda, he must have used an endearment too quickly. What sort of fools had attended her university for her to be so unaccustomed to cherishing? He backtracked quickly. "Relax, please, *doctora*. I give endearments only to very special people, not passing fancies. You are a very unique woman," he offered with a slight bow. "I would like to study you, as you would like to study me."

She flushed with embarrassment at being so obvious and twitched.

Maldita sea, she was nervous again. Rafael stayed perfectly still on the other side of the lounge from her, careful not to frighten her.

"How do I know that?" he asked rhetorically. "You saw me last night with the blonde. You have obviously satisfied yourself that she wasn't harmed, *querida*, or you wouldn't be sitting here so calmly with me. Correct?"

She nodded, stiff as the proverbial poker.

"So, what would you like to ask me, *querida*?" Rafael prodded gently. "I believe that the lady was content with the encounter last night."

"Yes, it seemed like symbiosis to me," Grania responded slowly, drumming her fingers on her notebook.

"Symbiosis?" Rafael echoed, startled at her description of an erotic event. *Just like that, she switches to a scientific discussion? When she herself had an orgasm from watching?*

"Exactly. She had an orgasm and you obtained some blood. But it didn't look like what the books say."

Rafael smiled privately. *At least she mentioned the word* orgasm. *Perhaps there is hope.* "Oh, most of the books are very wrong, *doctora*. A few have some elements of truth though."

¡Que jodienda! How can I get through to this female? She's so skittish, I can't push her. But how? Nothing else has worked, so why not try a gamble?

She took another sip of her soda.

"So here you are, interviewing a *vampiro*," Rafael remarked. "An unexpected event for both of us. I will answer your questions, *doctora*, as much as I can. It is a pleasure to converse with a beautiful, intelligent woman." He inclined his head to her and toasted her with his execrable drink. "But you must promise me that you will never tell anyone else, in any way, what you have learned tonight."

If she talked, he'd kill her, of course. Something inside him screamed in pain at the thought but he steeled himself. He'd spent five hundred years making sure he would survive at all costs, he and all the others who depended on him. One *prosaica* would not be allowed to interfere with his responsibilities.

A grin broke across her face and she saluted him in return. "You'll answer my questions? Cool! Let me get a pen and we can talk." She speedily retrieved a pen from her backpack and opened her notebook. She looked up at him more seriously, pen poised over the lined paper. "You have my word, Señor Perez, that I will never disclose my data or my findings without your explicit permission."

Rafael raised an eyebrow, recognizing her formal phrasing. *La doctora* had taken a scientific oath, the equivalent of a knightly vow. Honoring that, he bowed to her and waited for her first question.

Her eyes lit up and she put him through an interrogation whose relentlessness and thoroughness would have impressed even the Inquisition. She asked only about *vampiro* reproductive biology, nothing else. Not the wealth he might have acquired in such a long life, nor the friends, nor the power. Not even the Santiago Trust, whose land her employer would be exploring.

And she never, ever fully voiced any question that made her blush or look away from him. Oh, she'd start to say something, then blush, stammer—and change the subject back to something unexceptionable.

She was very focused on her questions, though. Perhaps now she'd allow him to approach closer . . .

Rafael stood up and stretched. He paced a bit as he answered her questions, occasionally coming close to her and seeing too much. Fair skin, inviting his touch. The faint scent of flowers in her hair. Her fingers curled around her pen as she drove it across the page; would she glide her hand over her lover with the same concentration? The fan of her lashes on her cheeks, the adorable tendrils of hair escaping from those tight braids to sweep over her ears and neck . . .

She ignored his movements, continuing to focus on her notebook, as she queried him.

A half hour later, he'd retreated to the far side of the lounge, where he would be less tempted to grab her and kiss the pulse beating in her neck. Grania was curled up on the lumpy sofa, studying his answer to the last sentence as she nibbled the tip of one fingernail, while he leaned against the wall.

He eyed her with pure irritation and frustrated lust. ¡Coño, despite five hundred years of experience in seducing women, he was still sitting on the opposite side of the room from her, as if there was a dueña on guard!

He fought the urge to crumple his can and hurl it through a window.

They were alone in a building at night, in a small, quiet room. Yet she still didn't feel comfortable enough to relax with him.

Somehow he needed to build a feeling of intimacy between them. Perhaps if he coaxed her to ask him that secret question, she might feel a bond between them. Perhaps she'd ask about another aspect of *vampiro* reproduction, such as the population size needed to nurse a *cachorro* through *La Lujuria*. Or the heightened senses, a subject she hadn't touched on, although she'd obviously done a great deal of research. Or . . .

He deepened his voice and slowed it to a social pace, escaping the scientific atmosphere.

"I've never before discussed *vampiros* with anyone who wasn't a *vampiro* or considering becoming one. Talking to you has been very enlightening for me."

Grania preened, sitting tall and smiling at him. She even closed her damn notebook. He considered taking another sip of the appalling pap in the can as a sign of fellowship, reconsidered, and simply swirled the stuff.

"But you still have one particular question for me, *doctora*. It has been burning your tongue all evening as you start to voice it, then quickly change your words. Do you believe now that I will be truthful with you? Come, ask your question."

She hesitated, her finger tapping the notebook. But she didn't immediately refuse.

He was too experienced a hunter to push her. He took a sip of the execrable, lukewarm sugar water, his eyes never leaving hers.

She swallowed hard. "Do you masturbate?"

His jaw dropped and he choked. Trust *la doctora* to bring up that topic in a scientific manner—and knock him off his feet!

She blushed and started to say something more.

But he closed his eyes and chuckled. She fell silent.

He opened his eyes, still laughing at his own idiocies, and crossed the room to her. He dropped to his knees in front of her, politely ignoring how she gaped at him. He bent his head and kissed her hand.

"You are truly the most incredible woman. So intelligent and so attractive." He kissed her hand again more slowly this time, exploring every delicate bone and tendon under the fine skin. ¡Ay, the slight tremors that ran up her arm into her heart!

He lightly rubbed his cheek against her hand, enjoying how his beard stubble made her shiver. What he wouldn't give to explore her between her legs the same way . . . "*Sí*, I masturbate but very rarely. I am seldom without sexual companions, as you have undoubtedly guessed. But sometimes, *querida*, I fantasize when I am alone and bring myself to a climax."

She trembled under his touch, a delicate flush of heat racing through her. She reached out, very tentatively, and pushed a strand of hair back from his forehead. He closed his eyes and tilted his head into her palm, savoring her touch. Finally, she was touching him of her own volition.

He'd widen this opening in her defenses as far as he could. She liked to observe, as he knew from the time in the park. So he'd offer her a performance to answer her *doctora*'s "scientific curiosity"—and start building the links he needed.

"Would you like to watch me, Grania?" Rafael asked, his voice a soft rumble in the quiet room.

She swallowed hard, hunger and indecision written across her face.

"I think it would bring you pleasure if you watched," he murmured.

She nodded, her tongue touching her lip. *Ah, sí, you do so like to watch*, doctora.

"But I would like to ask a favor of you in return."

She stiffened, eyeing him suspiciously.

"If watching me excites you, may I have a drop of your blood afterward? That would allow me a taste of your emotion, which is what I truly desire, Grania. I swear to you that you would be in no danger." Just a little thing, nothing too dangerous. Open the door for me, *querida* . . .

She considered the proposed bargain long and hard before agreeing. He waited patiently, truly not knowing what she'd choose. But that was the charm and the challenge of *la doctora*, the most unusual woman he'd met since becoming a *vampiro*.

"*Sí*, Rafael, you may have a sample of my blood. I put my faith in your honor."

Shock swept over Rafael. She agreed—but by relying on his honor? When she thought he was a supernatural monster? He felt exalted, lifted up and ennobled, as if he'd just been knighted.

For Grania, who knew so little of masculine cherishing, he would give the best show he could. He'd dance for her, for only the joy of the moment and the hope of seducing her into pleasure as well. But which style of dance? He'd learned so many in his lifetime.

He kissed her hand, bowing low in acknowledgment of the honor she'd done him, and stood up. He backed away, so she could see him clearly, and began to warm up, still wondering which dance would tempt her the most. Flamenco, perhaps?

He automatically planted his feet firmly on the floor, as far apart as his hips, and relaxed his knees. His back straight and his head erect, he rolled his neck. Only once or twice, to buy himself some time to decide. If the move startled her, he could always make a joke of it.

Instead, she leaned forward, watching him intently. ¡Ay, so he'd caught the *doctora*'s attention!

He did a few more neck rolls. She was definitely fascinated. He executed some arm and leg rolls, while still relaxed and smiling at her. He rolled his hips, just a little, not enough to move his shoulders or anything else. Grania put down her lab notebook to watch him. Her lab notebook, which she'd wielded like a shield the entire evening.

But the dance style that best suited these exercises was one he hadn't performed in five hundred years, not since he'd escaped his captivity in the eastern courts. Still, he'd been able to occasionally lose himself in it back then, one of the few relaxations he'd been permitted. Perhaps it would not be too bad to dance it once again, since it was the first thing that had cracked *la doctora*'s shell.

He hesitated, remembering so many old humiliations—and ecstasies. Surely he could manage it one more time.

He swayed a bit, trying to remember some of the music. He'd always loved dancing to the *tablah*, the hand drum, its strong, eternally changing beat underlying everything else. He swayed again, remembering how the reed pipe had woven its song of joy and yearning, into the *tablah*'s beat. He shook out his hair, letting it tease his neck.

Grania's tongue darted out over her lips.

Encouraged, Rafael strutted to the old rhythms and threw out his chest, drawing the dance from his center, deep in his belly. His arms twisted over his head, displaying his strength and ferocity. His lungs swelled, as his skin heated. He stroked his chest through the cloth and his heart started to beat faster at her wide-eyed fascination.

Her fingers started to drum on the arm of her chair, matching the rhythm of his hips and feet. His heartbeat speeded up even more.

Grania swallowed hard, her breasts rising and falling rapidly under her T-shirt.

Then he kicked himself. This was moving too far and too fast for his own self-control. If she looked at him like that much longer, he might be the one begging for a kiss. He stretched, rolling his arms up over his head and back down again, to close the first dance.

Then he sat down in the chair beside her and took his boots off. Grania stared at him and he chuckled. "Boots are easier appreciated at other times, *querida*, when they don't come between a man and what he wants."

She blushed and he tossed his head back, grinning at his sally's success.

He took his socks off and rubbed his feet, accustoming her to the sight of his skin. She reddened further, her eyes flashing away only to return. Her breasts swelled and tightened under her thin T-shirt.

Still, this was a very promising start to her seduction.

Rafael stood up again and let the old music, with its sensual melodies and unpredictable rhythms, ripple all the way up his body. When it burned its way to his bones, he began to dance again.

Hips swaying and shoulders high, he flaunted his masculinity—yet he never allowed her to look at him directly. He shook his head, rippling his hair over his skin—and exulted privately when lust leaped in her eyes.

He circled his hips, showing off his strong ass, and twisted to display his muscles for her. He caressed himself through his clothes—and saw her clench her fists.

Bien. Now *la doctora* was finally feeling the sting of frustrated lust.

Heat danced under his skin, lanced through his veins, every time he saw her gulp or lick her lips. His cock swelled and rose, straining against the tight jeans. He panted, gathering energy. Pulses began to build in his spine, to be used for his dance and his climax. Come gathered in his balls, begging for release.

All the while, he watched his beautiful audience, matching his every move to what most excited her. He could have danced like this for hours without ejaculating; *por Dios*, he'd learned how in the worst of schools. He'd avoided doing so since, disliking the memories. But *la doctora*, biting her lip as she fought not to show her excitement, was unschooled and irresistible.

All too soon, it was time to push her a little more. Make his nipples more prominent, perhaps. Or show off his ass more; Grania seemed to particularly enjoy that portion of his anatomy.

He plucked his nipples hard through his T-shirt, enjoying the little sting of pain. He circled his hips and squeezed his rear, thrusting his chest toward her in a show of dominance.

She gasped for breath and moaned softly, her hands clenching and unclenching.

Bien. He arched his head back and peeled off his T-shirt slowly. Slowly he slid it from side to side over his shoulders, teasing her more.

She hissed sharply, shuddered, and closed her eyes.

He froze. ¡*Coño*, he'd forgotten his scars! Would she make him stop? *Por Dios*, he didn't want to, not now, not with his cock weeping pre-come.

Grania's eyes opened slowly, the dark blue of the stormy North Sea. They fixed on his hand where it rested on his belt buckle. She gulped and swallowed, licked her lips.

His cock jerked and throbbed. ¡*Sí!*

He slipped his thumbs into his jeans' waistband and circled his hips, emphasizing the movement by keeping her attention on his belt buckle—and the bulge underneath his fly. He varied the tempo, remembering the *taqsim*'s ancient improvisations. He stroked himself lasciviously, slowly, fanned his fingers over himself. Then, still keeping his thumbs in his waistband, he rolled his hips again.

She whimpered, the merest hint of sound. She was almost quivering as she sat still, adorable in her desperate attempts to retain self-control. Beautiful beyond belief.

He ached for this moment to last so he took the longest possible time handling himself, before he unzipped his jeans. Her reaction was everything he could have wished when his cock bobbed free: a throaty gasp, followed by her low moan of desire.

His thighs tightened as orgasm's waves started to build in his hips. Not yet, he ordered himself, not yet. He could control his body through far more temptation than this.

His hand closed around his cock and he turned away from her, presenting his profile to emphasize the size of his erection. He enjoyed the sound of her protesting growls as she watched him. He played longer, teasing himself inside his jeans. Toying with his balls then pressing on his perineum to delay orgasm.

She cursed viciously under her breath and sat up straight.

He sniffed delicately. Ah, she was definitely creaming very well indeed. It was time to hasten matters.

He faced her again, stomping his feet and tossing his head. He slipped his hand inside his jeans and cupped his balls, lifting up his cock so it would look even larger than it was.

Grania stared at the subtle movements, riveted in place.

Ah, so she liked to be teased, not to have the answer flaunted in front of her, did she? Well, she was a scientist, who'd spent years studying and exploring. Her attitude appealed to him, given his long lifetime and fight against boredom. It was also frustrating, when every nerve in his body demanded immediate fulfillment.

Growling softly, he played with himself a little longer. Then he pushed his jeans slowly, oh so slowly, down his legs with little wiggles of his hips. He threw his head back and arched his chest, flaunting himself.

She whimpered again. The sofa squeaked, as she moved impatiently, before she settled back down.

Excelente. Pleasure for both of them looked closer and closer. But he needed to heat her veins further, until she ached as much as he did. If not, he'd shoot come across the floor.

He teased her by turning so she first saw his buttocks, then his hips and legs, and finally his jutting cock. She gripped the sofa arm hard, moaning softly.

¡*Gracias a Dios*, she finally sounded truly desperate!

Rafael stroked his cock firmly, the *tablah*'s beat echoing in his hips and the reed pipe's song running through his veins. He twisted his hand over his cock head when the *tablah* beat faster and heard her gasp. He shimmied, tilting his pelvis forward so he could cup his balls, so very sensitive now as they ached to unload themselves. Lust speared upward, tightening his nipples further.

She gulped.

Her face was as filled with unassuaged lust as his.

He took a deep breath—and she did the same.

He rocked his hips forward, thrusting his cock back and forth into his hands. Her hips moved in exactly the same rhythm, there on the couch. She was dancing with him, as she sat.

As passionate a woman as he longed for. *Mierda*, he could see her now when she sheathed his cock, with her legs wrapped around his hips, urging him on . . .

The image rattled his discipline and he began to move faster and faster. He fought to regain control, first by using only his left hand, with which he was slightly less skillful. She chewed on her lip, drawing blood, her eyes huge and her breasts heaving. His blood pounded desperately through his veins.

Still, he tried to slow down and managed to delay his orgasm longer than he'd thought possible, until his balls were tight beneath his cock, screaming for release.

Ay, mierda, she hadn't climaxed yet. He'd have to climax first and hope she'd let him take her over, if he was to taste her highest emotion. Easy enough to do normally but not when sanity was shredding under the pressure of an imminent orgasm.

He caught up his T-shirt and roared as he ejaculated into it. Climax shot through his body and he rode it out with gritted teeth, using all his experience not to lose control.

Then he dropped to his knees in front of her, betting she wouldn't let him drink from her if he dominated her physically.

Gracias a Dios, Grania reached out to break his fall, catching his shoulders, steadying him. He lowered his head, panting, ignoring his orgasm's aftermath, looking for her pulse.

She caressed his hair, crooning to him. She was vulnerable, poised on the brink of a sexual climax—and he could take her there.

He turned his head to find the pulse point on the inside of her wrist. She relaxed slightly, probably expecting another kiss.

He sucked her skin hard, preparing her. She choked.

Then he bit quickly into her vein, taking only a few drops of blood as he'd promised, no more. Given in complete trust and accepted in sheer joy of the moment, as he'd done so many thousands of times before. Her emotions tasted excellent, rich and dark, like an old burgundy. He'd want so much more of her, as often as he could have her, given that vibrant taste.

In the next instant, the world changed forever.

Grania's thoughts and pleasure came roaring into him. Her ecstasy in the midst of orgasm, pulsing brighter and deeper with every swallow he took of her blood, like a brilliant pinwheel of ecstasy, tumbling through him over and over again. The sting of his teeth in her wrist and the gentle wash of his tongue over her wrist. The feel of his hair—his!—through her fingers.

Her absolute trust that he was honorable and would never hurt her.

Shock raced through him, turning his veins to ice.

His fangs tied them together as he tapped her blood. The bond transformed pleasure into raw delight, blazing through Grania like the flame from a welder's torch. She cried out, as fire raced through her and centered deep within her. The orgasm burst through her in a series of shockwaves, tsunamis of feeling that consumed every cell and every thought.

But the aftermath, what the French call *le petit mort*, was different from anything she'd ever felt before. When she'd always before been separate somehow from her lover no matter how closely joined their bodies were, this time she felt Rafael somehow in her mind, part of her as she was part of him, ecstasy roaring through both of their bodies and minds together.

When she could think again, she was seated on his lap with her face buried against his chest. He smelled of sandalwood, sweat, and sex, and his heartbeat, like hers, was more than a little irregular. She snuffled happily and went to sleep, as comfortable in his arms as if they'd sheltered her a thousand times before.

Rafael glared at the unconscious innocent in his arms. A *conyugal* bond snapped into place between them and she had the nerve to sleep, instead of giving him an explanation?

A *conyugal* bond tied a *vampiro* and another person together at all levels of their minds, both conscious and unconscious. They could share both their thoughts and their instincts, to the point where they could share each other's senses during a duel, even give each other strength. Because the link was so complete, not even the slightest barrier existed between them. So a *conyugal* bond could never be forced in any way; it simply appeared when two people completely trusted each other and least expected it to happen.

All of which made it incredibly rare. A *vampiro* could spend his entire life—even become a *vampiro mayor* and walk in daylight—but never see two people who shared a *conyugal* bond.

Proof positive of a *conyugal* bond was knowing and feeling what someone else thought and felt, as if you yourself were simultaneously thinking and experiencing it. As had happened when he bit her wrist and somersaulted her into orgasm, the ecstatic waves ripping through him—he, the sated one!

If he'd known everything she thought and felt in that moment, then she must have known everything he thought and felt. His lip curled. After two hundred years as a tortured sex slave, he trusted no one that well.

And yet, how many *vampiros* had he heard say they would give everything to have the *conyugal* bond with someone, anyone?

What the hell was he supposed to do now?

EIGHT

Diego threw Rodrigo into the cell. "Did you truly think you'd dine tonight?"

Rodrigo rolled and staggered to his feet, glaring at his nemesis. "I feed on freely given blood, not on fear and death."

Diego laughed at him. "Pobrecito Rodrigo," he mocked. "Four years since El Abrazo *but you're still the toy of any* vampiro *who chances by. Whatever they want, sex or blood, you will give."*

Rodrigo gritted his teeth, ignoring the hunger roiling his belly. Gracias a Dios, Fearghus's *courage had gifted Rodrigo with the ability to feed from trust and physical pleasure. And with luck, if Rodrigo continued to distract Diego, the* pendejo *would never notice that he was learning to evoke carnal pleasure as a power source equal to death.*

"But I have never committed murder for pay, as you do," he snarled. "I have still kept my oaths, as you have not."

Diego slapped him, sending him back against the wall. "Our master—"

"Your *master*," Rodrigo corrected, *spitting out a tooth. It would grow again, as everything else had, thanks to the* vampiro *elixir in his veins. Only his head and heart could be broken now.*

"Feeds me *his blood regularly*," Diego spat, "*while you beg for scraps from any* vampiro *who finds you amusing. I am a mature* vampiro*, able to stand erect in a gathering of* vampiros*. While you, you grovel and cringe if so much as one* vampiro *raises so much as an eyebrow at you."*

"And you run to him like a mindless fool, whenever he lifts a finger," *Rodrigo snapped back.* Cachorros *matured fastest when they drank often from their* creador*, especially during* La Lujuria*. The bond formed then ran deep and strong, ensuring lifelong obedience.*

Diego had outgrown being a cachorro *in two years; he'd been a full* vampiro *when Rodrigo was forced into* El Abrazo*. He was infinitely stronger and faster than Rodrigo, as he delighted to prove time and time again. But Rodrigo would far rather take longer to mature, if he gained it through feeding on carnal pleasure and without The Syrian's blood.*

Diego lifted an eyebrow. "You are jealous of my status, as his adopted son."

"¡Nunca!" *Sometimes he was glad of the numerous* vampiros *who used his body, then grudgingly fed him their blood. Every taste of a different* vampiro's *blood was one more brick in his mind's wall against The Syrian and Diego.*

Diego snickered. "Of course you are. Look at you, wearing only that filthy loincloth, soiled with blood and—need I list everything else? Then consider my clothes. The embroidered cotton, the gilded leather, the Damascus steel—"

"The symbols of a coward who sold his soul for a comfortable bed," *Rodrigo sneered. His wife had warned him against this worm. He desperately feared he had fallen too far for Dios santo to hear him, now that the* vampiro *elixir ran in his veins. But if prayers from one like him were of any use, then may his wife and children be safe and well . . .*

Head held high, he looked straight back at Diego. At least he'd done his best to keep his vows.

"I love my father! He has given me love, not cold duty!" Diego slapped him, knocking Rodrigo's head against the stone wall and half stunning him. *"If he didn't want to see us fight duels, I would kill you now!"* he shouted, smacking his hand against the wall. *"I will ask him to reconsider, that I may paint the arena with your guts."* He stormed out, slamming the iron door. *Unfortunately, he remembered to lock it.*

Rodrigo allowed himself to slide down the wall, eyes shut. It smelled as if he'd left a blood trail a handsbreadth wide on the wall, which made it a nastier blow than usual from the pendejo. Not surprising, since The Syrian was teaching Diego his family business of assassination, which enhanced any tendencies he held toward efficient bloodshed.

Still, he'd be healed before sunrise. And tomorrow night, there'd be another vampiro—whether The Syrian, Diego, or someone else— to torture or fuck him, or both. And the night after that, and after that . . . ¡Ay, Dios!

Sounds reached him from the courtyard, growing louder and louder—steel against steel? His head came up alertly. Could it be? He sprang to his feet and went to the door, pressing his face against the bars to listen. Men's grunts and groans but no shouts. Yet.

Golden light slipped down the hall, astonishing in this place of shadows and foul smells. Borne by a clean man—a stranger—carrying a sword that dripped blood. "Tío Rodrigo?"

Joy flooded his veins. Every sense was brighter. Even the tiny cell seemed suddenly large and gracious.

Ah, family! And the hope of seeing Blanche and his children.

"Hassan, mi sobrino!" Achmed's son, now a man grown, holding aloft a glimmering lantern in his other hand. He could smell two men behind him, armed and watchful.

The door whispered open and, joy of joys, Hassan hugged him. Family touching him again. Treating him as a person, not a beast. Tears slid down his face.

"My wife? The little ones?" His voice broke.

"All well," Hassan assured him. "Your son grows more like you *every day and your daughters are enchanting. Your wife has refused all offers, insisting you are still alive."*

Madre de Dios, *she has remained faithful to me, despite untold pressures.*

Hassan tossed him a robe and sword. Rodrigo quickly donned the clothing, then swung the blade, testing the balance. Not his sword but a fine one; it would do for now. He'd return later at sunset, and kill The Syrian.

An instant later, Rodrigo and Hassan, with their men, were creeping through the corridor, alert to every sound. "There's a gap," Hassan whispered, "where the old Roman aqueduct comes in. We'll go back through there."

Suddenly voices sounded behind them. They froze, listening. Rodrigo cursed. "They know I'm missing. Hurry!"

They moved faster, trying to be quiet. Feet thudded, metal clanked behind them. Diego shouted.

Rodrigo froze, listening. How far away was the pendejo? "We have less than two minutes, mi sobrino. *Run!*"

Hassan stared at him but didn't argue. They ran.

The corridor twisted and turned, on its way to the old Roman aqueducts. At one of those turns, an arrow thudded into the wall above Hassan's head. "Faster!" he panted.

The arrows came closer and more often.

Rodrigo calculated the odds automatically. In a corridor this narrow, there could be very few bowmen. More to the point, they would be backed by multiple armsmen and Diego.

Still, one determined vampiro or cachorro could put up an effective defense, long enough for Hassan and his men to escape. It was almost dawn; if they could reach the bottom of the cliff then cross the valley floor, they'd be safe.

But he'd never see Blanche again. Never wrap his arms around her or laugh at her small jokes, or lie abed with her on a long winter's night. Never play with his children or stand proud of his grandchildren. Never, never, never.

The Syrian and Diego would deal out worse torments than before, if that was possible. And for how many years? Decades, even centuries, if his vision was to be fulfilled. He prayed that he would survive so long.

Rodrigo gathered his courage and came to a stop. "Take your men and go on, mi sobrino. I will stay here and fight."

"Impossible! They will kill you." Hassan waved his men forward impatiently. Good soldiers, they went obediently but reluctantly.

"They cannot. I will live for years yet, even centuries." I pray to Jesuscristo *this is true.*

Hassan frowned at him, his face unearthly in the lantern light. An arrow nicked the corner beside them and they moved back automatically. "There are rumors that this castle's master has lived longer than possible for ordinary men," he said slowly.

Rodrigo nodded. "Verdaderamente. But you must save yourself and go."

Hassan ducked for another arrow. "We cannot leave you like this."

He was too damn much like his father. Better give him a quest to fulfill, so he'd feel he was accomplishing something. "Tell your sons to return two centuries from now, at sunset."

"Two centuries?"

An arrow clipped Rodrigo's sleeve, drawing blood.

"Just come back then at sunset—and bring my knightly sword. Now promise and go, Hassan!"

His nephew's brown eyes, so like his father's, searched Rodrigo's. "Very well, you have my word and the family's. On our honor, we will return."

He kissed Rodrigo's cheek and ran to the next turn in the corridor. He paused at the very end to wave the lantern, which Rodrigo returned with his hand. Then they disappeared.

Rodrigo raced toward Diego, roaring his battle rage. Por Dios, he would enjoy killing as many of Diego's creatures as he could—and maybe Diego himself.

*   *   *

In time, he'd escaped that hellhole and built a new life, one based on service. For so long, he'd thought his *hijos y compañeros* were all the companionship he needed to be happy. But then the red-haired *doctora* had shaken him to the bone.

Dios santo, Grania had touched him with the heart-deep intimacy of a *cónyuge*, which was absolutely impossible. How could she have done it? They'd only known each other a few days, a handful of hours—when every other pair of *cónyuges* he knew had taken years to form their bond. Perhaps he'd been distracted and mistaken what had happened.

Impossible, impossible, impossible!

There was no way a man could keep secrets from his *cónyuge*; some of the things he'd done in his life were nothing to tell a woman. And if his enemies knew she was his *cónyuge*, they'd destroy her in a moment.

Even if he believed they were *cónyuges*—or trusted that she wasn't working with his enemies, since he still didn't know her motives—she was a *prosaica* and would be dead in fifty years, seventy at the most. If she tried to become a *vampira*, it was a near certainty she'd go mad and die. No man could ask that of his *cónyuge*. It would be far better to cherish her for the short time they'd have together, before she passed on. If *la doctora* waited patiently to be cherished, that is.

He was forced to laugh privately at the unlikelihood of her ever doing that and returned his attention to his surroundings. Three of his *hijos* were loudly arguing about Devol's most likely hiding places, while the others ran and reran search patterns for the options discussed. None of the actions discussed required his participation.

Again, he was waiting for others to act. Seven hundred years after his captivity and a hemisphere away from The Syrian's castle—but he still hated it, even when he fully trusted the men.

Rafael leaned back in his seat, surveying the gathering in the Austin Commandery's council chamber. He'd built this hall almost two hundred years ago to stand against Kiowa and Comanche attacks, but it remained remarkably useful against twenty-first-century attacks. The stout limestone walls were originally constructed to stand against cannon fire, and had recently been reinforced against modern bombs and mortar fire. Narrow windows high above admitted moonlight and permitted marksmen to dissuade attackers. Heavy steel shutters could be closed for additional protection, if needed. The walls were hung with magnificent Indian weavings, given as gifts over the years, while others covered the polished wood floor.

The furniture was equally massive and simple. An enormous, heavy table ran down the center, littered with paper and twenty-first-century electronics. It was surrounded by armchairs, upholstered in leather, all of them carrying scars from decades of close contact with booted and spurred feet. Narrow tables against the walls offered a variety of liquid refreshments.

The most impressive occupants were, however, the men.

Gray Wolf faced Rafael from the opposite end in his role as *adelantado mayor* and Rafael's designated heir. Caleb was at his right, his *cónyuge* and the other half of an almost invincible dueling team.

Ethan lounged at Rafael's right, as *alferez mayor* and the leader of Texas's armies, his hazel eyes deadly and cold as he considered how to hunt their enemies.

Jean-Marie sat on Rafael's other side as *heraldo*, his chief diplomat and spy. A litter of papers lay before him, as well as an exquisitely thin computer, all manipulated by his supple fingers. He'd also convey reports from the distant warriors, such as Lars, a World War I Marine who was currently worming his way into Madame Celeste's entourage.

Lars was a *vampiro* and one of Rafael's deadliest warriors, with an unspoken understanding between them—that of two men who'd stood on the precipice of mortal sin too often yet somehow survived. Only Rafael gave orders to Lars; none of his other *hijos* was permitted to.

Luis sat in the center, his headset all but hidden in his dark hair. He knew more of Austin and its defenses, the *esfera*'s center, than anyone else and could change them in an instant.

There were a dozen others, all deadly warriors. All of them talking, turning over papers, clicking keys on electronics, and pointing to bright lights on panels invisible a few feet away.

Rafael let his eyes roam over them one last time. They were all undoubtedly working very hard and very well, as they'd done so many other times before. *Excelente.*

They left him free to contemplate, yet again, exactly what had happened with the red-haired *doctora.* Instinct demanded that he seek out something so unusual that logic offered no explanation. Instinct insisted, yet again, that he occupy himself in her bed as frequently as possible—where he could lose control of himself and the situation without warning. *Mierda.*

He lifted his voice. "*Hijos y compañeros*, are we agreed then?"

They immediately fell silent and turned to him.

"One *vampiro*, at least seventy years of age."

"Most likely Devol of New Orleans," Gray Wolf said.

"No confirmation, either sightings or reports of attacks on respectable women," Ethan drawled, in the cold tones of a gunfighter ready for a shoot-out. "However, we are monitoring rape and suicide-prevention hotlines for unusual activity."

A muscle twitched in Rafael's jaw. Beau's passion for feeding on fear was sickening enough. But a monster that preyed only on respectable women was a demon to be sent directly to Hell.

"Devol's arrival can be either a direct attempt on us or a diversion," Jean-Marie interjected smoothly. "Beau has not been seen in New Orleans for the past four days."

An excited buzz broke out. Ethan turned to his second-in-command, growling commands, and pointed to a map.

Recognizing a report from Lars given through Jean-Marie, Rafael thumped his fist on the table. "Enough! Everyone knows what must be done, whether we hunt for one *vampiro* or twenty."

They fell silent, Ethan's eyes blazing as if he longed to personally rip Devol apart.

"Everyone has a sector to search in Austin." Rafael eyed them all sternly. "When a hiding place is suspected, Ethan's team will be summoned to flush the *vampiro*. Do not, I repeat, do not approach the hiding place on your own. Devol and Beau are extremely deadly. *You must obey me* in this."

He reinforced his instructions with the firmest *vampiro* mental order he could give. All bent their heads obediently, as befitted knights in his army.

Jean-Marie glanced at him sideways. As his eldest *hijo*, he had more latitude for independent thinking but was also clever enough not to express it in public.

"Now go find the enemy *vampiro* before he can harm a citizen of Texas."

"*Sí*, Don Rafael," they answered and rose to salute him.

Rafael came to his feet, his heart swelling with pride. It was the greatest honor in the world to lead them. *Dios mediante*, he'd do so for years to come.

They filed out, gathering up their notes and electronic aids, falling into groups as they did so. Gray Wolf dropped an arm over Caleb's shoulder as he spoke to Luis, Caleb leaning easily into the casual embrace.

Rafael's gaze rested on Gray Wolf and Caleb for a moment, considering for the first time in decades the implications of their comfort with each other. Trust was the essence of the *conyugal* relationship: love so complete that two people trusted each other on every level—physical, mental, and spiritual. It could not be forced or given; it could only occur. Each *cónyuge*'s thoughts were completely open to the other, since there could be no barriers between them.

He had heard of less than ten dozen *conyugal* relationships in his long life. Only two were known to openly exist in North America: Gray Wolf and Caleb, plus Donal O'Malley, the San Francisco *patrón*, and his lady wife.

So why the hell had he felt the openness of *cónyuges* between him and Grania a week ago? It was impossible, absurd, beyond belief. In seven hundred years, he'd only loved one woman, his wife.

Oh, he'd had lovers, many of them, but only his wife had ever captured his heart. And at that, they'd had so little time together, barely five years—the blink of an eye to a *vampiro*, no matter how he'd memorized every moment and retold it to himself. Since then, he'd given each lover the courtesy of complete attention, which included never comparing them in any way to his wife.

So how had Grania ensnared him when he'd met her so recently?

Could count the number of hours he'd known her on the fingers of one hand? Had tasted no more of her than her mouth and a sip of her blood?

And his instincts were snarling at him that he had to return to her. He'd awoken every night for the past week, aching like a young boy from carnal dreams of her in his arms. Insanity!

It had to have been a figment of his imagination. Of course, if it happened again, then he'd know she wasn't involved in a plot against him. Even the most cunning assassin couldn't not open up during a *conyugal* bond.

"Did you have a question for me, Don Rafael?" Gray Wolf paused before him, brown eyes quizzical, Caleb a polite half pace behind him.

Rafael started, caught by his own distraction. "I, ah . . ."

Jean-Marie glanced up curiously, from where he was neatly packing his computer into a leather satchel.

"Yes, I do," Rafael finished decisively. He might as well ask the experts. "Can you stay as well, Jean-Marie?"

"*Certainement, mon père.*" He propped a hip on the table and waited, blue eyes quizzical.

Gray Wolf set his PC on the table, casually resting his big hand on it. He'd set down his bow in the same way when he'd walked out of the night, the first time Rafael had met him over a century and a half ago.

Rafael drummed his fingers on the table, then took the plunge. "If I may ask, how long did it take before you and Caleb knew you were *cónyuges*?"

"Twenty years before the first mental touch, which was only the slightest hint," Gray Wolf answered calmly. "Another ten years before we could repeat the mind-to-mind touch at will."

"And another five years before it lasted throughout a duel," Caleb added.

"It was faster for the O'Malleys," Jean-Marie observed. "But that was during the Peninsular War."

"And wartime stresses can accelerate the creation of trust between a couple," Rafael agreed. "Have you ever heard of anyone recognizing their *cónyuge* sooner, say, within days?"

All three shook their heads in unison. *Mierda.* So what had happened between him and Grania?

"No, never," said Jean-Marie. "If anything, I would say that my brothers discovered their relationship's strength sooner than most. The few who become *cónyuges* seem to need a century or more together, according to all the rumors. At least enough to perfect the bond so they can fight as one during a duel, enabling them to defeat all challengers."

"If we had two pairs of *cónyuges*," Gray Wolf mused, "since Madame Celeste possesses only two truly dangerous assassins—"

"Consider Madame Celeste as well, *mi hijo*," Rafael drawled. "She alone is a most deadly opponent."

"The principle still holds," Gray Wolf pointed out. "The more *cónyuges* our *esfera* held, the safer we would be from any attack by enemies, since a pair of *cónyuges* can almost always defeat a *vampiro* of any age."

"It is a great advantage, especially in duels." Caleb's eyes lit up. "Otherwise, if one *vampiro* is older, even by a year, he will defeat another *vampiro*."

"Or if the other *vampiro* was trained as a *cachorro* to lose to the first *vampiro*," Jean-Marie interjected, "then he will lose again to the same *vampiro* even when he is a mature *vampiro*."

Rafael flinched inwardly at the many bitter memories evoked by those few words.

"But if he has a *cónyuge*," Gray Wolf added, "then the younger *vampiro*, allied with his *cónyuge*, will frequently defeat the elder *vampiro*."

"So we must do everything we can to find *cónyuges* for our brothers," Jean-Marie finished. "In wartime, doing so protects us all."

Rafael blew out a breath and accepted the inevitable. He'd been chasing this argument over and over in his head since that moment with Grania. There was too much at stake; he had to explore the bond with her, no matter how uneasy it made him. After a week of only phone calls, he'd have to seek her out again, now that she'd returned to the hills. He'd have her every move watched closely, to see if she truly was his *cónyuge*.

His instincts promptly, predictably, purred. His body tightened in anticipation, as his heart skipped then settled into a faster beat.

He snarled at his overanxious libido. The most likely result of calling on *Doctora* O'Malley was a discussion of reproductive rates among predators, not carnal satisfaction for a seven-hundred-year-old *vampiro*.

Still, his trousers were noticeably tighter when he left the council chamber.

Grania went through her routine warm-up, stretched, and looked down the quiet road. A line of fence posts was connected by barbed wire and mesquite. In the distance, a dozen Angus cattle ambled toward a placid pond sheltered by some ancient oaks. The sun shimmered over the low hills, hinting at the coming day's heat. A farmer's helicopter hovered overhead like a lost dragonfly.

Not a sign of Rafael. Of course, she'd been in Brownsville for the past week, filling in for one of Bob's college buddies. He'd used a lightweight gauntlet to handle a bald eagle and had twenty-two stitches across his palm and thumb to prove it. She'd spoken to Rafael by phone but that wasn't the same as seeing him.

She did some more stretches—the trickier ones that she usually saved for when she was training for a race.

All she wanted to talk to Rafael about was *vampiro* reproduction, nothing else. She'd read and reread her notes and compared his descriptions to other predators' metabolism. She'd used her time in Brownsville to prepare a long list of follow-up questions for him.

She was not, of course, hoping for another orgasm like the one he'd given her in the lounge.

She blushed furiously and started to run.

And she certainly wasn't hoping he'd cuddle her to sleep, a little voice in her head whispered. That's what a real lover does.

Grania ground her teeth, as she turned onto a quiet lane barely a mile from home, edged with red roses. That helicopter was really close to the ground; maybe one of her neighbors was loading it.

Rafael was a *vampiro* who drank blood, not a *man*, to use his terminology.

A very handsome man who knew more about sensuality than anyone she'd ever met before.

A predator.

Who gave her the best orgasm of her life. And where had she ever seen anyone half as sexy?

Well, she was finally established in the world. And she wasn't answerable to anyone for what she did in her private life.

The helicopter blasted into the air beside her. An instant later, when her ears had just started to recover, a man spoke.

"Buenos días, doctora."

Grania's head snapped around to see the man running so effortlessly beside her, as if her thoughts had conjured him out of thin air. *"Buenos días,* señor," she stammered and smiled.

Three bodyguards behind Rafael—one of them Emilio—two big Mercedes sedans puttering behind them, a sleek helicopter trying to look as if it was watching over a cornfield instead of him—he had more duennas than the king of Spain's virgin daughter. That assassination threat had to be real.

No way to talk to him about anything private. Maybe she should think about running, not him.

"Do you go jogging very often, señor?"

"Regularly, *doctora.*" He raised an eyebrow at her, a faint gleam of sweat on his face. He was wearing ordinary jogging attire for a hot day in Texas: tank top, running shorts, socks, and running shoes. It left a lot of him uncovered and very little to her imagination. Beautiful golden skin, those superb muscles flexing easily as he ran, like a poster child for an anatomy class.

She sighed. She could start listing the muscles, and the tendons, and the nerves. Or maybe discuss the chemical reactions needed to translate energy from his food intake into making his feet move forward. No matter how she said the words, looking at him made her mouth water and her fingers twitch with the need to touch.

"My muscles work like anyone else's," he observed, dark eyes amused.

She blushed but quickly recovered. Best to treat this encounter as an extension of the scientific conversation a week earlier, when they'd discussed *vampiro* reproduction at the raptor center. At least she knew he was safe in daylight, unlike Hollywood's vampires. "Like *prosaicos*? Is that for camouflage?"

He shrugged. "Probably. But also, it's how we were born, since we were all once *prosaicos*. Our bodies still remember and are comfortable remaining that way."

Grania considered the implications, her mind working rapidly. If a *vampiro* looked exactly like his prey, then it would be very easy for him to ambush them. A high-risk, but high-value, predation tactic.

"How far do you intend to run today, *doctora*?"

"What?" She looked up, startled, to see they'd arrived at her little bungalow. She wasn't ready to say good-bye, not when they'd just begun to talk. "Would you like to come in for some coffee?" She studied his bodyguards and the helicopter a little dubiously. "There's probably room for your men too, if they'd like some."

He frowned but nodded. "I would be honored to join you, *doctora*. My men will wait outside."

Grania frowned. "It's already hot and getting hotter." Then she put the pieces together. "Do you own the house down the road, the one that's being restored?"

Amusement danced in his eyes. "I have that privilege."

"So they're just going to walk over there and pretend to wait for you. Then they'll sneak back to my place and keep an ear and eye out for trouble. Probably call for either those two big Mercedes sedans to take you home or that helicopter, when you're ready. Am I right?"

He bowed. "You are entirely correct, *doctora*. Your powers of observation and deduction are indeed acute."

Grania shrugged. "Surveillance tactics aren't that much different for humans than for wildlife." She considered the men, dangerous as hunting cats, and the firepower they represented, before returning to him. "Do you trust me that far? Have they searched my place?"

He spread his hands. "Your house has not been searched. Trust has to begin somewhere. I do not believe you wish to kill me."

"True enough. Why don't you have the guys check out my house? Then they can set up their perimeter and we can have our coffee."

His eyebrows went up. "You're very matter-of-fact."

"Bodyguards seem to be a fact of life around you."

His mouth twisted. "At the moment. I thank you for your understanding. Gentlemen?"

Grania watched the covey of bodyguards pour into her little house, thoughts tumbling through her head. The easiest one was where would all those men fit in her house. The hardest one was why he was really willing to be alone with her, if he was guarded so thoroughly everywhere else. Then she shrugged the question off, as the bodyguards gave the all-clear for him to enter. He was a greater danger to her than she was to him.

She flipped the switch on her coffeemaker, starting the batch of coffee she'd prepared before leaving. "Do you take cream or sugar?"

"Black, *por favor*."

Something in the answer's speed triggered her medical instincts. "Is that by choice or necessity? Can you eat solids or are you confined to a liquid diet?"

He shook his head, coming into the kitchen from the colorful little living room. "Liquids only. Even cream, alas, is beyond my capability."

"A pity." So he could ingest blood and clear liquids but nothing else.

"Your house is very beautiful, *doctora*." He was standing by the center island, studying a glass-fronted kitchen cabinet full of Indian pottery.

"Grania, please." She smiled over her shoulder at him, as she set out mugs and napkins. "Places like this bungalow, with its bright-red cabinets, would have appalled the nuns at the group home where I grew up. But the warmth of all the colors makes me feel alive, after those boring whites and grays."

She poured coffee for them both and handed him a mug, then leaned against the counter next to him and sipped her own coffee companionably, trying not to think about that beautiful masculine body so close beside her. "Can I ask you some more questions? Under the same rules as before, of course: I'll never tell anyone else."

"Certainly." He waited, chocolate dark eyes slightly wary. Disciplined mouth, rather cruel but with a touch of sensuality. What would another kiss be like?

"You mentioned that all senses are enhanced when you become a *vampiro*: speed increases, sight and hearing improve, so on. What about any of the psychic abilities?"

"Such as?"

She reached for one of the more commonly mentioned abilities. "Telepathy?"

He froze, his face settling into a hard mask. The room's temperature dropped, recognizing a predator ready to pounce.

"You have my word and I will keep it," she assured him, keeping her voice calm and sweet as if coaxing a hawk to her fist.

His eyes were implacable. "If you don't, you will die."

Grania stared straight back at him, equally determined. It never worked to show fear to a predator. "My word is my bond. I will never talk."

He seemed to argue with himself, then slowly reach a decision. His face settled into its typically charming lines. He took a long drink from the mug before he answered. "Telepathy is one of the senses, usually much enhanced by becoming a *vampiro*. In fact, very few *cachorros* survive who don't have strong telepathy."

"Do you use telepathy for hunting?"

"Prey or other *vampiros*?" he asked dryly.

She raised an eyebrow. "Either."

"Telepathy among *vampiros* is like speaking aloud: difficult to do unnoticed. On the other hand, it's usually all too successful with *pro-saicos*. So easy, in fact, that boredom quickly sets in."

"Which leads to the very young behaving very foolishly, and many subsequent troubles caused thereby."

Rafael snorted in agreement. "Exactly. I teach my *cachorros* not to rely on it. They must use seduction instead."

"Since you look exactly like *prosaicos*, given enough experience, you can deduce who's susceptible to your lures—"

"After which, both parties enjoy themselves."

Years of scientific training revolted. "Impossible. Won't the *pro-saico* realize they were bitten by a *vampiro*?"

"Why should they? Do you remember everything that happens at the height of orgasm?"

Grania glared at him, unwilling to admit that until she'd met him, she'd never lost consciousness during an orgasm. She'd certainly never come close to achieving that much rapture with a partner.

Rafael set his mug down, his voice gentler as he turned to her. "Grania, we are skilled lovers and signs of the bite disappear within a few hours. As long as the *prosaico* thinks we're like them, why should there be any suspicion?"

She shook her head furiously. "But there's got to be some differences. A slight variation in body temperature or maybe how and where body temperature increases. Perhaps the texture of your body. Something."

"Grania, we're the same. Exactly the same on the outside."

"Under stress, your metabolism has to be different. Something has to be apparent to a trained observer."

"Do you want to test me?" he drawled, his voice deep and soft. "See just how much of an hombre I am, under your hands?"

Her body clenched, lanced with heat. Touch him, tease him . . . Oh yes! *Be professional, Grania*, she told herself. *He's just a scientific subject, the first predator you've ever been able to interview.* "Yes." She stopped, cleared her throat. "Of course I'd like to test you."

"I am at your disposal, *doctora*." He set his arms wide, his eyes still slightly wary. But there was definitely a noticeable bulge inside those running shorts.

Grania set her mug down on the far counter, beside the coffee-maker, and moved in front of him. He was so much taller than she was that she felt almost fragile.

She shrugged the sensation off. This was a scientific examination, just as she'd done before with large predators. It was certainly nothing like anything she'd ever done with a lover.

She'd already seen him, unclothed, at the raptor center. Now she looked him over thoroughly, trying to assess his physical condition. It would be easier to remain detached if she hadn't been jogging next to him and eyeing his sweating biceps. Healthy body, superbly muscled, moved like a god. Next step.

She took his hand. He gave it to her readily, letting it rest in her more slender hand. Dwarfing hers.

"Your hand is very scarred and callused. What happened to it? Shouldn't you have lost all the dead skin by now?" She traced the heavy lines and pads with her finger, before glancing up at him. Damn, how she wanted to touch him. How old was he anyway?

He watched her through shuttered eyes, a sensual half smile on his lips. "Swordplay and old battles," he dismissed. "Whatever muscles and scars your body has when you become a *vampiro*, it will retain."

Amazing physiology. She'd have thought a change so radical, as to convert his food source to blood, would also remake his body without visible blemishes, even though she'd seen the wicked ones on his back. "All of them?"

"Such as this on my chest?" He pulled his tank top forward to show a scar on his collarbone. "I gained from my brother as a child."

She traced it with a fingertip, her pulse racing at finally touching his body. "Take the shirt off, please."

One eyebrow lifted, Rafael obeyed silently.

"Scars on your ribs as well." Grania traced them delicately. None life threatening, all well tended. He caught his breath.

She ran her tongue over her lips, trying to think over the clamor in her head. This didn't feel like a medical exam, not when her heart was pounding in her chest. She wanted to incite him into lust for her own pleasure.

She ran her fingers slowly up his arms, feeling the glide of his sweat and the heat of his strength. She closed her eyes at the sensation, slipping back to how much she'd wanted to handle him like this, back there on that quiet Texas road. Her hands slipped over his broad shoulders, barely spanning the massive bulk of his muscles. Her core clenched and purred, cream edging onto her thighs.

"Rafael," she breathed and leaned up to kiss him, a whisper of a kiss, barely touching his lips. His answer was as light, his lips flickering, parting under hers, his tongue barely touching hers. She sighed again, her hand curling around his neck, and leaned against him. He stroked her waist gently as they kissed, the contact between them sweet and subtle.

Finally, she stirred and kissed his cheek, rested hers against him for a moment. "*Dulce*. But that kiss wasn't much of a test, Rafael."

He chuckled a little hoarsely, his chest rising and falling against hers. She laughed with him before easing away. She scraped her teeth lightly down the tendons in his neck, making him shudder. He groaned softly but stood his ground, his hips shifting restlessly.

So far, he was reacting exactly as she'd have expected a man to. Flushed, sweating, speaking her name frequently with some urgency. In fact, if she had to compare him to any of her lovers . . . No, that wouldn't work, if only because there weren't enough of them for a statistically valid sample.

She stepped back a little farther and spanned her hands over his chest, letting his crisp chest hair tickle her fingers and palms. Definitely furred but not much. Just a neat pelt that narrowed into a treasure trail pointing straight down to those running shorts.

Oh yes, he was definitely a fine specimen, something her breasts understood all too well as they ached, her nipples furling into tight buds.

Underneath that dark hair, his musculature would have made any men's fitness magazine beg to photograph him. Or maybe not; he obviously hadn't built that body in any gym. How could she describe her knight's body to them? Was there an Olympic sport it compared to? Heaven knows he made her body ache with hunger, as she fondled and kissed and licked and even—daringly—once nipped.

"*Por Dios*, Grania!" His eyes were brilliant with lust, his mouth a thin slit of control. Even his knuckles were white where he gripped the counter.

She glanced up at him, from where she knelt before him. If she lowered his running shorts just a little more, she'd uncover the head of his beautiful cock—or should she use another approach?

She bent lower and wrapped her hands around his ankles. "Kick off your shoes."

He did so with a ferocious growl, sending them thudding off the cabinets. "Grania, what are you trying to do?"

"I thought we discussed that," she answered demurely, tossing his socks aside. At least his were far cleaner than some of her friends'. "We're conducting a scientific experiment."

She lightly ran her fingertip under his foot, seeking out the sensitive spots. He cursed—and his cock jerked. Very promising.

She explored his other foot, establishing that it too had a direct link to his cock. She stroked and petted his feet for a few minutes, stretching out the aches from running. But there was little she could do, while he was standing, no matter how much her core hummed its approval of his shudders and growls.

She glided her hands up his legs, moving more and more slowly as her fingers reached above his knees. She kissed his thighs, enjoying how her simple movement made his strong legs spread.

Until finally her fingertips crept up the leg of his shorts, twitched his jockstrap just far enough away, and petted his balls from underneath. Definitely all man.

Fondled and played and cupped, while she purred, one hand inside her shorts playing with herself.

"Grania, *por Dios*, if you don't hurry, I swear—*Madre de Dios!*" His head snapped back as he gasped.

She wrapped her hand around his cock and squeezed, gently. Established that she could—almost—encircle it. Began to stroke him, up and down, while her other hand rubbed herself in the same rhythm.

"*Sí*, Grania, *perfecto*," he groaned, his hips thrusting hard against her hand. His face was a mask of pleasure, eyes half shut, utterly focused on what she was doing.

Given privacy by his self-absorption, her enjoyment built. Her hands moved faster and faster, so that exciting him was exactly the same as exciting herself. She sobbed, eyes shuttering, ecstasy coming closer and closer until finally, she climaxed. And at the same moment, he arched and howled, his hips pounding against her hand.

She sobbed happily, as the waves of orgasm rocked through her. Wonderful.

She settled into a kneeling position against his leg afterward, rather like a contented geisha. Pity she hadn't sensed even a trace of his thoughts, though, as she had at the raptor center.

The phone rang in the living room. Grania ignored it, in favor of stroking his thigh gently. As soon as she recovered her strength, the two of them could head for her bedroom and the narrow bed there. If she lay on top of him, there'd probably be room for both of them.

"Should you answer it?" Rafael murmured, stroking her head.

She leaned back against him, eyes closed. "Let the machine pick up."

A few seconds later, the machine buzzed, permitting Linda from the raptor center to speak. "Grania? Since you're not picking up, I'll assume that you're already on the way in and try your cell phone. The conference call with Cornell starts in an hour and Bob wants to review the Great horned's case notes before then."

"Shit!" Grania sprang to her feet and reached for the counter, a pivot to speed her way into the bedroom.

Abruptly, she found herself pressed against the wall oven by a very tall, very strong man whose dark eyes burned into hers. Her tiny kitchen, never spacious, became barely large enough to permit a deep breath.

"When do we finish this, Grania?" he demanded, his naked chest barely an inch from hers. Her breasts promptly tightened, as her body heated. He rolled his hips suggestively against hers.

She gulped and fought to think. Sex with a *vampiro*. *Soon,* her core entreated. *Madness,* countered her brain. *Now,* insisted the cream rushing eagerly out of her cunt.

"I'm supposed to be off tonight at six, so I should be back here by seven. Eight o'clock?"

"Excelente." His mouth came down on hers and she yielded in surprise. He kissed her thoroughly, passionately—and she was half witless when he lifted his dark head.

"Wear something very feminine," he whispered, his eyes hot and possessive as they roved over her. "Be a beautiful woman tonight, not *la doctora.*"

Her jaw dropped.

He bowed to her and was gone.

NINE

Rodrigo pounded his cell's walls, cursing his captors. His fists were bloody wrecks, every bone broken into a pulp. Yet the pain of his wounds meant nothing. He easily ignored the sun rising in the east, bringing with it the threat of imminent death.

As his master had taught him when he studied to become a knight, as L'Ordene de Chevalerie, the great tale of knighthood said, every knight was bound by the commandment to honor all women and damsels and be ready to aid them to the limit of his power. As he'd sworn holy oaths time and time again to do. Yet he'd failed to aid a damsel, especially one who so greatly resembled his beloved wife, with her dark hair and eyes, fair skin, and curving body.

The only thing that mattered now was her body, broken and battered on the castle's dung heap, reminding him of the trials she'd undergone. Of how he'd failed her.

How those devils had used their evil devices on her in the dungeon! Then Diego had proceeded to tear the poor girl's virginity away in every conceivable fashion, as The Syrian made sure Rodrigo under-stood how completely helpless he was.

He had offered himself in her place—and they had mocked him, listing all the times and places and ways they had used him.

Then they had offered him the Devil's bargain: He could save the girl's life—if he promised to become an assassin like Diego. A killing machine, murdering men for gold. Saving one life by taking others again and again and again, for eternity. Satisfy his knightly oaths to protect women by damning himself through repeatedly committing that heinous mortal sin.

The pits of Hell had opened before him at that moment, when the girl pleaded with him to accept their offer. To do whatever they said, if it would save her life. His enemies' eyes had gleamed with triumph, like jackals eyeing a fresh carcass.

But like a clean ocean breeze, he'd remembered his wife's words when she'd sent him off to battle, begging him not to dwell on soft thoughts, like her and the children, which might weaken him in time of danger and cost him his life—or worse. But instead, he should focus all his hopes and prayers on Dios santo *and his duty. If he did that, surely* Jesuscristo *would send his angels to protect him and bring him home safely.*

Somehow he'd managed to shake his head. Then he'd called on them to repent and turn from wickedness, using every holy verse he could think of. They'd quickly gagged him at that, as if he'd needed any further proof they were completely evil.

Diego's fangs had ripped open her neck as he'd raped her repeatedly—while The Syrian had held down Rodrigo and fed on his horror.

Diego had even gained enough strength from her death that for the first time, he'd changed shape—into a wolf, a howling creature of the night.

Dios santo, *how he prayed for their deaths.*

The dawnlight crept across the dung heap and toward his cell's wall. If it touched any portion of his skin, he'd turn to ash.

The memory of his helplessness rushed back over him, the com-plete hopelessness of being unable to do anything whatsoever. Surely

Hassan's descendants would come back in two centuries and he'd kill The Syrian, as the vision had shown him. But even if that happened, by then his wife and children would be dead, leaving him old and alone.

More likely he'd die here, a worthless, forsworn knight on a hell-hole's dung heap, drained dry by two demons from hell. Or worse, become like them and start exulting in his power to evoke horror from the innocent.

A burning tear escaped from his eye and slowly trailed through the dust on his face. First light touched the castle's rough stone wall and began to climb toward his window.

He was no true knight here, where he could no longer protect the innocent. Did he truly believe that Dios santo heard his prayers, when he wore the same body as those demons? Far better to die quickly than lend any portion of himself to those night-walking terrors.

If he held his hand out through the bars, into the light, he'd burn like a torch. Or he could wait until the sun entered his cell and let it wrap him like a blanket, the last touch of warmth in his life. Either way, he'd be gone so quickly that he'd have no time for second thoughts.

Pass by touching the sun again, as if he was truly human once more. A graceful thought.

But he'd be forsworn if he did so, unable to keep his vow to Fearghus of taking revenge for both of them. After last night, he had no illusions left of being able to protect any unfortunate prosaicas who came here: The Syrian and Diego would prey on them, no matter who was around. Everyone else in this valley was either too well bribed or terrorized to stop those two fiends.

The sunlight touched the windowsill and started to creep into his cell. He had but to reach out his hand and this agony would end, freeing him for the world beyond.

But suicide was a mortal sin. He'd be condemned to the lowest reaches of Hell for all eternity, never to see his beloved wife, who'd be with the angels in heaven.

His choices were therefore whether to spend eternity in hell on *earth or Hell with Satan's own demons. Neither was an appealing choice—but one saved a bit of his pride and offered a chance at revenge.*

Even if Dios santo couldn't hear him from this piece of hell on earth, Rodrigo could still act as a knight insofar as he was able. It was very little but it was all he had left. He'd have to do a great many things that the Santiaguista Rule had never dreamed of. But he'd do his best to cherish the principal virtues. And he'd have the chance in two centuries if Hassan's descendants came, to take revenge.

Far, far simpler to die now.

The sun was now a nimbus of gold behind his window's iron bars.

Slowly, agonizingly slowly, Rodrigo retreated deep into the shadows with the spiders and the rats. Two hundred years until he could easily look at sunrise and sunset again. Three hundred years until he could walk abroad at high noon.

He closed his eyes and wept.

"How many such rapes have been reported?" Rafael snapped out. Ethan, Jean-Marie, Luis, and Gray Wolf—accompanied by Caleb, of course—were in his office at Compostela, summoned to hear the disturbing news.

"Two so far, both in Waco," Luis gritted out as he paced restlessly, his white shirt brilliant against the steel shutters that protected them from daylight.

"But there've been a half dozen attempted suicides by healthy young women for no apparent cause. Or at least, no prior signs a mental-health professional noticed," Jean-Marie amended, double-checking the messages on his PC. "And one successful suicide."

"*Coño,*" Rafael growled. How many times had he seen women kill themselves in The Syrian's castle?

"The rapes fit Devol's pattern: respectable women, badly beaten," Ethan commented, a muscle ticking in his jaw. Today he wore two deadly accurate Super Redhawks in his shoulder holsters. "But the suicides?"

"Beau's doing," Rafael said flatly. "He feeds on fear then wipes the memory, but he's never been the best at controlling minds. Many times, the women remember something, even if it drives them insane."

There was a rumble of disgust. Rafael glanced around the room and allowed himself to smile at his *hijos*'s bloodlust. Hearing of women's peril and destruction had strengthened their protective instincts. "Jean-Marie, have your men watch all the mental-health databases very closely. We must be alerted immediately when young women commit suicide or suffer unexplained depressions."

Jean-Marie nodded, his fingers flying over the keys. "*Certainement, mon père.*"

"Every day those two live imperils the good people of Texas. Where are you and Caleb looking now, Gray Wolf?"

"Underground caves, quarries, and so on. According to all the records, Beau operated in cities with usable caves or subways."

Rafael thought back. "*Verdaderamente*, Beau has always slept in daylight, a habit he learned from his *creador*. Plus, Devol is so young that he must sleep most of the day. Hunting them in the dark places is an excellent idea."

Gray Wolf nodded, his eyes flashing with a hunter's fervor. "We've already searched most of the southeast sector."

They'd be able to do that quickly, thanks to Caleb's geological knowledge and Gray Wolf's tracking ability, plus their *conyugal* bond. They were the only one of his search teams who should be able to take on Beau and win. Still . . . "Be careful. The caves themselves can be tricky, with collapses or landslides, even if there isn't a *vampiro* to be seen."

Caleb grinned at the warning. "Don't worry, Don Rafael. I won't let anything happen to your *adelantado mayor*."

Gray Wolf huffed in mock indignation. Chuckles eased the occupants' tension somewhat.

Jean-Marie's fingers flashed over his PC. "We should probably scale back the Fourth of July picnic. It's also a First Saturday, so there'll be large crowds coming in for the music. We don't want our *prosaicos* wandering about when Beau and Devol are nearby."

"Agreed," Ethan seconded immediately. "It's also the only public event at which you, Don Rafael, are scheduled to appear at next month. Those two rabid wolves are certain to be lying in wait."

"Then you will simply have to chase them off," Rafael retorted. "I will not forego the Fourth of July. I am an American and this is my national holiday."

"You cannot risk yourself so foolishly!" Gray Wolf erupted, as Ethan slammed his fist into the fireplace. Jean-Marie and Caleb, both normally amiable, came to their feet yelling. Luis cursed Rafael in a steady stream of Galego, their mother tongue.

Rafael endured their tirade for a minute before putting his foot down. *"¡Silencio!"* he roared at the top of his lungs.

Small items on his desk trembled and slid sideways. Even his sword vibrated. He looked around the room, forcing each of his recalcitrant *hijos* to meet his gaze.

They growled deep in their throats, baring their teeth slightly, but stopped talking.

"You will obey me in this," Rafael ordered, enunciating every word. "I gave my word to the mayor that I would light the fireworks and so I will."

Jean-Marie snarled deep in his throat. Rafael's eyes flashed to him but his *heraldo* spoke nothing in words.

"Your duty is to secure the area—by whatever means necessary. Do you understand?"

"*Sí*, Don Rafael." Every syllable was pulled from Ethan's reluctant throat. "We can pull *vampiros* and *compañeros* from the commanderies to form a perimeter around San Leandro that weekend."

"Which will leave the borders very thinly protected, if many *bandolerismo* try to sneak into Texas," Gray Wolf pointed out, his fangs showing in a rare display. The courage to openly challenge Rafael on behalf on Texas's people was one of the virtues that had made him Rafael's heir.

Rafael nodded decisively. "For one night, we'll take the risk. What else?"

Gray Wolf inclined his head in acknowledgment and began to tick off points on his fingers. "Roving patrols of all likely *vampiro* hunting grounds. Parks, nightclubs, hotels . . ."

"And honeypots, of course. Using entrapment to pull 'em in, not just guns," Caleb added.

Rafael paced in front of his desk as he listened to their plans.

"And thin out the nightclubs in Austin and San Antonio, along the Riverwalk, to make it harder for *vampiros* to feed close by," Luis put in, pulling out his smartphone. "We can yank their ABC licenses and get half of them closed down within a week or two."

"Before the Fourth, kill every foreign *vampiro* who's entered Texas without a passport," Jean-Marie suggested. He shared a bloodthirsty smile with Ethan.

"I want to eliminate the criminal element too, especially the *prosaicos* who'd help Devol for money. Those bastards have enough guns to be dangerous, even if they're not *vampiros*." Ethan's eyes were as cold and deadly as a rattler readying to strike.

There was a murmur of agreement.

"Careful," Gray Wolf warned reluctantly. "Start in on them and you risk publicity."

"I'm sure you'd never hurt innocent bystanders, either," Rafael remarked.

Ethan flung up a hand in acknowledgment.

"If you'd like anyone in particular taken out," Jean-Marie drawled, "or more—just let me know. I'm not traveling much these days."

Ethan brightened, thoughts revolving behind his hazel eyes. Rafael watched and waited, patient and amused. What next?

"If Jean-Marie really does have some extra time," Ethan said slowly, drumming his fingers on the mantel.

Rafael raised an eyebrow. "What do you wish investigated?"

Ethan's head came up and he met Rafael's eyes across the room. "Something my *mesnaderos* and I can't handle, according to the code. One of the Houston federal prosecutors has been acting strangely recently, especially when smuggling and New Orleans comes up. It could be that he's recently divorced and has been burning the candle at both ends."

"But you don't think so."

"No, Don Rafael, I don't. But I can't dig deeper, since we've worked with him before."

And *vampiros* like Ethan, who enforced *vampiro* law, never punished *prosaicos* who assisted them. The code was similar to an old-fashioned *prosaico* cop's attitude: the worst cop was one who ratted on another, someone like the guys from Internal Affairs.

"I'll speak to him," Jean-Marie said smoothly. "I have to visit Houston in the next day or so, anyway. As I remember, this particular prosecutor had a variety of fine bourbons, which he once offered to show me."

Ethan laughed, a cold bark of amusement. "Just once, I wish I could watch when you speak to a dirty informer."

Rafael changed the subject, judging this topic closed. "Your target, Ethan?"

Ethan smiled, his eyes' intelligence startling as always in that incredibly handsome face. Too many people saw only his beauty, forgetting to look under the skin to their own downfall. "I'm personally concentrating on refrigerated warehouses, sir. Especially the meat lockers by the railroad yards."

A vision stirred behind Rafael's eyes. "Really?" he queried, waiting for it to clarify.

Ethan shrugged. "It's where I'd hide. No scent can escape from within those heavy walls. Or, at least, damn little."

The image blazed before Rafael, of a warehouse full of meat lockers. *Vampiros* raiding it in full disguise, with *compañeros* and *prosaicos* outside guarding them from being disturbed. Rafael blew out his breath, acknowledging his foresight's accuracy. "When you're ready to raid a warehouse, tell me. I'll be coming with you."

"Don Rafael—" Ethan began.

Rafael lifted a quelling eyebrow. "¿Sí? I'm the oldest *vampiro* in this *esfera*, with the best sense of smell, as well as being the single best fighter. Does anyone else have a chance of finding, or fighting, a seven-hundred-year-old *vampiro*? Given that the older a *vampiro* becomes, the fainter his smell becomes."

Ethan looked around the room for support and found none. Even Gray Wolf shrugged.

Rafael sighed inwardly. Everyone here was trained to obey him absolutely, no matter what, and never question a strict order. Once that had meant safety—why did it now mean loneliness?

Ethan yielded reluctantly. "Certainly, Don Rafael."

"*Excelente.*"

Abstracted, Rafael rose to show them out.

Perhaps he should seek simplicity and ease, by excusing himself from seeing Grania tonight and stay at Compostela. After all, this morning he had not felt a *cónyuge*'s closeness with Grania, as he had the night when he danced for her.

Or perhaps he was looking for it too hard. Tension would block a new *conyugal* bond as completely as if it had never existed.

On the other hand, there was no good reason for them to be *cónyuges*: they had known each other for only a few days and their acquaintance had undergone no great stresses, which might have speeded up the bond's formation. It was sheerest insanity for them to be *cónyuges*, especially since his heart had died centuries ago with his wife.

And yet. And yet, he could not deny that, in that cramped room at the center, he'd been as close to Grania's mind and body as to his own. He'd known her thoughts as if they were his own, felt her heartbeat in his body and the perfectly matching ripples of orgasm's aftereffects flowing through both their groins. He'd had the certain knowledge that if he'd wished her to stroke his hair, she'd have done so—because his wish was as deep in her bones as her own.

As a veterinarian, she might be an additional advantage to his *esfera* because of her detailed knowledge of animals. Donal O'Malley had once told him that if two *vampiros* were *cónyuges*, they even shared all mental and physical knowledge. If one was a great knife fighter, then the other would be as well, if the bond was open between them. Or one could shift into a shape the other had mastered, a valuable ability since alternate shapes were extremely difficult to gain.

Vampiro duels were fought hand-to-hand, with no man-made

weapons. Kicking, gouging, clawing, biting—any of that and more—
was entirely acceptable, all done at a speed and viciousness far greater than a *prosaico* could hope to comprehend. Shape-shifting—to a
predator's form, of course—was priceless. With a *cónyuge* for a second set of eyes and ears, a *vampiro* was unbeatable in a duel.

But even if Grania was his *cónyuge*, she was still a *prosaica*. If he
turned her into a *vampira*, the odds were excellent she'd go insane
and die. He'd sworn an oath never to give *El Abrazo* to a woman;
how could he break that oath and risk destroying his *cónyuge* to protect himself? *¡Nunca!* It was a knight's duty to protect women and
damsels, not the other way around!

So the best he could hope for, should Grania be his *cónyuge*, was
fifty years. Or perhaps seventy, if *Dios santo* was generous. A pittance
but better than destroying her.

He should think only of tonight, when there would be no interrup-
tions and he would finally become her lover. When he would explore
her as completely as she'd explored him, with eyes and tongue and
hands, and claim her femininity for their mutual pleasure.

She would be just another lover, during a long night of pleasure.
His heart had died centuries ago with his wife—his petite, sweetly
curved, black-haired darling.

Rafael knocked politely on the front door of Grania's little house,
then waited, ignoring Emilio and his cadre of *vampiro* bodyguards.
No amount of studying her movements for the past week (except for
the night Beau and Devol had slipped into Texas when she went un-
guarded), of searching her tiny house, or watching her neighborhood
since sundown could adequately assure them this wasn't a trap.

She opened the front door and smiled up at him. "Rafael."

"Grania." He kissed her lightly on both cheeks, a greeting she
returned in similar fashion. Best to keep their relationship publicly
formal, in case there were any watchers.

Tendrils were slipping free from her usually severe braid, and her
eyes were a bit heavy as if she'd just woken up from a nap. *Bien.* She

should have the energy for a long night of love play. An organized woman, she did not waste time by inviting him in but simply stepped outside, small purse in hand.

His libido saw her attire and promptly roared to life. A slim-fitting blue dress emphasized the superb lines of her long body and matched her brilliant eyes. Her only accessories were hoop earrings and simple, high-heeled sandals. She should be wearing the best of Paris and Milan, even if these thrift-store finds looked superb on her.

She closed the door, locked it, and came up beside him. His hand automatically, possessively, rested on the small of her back. She froze briefly and swallowed hard, before stepping off her porch. He matched steps with her, their hips brushing. She moved a little awkwardly, as if she'd never walked so closely with a man before. He allowed himself to strut a little, with a private smile, before handing her into his Mercedes. A moment later, his bodyguards had resumed their seats and the cars rumbled back onto the road, one of his helicopters flying guard overhead.

For a moment, Grania's pure profile was outlined against the dark bulletproof glass and the twilight sky beyond, then she turned to look directly at him. "Are you planning to feed from me tonight?"

Rafael froze for a moment, startled by her courage, before giving her the courtesy of honesty. "*Sí*, but only a few drops."

She tilted her head, considering his answer. "You took more from Brynda."

Why had he ever hoped *la doctora* might treat him solely as an *amante*, not a science project? Rafael resigned himself to conversation, at least until they reached his apartment. At least he'd never planned to seduce her in the back of a sedan. "She knows what I want and has agreed to it."

"In exchange for sex."

"Masturbation only," he corrected.

"Why the limit? She seemed ecstatic in your arms."

"Her choice, which I respect. Plus, a *vampiro*'s bite increases the emotion felt."

"Really." Grania settled back against her seat, clearly thinking hard. A few minutes later, they turned off the ranch road and drove into a well-tended pasture where dozens of fat, sleek Angus cattle ignored them, intent on strolling down the valley toward their dinner. There his sleek, private helicopter waited, blades spinning rapidly.

Grania spun around to look at him. "A helicopter? Where on earth are we going, Rafael?"

Rafael allowed himself a private congratulatory smile at having surprised her for once. "To my apartment, of course."

"What?"

The two cars came to a stop and Emilio ran to open Rafael's door. Rafael deftly scooped Grania up onto his lap. She choked, slid her arm around his shoulder, and tucked her head against him. He lifted her out of the Mercedes and ran to his personal helicopter, his men surrounding them protectively. He set her inside, careful to preserve her modesty.

She buckled her seat belt, all the while glancing around the interior. "Leather recliners? Plush carpets—and a bar? I should have known," she muttered.

Rafael kept a straight face.

A minute later, they were strapped into their seats and his helicopter took off, hurtling upward like a hunting falcon thrown into the sky. The other helicopter followed an instant later, protectively carrying the rest of his bodyguards.

Grania raised an eyebrow at Rafael. "Is this mode of travel really necessary for your safety, oh powerful administrator of the Santiago Trust, or are you just trying to impress me?"

He threw back his head and laughed. "How should I answer that?" he teased. "One answer would make me sound conceited, while the other would seem clumsy."

Her eyes danced as she laughed with him. They threaded their fingers together, sharing a companionable silence, while the bird flew fast and low over the quiet landscape.

"How soon will we arrive?" she asked, considering a herd of visibly sleepy cattle.

He kissed her hand, watching her face. "Very soon, *querida*."

She blushed an endearing shade of scarlet.

A few minutes later, the helicopter swept around a hill, revealing his favorite resort nestled among the hills. It was designed to fit into the natural landscape as much as possible, with natural limestone for the building materials, and surrounded by native plants and graceful watercourses. Even the marina, marked by the delicate masts of sailboats, looked as if it had occupied the lake for centuries. Just above the lake rose the resort itself, bordered by golf courses and nature walks. Saturday-night crowds gathered around the restaurants and nightclub, while others partied aboard their boats or frolicked on the shore. Farther back were villas and the single high limestone spire of the condominium tower, overlooking the entire complex.

Grania's fingers tightened on his, but she said nothing, her eyes scanning the scene below in between sideways darts at him. Her pulse beat high and fast in her throat, her breasts rose and fell rapidly. If he placed his hand on her knee, he could slide his fingers under her skirt . . .

The helicopter circled to the resort's rear, behind the villas. A helipad came into sight, guarded by more of his *compañeros*. A laconic all-clear signal was exchanged and the helicopter landed gracefully.

Five minutes later, he and Grania were alone in his penthouse apartment at the top of the condominium tower. He kept it primarily for meetings with business executives from outside Texas, who'd be comfortable in the resort setting. The furniture was accordingly casual and masculine—leather, massive, and practical—scattered across Native American rugs. A glass-fronted bookcase lined one wall of the great room, filled with some of his favorite adventure books. The longest wall was a sheet of bulletproof glass, its usual veil of white curtains pulled back now to show the famous lake view with Austin's high-rises barely visible in the distance.

Most guests never looked further than that window or the terrace outside.

"Oh, books," Grania cooed and headed for the other wall.

Rafael frowned and went after her. Inexperienced she might be, and therefore skittish, but there was too much unfinished business between them to allow her to escape now.

He wrapped his arms around her and breathed a kiss into her hair. "Grania, *querida*, are you running from me now?"

She gasped. The bookcase's door shook in her hand. "I, ah, was looking at your collection . . ."

He laid his cheek against hers, delicately. She closed her eyes, shivering, her pulse thudding. No scent of fear, thankfully.

He kissed up her spine and explored that fascinating point behind her ear. She sighed so he repeated the caress at some length, both there and on the other side.

When he lifted his head, her head was lying against his shoulder, her eyes half shuttered as she watched their reflections, her long red braid trailing against his arm. He caressed her, enjoying how his hands glided over supple midriff, spanning her with his thumbs on her ribs and little fingers almost reaching her hips. While all sizes and shapes of women had their attractions, there was an elegant simplicity in making love to a woman whose strength and size was such that he needn't worry overmuch about harming her.

He rumbled his approval. "Ah, *querida*, you are a marvel. So superbly shaped. Curved, with sweet long lines. Strong and smooth skinned . . ."

He kissed her neck again, sliding the zipper slowly down her back. She shuddered against him, whispering his name. He unhooked her bra and kissed down her spine, awakening those wonderful hidden spots in a woman. All the while, watching and learning her responses.

Rafael bit his lip, forcing himself to slow down. He had to stay in command of himself. He was a *vampiro*, who could easily break a *prosaica* if he forgot himself in the throes of passion. But, *ay, mierda*, how she tempted him!

He hummed his triumph when she rose up on her toes, gasping and crying, when his teeth first marked her at the top of her buttocks, next to her dimples.

Ah, *sí*, now he was finding the way to her passion. He immediately soothed her with his tongue, then gently repeated the caress. She bucked against him, sobbing.

His hands trembled, he who had pleasured women without number!

He wrapped his arm around her, steadying her. Waited until she calmed down slightly, then slipped one hand inside the front of her dress.

He stroked her belly gently, slow circles over her center. Gradually, her breathing matched his movements. His chest was tight, heat flushing through his body. Self-control was a distant thing, fraying under his pounding pulse. But he needed to soften and stretch her before she could hope to accept him into her.

He closed his eyes, forcing some discipline back into himself.

Her body's tension echoed the pressure of his fingers. He circled wider, deeper over her soft skin, her heat burning his fingers . . . And she moaned again, her head falling back against him.

The sound shook him to his bones.

He slid both hands inside her dress, moving closer so she stood astride his leg, her skirts rucked halfway up her thighs. Her hips rocked against his, her eyes shut in a sensual haze. He slid his hands up over her breasts, fondled, kneaded. He growled his approval when she reached back and stroked his hip, pulling him closer, fingers sliding over his ass. Ah, how he enjoyed that caress!

"More, please," she whispered, rubbing her ass over his thigh.

His breath hitched as he luxuriated in the feel of her soft flesh.

He pleasured her nipples—plucking and strumming them, until they stabbed against his palm and she was gasping for breath. He kissed her neck again and again, teasing and tormenting her sensitive spots. His cock was hot and hard behind his linen trousers, her every wriggle a torment.

Then he swept his hand down over her belly, repeating the circles that she'd enjoyed, savoring how quickly she found his rhythm again. He thrust his leg harder against her, opening her wider, needing to push her farther, faster, higher.

She gasped, struggled to find her balance—and his hand slipped deep inside her utilitarian panties. He rubbed her clit hard, in the rhythm he'd seen give her pleasure, and nipped her neck, careful to keep his fangs sheathed.

Grania screamed and climaxed, her cream gushing over his hand. His hips rolled against her, desperate to pound into her.

¡Madre Santa, but she was beautiful in the throes of passion! He closed his eyes, lest he be even more tempted to tear off his trousers.

When he thought he could control himself, Rafael deliberately slipped first one, then two fingers into her. He shuddered as her orgasm's aftershocks seized him. Biting his lip, he stretched her as much as he readily could in her orgasm's aftermath. All the while, he possessively watched the dazed satiation spread over her face.

Her eyes were heavy in passion's aftermath as she tried to stand up on her own. "Aren't you going to, ah, take your hand away?"

A smile played around his lips, as he gently twisted his fingers inside her, widening her further for his possession. "Why, *amante*? You have seen me. Two of my fingers are smaller than what you'll soon accept."

She turned even redder. "Your cock is a statistical outlier!"

He frowned and his eyebrows drew together. If that was an insult, it was the first time he'd heard it. "Please explain yourself, *querida*."

She wriggled, tried to get away, finally accepted that she couldn't, and settled back against him, almost with a flounce. "Your cock is so large that it's well outside the range of average men," she announced, staring straight ahead, chin held high.

Rafael threw his head back and roared with laughter. "In other words, enormous!"

She flushed, blushing again. He extricated his fingers and licked them clean in a salute to her. She blushed even deeper at the sight.

She was so beautiful that he tossed her up into his arms and kissed her.

"Caveman," she whispered against his mouth. Then she wrapped her arm around his neck and returned his passion, their tongues tangling eagerly as their mouths melded.

"Bedroom," he announced firmly, drawing back slightly. Her eyes widened before she nodded, gulping a little.

He carried her there too and laid her gently down on the enormous bed. The furniture here was as large and masculine as in the main room, with still more Native American rugs. Simpler windows and a stone fireplace covered one wall, with a bathroom visible beyond. This room was a sanctuary, rather than a display of wealth and power.

Rafael toed off his shoes quickly, before attacking the rest of his clothes. Grania leaned up on her elbows, looking around—his ever-curious *doctora*. He paused to cup her cheek, his shirt hanging open, his fingertips sliding into her escaping tendrils of hair. "Questions, *mi alma*?"

She rubbed her cheek against his hand like a cat, her fingers sliding inside his shirt to toy with his chest hair. "When you bite me, please take as much blood as you want."

What? She, a medical doctor, would ask this of a known *vampiro*? He drew back slightly to consider her expression. "Are you very certain?"

"Completely. I don't want you to feel limited in any way tonight. And, for Pete's sake, remember you're not stopping with masturbation!"

"If you insist." He laughed and kissed her. Then he released her and pulled her dress over her head.

Dios mio, she was beautiful with her blue eyes the color of the North Sea, the coloring Fearghus had always praised above all others. He freed her breasts from that utilitarian bra and worshipped them with his mouth. Every vein, every curve, suckling, nibbling, kneading. Blowing across her beautiful skin to enhance their sensitivity. Savoring every gasp, every time she sobbed his name, gasped, bucked.

Every lover was unique and enjoyable and valuable; exploring those differences was how he'd survived, how he'd stayed sane across the centuries. Yet Grania was somehow startlingly familiar, as if he'd known her somewhere before, done exactly this with her before.

She stroked his head and shoulders, pulling him to her, moaning his name. His own breathing turned ragged as her breath ruffled his hair. His chest tightened, heat raced through his veins as if desperate to find her. He fought for control, to keep a thin rein of discipline so he wouldn't hurt her.

He pulled away, stood up, and shoved his trousers down with little art.

"Condom?" she whispered, eyes enormous as she watched.

"No need."

"Really?" she muttered. "You must be so close to a different species that you can't catch human diseases or impregnate females."

He glanced back at her over his shoulder, as he tossed his trousers onto the chair. "*Verdaderamente.*" He spun to face her, displaying himself, stroking his cock that would soon—finally!—find its ease in her.

Grania studied him, eyes bright with lust and approval, teeth teasing her lower lip. The gesture was familiar but this was not the time for thinking.

His come burned in his balls, aching for release, as his cock rose and swelled still further.

Discipline, he told himself again. Discipline. You've had thousands of women. Do not let this one distract you.

He tilted her chin up with one finger. "*Querida.*"

Her tongue ran over her lips, her eyes sweeping over him in hunger, as her hands fondled his hips and squeezed his ass. "Rafael, please . . ."

Sanity fled and, with it, all traces of self-control. He growled in his throat, responding instantly to her invitation. He crushed her into the bed, moving so fast and hard that he slid her back a full body's length. His cock probed her sweet, creamy pussy—and he growled again when he recognized her complete readiness.

He shifted slightly, aiming himself, and entered. She gasped, nails scoring his shoulders. Her legs wrapped around his hips.

He pushed again and she bucked, moaning his name. His come built higher, more insistent. He groaned her name against her throat, locking his arms around her. His, *maldita sea*, his.

He thrust and she took him cleanly, their bodies melding as if they'd done this hundreds of times before. Their tempo increased, passion building in both of them.

She begged for more of him, with her voice and her body. His fangs descended, pressure built higher and higher from his spine through his cock. Every inch of skin was fire bright, sensitized and alive to the feel of her skin, her muscles, her sweat, gripping and sliding over him.

Something gleamed, just out of sight, like the scintillating pinwheel he'd felt during the *conyugal* bond. He concentrated—and it vanished instantly. He snarled but he had no energy to worry about seeking it again, not when his come was boiling in his balls.

He pounded harder into her, listening only to *vampiro* instinct for when she'd climax, when he could taste her and trigger his own ecstasy. He shifted, desperate to increase her rapture and speed her climax. Found the point inside her that would send her into rapture—and felt her stiffen. Saw the shock of sudden bliss touch her face. Triumph touched him then, as orgasm's first shockwave swept her.

Perfecto.

Rafael bit down, fast and deep, on her neck. She convulsed again, as the *vampiro* elixir immediately strengthened her orgasm. She screamed her release as wave after wave rocked her body. He drank deep, glorying in the taste of her ecstasy, sharply brilliant on the tip of his tongue, rich and dark against the back of his mouth. It raced through him, exploded down his spine and up through his balls, shooting him over the edge.

He shook, silently, over and over as he drank, every swallow of her blood driving a fresh rapture through every fiber of his being. Pumping his come into her as he too climaxed, still holding tight to that thin thread of discipline, lest he harm her as a *vampiro* could so easily do to a *prosaico*.

He withdrew carefully when her orgasm ended, cuddling her as echoing tremors rocked her beautiful body. Next time perhaps, he'd unbraid her hair and thread his fingers through all its silken glory.

He lay with her afterward under the sheets, gently licking the puncture marks on her neck. Even without additional care, they'd disappear within twelve hours. While yet again, there'd been no *conyugal* bond, she'd still been a remarkable *amante* and deserved special care.

Perhaps he'd been watching too hard for the *conyugal* bond, since even that slight tension could push it away. Perhaps.

Grania shifted slightly, caressing his back. Rafael stiffened slightly, ever wary of attention to those scars, then nuzzled her neck. "Do you want something, Grania?"

"Just curious."

Rafael sighed, resigned to yet more questions from his scientific *amante*. He shifted so both their heads were lying on the pillows and they could look at each other. "What do you want to ask me about?"

"How old are you? You don't have to answer, of course." Her eyes were direct and sympathetic.

Knowing Grania, he wondered what had brought the subject up, since it probably wasn't related to carnal expertise. "Why?"

His *amante* promptly reverted to *la doctora* as he'd seen her at the raptor center, a fierce protector of the wounded. "I treated a bobcat once who'd been tangled up in a roll of barbed wire. He lost almost all his skin and nearly died but his scars weren't nearly as deep as yours. Yours must have taken years to acquire—years of being whipped, then healing, then whipped again. Whoever did that to you," she growled, her fists clenching the sheets.

Rafael's heart turned over at her willingness to fight for him. But what could she have done against the likes of The Syrian and Beau? "Don't fret. It was over seven centuries ago," he soothed, cuddling her.

She was rigid against him. "Brutes," she growled, thumping him. "Abusers of innocents. All of them should have been shot."

He caught her hand and kissed the top of her head. If she tried to fight Beau . . . "*Relajate*, Grania. Don't worry about it."

"Shoot them all," she muttered but allowed him to soothe her. Gradually, she relaxed against him, snuggling with her arm around his waist and their legs tangled together. He knew the instant her agile brain found a different thread but he couldn't quite see her face.

"If you've been alive for centuries, how long have you been lived in Texas?"

"Two centuries, *querida*," Rafael answered, wondering where this was leading.

"Back then, Texas was a frontier with less than two people per square mile. Whether you counted Anglos, Hispanics, or Native Americans." How could a woman with her pussy tucked up against his cock sound so dispassionate?

"*Sí.*" Why was she asking about such a well-known fact?

"There were very few people around back then and most of them were men, given the classic frontier imbalance of men to women. But you were feeding on sexual energy," she mused, stroking his waist. "So logic says you must have had sex with men. After all, would a tiger refuse a goat because it was the wrong gender?"

Rafael gawked. Given the exigencies of hunting prey, all *vampiros* were assumed to be bisexual unless they explicitly stated otherwise— like Gray Wolf. However, not all *prosaicos* were as pragmatic as *vampiros* had to be.

"That is a very scientific analysis, Grania," he ventured, extremely aware of their musks' combined scent. "Does it disturb you?"

Her head snapped back and she glared up at him. "If your long life included encounters with brutes, like the ones who scarred your back, then I pray to God it also included some joy wherever you found it."

He was speechless. Grania sniffed and rested her head back against his heart. "Still think the other bastards should be shot."

TEN

Rodrigo snarled, baring his teeth in a wolf's grin. His first time in the arena, after learning to shapeshift into a wolf.

Diego snarled back, the ritual beginning to a shapeshifter duel. He was also in a wolf's form, something he'd mastered years ago.

The Syrian watched from above, his hand held high. Then he dropped it and Diego lunged.

Rodrigo dodged and bit hard at Diego's flank, gaining only a mouthful of fur. Then teeth came down hard into his leg, with a loud crack of broken bone. He fell helplessly to the ground.

Diego stood up in human form, laughing.

"Yaa ibni l-'aziiz, you were perfect!" The Syrian applauded. "Dodging the infidel, then leading him into a trap. Do that often enough, with ever more complex moves, and you'll train him to always be defeated by you."

Rodrigo staggered to his feet, shifting back into human form—the rest form for healing as a vampiro. *His right leg couldn't bear much weight.*

Diego bowed with a flourish. "May I do it again and feed on him this time?"

"Certainly!"

Hell. Rodrigo came on guard.

"Prepare yourself, unbeliever!" The Syrian shouted genially. He raised his hand and dropped it immediately. Diego charged.

An instant later, Diego bowled Rodrigo over, knocking the wind out of him. Then the pendejo *ripped his thigh open with a ragged nail and started to feed . . .*

Beau strolled down the Dallas hotel's corridor, truly relaxed for the first time in centuries. Once again he had luxurious surroundings and an obsequious flunky showing him the way, after a scented bath, manicure, and pedicure. The finest of clothing caressed his skin, with soft leather shoes protecting his feet and the sweet taste of blood and terror on his tongue from that young coed. She'd unaccountably died—but no matter. The authorities would never decipher the cause.

This was exactly how life should be spent, as it had been for those two wonderful centuries in his true home. When The Syrian had captured him at Ecija and offered to adopt him if he'd convert, he'd promptly agreed, knowing he was too poor to ransom himself. But he'd gained so much more than he'd hoped that day. He'd been safe in the care of a loving father for the first time in his life, cherished in a way utterly different from Rodrigo's eternal sermons on duty and honor.

He'd enjoyed learning the tricks of being a *vampiro*, such as different animal shapes, then practicing them by tearing into Rodrigo. He'd always won, of course, since he'd matured first as a *vampiro* and Rodrigo's *vampiro* body was trained, from its earliest days, to expect defeat at his hands.

He glanced at his reflection and smiled. Damn, he'd been good. He tried out a few steps, the better ones—fast, like a salsa dance. Just like the best dance partners, Rodrigo had always wound up at the perfect point in the end. It was always so enjoyable to see the sanctimonious wretch lie bleeding at his feet.

His face tightened as he remembered all that *sharmuuT* had done, then relaxed. Revenge would be very sweet when it finally came.

His grin widened further. He just needed to finish setting up that final dance and then he'd have Rafael right where he wanted him. But this time, he'd be dead.

The hotel manager knocked on the conference room's door and Devol's rough voice answered promptly. The manager opened the door and stood aside for Beau. "Here's your meeting, sir, with everything as you requested. If not, please give me a call at this number."

Beau favored him with a sweet smile. "You were recommended as the best and you've more than lived up to that reference. Thank you."

"It is our pleasure to serve you, sir." The manager accepted his enormous tip with a bow then departed, without once looking at Devol.

Beau sauntered in and surveyed the refreshments on the sideboard. Cristal champagne, as he'd requested. A variety of beers for Devol—one could not be expected to remember a brute's preferences. He plucked the champagne bottle out of its ice bucket and began to open it.

The small conference room was lavishly paneled and designed to encourage conversations among small groups. A few paintings of expensive racehorses provided touches of color, in between heavy green curtains. The only exceptions to the atmosphere of old-fashioned masculine clubbiness were the high-tech screen covering one wall and its complicated controls set in the central table.

A lavish, silk-draped bedroom was displayed on the screen, Madame Celeste's favorite chamber for feeding on *prosaicos* plucked from her nightclub. A black box, smaller than a cigarette pack, was the only hint her bedroom had any relationship to modern technology.

"I don't see why you pamper those stupid *prosaicos*," Devol growled. Shit, he should have had a beer by now, not be standing there sweating. Why had he arrived so late? "Give me ten seconds and I'd have him terrorized into doing what we want."

How had he survived seventy years without learning even a trace of caution? "Do you truly believe Don Rafael's men aren't watching every place that has what we need? And couldn't tell when someone has had their memories wiped by a *vampiro*?" He finished easing out the cork and poured himself a glass.

"Madame is impatient."

Ah, now we come to the real problem. She has you by the balls, my friend, and you're only thinking about what she wants. "Is she ready?"

Devol snorted. "*Certainement*—and she'll be back any minute."

"Where the fuck have you been?" snapped an electronic voice.

Both men swung to face the screen. Beau bowed as elegantly as the centuries had taught him.

Madame Celeste was pacing the room in front of the bed, dressed in an almost transparent mini slip dress. Eleven o'clock and she hadn't fed. Damn.

"A pleasure to see you again, madame."

"Why is Don Rafael still alive?" she snapped. "You've had over a week to kill him." The videoconference connection between them conveyed her foul temper all too well.

At this distance, she couldn't kill him immediately and Devol was too young to be a threat. Beau chose to speak part of the truth. "The only *compañero* we managed to subvert was immediately discovered and executed. We can only buy spies in the cities, not in the Hill Country near his estates. He's smart enough to stay where we can't reach him."

"Or cowardly enough," Devol sneered.

"Don't underestimate him, Devol," Madame Celeste retorted. "If he's staying at Compostela, it's probably because he can best control his damn spies and saboteurs from there. We must stop him now before I lose any more money."

"I'll have to spy on him personally, in order to plan the ambush," Beau offered. *Give me permission to go in close, bitch; you still hold the purse strings.*

She pursed her lips as she considered his suggestion, her magnificent breasts displayed to full advantage by the dress's deep neckline. "You could shoot him from hiding, as you did that party flunky in Kazakhstan. Just tell me before you do it, so I can be ready to move in and take over."

"No!" How the hell was anyone supposed to crawl across ten miles of rough country, every inch guarded by the best *mesnaderos* in the world? Even Kazakhstan hadn't had such strong defenses.

Devol started to pull a Smith & Wesson revolver. Irritated beyond endurance by his idiocy, Beau whirled and gripped his wrist, stopping him before the revolver had lifted so much as five millimeters from its holster. He snarled and Devol jerked, then glared back.

Beau tightened his grip, impatient to end this. Devol's lips tightened stubbornly. Beau ground the bones together, breaking the man's wrist. The gun slid back into the leather. Beau released the fool and Devol sullenly retreated to the bar.

Beau finished his champagne. Devol would heal within a few hours, sooner if he killed someone before then.

Madame Celeste's chilly voice cut through the room again. "No? Why are you refusing me, golden boy?"

He poured himself some more champagne. When would the young bitch start thinking about what was readily achievable, not what she wanted? "Do you want him to die that easily? Don't you want him to suffer before he dies? To humiliate him?"

"What are you thinking of?"

"Making Don Rafael crawl."

"*Ce n'est-ce pas possible, cher,*" Devol remarked and opened his beer bottle with his teeth.

"If I destroyed something that he valued above anything else, he'd break." Beau was certain of this, more certain than anything else. If Rodrigo's wife and children had faced the rack then died, Rodrigo would have broken.

There was a long, considering silence. Devol glanced at his mistress for guidance. She studied Beau, a crimson fingernail tapping her bedpost.

"Don Rafael is a very sentimental man," she drawled at last, "with some ridiculous soft spots, like those horses of his. Very well, you may have two more weeks."

Beau bowed low. "*Merci beaucoup*, madame."

"Don't push your luck, golden boy." She turned to her enforcer. "Devol, start recruiting the army we spoke of."

Army? Beau came on alert. He didn't want any extra complications in his plans to kill Rafael.

"*Oui*, madame. The Mexican *vampiros* have agreed to let other *vampiros* come through their *esfera* under escort. Your army should start arriving in Brownsville within a few days."

"Congratulations, Devol. You've accomplished what no one has managed in two centuries," Beau remarked, swirling his champagne in the delicate glass. He kept his face a mask of angelic agreement. He'd have to slaughter at least some of those newcomers, after he killed Don Rafael, thereby delaying his enjoyment of the Texas *esfera*. "Don Rafael's *alferez mayor* is legendary for his ruthless destruction of any *bandolerismo* who try to enter Texas."

Devol preened, his wrist now bandaged in cloth napkins. "Give me the chance and I'll show Ethan Templeton who's the better enforcer!"

"Gentlemen, enough of this backslapping," Madame Celeste broke in impatiently. "Hide the hired guns in San Antonio as soon as possible. They must be able to move on Austin and Dallas the minute that cretin Don Rafael departs this earth."

Devol bowed. "As you wish, madame."

"Any questions, gentlemen? *Magnifique*; you're finally learning to obey." Her voice dripped acid. "Now go and make yourself useful, while I dine."

She pointed the small black box at the screen and clicked the videoconference off. An instant later, Devol finished his Corona.

Beau smiled sweetly at his fellow conspirator, considering then discarding ways to kill the brute. He'd need to destroy both Devol and Madame Celeste far sooner than he'd planned. *Bandolerismo* in Texas would raise a *prosaico* mob faster than the ones he'd heard howling in Moscow.

*   *   *

Jean-Marie trailed Hollingsworth's stooped figure through the old house, eyes and nose alert for anything out of the ordinary. He'd met him here after the federal prosecutor had worked late into the night in his usual pattern. No one else knew Jean-Marie was here, his usual approach to handling situations like this.

The lumber magnate's nineteenth-century mansion had recently been restored to its original glory, replete with period wallpaper and carved wood paneling on every wall and ceiling. Genuine paintings from its birth, including a pair of Sargent portraits worth far more than its owner's annual salary, occupied strategic positions, emphasized by professionally hidden lights. Antique Bokhara and Turkistan rugs covered the floors. The furniture was a mix of comfortable modern reproductions and excellent antiques, all extremely expensive.

But underneath the scent of ostentatious floral decorations and frequent applications of lemon furniture oil was the faint, distinctive odor of Madame Celeste's perfume, made exclusively for her in Paris.

Jean-Marie smiled politely again and again, no matter what he saw or smelled. He wore it when he nearly gagged over Madame Celeste's rotten scent. His hands tightened convulsively, causing his knives to shift slightly in their leather sheaths. He forced himself back to a guest's polite appreciation of hospitality.

Finally Hollingsworth stopped in the library and waved Jean-Marie to a chair. Here, leather-bound books lined the walls from floor to ceiling of the two-story room, hidden from daylight by heavy draperies. A superb Victorian humidor had pride of place on the central table, while the walls and ceilings bore subtle testimony to the ventilation and fire protection needed to permit men to enjoy cigars in an old wooden structure.

The entire space reeked of Madame Celeste.

Jean-Marie prowled around its octagonal boundaries, observing everything he could. *Chère* Hélène had once teased him that, at six feet three, he was far too tall to behave so much like a cat.

"Cigar?" Hollingsworth asked, his gray eyes wary above his white mustache. He cultivated the image of an old Southern aristocrat, although his father was unknown and his mother had been a Laredo barmaid.

"Yes, thank you," Jean-Marie agreed. He settled himself into the wing-backed chair offered and stretched his legs out. He'd introduced himself as a lawyer from the Santiago Trust, which was true enough. But anyone who tried to swim with big money in Texas knew that very few lawyers openly admitted to being from the Santiago Trust—and the ones who did talk about it weren't the fellows you wanted to meet.

Thankfully, the rituals of lighting a cigar would speed learning what Ethan wanted.

Hollingsworth's eyes flickered at Jean-Marie's fast agreement but he quickly recovered. He unlocked the humidor, using a key on his watch chain, and extracted a tray of cigars. He offered it ceremoniously to Jean-Marie, who coolly considered the various cigars for the expected factors—oiliness, firmness, texture, consistency of wrapper color—while expecting them all to be fully satisfactory. Then he selected the one he'd wanted all along and waited for his host.

The gray-haired lawyer chose one, returned the tray to its source, and sat down opposite his guest. Fingers steady but pulse just a little too fast, he unwrapped his cigar, never once looking at his guest. Still moving in the fixed pattern of the habitual smoker, he reached for the table drawer.

"What do you use to cut your cigar?" Jean-Marie asked conversationally, balancing one of his knives on his finger. Emilio had given him one of the deadly, black SEAL knives, so superbly effective and frightening.

Hollingsworth's head came up—and he froze. His Adam's apple bobbed up and down in his throat.

"Personally, I prefer a fine knife," Jean-Marie continued, keeping the weapon rock steady. "What do you think?"

The other's throat worked but no sound came out.

"Knives do have the advantage of being useful for other purposes, such as eating. Or persuading traitors to talk."

Hollingsworth's eyes grew bigger. He clutched his cigar as if it could protect him. "You must be speaking of someone else," he began, his heartbeat skyrocketing, according to Jean-Marie's excellent *vampiro* hearing.

"Or killing, especially men who consort with enemy *patrones* from other *esferas*." Jean-Marie's hand twitched—and the knife thudded into the chair beside Hollingsworth's head.

The man gasped and dropped his cigar. A foul odor uniquely *prosaico*, that of empty bowels, poured into the room.

Another SEAL knife appeared in Jean-Marie's hand, this one held unabashedly ready for immediate use. "You have seen the *mesnaderos* work on others and believed you were immune, because they swore they'd never touch you. I swore no such oath and can do whatever I please."

Hollingsworth fought to recover himself. "I have nothing to confess," he declared, head held high as if he stood on a courthouse's steps.

Jean-Marie tsked. "Try teaching your grandmother to suck eggs, fool. Any *vampiro* could tell you this house reeks of Madame Celeste. For consorting with her without our permission, you know you deserve death."

The man flinched, mouth drawing tight, acknowledgment in his faded eyes. Jean-Marie tested the blade's edge on his thumb, watching the other hunt for an escape. His voice was deadly soft when he spoke again.

"Which category do you want to fall into, *m'sieu*? Someone who lived to speak—or the dead? It makes no difference to me which you choose. You have one minute to decide."

The old lawyer drew in on himself, eyes darting around the room. Jean-Marie waited patiently, knife at the ready.

Fifty seconds later, Hollingsworth began to talk.

Rafael turned the doorknob and stepped into the bungalow's small living room. A message left on his answering machine was not the same as speaking to his frustrating new *amante*. He heard Emilio and his bodyguards take up position outside, confident after a week of this unusual relationship that no one else could readily observe his arrival here.

"Grania?"

"I'm in the bathroom. You can come on back; I'm dressed," she called, her voice slightly muffled. "Just braiding my hair."

Rafael stepped into the tiny bedroom, shaking his head. One touch of a *cónyuge* bond but little hint of anything since, even though he'd spent every night in her bed. Surely he'd dreamed that moment. And yet—could he afford to deny his *esfera* the chance of such a weapon, even if she was a *prosaica* and would die in a few decades? No.

It was the only reason for being here—that, and the ever-astounding twists and turns of her mind, and the pleasures of her superb body, and . . .

"Sorry I'm running late." She smiled at him in the bathroom mirror.

"*De nada, querida.* One of the joys of dating a *doctora* is waiting for her." He smiled at her as charmingly as he could, eyeing how her hands rapidly tamed her heavy mass of hair, as he leaned against the bathroom door. One day, *Dios mediante*, she would make a display of her fiery hair for him.

She blushed scarlet. Her hands fumbled and stopped, forgetting the braid's pattern. *Ay de mi*, Grania truly had so little idea of how magnificently sensual she was.

"Uh, ah, why don't you wait for me in the bedroom?" she suggested. "There's not really enough space in the bathroom for both of us."

Rafael considered the bathroom's potential for lovemaking, as compared to his Mercedes, his helicopter, or his penthouse.

Grania followed his eyes and flushed again.

"Of course, *querida*. Anticipation"—he caressed her with his eyes—"will make the heart beat faster."

She choked.

Well-pleased with her response to his flirtation, he stepped back. A narrow bed, small as a monk's cot, sliced diagonally across the room.

A large, green armoire and matching bookcase covered the only sizable wall. Rafael edged carefully around the bed, automatically crossing himself before the crucifix at its head, and headed for the books.

The ones in the living room were scientific tomes, school textbooks, and great works of literature. But these well-thumbed, frequently ragged volumes held entirely different subject matter. A few were adventure novels, while some were romances. But much of it composed one of the best small libraries of sexuality he'd ever seen. Nonfiction and fiction jostled each other for space. *Guide to Getting It On!* sat cozily with the superb books from Good Vibrations and a huge array of scientific tomes, self-help guides, and highly specialized small references. Classics like Sappho and Catullus, great BDSM literature such as *Venus in Furs* and the *Beauty* trilogy, were wedged next to still more novels. She had a particularly large number of art books—but perhaps that wasn't surprising, considering how much she'd enjoyed watching him pleasure Brynda.

Rafael lifted an eyebrow as he considered the wide range of subjects represented, as well as Grania's evident appetite for carnal education. Even if obtaining a *conyugal* bond with her proved impossible, he would greatly enjoy introducing her to a wider range of sensual activities.

This did mean a great deal of involvement with her, which could endanger her. If his enemies decided to take her hostage . . . His blood boiled.

¡Nunca!

He'd order Ethan to protect her very carefully. Whether she was his *cónyuge* or not, she was his *amante* and he would look after her.

"Train coming through," reported Emilio.

Ethan affirmed his understanding and shifted slightly, careful to keep the refrigerated warehouse in sight from behind the big truck. As soon as the late-afternoon train was past with the last possible witnesses, they'd go in.

He glanced sideways at Don Rafael, who stood at the narrow

road's edge with his visor open, testing the air for their quarry. He twitched, silently longing to shove his *creador* into a truck and send him back to Compostela and safety. Even if he could pull that off—hah!—only a *vampiro mayor* could track another *vampiro mayor*, because only a *vampiro mayor*'s senses were sharp enough to catch the few faint whiffs of scent emitted by another. So, like it or not, Don Rafael was a member of this raid.

The two of them, plus their fellow *vampiros*, were sheathed in black body armor from head to foot, complete with black shields, batons, helmets, and tinted visors. Its layers of Kevlar were sufficient to keep the deadly sunlight from their skin, thus protecting their lives. Faceless and deadly, they had the look of medieval knights rather than twenty-first-century men, except for their shotguns and revolvers. Even the small grove of oak trees and green grass where they waited, once a corporate park, seemed more attuned to centuries past than modern days.

"*La Compañía* Wolf ready," Gray Wolf reported. He and Jean-Marie led the two other *vampiros compañías*, also waiting downwind of the warehouse. Caleb would be the only non-*vampiro* inside, guarding Gray Wolf's back through the adamantine *conyugal* bond, as Gray Wolf guarded his.

The ground trembled underfoot as the big freight train began to roar through, flooding the air with the heavy, rich aroma of cattle.

Even so, they took no chances that their prey might be spooked by a stray whiff of other *vampiros*. Their armor's scent was a disguise—pure *prosaico*. Every item on their bodies had last been worn by a *prosaico* policeman who'd gladly traded it for a new, top-of-the-line outfit. Don Rafael's *prosaicos* had carefully handled the armor every step of the way since then, including fastening every buckle and strap today.

Compañero snipers guarded the rooftops, too high for the enemy *vampiros* to smell. Trusted *prosaicos* drove the big police trucks. Helicopters circled at a distance suitable for traffic helicopters, and would rapidly move closer as soon as the *compañías* entered. Thankfully, the warehouse was slated for remodeling and therefore empty. The local

police had been told this was a movie company shoot, involving live fire.

The other *vampiros* on his *compañía* were lounging around, most watching Don Rafael. His best men, they'd all been on raids with the Old Man at least once before. They'd form a lethal buzz saw behind him on this one, should it come to violence.

Don Rafael's head came up, his eyes narrowing. The men stiffened and Ethan's hand automatically dropped to his Ruger. Good revolver, deadly accurate, perfect for the one-shot stop necessary in *vampiro* duels.

"Your report was correct," Don Rafael remarked slowly.

"Two *vampiros* inside?" Ethan asked. "Each fifty years old?"

"*Sí.*" *And yet, I wonder . . .* he added, mind to mind.

Ethan gripped his Ruger, ready to draw it from its holster.

The ground shifted, began to steady in the distinctive pattern marking a train's end.

Never mind. Don Rafael shook off his momentary abstraction. *Ready?* he asked Ethan, mind to mind.

Ready. He found that familiar, fractionally greater alertness and settled into it, perfectly calm now. Death didn't matter, only serving the man and the *esfera* who'd salvaged him.

"Mount up," he ordered and the men headed for the trucks. Moments later, they were hidden inside, as the trucks waited, engines rumbling at a low roar.

The last train cars clattered down the tracks. The big vehicles burst out of the grove, bouncing down the road as quickly and precisely as their ex-cop drivers could take them. Each *compañía* simultaneously roared up to their assigned door, a full city block apart, just as the train dropped out of sight beyond a dry river bed. An instant later, the *compañías* leaped out of the trucks onto the warehouse's loading dock, under the last blood-red rays of the setting sun.

The doors were unlocked and well oiled, as promised. The *vampiros* entered silently, guns drawn, and closed the doors behind them, leaving edgy *compañeros* and *prosaicos* on the outside.

Once inside, they raised their visors for better observation and fanned out, moving as stealthily as possible in the heavy body armor and boots. Don Rafael was in the lead, with Ethan covering him from the right.

The big refrigerated warehouse was a half mile long and two blocks wide, designed to hold meat. It was solidly built, in order to hold the low temperatures necessary to keep the valuable cargo frozen. Doors, at either end and along the sides, were large enough to admit forklifts, while a huge conveyor belt ran along one side. A single row of bare industrial light panels burned high along the ceiling, providing starkly brilliant illumination.

Outside, the trucks backed away from the loading docks, sending faint vibrations through the warehouse's floor, their drivers careful not to become hostages—or meals for the enemy. The helicopters sidled closer, their rotors' beat faintly reaching Ethan.

Small bits of scent eddied past—motor oil, a long-dead mouse, a bit of cattle meat. Ethan sniffed the air warily, both guns ready, the skin on the back of his neck itching as it had before that Abilene gunfight so long ago.

Suddenly a padlock snapped and two snarling *vampiros* erupted into the big center room, in front of Ethan's team. The ones he'd expected, each fifty years old—and unfortunately, well armed with shotguns.

An instant later, another, far older *vampiro* jumped down behind them. Shit, this brute was two centuries old—more than a half century older than Ethan.

Instantly, the Texas *vampiros* shifted to cover all three.

Ethan held his fire, waiting for Don Rafael's signal. He could barely hope to wing that old buzzard, given the bastard's greater speed, but he could surely create a diversion. Behind him, he could hear Gray Wolf and Jean-Marie's *compañías* moving closer.

The older one, a singularly ugly fellow even for a *vampiro*, sneered at Don Rafael. "You're remarkably handsome for a dead man walking. Fifty million dollars for your hide—which I will enjoy spending."

Don Rafael's mouth curved. Ethan shivered, remembering the times he'd felt the lash of that cold greeting decades ago, and turned his attention fully on the two younger *vampiros*. The fight would turn openly nasty very soon.

"How many children did you kill this week, Lorenzo?"

"Not enough," the old buzzard purred. "There's not much blood in them but a mountain of pleasure."

Only decades of hard discipline kept Ethan from blowing the bastard's head off then and there.

Don Rafael raised an eyebrow. "My condolences on still needing to roost in dusty barns like a bat, Lorenzo," he remarked. "I'll see that your ashes are properly washed when you're gone. No doubt it'll be the first time they've been cleansed."

"Cleansed? You say I, a devotee of the great baths, need washing?" He spat. Claws leapt out from his fingers as he suddenly shifted into a great bear.

Don Rafael snarled something deep in his throat. By the time it finished, an enormous wolf was leaping from Don Rafael's armor toward the bear's throat, almost faster than Ethan could follow.

Don Rafael's armor fell to the floor in a series of thuds, followed by his clothing, empty of the man it had once covered. A few feet away, Lorenzo's chambray shirt, jeans, and boots also lay on the warehouse floor. No *vampiro*'s attire went with him when he shapeshifted.

The younger *vampiros* screamed insults and began firing, methodically trying to take down the Texas *vampiros* around them.

Ethan shot fast and accurate, gunslinger instincts paying off again. A young enemy dropped, his shotgun's last blast ripping open a refrigeration line. Coolant hissed into the air. Ethan's men's shots ripped into the walls, whined off metal, and thudded into the concrete floor.

The last enemy youngling swayed, shotgun still at the ready, then slowly crumpled to the floor. His hands turned to ashes, as more ashes fell out of his shoes and clothing. The last thing to go was his head— but no Texan watched that.

Every Texas *vampiro* now surrounded the fighting wolf and bear, in the classic dueling circle for *vampiros*. Nostrils flared, as they scented the spilled blood. Hunks of flesh, with fur still attached, flew across the warehouse.

Suddenly the bear lunged at the wolf. The nearest *vampiros* jumped back, quick to give their *creador* room to fight.

Rafael panted, tongue lolling out and rich scents rolling in. Blood painted his muzzle, while a tuft of fur clung to the corner of his mouth. He shook his head fiercely, cleaning himself. Kill. He needed to kill.

Once he'd smelled the blood of another *vampiro* determined to kill him, his own blood had risen in response, also driven to kill. Nothing could stop them until one, or both, were dead. Instinct and bloodlust ruled now. Only through a link as deep as the *conyugal* could anyone have reached him now. His tools were his centuries of dueling in this form. He'd fought so often as a wolf that every move came readily to him, as easily as he'd once used his sword.

A great flap of skin hung from the bear's throat, half hidden by matted blood, the legacy of Rafael's last attack. He spat the last bits of fur from his mouth and charged in.

It snarled at him and swiped with those great claws. Pain streaked down his ribs.

Rafael leaped for the bear's throat and ripped out the life of a man who'd tormented so many innocents.

Ethan relaxed finally. He was also damn glad he'd never come up against Don Rafael in a duel.

A moment later, Don Rafael stood in the center of the circle, swaying slightly over his would-be assassin's ashes. Crimson painted his chest.

Ethan handed him a survival blanket for temporary clothing and stripped off his glove, preparing to offer his master his own blood.

"*Gracias*, Ethan," Don Rafael murmured. "Did you smell the locker that Lorenzo came from?"

Ethan shot him a hard look. "No."

"Beau was there, less than a day ago."

*   *   *

Grania sat on the floor, shaking, as exhausted as if she'd run a marathon. She gazed around the prep kitchen, an island of light against the darkness outside, and fought to catch her breath.

She'd been a nervous wreck all afternoon, the way Blanche had paced before the *Princesse* confronted her. Her stomach had been tied in knots, as if part of herself was about to go into combat, which was a truly ridiculous notion. The only thing that had saved her from taking a sleeping pill, to block the sensation out, was hard physical labor—scrubbing anything and everything first at home, then in the center. She'd called Bob and taken over as on-call vet, then spent her time acting like a charwoman, even putting a mirror polish on ancient stainless steel.

But a few minutes ago, out of the blue, a flurry of intense concentration had overwhelmed her, demanding the utmost from every cell in her body. It was over in a few minutes, leaving her as drained as when she'd performed major surgery—and sitting on the floor. Well, at least she wasn't desperate to find something else to clean any more.

Grania rested her chin on her knees and hid her face in her hands, pushing tendrils of wet hair out of her face. Sooner or later, she'd need to stand up and drink a lot of water. But not quite yet.

She'd behaved entirely too much like Blanche today, nothing like how she'd ever acted before, even during her worst finals week. But everything was different here in Texas.

Her dreams, those nighttime fantasies, had changed after she came to Texas. Before then, she'd often dreamed about Rodrigo but the episodes had always had a pleasant haze around the details. Very enjoyable, very comforting, but easy to forget in daylight.

Last April, she'd arrived for the interview and slept in that tiny but painfully clean motel. There she'd had her first wet dream of Rodrigo, experiencing it as his pregnant wife being well loved before he went to war. It had to be a sexual fantasy—and yet, it was far too vivid. It had held too many details for a pure fantasy, like the names of the young princes.

When she'd started to work here, the dreams had returned in earnest, demanding her attention as they vividly told the story of Rodrigo's life. They'd included so many elements, like the battle at Ecija and The Syrian's castle, that they felt like memories. But how could that be? They couldn't be her memories unless she was Rodrigo reincarnated.

Everything in her rebelled at the thought and she smiled ruefully. Given the number of sexual fantasies she'd had about the man, both waking and sleeping, she'd hate to think she was narcissistic enough to lust after herself in a previous reincarnation.

No, that couldn't be it.

Grania reached over her head to the counter and pulled herself up slowly. She turned on the faucet and rinsed her face with ice-cold water. Cupped her hands and gulped the precious liquid. All the while, her brain kept worrying at the problem.

Rafael looked like Rodrigo, except for that appalling scar on his forehead. If she was the reincarnation of a *vampiro*'s long-dead wife . . .

She stared at herself in the window, reflected against the darkness outside. Impossible. He'd never given any sign of recognition. Sexually interested, yes, and courteous—but hardly obsessive, as Rodrigo always seemed to be around Blanche. Science or no science, reincarnation didn't come into this.

He was simply a fascinating predator—who happened to also be an excellent companion and a superb lover. Nothing more.

She turned away from her disbelieving reflection and headed for her pickup. Hopefully if she came up with a list of questions, she could pretend their relationship was mostly scientific. Maybe.

ELEVEN

Grania drove her pickup down the badly rutted dirt road carefully, trying to avoid the worst of the monster potholes left by last night's thunderstorm. She had no objections to washing more mud off this old truck but she did not want to break an axle on her way to a date, especially just after dawn.

Not that she could say when the storm had started or how long it had lasted, since she'd been in Rafael's arms the entire time. She'd only known there'd been a meteorological event because of the wet pavement and the many branches across the road on the drive home.

She spent part of most nights with Rafael now and had for over two weeks. They'd meet well after she'd left work, changed, and eaten. Later she'd return home well before dawn. They'd talk, argue, listen to music—and make love. She'd never thought she could have this much fun spending time with a man.

Her dreams of Rodrigo also continued, vivid as ever. She still didn't know what she'd do if Rafael proved to really be Rodrigo.

Just ahead of her was one of Rafael's big Suburbans, loaded with four of his men, her near-constant companions now. She'd talked them out of riding in the cab with her only by allowing two to ride in her pickup's flatbed. One of them was Emilio, the SEAL she'd met weeks ago. Rafael's paranoia about security was spilling over into her own life. She shook her head and kept driving.

She slowed to make a hard right turn past an enormous granite boulder and waved at the totally expected sentry on top. He lifted his hand to her in response, with a quick flash of white teeth.

An old ranch house appeared ahead, whose driveway sported some very elegant horse trailers as well as more armored Suburbans. A dozen deadly-looking men milled around the property, drinking coffee and carelessly tugging their jean jackets down over their holsters. Beyond them, a half dozen saddled horses were patiently waiting in a corral. They were stunning Andalucians, too, with a few elegant Arabians in the next corral. Overhead, Rafael's sleek helicopter flew lazy dragonfly circles in the dawn sky.

She pulled her pickup to a stop in front of the house and hopped down, grabbing her battered old Stetson as she went. An entire day off and Rafael to spend it with. She was perfectly happy to spend her time with him in the open like this, or at fancy hotels. She didn't think she'd be comfortable in the kind of mansion he was likely to frequent. "¡Hola, Rafael!"

The one man who wasn't wearing a shoulder holster reached her. "Querida." He stroked a finger up her throat, her chin lifted to follow it, and he kissed her.

Long minutes later, she murmured, fingers deep in his thick, night-dark hair, "I thought we were going riding."

"Bedroom's right there." He made as if to turn for the house.

"You have a dirty mind, mister." She swatted his ass. One of his bodyguards gasped in shock. Her eyes met Rafael's, sharing his amusement.

"We'd best move out now, while the day's still cool."

She nodded in agreement. With one accord, they turned for the corral.

"Andalucians?" she asked, considering the beauties. "You bred them, of course."

"*Sí.* We use them mostly for working cattle."

Since they're extremely intelligent. "Except for the ones who don't go into show jumping or dressage."

"Or competitive driving," he agreed amiably. "I hope you'll like Atalanta."

A pure white horse named Atalanta, the name of a famous runner in Greek mythology?

"Do you like Golden Delicious apples, sweet Atalanta?" she cooed to the mare.

The horse whickered eagerly, tossing her nose up.

"Now I wonder who might have taught you that," Grania mused. She gave Rafael a very long look, which he returned with laughing innocence before tossing her a Golden Delicious apple. She offered it to the mare, who accepted it graciously. Soon she and Atalanta had established a warm understanding.

"Ready?" Rafael asked, astride a big gray Andalucian stallion next to her.

Grania gathered up the reins and smiled at him. "Let's go."

They started down the narrow valley beyond the ranch house, closely surrounded by the mounted bodyguards. Sentries, equally wary, watched from the hilltops, while the helicopter patrolled the skies. Voices buzzed briefly over radios and rifle stocks flashed from saddle holsters. A president couldn't have been more closely guarded.

It was all utterly different from a quiet ride with her godfather, especially when Tom was tracking a lost child.

Grania ignored them all, as she would have mosquitoes and black flies. They were at least polite enough to pretend they couldn't hear what she and Rafael talked about. Besides, they kept Rafael alive from whatever the hell threatened him.

It was a glorious summer morning, that she spent riding across the quiet Texas countryside with Rafael. They climbed rugged limestone ridges, made their way through heavy mesquite and white brush, and stepped carefully around prickly pear. She even spotted a white-tailed

deer in the shadows once. She grinned happily, thinking of how much
Tom would have enjoyed hunting here.

"I started working with Houston, that great horned owl, yesterday," she remarked, eyeing a faded poster about the Alamo, as they
reached a rare reminder of civilization. "He should be ready to release
in another two weeks."

Rafael glanced sideways at her, obviously reading her excitement.
She grinned back at him, more than willing to show her enthusiasm
at the bird's difficult, successful rehabilitation.

"Why are you, a *doctora*, working with the owl? Shouldn't one
of the techs be doing so? Testing his wings, making sure he can hunt,
and so on?"

A brook sang, full of last night's rain, as they picked their way
over a hillside. Atalanta was a pure pleasure to ride, seeming to enjoy the challenge of this terrain as much as her rider did. She waited
to answer him until they reached a narrow trail. "Yup, Ryan's been
Houston's tech for the past eighteen months. But he sprained his
shoulder working on his pickup."

"So he can't have a bird sitting on his fist, certainly not one as
large as the great horned owl."

"Correct. We'll both go into the biggest flight pen, with Houston
on my fist, and Ryan as backup. But the last couple of times, I'll do it
alone, so Houston is as untamed as possible when he's released."

"Untamed and dangerous. They're not called the tiger of the woods
for no reason." Rafael's voice was quieter as the hills narrowed above
them, blocking the sky, as the trail turned and descended precipitately
between the rugged limestone ridges. His men moved around them,
like a deadly river sweeping in and out as the terrain dictated, weapons never far from their reach.

"Which is why Houston should be returned to the woods as soon
as possible," Grania answered serenely.

"He could fly at your face, rip off your scalp . . ."

"And that's only what his talons can do. Plus there's his beak,
which is also intimidating," she agreed. "I first met a great horned
when I was four, Rafael. Trust me: I'll be okay."

"Grania . . ." He sighed. "Of course you will be."

She considered how to reassure him with more specifics—the heavy gauntlets and clothing she'd be wearing, the years of experience she had, the size of the flight pen, and so on. An appeal to his emotions might silence him but she'd always been better at logic. She summoned up a description of her gauntlets, dwelling particularly on the leather's thickness, just as the trail emerged into a small valley.

It was scarcely more than a wide place in the road, with a handful of houses scattered along the asphalt and separated by magnificent old oak trees. Beyond them on either side, white goats and black goats grazed happily in quiet pastures, threaded by delicate streams. A dairy's unmistakable, well-scrubbed bulk sat comfortably at the road's other end, just before it swept back up into the hills.

Rafael's pace slowed as they reached the first house. Grania stared at him, perplexed, and held her tongue about how she prevented being hurt by owls. His bodyguards drew closer, encircling him. He came to a complete halt in front of the third house and revolved slowly, eyes searching everything in sight. It was a little place, one story with a single attic room above, and painted immaculately white.

"What is it?" Grania demanded, following his moves along with his men. She could find nothing except a remarkably bucolic scene.

"It's too damn quiet."

"It's a goat dairy. You can hear plenty of goats and the dairy machinery. Plus the brook," she pointed out, watching him. She didn't mention the helicopters overhead. After all the time he spent with those mechanical beasts, he had to have filtered them out by now.

"*Sí*—but there should be more."

"Like what?"

His face hard, Rafael looked over at his nearest bodyguard. "No other *vampiro* is here, Emilio, nor an enemy *compañero*. But something is very, very wrong. Check it out."

Emilio nodded. He and another man sprang down from their horses, tied the reins to an old hitching post, and ran up to the house. The building remained silent, with every window tightly shut.

"Get down," Rafael ordered imperiously.

"What?"

"It could be a trap. At least put the horses between us and danger." He started to reach out to her.

Grania opened her mouth to protest but obeyed. The odds of him being correct were smaller than the chances of him turning violent if she disobeyed.

"*Ay, mierda*, their dogs should be barking," Rafael cursed softly.

Emilio rattled the door knob fruitlessly. "Señora Perez?" he called and pounded on the door.

A pang lanced through Grania at the name. "Your relative?" she asked quietly.

"No, an employee's daughter. Her husband is serving overseas with the Army."

"Señora Perez?" Emilio shouted again.

Still no answer.

"Break it down!" Rafael shouted.

"Perhaps if you tried the back door, or a window—" Grania began.

A single kick sent the door swinging open and the two men disappeared inside, guns drawn. Well, at least Rafael had more than enough money to pay for the damages.

It seemed forever as Grania and Rafael waited, although it was only a few minutes. Finally, Emilio reappeared in the doorway, looking puzzled.

"All clear. They're all inside, Don Rafael, sleeping peacefully in the children's room except for the dogs in the living room. I couldn't wake any of them. The only oddity is a space heater turned on."

Rafael tossed the reins to one of his men and headed up the path between magnificent summer roses, Grania a half step behind him. The bodyguards clustered around them, their guns all too evident.

"Don Rafael," began Emilio, shifting as if to block the doorway.

"Guard *Doctora* O'Malley with your life while I investigate. She'll want to tend the dogs."

Grania's mouth fell open when Rafael disappeared down the hall. Rafael, who'd always accepted the need to be guarded, had put *her* safety first?

She blew out her breath and started acting like a vet. She found the living room full of well-used furniture and overflowing with children's toys. Two big Border collies slept unmoving, sprawled between a slip-covered recliner and the hallway. It was incredibly hot inside.

She started to examine the still-sleeping dogs, trying to remember canine basics from first-year veterinary college. Neither of the Border collies would wake up. Actually, she'd describe them both as being in a coma.

Both dogs' normally fluffy black-and-white coats were badly stained with vomit. Her careful testing evoked an extremely bizarre set of reflexes. She peeled back eyelids and studied their eyeballs.

Grania sat back on her heels and thought.

Down the hall, Rafael sounded furious about how slowly the mother and children were waking up.

Emilio was watching her closely.

Grania came up onto her feet in a rush. "Rafael, get them outside. Now!" she yelled. The diagnosis wasn't one commonly taught in veterinary school, but she'd had enough first-aid training to recognize it.

Glass shattered in the bedroom.

"Emilio, call 911 and have the men start CPR. And bring oxygen, if you've got it. Don't just stand there, looking at me like a dolt—*move your ass!*"

"Yes, ma'am!" He saluted and ran.

Grania shook her head and hoisted a Border collie over her shoulders. She needed to get them both out of here as soon as possible, before they too succumbed to carbon monoxide poisoning.

An hour later, Grania finished describing how she'd made her diagnosis to the local sheriff and fire chief.

The last ambulance had long since taken the small family to the hospital. More than that, the early prognosis for them had come back so she'd have something to tell Rafael.

Much to his resigned disgust, he'd been bundled off by his bodyguards before the first ambulance had arrived. She'd fought to remain with her patients, insisting that the local medical personnel would need an accurate account of their symptoms. Her head and heart were glad she'd insisted but, damn, the rest of her was exhausted.

She glanced over her shoulder when steel fingers closed lightly around her elbow. Behind her, two more helicopters came in fast and hard.

Emilio tipped his Stetson. "This way, ma'am."

Grania raised an eyebrow and followed him into a small, purely functional helicopter. She folded herself into a seat and was totally unsurprised to see Emilio take the one next to her. Ever since Rafael had ordered him to guard her, the only time he'd left her side was when he'd run to fetch the oxygen.

A hard-faced man, with a Kevlar vest barely hidden under his denim jacket, took the seat beside the pilot, a compact submachine gun across his lap. Her eyes widened briefly before she recovered. Good God, had the threat to her gone up that much?

She barely finished strapping herself in before the chopper flung itself into the sky and hurtled west. The bird was flying really fast, in fact, damn fast—and low.

She cast a suspicious eye outside, checking their altitude against what she'd previously experienced during helicopter flights. They were definitely flying at a far lower altitude than she'd expect for a commercial flight, even over private land. Much more like a military flight, trying to avoid being shot down.

Emilio, of course, was totally undisturbed.

Only a few minutes later, they flew up a small mountain, whose crest was covered by a beautiful, low limestone ranch house and outbuildings. A network of roads connected the buildings, pastures, gardens, and fields, even those in the valley below. Fountains danced in a rose garden and spilled into a swimming pool. It was a big estate but surprisingly, also a home. This had to be Compostela Ranch, the legendary but secretive headquarters of the Santiago Trust.

Rafael's home. She wasn't going to be seeing him only in hotel rooms anymore. She wasn't just the well-guarded girlfriend, kept around to be played with. She was now important enough to be a part of his true life.

Unexpected moisture touched Grania's eyes but she blinked it back fiercely.

The helicopter touched down on a well-used helipad, near several other helicopters clustered under the watchful eye of a small control tower. Emilio jumped out and bustled her off, trotting her up a flight of stairs, then down a long porch. He entered the main house with scant ceremony and towed her across the great central room, leaving her no time to absorb its details.

They paused just outside a very masculine office. Its windows were covered by thick steel shutters, blocking all daylight, so that artificial light focused attention on the men there. Inside Rafael's cold, angry voice was dressing down someone.

Emilio held up his hand, but Grania didn't need the warning.

"It does not matter what you thought, Ethan, or you, Gray Wolf. The enemy penetrated into the heart of my lands, something you said was impossible. He injured my people—innocent people, solely because of their likeness to me."

"My humblest apologies, *patrón.*" A Texan's voice, who sounded truthful but not the type to often apologize. "It will not happen again."

"*Bien,*" Rafael all but snarled. "And you, Jean-Marie, your networks should have done better than this."

"*Mille pardons, patrón.*" A Frenchman's fluid tenor.

"Take the men away from guarding me and set them to hunting these devils."

Good God, no! Ice crowded Grania's veins, as her heart choked her throat. If she lost Rafael now . . .

"No!" The men shouted their objections, adding curses to their logic.

"Yes!" Rafael roared.

The others snarled and growled but reluctantly fell silent.

"We must stop them, no matter what. The penalty for failure is death, *mis hijos*. You do not like my punishments—but you will hate those doled out by the enemy more."

No! Grania took a step forward, her boot heel striking wood floor instead of carpet. Silence fell for an instant before Rafael spoke.

"*Doctora* O'Malley?" he called. "Please come in."

The men inside turned to face the newcomers, as politely as if they hadn't been fighting like wolves an instant earlier.

Rafael, dark and coldly angry, was standing by the steel shutters. "*Doctora,*" he began.

Still dusty and sweaty, reeking of dog and horse, she tossed her Stetson onto the hatrack, went straight past every other man to Rafael, and wrapped her arms around him. He choked with laughter and hugged her close.

The others started to file out quietly. Rafael lifted his head. "Gentlemen, another minute of your time for introductions."

Under different circumstances, she'd have laughed out loud at how they promptly came to attention, like puppies at obedience class. But she had to comfort Rafael first. That was more important, even than thinking about these men's resemblance to the ones she'd seen in her vision at the graduation party.

"*Doctora* O'Malley, may I present to you my *adelantado mayor* and heir, Gray Wolf? You've already met his partner, Caleb Jones."

A Native American, tall and handsome, bowed. She nodded politely.

"My eldest *hijo* and *heraldo*, Jean-Marie St. Just."

Another tall man only an inch or two shorter than Rafael, with light brown hair, brilliant blue eyes, and a much too charming smile, bowed. "*Enchanté, mademoiselle.*"

"My *alferez mayor*, Ethan Templeton."

So this was the Ethan who'd had her in the choke hold? He was blond, extraordinarily handsome, with cold hazel eyes. She'd rate him as intellectually brilliant and fully capable of killing at any time, in any place. He nodded politely, a salute she returned in kind.

"And Luis Alvarez, my *siniscal*."

Now this gentleman looked almost enough like Rafael to be his older brother, albeit a few inches shorter and without the scar. His hard, wise eyes searched hers, almost as if checking her intentions toward Rafael. Startled, she opened herself to his inspection, as if facing a new professor. He studied her for another minute before nodding. She relaxed, eased by his acceptance.

Luis turned to Rafael. "I myself will go to San Leandro on the Fourth."

Rafael stiffened.

Luis shrugged, his eyes alight with a rueful triumph. "I am the best one to check the preparations, since it must be done in daylight, as you know, *patrón*."

Grania's gaze shot back and forth between the two. If Rafael had had any choice, she was sure he'd refuse.

"Very well," Rafael finally yielded. "The children cannot be risked at the picnic."

Luis bowed and turned to go.

"But I swear to you, Luis, as soon as this is over, you will receive *El Abrazo*, no matter what excuse you offer next."

Luis spun, his mouth gaping open. An instant later, he'd returned to being the polite caballero and gave Rafael a sweeping bow.

Rafael shook his head and hugged Grania closer.

"*Querida,*" he murmured, stroking her cheek. "Will they live?"

"Every one of them will be fine, even the little baby, especially since you gave the hospital a hyperbaric chamber." She kissed her fingertips and touched them to his lips. "The fire department sent their thanks for the full set of the latest oxygen masks you gave them. Because they had canine oxygen masks, the dogs will make it through too."

"*Gracias a Dios,*" he murmured against her hair.

"It was carbon monoxide poisoning," she added. "The space heater in the bedroom had been sabotaged."

Ethan growled. "It will be a pleasure to destroy those devils."

Rafael lifted his head. "You have your orders, gentlemen. *Buenas nochas.*"

Rafael's men left quietly, closing the door behind them.

She caressed his cheek. The grooves bracketing his mouth seemed to have deepened since that morning. "Did I disturb you too much?"

"No, we were done. Our enemies will regret escalating the war in this fashion."

The confirmation hit her like a blow to the stomach, knocking the breath out of her and tensing every muscle. She cursed under her breath and prayed she'd misheard him. She tilted her head back to look at him better. "War? This morning wasn't an accident?"

He shook his head. His mouth was held so tightly, the skin around it was almost white. "No. Bianca Perez and her children—Fernando, Beatriz, and Inez—are the same names and ages as my family was, when *El Abrazo* was forced upon me. My greatest enemy, Diego Sanchez who now calls himself Beau, did this, as a sign that he's close and plans to kill me."

Grania's brain whirled at the names: Bianca, Fernando, Beatriz, Inez. The Christian names were very common but to have them combined in one family? Especially with this mix of ages and the names of the twins?

All of the names from her dreams and her knight's face in front of her. Her heart stuttered to a stop. "Are you certain?" she asked faintly, not sure what she needed reassurance of.

"*Verdaderamente.* I smelled him upon the bedroom's windowsill when I carried them out. How that devil must have danced when he found that family, with their names so close to those I loved."

"No, there can be no doubt at all," she whispered, her stomach clenching as it never had during a college exam. But if the assassin had been so close . . .

"What if he was watching us, while we tended the victims?"

Rafael shrugged that off immediately, with complete and utter finality. "In all the centuries I knew them, Beau and his *creador* always stayed indoors during daylight, a habit he has continued ever since. He would never have stayed outside, in the harsh sunlight."

"You are certain."

"Completely. It is a very easy habit for *vampiros* to form as *cachorros*, when sunlight means death, and a hard one to break."

Grania nodded, accepting his summary. But if Beau had attacked, as a reminder of Rafael's family, then that was verification that Rafael's family was named Bianca, Fernando, Beatriz, and Inez. Bianca was the Spanish form of Blanche, a French name. Rodrigo's wife had been Norman-French in her all-too-vivid dreams.

She must be comforting Rodrigo.

But if that were true, then what about those dreams she'd had, the ones with too much detail to be fantasy? Like the one in the cathedral or where the *Princesse* had attacked his wife? Rodrigo could not have known that the *Princesse* attacked his wife; only Blanche would have known that. It had to be a memory, and Blanche's memory at that.

Reincarnation? Could she be the reincarnation of Rodrigo's wife, Blanche?

"How did you ever survive so many centuries if you lost such a young family?" she mourned.

He sighed. "I prayed regularly for them, for my children, and my grandchildren, and my great-grandchildren."

"But your enemies . . ." She stopped. She couldn't find words yet to speak of the dreams, especially to him. *How do you tell someone you might be their long-dead wife?* She needed to think about this some more. "You just said you were forced into *El Abrazo.* How did you keep yourself sane?"

He laughed, not a happy sound, and shook his head. Then he gathered her up and settled into the big leather chair behind the desk, cuddling her on his lap. "I plotted and hoped and prayed to take my revenge. I was a sex slave to both men and women, good and bad. I never killed for blood. But there is no sexual act that a human being can participate in that I have not performed or assisted in, whether I enjoyed it or not." His eyes were resigned and bleak, slightly defiant.

She caressed his cheek. "I don't judge you. You did what you had to do to survive."

He kissed her hand. "You forgive more than you understand, *mi corazón.* These things are not easy for me to speak of. For so many years, I was alone with no one to trust, no one to talk to."

Grania bit her lip. But she could share this with him, as she'd never shared it with anyone else. Her knight needed to know that she too had spent long years of bitter loneliness.

She looked him straight in the eye, dropping all barriers, even the angry defensive ones, so he could see she told the truth. "I'm a foundling, Rafael. I was found abandoned as a baby, in a filthy drug smuggler's tunnel, screaming from colic."

His arms tightened around her. "A magical survival."

She smiled at his silliness. "Couldn't tell that by the legal record. The courts declared me a ward of the state, and sent me to a Catholic group home on the wrong side of Tucson. An Irish nun named me for the Irish pirate queen, Grania O'Malley, given my coloring and how so many law-abiding men didn't know what to do with me."

Rafael chuckled, his breath stirring her hair. She smiled with him, then gathered her courage and went on.

"I was unadoptable without known birth parents to sign the release forms. There were always so many orphans there, that assembly line was a better description than family life."

He cursed under his breath, not in English or Spanish. "No one? No family at all? No love, no hugs?"

She shook her head. "Very little. When I was a little older, the church was so proud of having one child with good grades that they shunted me from boarding school to boarding school, each chosen only for needing a student to show off. I attended a different school—or two—every year."

His eyes glistened suspiciously. "And no friends."

"Just my godfather, Tom McLean, the deputy sheriff who found me. He was a widower so he couldn't even be my foster parent. But he saw me on vacations, since I always came back to the group home. His father learned tracking from one of Cochise's last surviving braves," she added slyly.

"And he taught you, which is how you could surprise me that first night!"

She grinned triumphantly and laid her head back against his shoulder. "*Seguro*," she drawled.

He kissed her hair. "Any idea of who your real family is?"

Besides you? She roused herself. "There's no proof, only speculation," she warned him. He shrugged impatiently.

"The cops think my mother was a showgirl, whose family threw her out when she started dating a Colombian drug lord's eldest son. He vanished when she got pregnant. The last time she was seen was in southern Arizona with another showgirl, who was also pregnant, a few months before I was found."

"Why do the police think these people are related to you? ¡Ay, *querida*, forgive me if I tread on painful ground!"

"It's not as difficult to talk about anymore," she assured him truthfully. "They think we're related because my height and coloring are a match for hers. My intelligence is said to be very much like my father's, as if I gave a damn about him!"

"I could have him killed for you," Rafael suggested.

She stared at him, frankly nonplussed. He met her eyes levelly and she was forced to take him seriously. "Not today, thanks," she declined, keeping her voice light.

"If you insist." Rafael kissed her hand and she smiled at him a bit wryly, before going on.

"My mother and the other woman were with a notorious Mexican drug mafia, which owned the tunnel where the police found me. During the raid, the police found that the smugglers had fled a few minutes earlier into a particularly deadly stretch of desert. A few bodies were recovered days later but never the women, nor any other babies."

"Your mother saved your life," Rafael said slowly, considering her account.

Grania had always hoped so but nobody else had ever agreed. "Why do you say that?"

"A colicky baby is a very noisy one. A bad-tempered smuggler would have quickly killed anyone who threatened his escape. Your *madre* must have known that the only chance to keep you alive was to give you to the police."

His arms tightened around her. "Take joy in the small pleasures of life, *querida*, in her honor. If your intellect comes from your father, then your hunger for life is hers."

She stared at him, baffled. "What do you mean?"

"Just once, when you're engaged in something intense"—his slumberous eyes hinted at carnal delights—"don't think, just enjoy."

"Are you saying that I overanalyze?"

"Not at all. Every approach has its benefits, as I have had the opportunity to learn." For an instant, his eyes looked inward and she shivered slightly at their coldness. "But sometimes, it's also good to try something entirely different."

"Just wallow in the simple things?" Grania turned the concept over dubiously. "I don't know that I can. It sounds very passive, almost boring."

"Is that a challenge?"

Her head snapped up. "Oh, dear."

"Precisamente."

She eyed him suspiciously. "What are you thinking of?"

"The day has already been an exciting one, Grania," he observed. "Perhaps a bath will make both of us feel more relaxed, and a massage as well."

She couldn't deny that she needed to clean up but his tone sounded like he was plotting something. "A shower would be much more efficient."

"Indeed it would," he agreed, standing up with her in his arms. She squeaked and clutched him. "Are you going to demand to be put down?"

"Would it do any good if I did?"

He pretended to consider her question as he opened the door. "Very little, I'm afraid. I have my heart set on seeing you relaxed and sweet smelling, as you emerge from a sea of bubbles."

The image rendered Grania speechless. Her, in a bathtub like a 1950s Hollywood goddess? She opened and shut her mouth as he carried her all the way across the great hall with sweeping views and massive ceiling beams, then down the hall to a bedroom. This room was as simple and spacious as the others she'd seen, with an antique wooden bed, chest of drawers, and nightstand, plus crisp white bed linens under a Lone Star quilt.

He pulled the door shut behind them, set her carefully down in an old rocking chair, and went into the bathroom. Water began to run fast and hard. Grania's head swiveled as she absorbed all of the room's details.

The bathroom door thumped open and he beckoned.

She followed him and sighed happily. Like the bedroom, this room was classic rural comfort and simplicity, albeit on a Texas-sized scale. Two—or three—adults could have washed in either the bathtub or the shower. Soft blue rugs covered the white tile floor, while blue tiles accented the crisp white walls.

But he was more appealing to her eyes than any of those man-made attractions. Prowling like a great cat in his simple clothes, even his cowboy boots almost soundless, he tossed bath salts into the tub, then pulled towels from a hidden cupboard. Her heart twisted. She leaned against the doorway, trying to conceal her reaction to her man. This wasn't the time to talk, even if she knew what to say.

"Did you want to wash off the worst in the shower or just jump straight into the tub?" he asked quietly.

Grania straightened, eyeing the tub. It was a monster, which would take forever to fill. She moved forward, unbuttoning her shirt. "Shower first. What about you?"

"I have already washed. But I need to give some orders first."

He kissed her mouth gently, the relaxed greeting of a lover confident of his welcome. She responded willingly, her hand sliding up to his cheek to bring him closer.

"Unbraid your hair, *querida*," he whispered into her ear.

Instinctively, she started to object, thinking of the hours it would take to dry.

He put his finger over her mouth. "Just pin it up loosely with these chopsticks. For me, *por favor*?"

How could she refuse? She kissed his hand. "If you hurry back."

His eyes flared with lust, sending a matching fire through her. She flushed, gazing at him. He kissed her hand and slipped out the door, his eyes never leaving her.

She swallowed hard, all too conscious of her rapid pulse, then shook herself back to reality. She needed to pull off her boots first, so she could be out of the shower and into the bath before he returned. There was still enough of the orphanage-raised girl left in her that she couldn't stand naked before him, even if she was sleeping with him.

She barely made it, leaping into the bathtub just as the door opened, splashing water across the floor. He raised an eyebrow as he propped his chin on his fist. "Did something disturb you, *mi corazón?*" he drawled. "Has an earthquake struck Texas that I should know about?"

Grania crossed her eyes at him, bubbles safely up to her shoulders and her hair atop her head. "An earthquake, indeed. A very large, opinionated gentleman has walked into my bathroom, upsetting my delicate sensibilities." Was that the appropriate term? "He should wash himself immediately." She sniffed disparagingly.

Rafael clucked his tongue. "*Pésimo.* It shall be taken care of immediately." He began to strip, unbuttoning his shirt first.

Grania's mouth went dry at the sight of his magnificent chest, the strong muscles and dark mat of hair, which narrowed to disappear behind his silver belt buckle, like an arrow pointing to further delights. The warm gold of his skin, surmounted by the darker copper nubs of his nipples on his chest. Those wonderful, sensitive clues and triggers to his sensuality . . . Weeks of being his lover seemed to have only whetted her appetite for him. She sighed, eating him with her eyes.

His trousers swelled behind his fly, as he slowly unbuckled his belt. He was barefoot now, having discarded his boots and socks in another room. "*Calor de mi vida*, do you wish me to join you?"

"Right away," she sighed, memorizing every movement of his strong fingers as he unbuttoned his jeans.

"It will be to wash you," he warned. "You will need to yield yourself utterly to me and your body's needs."

Yield utterly? But if it was to him . . . "Will you be in the tub with me?"

"*Sí.*" Laughter underlay the single syllable and a dark masculine certainty.

"Very well. Just hurry up, please."

He bowed to her, his eyes as rich and caressing as dark chocolate. In a single smooth movement, he divested himself of his jeans and tossed them aside. His cock was full but not rampant as he stepped into the tub. He sat down next to her and tucked her against his side.

She stiffened, startled. He caressed her arm lightly, humming an old folk tune.

After a few moments, she started to run her fingers down his chest and over his stomach under the water. He stopped it immediately, his grip ruthless on her wrists. "No, *querida*. Just soak."

She was appalled. "Soak? Without touching you?"

"Relax and listen to your heart and your body. The sound of the waves as they lap against the walls of the bathtub. The feel of our wet skin sliding over each other. The scent of the herbs and the water's warmth."

She worried her lower lip with her teeth, wretchedly disappointed and all too aware of his closeness.

His eyes widened briefly, staring at her face as if he'd never seen her before. He quickly recovered himself and kissed her cheek. "The rest will follow, *querida*. Trust me; you will be more than satisfied."

"If you insist." She sniffed in disbelief and began to silently recite multiplication tables to relax. He continued to gently pet her, as he hummed under his breath.

The room's peace slowly seeped under her skin and into her bones. She began to take longer and longer between steps in the multiplication tables. Her eyelids drooped. Her recitation slowed and finally stopped, as her breathing matched itself to the gentle waves in the tub.

She barely stirred when Rafael began to wash her hands, his touch as light as the herbs' scent. He cleaned her feet and legs, then her face. She murmured, when he rearranged her so he could attend her torso. She quirked a lazy eyebrow when he washed between her legs. But his touch was so gentle and deft, if remarkably thorough, that she closed her eyes again without speaking.

She muttered against his shoulder when he lifted her out of the tub. "Are you showing off again? Doing that big, strong he-man thing?"

He wrapped her in layers of warm, fluffy towels. *"Precisamente."*

"Good." She went back to not thinking.

He laid her facedown, still swathed in towels, on a thick rug. A minute later, he peeled a towel off her shoulder. Warmth immediately poured over her, either sunlight or lamplight, and his strong hands gently rubbed a light oil into her skin. Instinctively, Grania purred like a kitten.

More towels were replaced by the light, more warmth and oil entered her skin under those big hands. His calluses and scars were simply a delicious contrast to the oil's smoothness, enabling him to work the moisture in deeper. She was supple under his hands, entirely his, alive in the moment.

His touch shifted. He worked a spicy oil into her now, finding and inciting every pleasure point. He twisted and tugged, even used his teeth gently, as he worked down her back. Fire awoke in her, sparking through her veins, and flickered along her nerves. Her core clenched, bringing liquid heat to life deep within. She arched under him, her body twisting and writhing to follow him.

He stroked and nibbled her ass and thighs, the sharper touch arousing her as she'd never thought possible. Sharp spurs of lust darted from his teeth to her breasts and her clit. She twisted and rubbed herself against the rug, moaning. Cream rose, seeking him. She whimpered and tried to clench her thighs around his hand.

He slid his fingers slowly through her folds, harvesting her cream. He rubbed it into her skin together with the oil, his dark voice telling her in Spanish how richly it made her gleam, like a goddess of the bedroom. She moaned, more excited by the image than she would have thought possible.

When she knew she'd die if he didn't finish her, he stopped seeking out her cream and returned to working only oil into the long muscles of her thighs and legs. He kissed the backs of her knees, arousing every sensitive, delicate spot, holding her legs down, until she sobbed and begged him for more.

He rolled her over gently, so she was barely aware of the movement. Then he rubbed her feet and worked oil into them, until her legs lolled open and she could barely breathe for sheer boneless bliss as he worked up her shins.

When he oiled her shoulders, her head dropped back against the rug. His first touch on her breasts was innocent enough, with only the slightest attention paid to her nipples. Then he swirled the oil around and around, plucking and twisting, until she moaned, shuddering in unison with every movement of his hand.

Another big hand slid through her folds again and began to delicately tease her clit. She gasped, arching up against him.

"*Ay, querida*, you've the knack of it now. Just give yourself over to the pleasure," he crooned. The words slipped into her, bypassing her brain. She sighed, tightening her legs around his hand as her hips began to rock.

A minute later, he oiled her breast again, kneading it in exactly the fashion that sent shockwaves surging to her core. She moaned again and again, heat building within her until her skin seemed barely able to contain it, writhing and twisting, her body still supple under his touch, as he worked first one breast, then the other.

The first orgasm, a sweet one, took her when he rubbed her clit in her favorite stroke. It rippled through her body, relaxing her like fine wine.

"Grania, *mi corazón*," he whispered.

He continued to knead her, skillfully working her breasts and her stomach with one hand, while the other played first with her clit, then worked finger after finger inside her. Orgasm after orgasm washed over her, shaking her, arousing her until she no longer knew where the boundaries were between normal and the heights of pleasure. Only that her beloved knight had brought her here.

A moment later, a kneeling Rafael lifted her hips and his cock slipped easily and deeply into her. Even his enormous cock head only evoked a contented grunt from her now. His big hands stroked up her legs, placing them on his shoulders. Then he gripped her carefully, around the ribs, and began to thrust.

She groaned happily, immensely pleased by just how completely stuffed she was. Her body was now one long, sleek sheath for him, hot and wet and gripping him passionately. She was hot for him, and so full of him that every movement excited her oversensitized nerves. Fire raced and blazed through her nerves as he thrust. Liquid heat, the wonderful sound of their bodies slapping together, his grunts of effort made lust clench her body again until insanity and ecstasy were the only solution.

She grabbed his forearms, clawing him as she climaxed. "Oh god, Rafael!"

Still kneeling, he dropped her legs off his shoulders and pulled them around onto his hips. He pulled her onto his cock again, holding her by her hips, filling her to the hilt again. She shuddered, tremors racing from her clit up her spine as if she'd never been satisfied. The chopsticks were long gone and her hair was a tumbled mass around her head and shoulders.

He growled her name and began to thrust in earnest, patience gone as he watched her face. She stroked the scars on his chest, teased his nipples—his wonderful nubs stabbing her fingers and palms with his arousal. Her eyelids drooped as she lost herself in the delicious sensations shattering her, thanks to his big cock in her pussy, her man making love to her. She was a being of pure sensation, ready to fly. Only the feel of his arms under her hands kept her connected to earth.

He shifted subtly within her, finding a new spot. She arched, her hair tossing wildly, and sobbed his name as she orgasmed again, the tremors shaking her.

Then Rafael knelt up over her, still joined to her, his arms braced on either side of her head. He kissed her in a passionate tangle of their lips and tongue—before his hips began to rock. Soon he was pistoning into her, as if they'd only begun. She wrapped her legs around him, locking her ankles in the small of his back to hold him closer.

His chest rasped against hers, her breasts stabbing at him as if desperate to catch him and hold him. She dug her nails into his shoulders and sobbed his name, her breath as harsh and agonized as his. He stiffened, bit her, and climaxed, spilling himself into her.

Grania screamed and bucked, as the last and greatest climax swept into her with his come, shaking her to the bone.

In the aftermath, she lay sated and limp under him. For an instant, she felt his heartbeat as her own, blood flowing through his veins as if it was her own. The brilliant glow of warmth flowing through him from where he'd tasted her orgasm. The final drops of semen rising from his cock. The masculine satisfaction of sexual pleasure achieved, for himself and his lover.

Her man, her lover, her knight. In this life and any other.

Blanche dozed lightly in the mid-afternoon sunlight, as she listened to her daughter Inez tell the familiar story. Behind her stood the beautiful chapel, dedicated to San Rafael Arcángel, that Fernando had built in his father's honor. It was framed by the beautiful Galician mountains with their tall, verdant forests. "And that is how your Abuelo Rodrigo—"

A young boy's voice interrupted her fiercely. "No, mamá, it was not like that! Abuelo Rodrigo first parried left, then thrust right to defeat the French champion. Is that not so, abuela?"

Blanche opened her eyes and smiled at Rodrigo, Inez's youngest son. Like the rest of his eight siblings, he was gathered in the herb garden on the chapel's south side, waiting for the arrival of their Aunt Beatriz and her family. Fernando and his family would arrive tomorrow, in time to celebrate the feast day of San Rafael Arcángel on the next day, the twenty-ninth of September. They always tried to come together at this time of year, as they had when the chapel was dedicated, to pray that Rodrigo would have a safe journey home and be healed of all his wounds.

They were a very large family now, every babe born healthy and all growing strong and tall. Thirty-one grandchildren would stand under the blaze of light from the chapel's rose window, while Beatriz's Violante was expecting the fifth great-grandchild early next year. Truly, a guardian angel watched over all the children. Her own aches and pains were unimportant, linked as they always were to thoughts of her husband.

Blanche straightened herself, shifting the pillows they insisted on providing her. She was no more infirm than the chapel behind her, which would stand for centuries here on Rodrigo's lands in Galicia. It was built in the very latest fashion, a miracle of lacy stonework and pointed arches that seemed to fly. The inside was even more breathtaking and had been provided by Rodrigo's Moorish cousins, who'd said simply that prayers for his safe return should be said in his faith. When the time came for her to leave this earth, she'd be laid to rest there in the crypt under the high altar.

"Well, abuela?" little Rodrigo demanded.

His sister hushed him and Blanche realized she'd been dreaming again, seduced by the scent of late summer roses, her husband's favorite flower.

She folded her hands on her black habit, the mark of a married sister of Santiago, and smiled at the young rascal. "Sí, nieto, you are correct. I remember that day as if it was yesterday. My Rodrigo did parry left, then thrust right to defeat the French champion at the tournament."

He sprang to his feet, roaring triumphantly, tripped—and fell backward into the mint bed. His siblings shrieked with laughter and sprang upon him. She smiled at their antics and shared a fond glance with Inez.

Twenty years from now, all these niños would teach their children this story and others, so that her Rodrigo would be remembered. As their cousins and their children would also keep his memory alive here on these lands when she was gone. Forever, she prayed.

Even forever doesn't seem long enough for loving him . . .

Amarte para siempre, no sería suficiente.

TWELVE

Rodrigo thrust hard, whirled with vampiro speed, lifted his shield arm—and fought not to scream as healing flesh tore. Crimson blood gushed from his armpit, a life-threatening weakness he couldn't afford, especially when he hadn't fed for three days. Gritting his teeth, he immediately dropped his wooden practice sword and clapped his hand against the filthy bandage. He leaned against a stone pillar and forced his heartbeat to slow, an old swordmaster's trick that seemed to help even in this hellhole.

His skin was cold and clammy when the blood flow finally stopped. Rodrigo closed his eyes and began a Pater Noster. He prayed every dawn, sunset, and midnight now—committing his soul to the Lord, the closest he could come to communion without a priest.

The twenty-eighth day of September in this year of Our Lord 1487, or the eve of the feast day of San Rafael Arcángel. More than a century ago, a sword of ice had ripped through his heart and he'd known immediately that his beloved wife had died. He'd cried then and, afterward, when his first child had died. But his heart had been *too frozen for any tears by the time his third child left this earth. His nietos and even his bisnietos must also be dead by now. He still prayed for his descendants and his lands, but with only slightly more fervor than he sought blessings for all of Christendom.*

More important was counting the days and years since he'd seen Hassan. Two centuries and a few months had passed but still no sign of Hassan's descendants, come to fulfill their father's oath.

Recently, The Syrian had taken to staging duels in western armor, which were little more than an excuse for Diego to dismember Rodrigo—with the minimum time in between for his limbs to grow back. The most damage Rodrigo had yet done to Diego was to nick an ankle. But the intervals between bouts were growing shorter, as The Syrian's temper worsened. Rodrigo feared it was only a matter of time until Diego killed him.

During the last bout, Diego had carved off Rodrigo's left arm and much of his left shoulder, until only The Syrian's order had spared his life. Then Diego had gone off to assassinate a Turkish general, but this reprieve wouldn't last long, a few days at most.

He might not be able to feed but he could at least go down fighting.

His pulse finally steadied. He glanced around the filthy dungeon cell, looking for a fresh cloth to use as a bandage.

"Psst! Rodrigo," a girl's soft voice whispered. Iron moved in the lock, loud as a blacksmith's forge to his vampiro ears, and the door swung open. There was no use in trying to escape the castle though. The Syrian kept the keys to all external doors, including the secret passages, on his person.

He tried an unsteady bow, cursing his weakness. "Señorita Sara, you should not be here. You will disgust yourself."

She closed the door softly, pocketing the key in her cloak, and came to him quickly. Involuntarily, his nostrils flared and he cursed silently, bitterly.

She was of average height and build, albeit more slender than she should be. But she put her arm around his waist and took his weight with a vampiro's full strength. "Lean on me, Rodrigo. You must sit down on your cot."

Still cursing but helpless in his weakness, he did so. She eased him onto the pallet, sitting down as he did.

"You should not be here," he repeated, revolted to his core by what she must have done.

She put back her hood and gazed at him with those great, dark child's eyes, haloed against the torchlight from the corridor beyond. "How should I not come to the aid of my only friend?" she asked in her little girl's voice, the same as when Diego had brought her to this pit of iniquity. Their abuse had frozen her mind into that age. But her face was that of the forty-year-old woman who'd fought El Abrazo tooth and nail.

Her expression shifted, suddenly displaying the century she too had suffered here. "If you die, how much longer will I walk this earth? I am only allowed to live so they can torture me, in hopes of breaking you."

He had no answer for that. Sabe Dios, The Syrian and Diego had told her so often enough. And it was God's own truth.

Guilt twisted his gut yet again and he vowed to protect her as best he could. He'd have saved her from it if he could have done so without pledging to commit mortal sins at The Syrian's command.

But still, what she must have done tonight to be so replete with blood. He shook his head. "How many—" He cut himself off.

"How many partners did I seek?" she asked. Her mouth took on a mocking curve. "Five women and two men. I still cannot persuade myself to trust the male of the species very much, except for yourself. But you are my brother."

Rodrigo took her hand in his, chafing it gently. "There is love in the world for everyone, Señorita Sara. Be patient and you will find it somewhere."

The torchlight grew into a nimbus around her dark hair. Her face grew indistinct. Behind it, he saw a man's handsome face, with brilliant blue eyes, light-brown hair curling onto his shoulders, and a mobile mouth. Clad in a broad-brimmed hat with a great feather and a velvet suit trimmed with wide lace collar and cuffs, at first he was laughing as he looked down at Señorita Sara.

*But then his expression closed as his costume changed to a plain
one of black, the coat cut short in front but long in the rear, over a
white shirt with linen wrapped high around his throat. Great sadness
built in his eyes, while his mouth tightened until it held only agony.*

"*You have seen a vision! Of someone for me—a man? I can see
him now, as you see him. The handsomest man in the world with the
most beautiful blue eyes!" Impetuously, she threw her arms around
Rodrigo and kissed him on the cheek, like a child promised a Christmas sweet.*

*Rodrigo vehemently cursed the link between all of The Syrian's
hijos, which left him unable to keep her out of his mind, especially
when he was so weak and they were physically close. He must practice his shields more fiercely. "Por favor, Señorita Sara, do not assume
this man belongs to you. He might simply be someone you meet, or
a good friend."*

*She bounced up and down on the cot. He gritted his teeth against
the pain in his shoulder.*

"*Oh no, that is impossible," she cooed. "He will be the one for
me, I know it, and we will have such fun together. A cavalier to squire
me to all the best parties, where I shall feed on so many beautiful
people before falling asleep, safe and sound, in my lovely, narrow
coffin."*

*His stomach heaved. Arriving here at such a young age, The Syr-
ian and Diego's insatiable carnal usage of her seemed to have taught
her that the only survival techniques were carnal. As an adult and as a
vampiro, she thus insisted on feeding on as many partners as possible.
Furthermore, it had amused The Syrian to never disturb her if she
slept in a coffin. Even now, a century later, the only place she could
sleep was in that ill-omened box.*

"*Oh, I am so sorry, dear Rodrigo. Your poor shoulder must be
causing your agony," she crooned, her dark eyes filling with concern.
"Here I am, thinking only of myself, when I came to help you." She
caressed his cheek, smiling up at him. "I am stuffed with blood, all
for you. If you need more, I can obtain it quickly so you'll be healed
by tomorrow night when Jamil may return."*

Tomorrow night? Despite his worry for her, his mind raced quick-
ly. Daylight was such a mortal enemy to a cachorro *that avoiding it*
usually became a habit, even as an adult vampiro. *The Syrian had*
retained that weakness and passed it on to Diego, who never went
outside in daylight or even twilight.

If he was healed by the next evening, he would be able to fight
Diego again. Not that he honestly thought he'd do much better the
next time, after two centuries of Diego learning how to defeat his
every move. But if he was healed, he could at least make the pendejo
work his ass off.

Rodrigo bared his teeth in a predator's invitation to fight. If you
want to see me dead, treacherous brute, you'll have to work for it.

Grania glanced at the clock above the big sink at the raptor center's
lab. Two minutes, five at most, before one or more of Rafael's men
burst through the doors looking for her. If she was lucky, it would be
Caleb, who might understand why she was still here. If it was Emilio,
on the other hand . . . She winced and kept talking.

At least everyone else had left for the Fourth of July, off to family parties or the Fourth of July picnic in San Leandro. Combined
with San Leandro's famous monthly First Saturday festival, which
celebrated amateur musicians, this year's picnic promised to be quite
a festivity.

"I'm telling you, Bob, Houston's ready *now*, not two weeks from
now. You know the signs as well as I do, including all the wildness
coming back in him. I'm sorry if you want to delay until the senator
can fly back to release him. But Houston won't wait, with or without
the big photo op."

An explosion of Texas-flavored static burst from the cell phone in
her ear. Dammit, he wasn't usually this stupidly obstinate.

Her temper slipped a gear. "I know exactly how wild a male great
horned owl is supposed to be. This one's tougher than most or he'd
never have survived a close encounter with a cop car's light bar! You
understand—you're the one who named him Houston for the victor

of Goliad. You know: the guy who shouted 'Remember the Alamo!' then smashed Santa Ana's army to smithereens?"

A merciful silence on the other end of the phone. She risked a glance at the clock. Ouch.

Time to try a little sugar. "I'm sorry you're in Dallas today, for that Fourth of July party, and missed Houston's evaluation. Since you're driving back tomorrow, what if we meet here at the center and I can quickly show you just how ready Houston is?" Sweeten the deal a little more. "I'll also bring my books on North American fossils so your son can write that paper on sabre-toothed tigers for summer school."

Grumbling noises, not necessarily intelligible. She didn't dare look at the time. Loud boot heels, too many for one man, pounded up the steps. She closed her eyes and tried to end the conversation in a professional manner before they were interrupted.

"Yes, I do think it's that important." More muttering followed by reluctant agreement. "Thank you, Bob, I'll see you tomorrow at seven p.m."

The double doors into the lab slammed open, framing a very irritated Rafael, flanked by two glowering men cradling MP5s. Grania grinned, dropped the phone's handset into its cradle, and ran to him.

He caught her up in a crushing embrace. "You are lucky I don't wring your neck, *solaz de mi corazón*!" he scolded.

She kissed his cheek, thrilled to be considered the comfort of his heart. "Later. After I ask you some questions."

"Always the *doctora* with the questions." He pretended to frown but his eyes were gentler now. "You're truly safe?"

"Extremely."

She bit back a sigh as Emilio retrieved her knapsack. Life would be much more normal if she could take care of the little things for herself. But if life was normal, it wouldn't have Rafael in it.

She still hadn't figured out how to broach the subject of reincarnation to him, something she'd have to do soon. But not yet, not with the big dance coming up. She'd never gone on a date to a dance before. While she trusted Rafael a great deal, she didn't know how he'd react to her belief that she was his reincarnated wife. If he took it poorly—at least at first—she could miss out on going to the dance, something her newly discovered femininity didn't want to risk. Surely the conversation could wait until tomorrow, after the dance, when he'd seen her new clothes and new hairstyle.

She happily settled herself next to him in the Mercedes, admiring how the late-afternoon sun highlighted the contrast between his soft, thick black hair and the hard-cut lines of his profile. If she didn't start thinking about something else, she'd go down on him here and now. It was a long drive back to Compostela, given that she was now living in the guest bedroom there.

"Rafael?"

He raised a quizzical eyebrow. "You wish to begin the inquisition now, *querida*, rather than wait for an iced drink at the ranch?"

"I won't have time then. It'll take me a while to get dressed."

He couldn't quite hide his surprise. Grania smirked privately but adopted a serene, butter-wouldn't-melt-in-her-mouth expression.

To her shock, his dark brown eyes grew slumberous and his voice deepened, as if they were in the bedroom. "¡*Ay, querida*, you have whetted my appetite most magnificently with your hints! Let us discuss your questions quickly so that you will have ample time to prepare for tonight's fiesta."

He kissed her hand and she blushed scarlet. Someday, perhaps, she'd know Rafael well enough to flirt with him. For now, it was better to stick to subjects where she felt confident, like science. "I, ah, I was thinking about the night we met."

He ate her with his eyes. "As do I, *querida*, very often."

It was a wonder no husband had killed him before now, given how he could upset a woman's pulses with a single glance. "When you turned into an owl and ran away from me?"

He frowned. Her heartbeat steadied slightly. Much better; now she could talk to him as an equal.

Encouraged, she went on. "How did you learn to become an owl?" She wasn't about to discuss his being a wolf, since she couldn't tell him she knew he'd become one. But surely she could safely ask him about changing form into an owl.

His expression changed, moving from seductive lover into professional colleague. One of the things she most enjoyed about him was being able to converse with him as an intellectual equal. There were so damn few people in this world that she could talk to about anything and everything.

"I knew how an owl behaved—how it launched itself and flew—by watching them. You know we spend most of our time awake during the night for the first few centuries?"

She nodded eagerly, memorizing every word. She'd long since burned and flushed all her notes, refusing to take any risk of endangering him or his people by exposing them to public scrutiny.

"Changing to an animal shape means knowing the beast so well that we understand them instinctively, at a level below conscious thought. Usually this is done by many, many hours of observations until the beast's every move is burned into our brain and every cell of our body. After that, when you wish to behave as the animal did, you simply summon up a picture of it and you become one."

Grania sorted through her memory for similar examples. "That sounds like how the Wright Brothers learned how to fly. They spent months watching buzzards fly before they went to Kitty Hawk."

"Until the men also learned how to soar and could make their mechanical wings do the same. *Precisamente*. I have a similar ability to reshape individual pieces of my body, which is how I have fangs. But to change my entire body requires a great deal of knowledge, which takes time and extreme amounts of nourishment."

"Few *vampiros* can do this," she said slowly, considering the benefits and costs to a predator.

He studied her, effortlessly balancing himself against the sedan's dance through a hairpin turn. "All *cachorros* learn some of this early, or they will have no fangs and must die. Also, if a *vampiro*—or even a *cachorro*—has a very strong link to another *vampiro*, the other can show him an animal in sufficient detail to change shape. Then he too can change his body."

"How many different animal shapes does a typical *vampiro* know?"

"None. An expert duelist, who has survived fifty years or more, probably has one or two. I personally know better than a dozen but I have worked hard to learn so many. It takes decades to perfect an animal shape."

"What are the shapes used for?"

"Usually for dueling, which is a hand-to-hand, fang-and-claw fight to the death."

Grania tilted her head, comparing his answer against what she'd learned in her years of study. "Fighting for territory?"

Rafael's mouth twisted. "Almost always. Occasionally, a challenge can be issued to bring judicial combat."

She stared at him. "To settle a legal dispute?"

"If two *vampiros* come from different *esferas*, a duel may be the only way to settle their differences, even if no land is involved. So one *vampiro* will issue a formal challenge, listing his grievances. The other almost always answers it."

"So he won't be thought a coward."

"Such a reputation would cause every other *vampiro* to attack him at any, or no, provocation. Refusing a duel is essentially suicide."

She whistled softly. "Sounds like lions fighting to take over a pride. Very bloodthirsty."

"We *are* predators, Grania."

"True." She linked fingers with him. Her predator—and her knight.

Grania considered herself one last time in the long, three-way mirror, while the last of her dinner grew cold behind her.

She'd dragged her cadre of bodyguards all over Austin to find an outfit she liked for a price she could afford, scorning any mention of Rafael's money. It was the first time in her life she'd bought sexy clothes.

Now she wore a sleeveless, blue, silky, empire top, cut low to show her breasts and shoulders, with matching, knee-length skirt. High-

heeled sandals—well, Brynda probably wouldn't consider them high
but she did. Long, blue, dangly earrings and matching bracelets—she'd
been very careful to make sure that Rafael could nibble on anything
he wanted to. She'd even gone without a bra—she shivered again at
the sensations *that* created—and she was wearing only a thong under
the skirt.

Most astonishing of all, she was wearing her hair in a high ponytail, caught up at the back of her head and falling to her hips. She'd
braided her hair all her life. In fact, she always put it into the braid
while it was still wet. This was the first time she could remember seeing it loose and dry since she was six years old and had cleaned up
after an unexpected thunderstorm while hiking with Tom.

She shook her head from side to side, letting her long hair chafe
her shoulders and arms. Her clothes were so thin, she could feel her
every strand brush against her back and elbows. She tipped her head,
letting it veil her expression, and laughed at her unexpected secrecy.

She drew a few locks forward, so the ends curled over her breasts,
teasing her sensitive flesh through the delicate fabric. A sudden spark
flashed through her, dancing down to her core and all the way to
her legs and toes. She shivered, her other hand coming up over her
mound.

Mischief bloomed in her eyes. If she excited herself before she
joined Rafael, she might drive him wild. One of the few things calculated to fray his concentration was the scent of an aroused woman.

Her hand promptly dived under her skirt and into her thong.
Sparks gathered under her fingers, turned into a flame, which became
wet heat and coated the thong. It tightened her belly as she breathed
and swelled her breasts, lifting her nipples. "Nice," she sighed. "But
more, I think."

She played with herself further, flicking the thong across her labia
until she moaned, swirling her finger inside herself. She added a second finger and rubbed her clit lightly, approving of how her cream
rose and dripped onto her thighs. She closed her eyes and thrust her
fingers faster, rocking back and forth as the familiar pleasure built.

"Rafael, ah, yes," she moaned, as she climaxed, a sweet orgasm that sent waves of cream gliding onto her thighs. She laid her head against the wall until she regained her self-control. Then, while very carefully holding her skirt up with a tissue, she carefully rubbed her cream into her thighs.

Rafael might have to talk to politicians tonight at San Leandro's big Fourth of July Picnic, but she'd have at least some of his attention.

Head held high, she sashayed out of the bedroom and down to the great hall, where Rafael was talking quietly and intensely to a few of his more dangerous men.

"Evening, gentlemen," she said sweetly. "Ready to go, Rafael?"

Her reception was everything a girl could have wanted. Rafael came to his feet immediately, his dark eyes drinking her in like wine. Ethan's hazel eyes flashed hungrily, before he quickly leashed himself and reverted to a gentleman's stolid propriety. Emilio frankly stared before he grinned and bowed low, in one of his Zorro impressions. The others gaped before Ethan's elbow reminded them of their manners.

"Grania, *mi corazón*, the stars above will be jealous of me tonight." Rafael kissed her hand, drawing her close. His hand cupped her cheek, his fingertips stealing into her hair. "You left your hair unbound."

"To tease you," she whispered.

"More than your scent? Impossible," he breathed against her mouth and kissed her gently. She answered him, their tongues dancing together, as his fingers slipped over her back.

His big hand slid down over her ass and stopped.

Grania waited, suddenly nervous of his reaction. Would he be offended that she wasn't wearing panties?

His fingers stroked, explored, found the edge of her thong, froze. She pressed against him, seeking more.

He lifted his head from hers, with a barely perceptible quiver. "*!Ay, querida!*" he breathed. "You will drive me insane tonight."

"*Excelente,*" she answered, caressing his cheek, confident again.

San Leandro was over a century old, founded just after the Co-

manches had left, and built in the true Old West style beside the San
Leandro River. The small town was centered on a courthouse square,
where a World War II soldier still threatened enemies from high atop
a granite plinth. Its two-story buildings were formed of limestone and
granite, with boardwalks circling the courthouse lawn.

Tonight red, white, and blue bunting hung above the boardwalks,
patriotic ribbons decorated every door, and American and Texan flags
flew proudly on every pole. Pictures of Texan heroes, both modern
and historic, papered every window. Twinkling lights decorated the
courthouse roof at the moment, although they'd be turned off during
the great fireworks display.

Normally sleepy with barely enough vehicles for its sole traffic
light, now San Leandro was crowded with people wandering between
food booths and devouring their findings. Since this was a family picnic, nonalcoholic beverages were readily available. Beer could only
be found at one truck on the edge of the square, conveniently close
to the jail.

As befitted a town close to Austin, San Leandro's world-famous
festival focused on music. First Saturday celebrated amateur musicians, rotating the type of music every month. Many famous professional musicians had gotten their start at a San Leandro First Saturday
and still came back to sit in on a jam session. For big holidays, especially in summertime, First Saturday would be stretched over two
weekends, allowing extra time for the pros to play.

Tonight live music provided the underlying beat, not a radio DJ.
Bluegrass musicians kept people's toes tapping with their lively banjo
and fiddle playing, while Tejano bands warmed up on the bandstand
overlooking the park.

Rafael and Grania strolled quietly through it all, hand in hand.
Or, more likely, with his arm around her waist and her head resting against his shoulder, all too conscious of how neatly his chest
curved against her jaw. Or the light glide of his fingertips over her hips
through her skirt's thin silk.

Their bodyguards were working a layered defense tonight, both
on the streets near them and on the rooftops. Changing positions

with each other and trying not to be too conspicuous, especially before darkness fell. Frankly, they were just part of the scenery around Rafael to her.

She smiled and said the right things to the people she recognized. Rafael always knew all of the children's names.

They wound up at the park by the river, just as the first Tejano band started playing. Excited, happy cries went up and couples surged onto the grass—young lovers but also married couples and children. Grania grinned at their enthusiasm, which so matched her own. Rafael wrapped his arms around her and she leaned against him, watching the dances. Most were country-western, with some pure Tejano dances thrown in, including a polka, Cotton-Eyed Joe, Texas Two-Step, the cumbia, and more.

Rafael played with her hair, caressing her shoulder. "You seem to recognize some of the dances," he commented.

"We did a lot of folk dancing at the group home," Grania answered vaguely, wishing they were back at Compostela, where she could have fondled him without worrying about an audience. "The nuns found it a good way to burn off our excess energy on days when we had to be indoors."

The music shifted to an infectious, slightly irregular, very Latin beat. Similar to a polka, it was obviously the rhythm section for the next dance. The Tejano band's lead singer urged people to come down to the dance floor.

"Would you care to try the cumbia? After that, there's another polka, then the patriotic concert and fireworks."

Dance with Rafael? "Of course I would. Can you prompt me through it?"

"My pleasure, *querida*."

He led her out onto the dance floor and took position behind her, left hand holding her left, right hand to right, hands caught at shoulder height. His long fingers gripped hers lightly, giving the barest hint of their rough calluses.

Her head came up and her shoulders straightened as her body

started to purr. His scent wrapped around her, with his heat and his strength, as she waited for the dance to begin.

Then the music started, its rhythm pulsing through her skin and into her bones. The female singer caroled the melody's first notes.

"Forward." Rafael took a step, his muscular horseman's thighs brushing against her. How soon could she have his legs against hers without denim's intervention?

Grania instinctively moved on the same beat, responding to his lead.

"Spin." Rafael's deep voice resonated through her and set her body throbbing.

He spun her in a circle, rumbling something softly as her long hair brushed against him. But he recovered quickly and gracefully finished the move, leaving Grania behind him, still holding both his hands. She found herself so temptingly close to his firm backside above his strong, narrow hips. If she let go of his hands, she could fondle him there . . .

"Come front," he whispered, the words sinking into her bones like an invitation to sin.

He twirled her and she ended before him, tucked against his hip as at the beginning. Now she could clearly feel the hard ridge behind his fly and a sharp stab of desire ripped through her, weakening her knees.

She looked up to see his dark eyes intent on hers. She could almost taste his sensual mouth when it would finally cover hers. She shivered at the thought, regardless of the Texas night's heat.

"Spin."

Then he rotated her again, proclaiming her desirability to the world. Her body burned under his glance, even when she couldn't find him with her eyes.

The singer sang again, urging everyone to dance the cumbia.

Sweat trickled between Grania's aching breasts when she brushed against his massive chest. Her skin prickled as Rafael watched her, spinning and dancing with her as if she was the most beautiful woman in the world.

"Turn. Reverse."

A pattern of repeated turns came, first one direction then the next, always next to his heart. She deliberately tossed her head to sweep her hair over him and his eyelids drooped, half veiling his passion.

Longing to feel more of him, she ran her fingers across his shoulder as she slipped behind him, letting his strength flow into her. She leaned against him a little, his black hair brushing her arm. Her nipples hardened into spear points against his back, shielded only by thin clothing.

A long shudder ran through him. His eyes snapped to meet hers and her body melted before his hunger.

"Can we leave now, please?" she begged softly, spinning around him again to the starting position and snuggling herself as close to his crotch as possible. Every button in his jeans' fly rubbed against her ass.

"Not yet, *querida*." His voice was all too husky. "Three more circuits around the floor."

He stepped forward, his cock as hot and hard against her as if she wasn't dressed. She moved with him obediently, their thighs sliding against each other, and he dragged in a harsh breath. "Plus the fireworks."

"Good thing it's dark and nobody's watching," Grania commented before slipping around to his back. She was damned if she'd be cautious tonight about anything.

Beau closed the binoculars slowly, enjoying every subtle click as its mechanical elements and his long-held plans simultaneously fell into place.

Rafael had smiled at the red-haired bitch even more fondly than he'd looked at his wife. Destroy her and he'd finally crawl.

"*Yaa 'abi l-'aziiz*, his blood will run like water for you," Beau whispered.

Cursing the fire ants eating every inch of his flesh, he started to crawl carefully back to the ravine where he could shift and free himself from their sting. If Rafael's roving *mesnaderos* hadn't forced him to stay so far away that he had to use binoculars to see anything, he wouldn't have had to be tortured by these insects.

It would be a delight to finally set Rafael's downfall into motion.

THIRTEEN

A whisper of sound, scarcely louder than a mouse cleaning its whiskers, but unusual.

Rodrigo came awake instantly, straining his ears to hear. Less than an hour before sunset on the feast day of San Rafael Arcángel, in the Year of Our Lord 1487. Thanks to Señorita Sara, he was fully healed and could fight again.

There! It came again, a scratching noise just outside his door. A man whispered in purest Castilian, "Tío Rodrigo?"

¿Uncle Rodrigo? His heart leapt for joy. They came, they came, they kept their word after all these centuries!

Santísima Virgen, I will begin every day, for the rest of my life, with thanks to you and your Son for answering my prayers.

"Here." Rodrigo scraped his door very lightly in answer. "Hassan?"

"His descendiente, yaa 'ammo, also named Hassan. Let me pick the lock so you can finally be free."

Dear uncle. Rodrigo smiled at being given an affectionate title in Arabic again, after all these years, and waited, eyeing the sunset through his window. If he didn't kill The Syrian before nightfall when that demon awoke, all would be lost.

Hassan oiled the lock, latches, and hinges thoroughly before setting to work. Metal scratched metal delicately as he worked, almost as quietly as his arrival. Suddenly, he paused, scraped again, and the lock turned.

An instant later, the door opened soundlessly and Rodrigo beheld a kinsman's smile. "Tío Rodrigo. Praise be to Allah that you are still alive."

He bowed, offering Rodrigo's sword in its scabbard, its silk wrappings pulled back. Behind him, two other men—closely related by their scent—kept watch in the corridor.

"Mi sobrino." Rodrigo embraced him hard, unashamed of his tears. He released him and began to buckle on his sword.

Hassan's eyes also glittered. "My brothers, Achmed and Hamza."

Two brief nods from the others, their eyes remaining on the corridor not Rodrigo, and their weapons at the ready.

"As the fastest one of us to pick locks, I had the honor of being first down the corridor, even though I am the youngest. We came on the twenty-ninth day of September, the day Tía Bianca always kept vigil for you. My ancestor said it would be the safest time."

Rodrigo's fingers froze for a moment. Blanche had kept vigil for him on the feast day of San Rafael Arcángel, guardian of travelers and healer of the sick? He would ponder that later.

"Did you lie up during the day?" He drew his sword and slashed the air with it, grinning like a fool at the still-perfect balance.

Hassan's face held the same delight. "Sí, Tío Rodrigo. There is a small, half-ruined cistern just below the aqueduct."

"Return there and I will find you, bringing a gentle lady with me, who is distressed of mind. But we may have pursuers. If we are not there by an hour past sunset or the guards find you first, then save yourself."

Hassan's mouth curled in a warrior's hard grin that promised death to all enemies. "Let them come. We have more men waiting for us below and the Turkish overlords wish this evil gone."

Rodrigo nodded, well aware that neither Hassan nor any Turkish overlord had any chance of destroying The Syrian. "Go then and be quiet. You must be hidden before it is dark."

The castle held only its usual sullenness as he crept toward The Syrian's quarters. Given that their masters lived by night, the servants tended to do so also, and he needed to dodge very few in the corridors. Still, very few minutes remained before sunset when he reached those great studded, double doors.

He crossed himself and said a prayer, committing his soul one last time to God. He reckoned up yet again—as he had every night for two centuries—all the women he had failed to save and their mothers who must have wept for their lost children.

His fingers flexed on his sword's hilt. He went into battle now as the champion of all those girls' fathers and brothers, who could not themselves destroy The Syrian.

"Fearghus," he whispered, remembering his friend, "this is for you."

He lifted the great shining blade and set his lips to it, sealing his dedication to the fight.

Then he set his palm to the door and pressed lightly. It swung open quietly and he slipped inside, closing it behind him.

The entire suite was laid out and decorated reminiscent of an Arabian tent, with hanging lamps and carpets. The carpets were layers thick, matted deep with blood and worse. Eventually they'd be thrown out and burned, rather than cleaned, as would those on the wall.

Rodrigo's nostrils twitched and his stomach heaved. The room reeked of foulness, of blood and death and agony beyond belief. Every scent was wrenchingly familiar to him.

The room's most prominent feature was the balcony overlooking the garden and the western sky. The sun hung blood-red just above the horizon like a baleful eye, casting its heavy, rich light over the bed and its occupant—just as it had in Rodrigo's vision two centuries ago. The vision that Rodrigo had rarely allowed himself to remember, lest The Syrian or Diego snatch it out of his head and kill him for it.

Rodrigo stepped forward, raising his sword, first given to him in the cathedral with holy oaths.

Suddenly The Syrian awoke and rolled to face Rodrigo. Irritation flashed in his eyes. "Yaa ibn sharmuuTa," he barked, "get back to your cell immediately. Diego will deal with you tomorrow."

A spark of anger lit deep within at hearing his mother called a whore. Rodrigo braced himself against the ingrained need to obey his creador's order and fought to complete his sword's downward strike. "I will not," he bit out.

Cursing viciously, The Syrian climbed out of bed and drew his great, curved sword from its display stand. "Yaa Himaar, I will not listen to your insolence any longer, no matter how much I have enjoyed your torments."

Light flashed along the blade's edge as he lifted it, and lit up his features. The Syrian squinted against the glare, which was suddenly as bright as daylight—and probably something he hadn't experienced in centuries. Snarling, he whirled it around his head and swung.

Rodrigo ducked instinctively, his hair lifting as the sharp edge passed just above his head. He lashed out stiffly—but it was the first move he'd ever made against his captor. He bared his teeth in determination and leaped back, agility returning to his limbs.

The Syrian stared at him, baffled, a curse hanging half said on his lips. Then he gripped his curved blade with both hands and came after Rodrigo, the vampiro *link between them silent. "I will butcher you myself, yaa sharmuuT, like the donkey you are. Crushing you is not worthy of* vampiro *gifts!"*

He swung hard, arrogantly—and just a little too slow, compared to someone who'd been training against another vampiro *for fifty years.*

Rodrigo parried the blow, his sword ringing like a bell as the two blades came together—but the fine Toledo steel held. Ah, sí, he was finally fighting back!

He disengaged and brought his sword up, to begin the true duel. The Syrian slashed sideways and the battle was on. They fought silently, viciously, across the room and back toward the balcony. Ro-

drigo had the advantage of stamina and strength from a more recent feeding but The Syrian had the greater speed.

Then The Syrian slipped in a patch of foulness, on a decayed carpet that hadn't been removed yet. His sword's point dropped a little, giving Rodrigo the chance he'd prayed for.

Rodrigo saw his opening and took it. He lunged, twisting the great scimitar out of his captor's hand and sending it flying across the room.

The Syrian stared at him for a long moment, angry realization dawning in his eyes.

Then Rodrigo swung. He sliced The Syrian's neck in a single blow, sending the head rolling onto the balcony.

Instantly the snarling visage with its matted hair burst into flame and withered into a puff of ash. A moment later, The Syrian's body was only a slightly larger heap of dirty powder that a vagrant draft quickly dispersed.

Fireworks burst over the river and collapsed into puffs of ash drifting slowly through the sky. Rockets leapt into the skies in a frenzy, only to explode in brilliant flowers of light. Gold and white stars outshone the Milky Way, quickly followed by red, white, and blue powder puffs.

Rafael's helicopter settled down gently on Compostela Ranch's helipad, sending the dust swirling into the surrounding gardens. Grania took her eyes away from the last of San Leandro's fireworks and quickly climbed out, her hands—and arms—tingling from how Rafael had played with them throughout the flight. The man could have seduced a nun in a movie theater's back row without touching her above the elbow.

He wrapped his arm around her waist, gallantly protecting her and her hair from the worst of the helicopter's rotor wash as they moved away. A few minutes later, they paused to look at one of the beautiful fountains in his rose gardens, a single jet shooting straight up into the air before falling back into a smaller pool, where smaller jets arched into the water. The steamy air was heavily perfumed with roses and herbs, while the only sounds were the gentle ones of water and wind.

"Lovely, truly lovely," Grania sighed.

"*Es verdad,*" Rafael agreed.

Caught by his tone, she glanced over at him. "*I* was talking about the garden's beauty."

"*Sonrisa de mi corazón,*" he purred, his dark eyes like velvet in the moonlight as they caressed her, "you shine brighter than fireworks and far brighter than the moon."

She pushed his hair gently back from his forehead, lingering. "Flatterer," she whispered through a lump in her throat.

"*Querida,* thou art the most adored of all women, *la luz de mi vida,*" he whispered. He went down onto one knee beside her.

"Rafael?" Grania whispered and reached for him. "What are you doing?"

"I wish we could spend the rest of our lives together but it is too dangerous for you." A tear glittered in his night-dark eyes. "If I shared *El Abrazo* with you, the odds are too great that you would become insane and die."

Maybe, but I'd sure as hell try it, just to have a chance at forever with you. She caressed his head. "Yes, I know, you told me that the first night, when we talked about *vampiro* reproduction. Let's sit on the bench over there, *cariño,* where we can be comfortable." And private.

After they settled into the bower's fragrant seclusion, he took her hands. "If you remain a *prosaica,* then we only have fifty years, maybe seventy. Not very long to my eyes."

She flinched and shook her head, unable to say anything.

"There's another way but it's difficult, especially for women. You could become my *compañera.*"

Her pulses leaped at another option and she forced them to steady. If she had an alternative, then she sure as hell wanted to know more. "You haven't mentioned this before. Tell me about it."

"If a *prosaica* drinks a *vampiro*'s blood regularly but not much at any one time, she will gain many of the benefits of the *vampiro* elixir. This includes longer life, more powerful senses, and greater strength. You could easily live for a century, and possibly even two centuries."

He was phrasing this too carefully. "What's the catch?" Grania asked bluntly.

Rafael met her eyes directly. "A *compañera* is unable to bear children. After a century or so, she will suddenly collapse and die, usually within a matter of days, unless given *El Abrazo*. For men, becoming a *compañero* apparently makes it easier to receive *El Abrazo*."

No children but Rafael for a lot more years? Grania snorted silently at the obvious choice. "I'd rather have you than children. Can we start tonight?"

A slow smile began to grow on his face. "Are you certain? Giving up the chance to bear a child—"

"Extremely. You're the only family I want or need."

"*Mi alma!*" He kissed her passionately.

"It can take months to become a *compañera*," he murmured minutes later.

"So? As long as we start tonight, who cares?"

"Of course." He lightly scraped his teeth over her earlobe, not drawing blood.

"Will this change my ability to know what you're feeling after we make love? Or when you're fighting?"

"What! When I'm fighting?" He disengaged himself, staring at her. "*Por favor*, explain yourself."

He was pale, even allowing for the moonlight.

Grania gathered her courage. Telling the complete truth was the only way to handle a scientific inquiry into a very large issue, especially when no theory had been formulated to cover the observed facts. "The first time it happened was the night you showed yourself to me at the raptor center. When you bit my wrist, just after I orgasmed, I knew what your thoughts were—and you knew mine too."

His face could have been carved out of stone. "Continue."

"One afternoon, I could see you—no, feel you down to my bones!—searching a building in high-tech body armor, then fighting as a wolf." Her chin went up stubbornly. "I don't know how you went from the armor to the wolf shape but I know it happened. I felt your claws slash a bear's muzzle and your teeth bite through his throat."

"What else?" he gritted out.

She eyed him warily. He had asked her to spend centuries with him, so she knew he cared for her. She went on. "Another time after we made love and you drank my blood, I felt the energy from my blood flowing through your body, as your orgasmic contractions continued."

"It cannot be true," he muttered, his thoughts obviously racing. "I wish to God it was, though. But there is no way for us to already have the *conyugal* bond when we have loved each other for only a month."

He knew how to explain this? "What's a *conyugal* bond?"

His attention came back to her. "It is a soul-deep link of complete trust between *cónyuges*, which can only be given and never be forced. It takes years to grow between two people, *querida*, not days or weeks, because it governs instinct and reflexes, as well as intellect."

"Why do you wish we had such a bond?"

"I love you dearly. It would gladden me greatly to share such communion of heart and soul with my beloved."

She raised an eyebrow quizzically. "And?"

He shrugged. "I am fighting for my *esfera*'s existence, *mi corazón*. I will not deny I would welcome any weapon that comes to my hand. A duelist, backed by a *conyugal* bond, is nearly unbeatable."

"His *cónyuge* acts as his second set of eyes and ears, so he can't be surprised in a duel?"

Rafael nodded. "The *cónyuge* can also provide the duelist with additional fighting styles to use or shapes to shift into."

Grania studied him, looking so serious, even sitting in the moonlight with roses all around. "A *cónyuge* could be the reincarnation of someone you loved deeply," she suggested, choosing her words carefully. "That would explain how trust came so quickly."

His eyes blazed with hope for a moment then steadied, level and dark. "There was only my wife but she is gone to heaven, far from this world's agonies. I cannot ask her joyous spirit to be shackled to this earth again, not even to have her wisdom in my life, she whom I trusted as I have trusted no other until you. Your love is a gift from above, *gracias a Dios*, and needs no further explanation."

He pressed a kiss in each of her palms, then wrapped her hands in his big, scarred ones. "I too have felt much of the same *conyugal* bond. But to be certain we are *cónyuges*, messages would have to flow from you to me across the bond when we are *not* in physical contact. Your mental shields are incredibly strong, *querida*, and, so far, they've only lowered during passion."

She nearly cursed. The man was stubborn beyond belief but they'd have time to talk about it later.

She smiled at him, then bent her head and kissed his hands. "I will dedicate my life to making you happy, Rafael."

"*Te adoro*, Grania." He gathered her close and kissed her, his tongue curling around hers. She tasted herself on him and moaned hungrily, wrapping her arms around his neck and rubbing herself against him.

He nuzzled her hair, little kisses that led him down past her temple, and undid her ponytail with a growl of delight. She trembled under his touch, her arms sliding around him, feeling his heart beat faster under his white shirt. His lips trailed over her nose and her head fell back to meet him. Their mouths met and melded, breaths heating each other as their tongues danced and twined together.

She sighed, pressing closer, and he pulled her to him, his strong fingers kneading her ass and burning through her thin skirt into her skin. She stretched up, shaping herself to him, opening her legs so the hot, hard ridge behind his rough denim jeans would ride exactly where she needed it against her mound. She jolted in shock at feeling the denim's harshness against her bare skin. Her thong might as well not have been there, for all the protection it offered.

Her fingers dug into his shoulders at the increased heat, her hips surging against him, as his hands pulled her closer. Her clothes were no barrier at all, not with the heat of the night and the passion between them. She moaned again and tried to move closer.

He swept her up into his arms, still kissing her. She automatically adapted herself to the new position, happy to be touching him. But she forced herself back to sanity when he set her carefully down onto her feet, steadying her. "Grania, *mi corazón*."

She tried to lift eyelids grown heavy with sensuality and assess her surroundings. A bedroom, bigger than any she'd seen, so it definitely wasn't hers. Moonlight poured in through a long row of French doors opening onto the gardens, showing a room lit with candles rather than electricity. An enormous, carved four-poster bed held pride of place. Together with its matching tables, chairs, and chests, the room looked like something from a film about Washington. And every surface was covered with red and white rose petals.

He drew her up against him. "A bower for the lady who holds my heart in her hands."

She managed a chuckle at his fanciful thought, sparks flying through her at the look in his eyes. "My love."

They kissed as tenderly as if it was their first kiss, as if they were only now learning each other's taste. His hands drifted gently up and down her arms, the light touch sending prickles of heat through her veins and into her breasts. They firmed, lifting against him. She sighed, moved closer and rubbed her leg over his calf. "More, please, more."

A flush rode high on his cheekbones when he looked down on her. "As the lady of my heart commands."

He lifted her up and set her down on the bed, settling her so her head and shoulders rested on the pillows, her hair spilling behind her. Petals floated up then drifted back down over her, as light as thistledown. He gently eased off one flimsy sandal. Then he produced a rose from the table and lightly ran it over her foot, down the side, outlining every toe, then underneath the instep.

Grania gasped and stared at him. "Rafael?"

He repeated the caress, very, very delicately. A tremor ran through her body straight up to her core. She moaned involuntarily, her eyes closing against the unexpected pleasure.

He did the same to the other foot. Even knowing a little of what to expect didn't stop her pussy from clenching and dripping cream. When he brushed a rose over her thighs, it set off shockwaves of sensation that raced through her bones, arching her up off the bed as lances of desire wracked her spine.

"You are so beautiful, *mi corazón*, when you are aroused," he murmured. "Your skin soft as silk, with heat running under it and the dark fire of your hair. A man would willingly die for an hour with such a priceless treasure as you."

He traced another rose across her other thigh, teasing her skin there as delicately. She gasped in shock as her toes curled in pleasure, when the velvet soft flower teased her. She tossed her head back and moaned, her skirt heaped almost to her waist.

He opened her legs wider and eased her thong off. Then he found another rose and another to stroke over her nether lips. Desire strummed her veins with every soft touch, and cream flowed quickly for him, urged on by his praise. She begged him for release but he whispered to her of patience, swore she was beautiful beyond compare. And still she writhed and twisted and arched under the caress of the flowers and his voice, filled with desire and desperation.

His mouth found her, latching onto her clit just as his finger slipped into her. He sucked hard, pressuring her exactly where she needed it. She climaxed, tumbling over the cliff into fulfillment while her body spasmed between his expert hands.

She started to recover her senses, gasping for breath, still unable to find words.

His hands slipped up her back, underneath her top. "Lift your arms, *querida*."

She quickly did so and he pressed a kiss to first one, then the other aching, ruby-red bud of a nipple. She pulled his dark head closer, sinking her fingers into his silken hair and sighing as each swirl of his tongue sent more lust spiraling through her. Her clothes quickly fell away before his wickedly enticing mouth and hands, while her restless hands demanded similar availability from him.

Soon they were lying side by side, kissing, Rafael caressing Grania's breast while her leg rubbed his in a silent plea. Her nerves were a coil of lust, while liquid heat rippled and gushed over her thighs at every touch of his lips or hands.

"Rafael, please," she moaned, her hips rocking against his fiery hot cock. Pre-come slipped from it onto her skin, marking her with his hunger.

He shuddered, thick fans of eyelashes sweeping down, visibly leashing himself. "Grania, I wish you to be very certain."

"Silly man." She gave him a totally incredulous look and tried once again to capture his cock between her legs.

Suddenly, he rolled onto his back, bringing her up, astride his thighs. She stared down at him. "What are you doing?"

"Ride me," he bit out. "It's not so very different than with horses. Just before you climax, I'll open my jugular and you can drink from me, if you still want to."

She hesitated, worrying her lip between her teeth. "You've always been so dominant. Why are you letting me be the one on top now?"

His gaze swept to her mouth before returning to her eyes. "So you will always know that this is completely your choice. No force of any kind will be involved."

She relaxed, accepting his logic, and leaned forward. "Do you honestly think I'll know how to treat you right?" She wrapped her fingers around his cock, admiring how massive he was. Slowly she ran her hand up it, with a very slight twist, repeating the move with her other hand.

"¡*Dios*, Grania!" His hips bucked off the bed, shaking the rose petals.

"Am I doing something wrong?" Wonderful how his excitement was echoed in her body. Her fingers shook slightly as she masturbated him.

"No!" His face was etched in passion, barely leashed.

She smiled in pure joy. "You will always have my heart, Rafael."

His gaze dropped to her breasts, flushed and full, aching for him. His big, dark hands cupped them, lifted them, and excited them irresistibly.

She tossed her head, sending her hair spilling around them like a curtain of living light. She moaned, hunger for her man tightening in her belly, stronger and stronger. She cupped his balls gently and he rumbled his pleasure, the muscle twitching hard in his jaw.

But that was only a moment's diversion before she returned to her true goal, his beautiful cock, rearing up like a scimitar pointing toward his heart. She straddled it, rubbing herself over it, claiming him with her cream. He moaned her name, his eyes falling shut as his hips rocked under her in a demand for completion.

She knelt over him and kissed his mouth. He answered her, their tongues twining in a silent communion, confirming everything their words had said.

Then she gathered his cock in both hands and slowly, very slowly, watching his expression every moment, she sank down onto him. Small wriggles and moans marked her journey, her inner muscles clenching and releasing him. He shuddered under her, his chocolate eyes wild as he watched, his hands shredding silk bedcovers and rose petals alike. Finally, she held him completely, her legs straddling him like the finest of stallions. She was so very, very full of him that it was hard to think over her body's clamor for completion.

But she managed to look him in the eyes and speak logically. "Now do you believe I choose you?"

"*Sí*, Grania, I believe you," he gritted out, his hands coming to her hips at last. "Now will you finish this before we both go insane?"

"Damn right I will." She rose up and sank down hard, freely enjoying herself. She braced herself on Rafael's chest, sinking her fingers into him. But it wasn't quite right for what she wanted. She wriggled and Rafael's strong hands helped her.

Two strokes later, she was drilling the perfect pleasure point with every rise and fall, while the wet slaps of their bodies were a strong counterpoint to the fountains' music from outside. Her skin was flushed, tight and aching, as if it would burst unless the drumming pulse in her blood and bones was satisfied. Everything in the world narrowed down to the man under her, united to her through his great dark eyes, hands of steel, and fiery cock.

The pulses built higher and higher in her bones until she abandoned herself to her climax. Her fingernails drew blood from Rafael's chest, making his head snap back in pleasure. Lightning fast, he sliced open the great vein at his throat and pulled her down.

His blood filled her mouth, just as the first orgasmic pulse tore through her. The rich coppery taste was intoxicating, heightening her orgasm, until her senses exploded. Waves of sensation pounded up her spine as she greedily gulped his blood, while stars shattered before her eyes and his come filled her. She was deaf to everything but the sound of his pulse, drowning out the beat of her heart. Ecstasy tore her apart, as she lost consciousness in the safety of Rafael's arms.

FOURTEEN

"This should only take a minute, Emilio." Grania entered her little bungalow, past the ever-wary bodyguard who'd just declared it safe. "I just have to grab a couple of books before we go to the raptor center."

"Yes, ma'am. But I wish we had more time to prepare than this."

Grania sighed. "Yeah, Bob's call moving the time up did throw everything out off. Worse, Houston's a nocturnal bird so he'll be extra grumpy being woken up so early."

"Could be worse. At least we can figure that an ad hoc meeting like this will throw off the bad guys too." He swept the room with yet another of those all-encompassing stares, which assessed every possible hiding place for an enemy.

"We'll both still be a little skittish, especially with Don Rafael at the ranch," Grania agreed ruefully. He'd needed to phone Jean-Marie, now in New Orleans, about something which Rafael, that over-protective male chauvinist, wouldn't tell her. Now only *compañeros* were around to protect her, not *vampiros*.

She turned for the bookcase and her eyes met Tom McLean's, in his photograph as a deputy sheriff. His eyes caught and held hers, making him look alive.

A draft of cold air feathered across her cheek, as if he was talking to her. She shivered, her hands opening and closing. "What if Beau decides to break his usual pattern and do something while the sun's still out . . ."

"You could be in serious trouble, ma'am," Emilio agreed, eyeing her with interest.

"Yeah, I could be—but I'll fight it as hard as I can, to stall until Rafael can come." She sighed. "I wish I could stay in today. That's not possible, but at least I can arm myself with something."

By the time the big Mercedes turned down the road leading to the raptor center, Grania was almost wishing she hadn't dressed for a hunting trip with Tom. Cowboy shirt, jeans, and high boots were fine; they were what she'd usually wear to work in a flight cage, given the frequent mud. Her heavy twill jacket was also fairly typical attire, since it provided excellent protection from irritated raptors.

She adjusted her jacket's cuffs again. She'd love to have her sawed-off shotgun or her big Colt .45 but her jacket wasn't long enough to completely hide them from Houston.

"Would you like to take the jacket off, Dr. O'Malley?" Emilio offered. "Don Rafael says—"

She raised an eyebrow, just as if he was a first-year vet school student. "That our enemies never come out in daylight?"

"Even if they do, we've got a full contingent here. You should be safe." At least he was being direct with her now, rather than formally polite and noncommittal as he'd always been before.

Grania shrugged, half smiling. "I worked my way through college by surveying owls in ecosystems where they've never been counted before. Many such places aren't very comfortable, either because of the weather or the two-legged residents. I've carried a knife up my sleeve before. The jacket's also handy, even if it's hotter than hell, because it protects me from the owls' talons."

Emilio frowned. "How big are they?"

"A great horned owl has the largest claws of anything in North America except eagles," she answered dryly.

He winced, clearly assessing her jacket from a totally different outlook.

"They're also very aggressive, with a nickname of winged tigers. As my boss says, you can usually tell how a great horned is feeling by how eagerly he tries to kill you."

He chuckled at the old veterinary joke. "If they're that dangerous, then I should be in the flight cage with you."

She snorted. "And piss off Houston more? Hardly. You can stay outside and keep an eye on things from there. There's only one door so I'll be fine."

They were silent for a few minutes, as the cars turned down the lane into the raptor center. A pickup headed toward them, moving at interstate speed on the rutted side road as it headed into the thunderstorm coming up from the west.

Her head came up as she saw the truck's driver. "Ryan? What the hell?"

The old Ford went past without slowing. She swiveled to watch it then settled back in her seat. "Crap. Hopefully, my vet tech left the raptor center for a really good reason." Not because the bad guys scared him off.

Bob's old Suburban was parked in front of the raptor center, in one sign of normalcy. Otherwise, the center was empty, as she'd expected for the Sunday after the Fourth of July.

But the alarm was off and the main building held no sign of him. They searched everywhere: the offices, the conference room, and the lab. Even the glass-walled barometric chamber that doubled as an operating room.

Or rather, Emilio and his men did, while Grania waited, guarded by another pair of men. All of them, except her, had their guns out with the safeties off.

At least there weren't any convalescents in the ICU, so she didn't have to coach them in how not to disturb birds.

Still, she reset the electronic lock on the ICU, the best hiding space around. She was damned if any bad guys were going to take cover in her hospital.

The last room was the prep kitchen, with its view of the pens holding the resident and convalescent birds. The smaller pens stood on legs to avoid snakes, while the larger ones were up to fifty feet wide. They were so widely spaced that men could easily hide amongst them.

Beyond those pens lay the neatly paved path up the hill past the long, narrow flight cages. The farthest one was also the biggest, where she'd planned to show off Houston for Bob. The entire area was heavily wooded, in order to provide shade for the birds. Of course, the same trees could also provide cover for stalkers.

"Should anyone else be here, other than you and Dr. Bob?" Emilio asked.

"No. All the birds have been fed and exercised by now, so those volunteers and techs are gone. Only Bob and Ryan should be here, plus me."

"But Ryan left."

"Yeah." She tallied up the resident birds one more time. Every one of them was here; since it was a holiday weekend, they weren't traveling to teach people how wondrous and important raptors were. Like those of the convalescent birds, their pens were mostly made of wood, which would never stand up to a gunshot or an angry *vampiro*.

"I'll get the gauntlets, net, and the crate. Then we can fetch Houston and go to the flight cage. We should see Bob along the way," she declared with more optimism than she felt. A walking, talking Bob, of course.

Once outside, the birds proved to be uneasy, the rising wind ruffling their feathers as they shifted from side to side or swooped between perches. A resident golden eagle was drumming its pen's wall with its beak, while a pair of western screech owls hooted fiercely. But thankfully, there were no major upheavals such as birds flinging themselves against the walls in a frenzy.

The farthest, and largest, convalescent pen held Houston. Grania double-checked her jacket's buttons, making sure his sharp talons couldn't reach her skin, then pulled on the heavy leather gauntlets and safety glasses. "I'll catch Houston, Emilio. Then you bring the carrier in and hold it open for me to put him inside."

There was a pause before he answered. "Yes, ma'am."

She glanced over at him. "We'll both be fine. I've done this hundreds of time before."

"Sure hope you're right. I just wouldn't want to face Don Rafael if anything goes wrong."

Grania smiled in agreement.

She slipped inside the pen, while Emilio and the other bodyguards kept watch, as wary as coyotes caught in the open. Overhead, Rafael's helicopter circled patiently, so high its usual aggressive buzz was muted to a distant rumble.

Houston eyed her suspiciously from the top perch, leaning forward and spreading his wings. Grania raised an eyebrow at him.

Houston hooted, emphasizing his unhappiness with the situation, the long, deep, resonant call echoing through the hills. Even for a great horned, he was a big owl, with a wingspan of over four feet and weighing almost five pounds. His huge yellow eyes watched her narrowly over his great beak.

Then he swooped across the cage to attack her.

"Look out, Dr. O'Malley!" Emilio shouted.

Grania watched Houston narrowly, timing his move. At exactly the right moment, she whipped up the great bird net and caught him, then flipped it onto the ground, trapping him.

He screeched furiously, no doubt describing her ancestry in very unflattering terms. He flopped furiously back and forth under the net. Finally he managed to roll onto his back and put his deadly talons up to where they could attack her as soon as she approached him. They were black and almost as long as her hands, sharp and strong enough to kill most prey with one stab.

She crouched down warily and watched for her opportunity. When it came, she quickly grabbed his feet with one gloved hand, thereby controlling his talons—and causing him to emit a blood-curdling shriek. Having thus mastered his most deadly weapon, she soon managed to slide her other hand up his back and pin his head, thus controlling his beak.

"Emilio? You can come in now."

A pause. She glanced at the door. Emilio was holstering his gun.

The previously rock-steady Navy SEAL slowly unlatched the door, slightly shamefaced. "If you'd seen the look in his eyes when he dived on you, ma'am, with those sharp claws pointing at your face . . ."

He came inside, eyeing Houston like a ticking time bomb.

Grania concealed a smile. "That's okay, Emilio. It's mostly a matter of knowing how to behave around them. You'll do fine."

A few minutes later, with Houston seething inside the carrier, Grania stretched. Experience had taught her that an easy capture of Houston was absolutely no predictor of his good behavior later.

The biggest flight cage was hundreds of feet long, nestled just below the top of the hill and far enough away that gunshots fired here probably wouldn't injure any other flight cages. It was tall and lightly built, so that breezes could freely enter. Slats were woven into the sides, plus a lightweight roof above, to protect the birds from distraction. One door opened from the center, to reduce the opportunities for birds to escape.

Thunder rolled in the distance. She glimpsed the rest of the bodyguards moving between the pens and the trees below, as they took up their posts.

"Bob! Are you here? Bob!"

No answer. No sound at all, except the wind in the trees and the unhappy birds.

Grania's eyes met Emilio's. He held up his hand for patience, while the remaining bodyguards fanned out around the flight cage.

"Clear." "Clear." "Clear!"

Damn, she wished Rafael was here. Logic told her that the bodyguards were correct. But she'd have felt better if he was present to confirm it.

Emilio opened the door for her. "I'll come with you."

"Don't be crazy. Houston would rip your head open and the test would be a loss."

He hesitated. "I can't let you out of my sight."

"You can still see me through the slats and hear everything that goes on," she pointed out. "Besides, Bob will be here in another minute or two." I hope.

Houston chose that moment to attack the crate, worrying at the bars with his beak. Emilio eyed the bird narrowly. "He gets worse than that?"

She nodded. "He can rip your face open without trying. Honestly, I'm only afraid of Houston if you come inside."

Emilio shook his head and held the door for her. "Okay, we'll play it your way. Just try to stay within sight of the door, where I can keep an eye on you."

Grania tossed him a salute and wished once again she had more than a knife. She tried to laugh at herself for such fancies. Why would she need Tom's ninety-year-old guns, if she had all these trained pros with state-of-the-art weapons handy?

She entered the flight cage, carefully carrying Houston in his crate. She bit her lip hard enough to draw blood when a quick glance showed no sign of Bob. Maybe he was taking in the view from up above; there was a flat stretch there, almost large enough to take a helicopter.

She took Houston out of the crate, hoping her boss would show up soon. He was, after all, notorious for never being late. The big owl hooted and snapped his beak angrily, then flew to the perch farthest from the door. In fact, for a nocturnal bird, he'd chosen almost the sunniest spot in the flight cage.

She frowned, smoothing her gauntlets.

The door opened. "Grania?"

She glanced over her shoulder. "Bob?"

Her boss smiled broadly at her, which was a very unusual expression for him. What the hell was he doing with all those mesquite and live oak leaves on him? Had he been crawling over the hillside behind the flight cage?

Her skin crawled and she stopped moving toward him. "What happened to you, Bob? We didn't see you down at the offices."

Strange; he wasn't wearing his safety glasses, which he always did in a flight cage. An appalling headache suddenly attacked her, just like the one Rafael had sent her in the park when she'd spied on him and Brynda.

Bob grinned even more. "I decided to meet you up here."

She backed up a step, closer to Houston, and tried to decide what to do next. Bob looked like himself but he really wasn't quite behaving normally.

Then Emilio marched jerkily into the flight cage like a tin soldier. He closed, but didn't latch, the door. His eyes were furious and his mouth tight.

Grania opened her mouth to scream.

An instant later, she lay flat on her back in the leaves, with Bob lying diagonally across her and his hand wrapped around her throat.

She spat in his face and fought to throw him off. But he was infinitely stronger than Bob had ever been. *Vampiro* strong, in fact.

Finally, she exhausted herself and lay still under him, glaring. Emilio was still standing stiffly, his eyes alive with anger.

Bob shimmered above her and changed into a handsome young man, with blond hair and blue eyes. He was just as beautiful and arrogant as Lucifer must have been. Her stomach plummeted into her boots.

"Don't bother calling for your men, Dr. O'Malley. They're dying, except for this one."

Damn him to hell!

She fought back her temper. His hand loosened slightly, enough to let her whisper, "Good afternoon, Beau. Or should I say—Diego?"

"So the fool's told you that much? Excellent, that will save me time."

Save *him* time? The saving grace of anger flashed through Grania. She became preternaturally calm, as when she was standing in her operating room, fighting for an injured owl. Now only her nerves and skill could prevent injury to the helpless ones around her, like Emilio and his men, or the birds.

"And you're also the man in the bookstore, who helped me find vampire books," she remarked, playing for time. Surely the body-guards would notice something soon.

If only Rafael were here . . .

Ten miles away, in his well-guarded office, Rafael was speaking to Jean-Marie over an encrypted phone line. Suddenly ice formed in his veins; his fingers curled to slip a knife out of his sleeve.

Grania was pinned to the ground in a cage. A rock dug into his shoulder blade—exactly as it did into hers.

A link snapped fully into place between them, carrying her body's sensations as clearly as if she'd been wrapped in his arms.

Time slowed to a stop, while his thoughts tumbled into new patterns.

Madre de Dios, she was at the raptor center, miles away.

This time he could not claim that he felt that rock, the roughness of her jeans, the hard protection of her boots, because of his telepathy opening a channel for her senses to walk through into his own. No *vampiro's* telepathy operated at so great a distance—only the *conyugal* bond could accomplish it, as Gray Wolf and Caleb had proven time and again.

But it was too soon! shrieked his brain. He'd only known her, adorable as she was, for a month. Yes, he'd committed to her as his *compañera.* Yes, he wished she could live longer than a century or two—but not at the expense of her sanity. A month was too soon for the soul-deep trust and understanding needed to become *cónyuges.*

Even the five years he'd cherished Blanche would have been barely enough to become *cónyuges.* And yet . . .

Blanche and he had shared a strong bond. She'd known whenever he was wounded, although she didn't speak of it to him, lest she distract him. He'd known when she was in agony, such as when the twins were born. He'd been in Ciudad Real, leagues away from Toledo, when the first pangs jolted through him, an agony like nothing he'd ever felt before. He'd begged permission from the *Infante* Don Ferdinand to return to court and barely arrived in time for his son's birth.

Blanche had remained loyal to him after Ecija, had built the chapel, had prayed constantly, had established his legend, and been buried there, as close to his heart as possible in Galicia. A life of dedication to him—as he had prayed for her constantly, until the ice-edged sword had lanced through him, telling him of her death.

Couldn't that have formed a *conyugal* bond between them?

If Grania was Blanche reborn, then his heart and soul must have known her immediately, without any need for intellect's icy reality. How nonsensical that he'd made her prove herself to him when he should have known her immediately, as soon as their hearts touched in the raptor center's lounge.

Grania must know of this, since she had mentioned reincarnation last night. So she must have at least some of Blanche's memories— joy danced through his veins for an instant at the possibilities—or his *doctora* would not be so certain. But Grania was different from Blanche in some ways, such as her never-ending inquisitiveness.

If the *conyugal* bond had happened only because Grania was his delight and not because she was Blanche's reincarnation, he would be very happy. But if *Dios santo* had greatly blessed him and Grania was Blanche reborn, then life's joys were a cup full to overflowing.

Rafael, his *cónyuge* whispered, *Beau is here.*

And then, horror of horrors, he heard his enemy's voice, clearly saw the man pinning her to the ground.

Grania at the mercy of that fiend, that annihilator of innocence and virtue?

He leapt to his feet, a guttural shout of denial surging from the depths of his soul.

Beau nodded mockingly. "Indeed. I'm glad I left you alive, instead of dining on you back then. It will be so much more satisfying to destroy Rafael's slut."

"Why did you bring Emilio in here?" Grania demanded. "Let him go; this is just between you and me."

"Don't be silly, *sharmuuTa*. He's the irreproachable witness, who'll tell Rafael exactly what happened." He looked over. "Go sit down. You will not speak or move until Rafael arrives, unless I say so. Do you understand?"

"Yes." Emilio dragged his feet to the flight cage's edge, glaring at Beau the entire time, and sat down directly under Houston.

The great horned ruffled his feathers and hooted his displeasure loudly before flying to another perch.

Beau clucked his tongue. "Really, you'd think Texans had better manners, the way Rafael dotes on them."

The breeze strengthened, stirring the leaves inside the flight cage. Clouds flickered over the sun, darkening the flight cage until Houston disappeared into the shadows.

Beau smiled down at her, displaying long yellow fangs totally unlike Rafael's clean white teeth.

She managed not to gag.

The door tapped against the frame and creaked in the wind. It swung open slowly.

Hold on, Grania, hold on! It was Rafael's beloved voice, through their *conyugal* bond. *I can't reach the bodyguards but we're leaving now in the helicopters. Remember—Beau can't read your thoughts.*

"You will become my first *hija*, after which I'll leave you behind for Rafael to find and weep over. The fool can watch the woman he loves die, when you awaken to *La Lujuria*. Or he can see you run to me, your *creador*, when I summon you after he's tortured himself by nursing you. A perfect way to destroy him, don't you think?"

She stared at him, shocked. Rafael's objections to *vampiras* were too deep-seated to be negated by sentiment. Otherwise, he'd have asked her to be his *hija* instead of his *compañera*. "It won't work. Rafael's too strong to fall prey to emotional tricks like that."

"You never saw him with his wife and children. Losing you to his worst enemy, for centuries to come, will break him. Then I'll kill him, slowly of course."

"If you touch him, I will destroy you myself, no matter how long it takes," Grania announced coldly. She didn't give a damn if it took ten thousand years. If Beau hurt a hair of Rafael's head, she'd ruin him. Utterly.

Beau threw back his head and crowed in triumph. "Perfect! You love him too! He'll be heartbroken to lose you."

She bucked furiously again but to no avail. An instant later, he had her jacket collar ripped aside and his teeth in her jugular.

Fire slashed through her as he ripped the vein open and began to suck. Every pull was a vortex dragging her away from sanity and health.

Grania, please focus on fighting him. Rafael was crying. *You'll go insane if you let him take control of your emotions.*

She writhed, cursing Beau. Her eyes blurred, as her struggles grew weaker.

He shoved his wrist into her mouth, pouring his tainted blood down her throat. She choked and tried to turn her face away. Ruthlessly, he imprisoned her jaw and forced her to drink. Her hands and lower arms were free, since he was holding her face. But they felt heavy, as if they were slowly turning into stone.

She grew dizzier, and her stomach cramped. She started to hallucinate, images whirling past of Beau, wearing horns and capering in triumph, as Rafael broke into pieces. Beau's foul poison continued to pour into her mouth and he laughed triumphantly.

She struggled weakly against him once again—and her knife slid into her hand. She opened it instinctively and shoved it into his thigh, the closest part of him. She twisted it, as Tom had taught her before her first long field trip, to cause the maximum pain.

Beau shouted and started to pull back, grabbing at her wrist and the knife.

Suddenly, someone hooted in the distance. Beau's head and shoulders fell forward to within inches of her face. Blood gushed over her. He screamed, released her, and sprang away.

She choked and desperately spat out his foul blood.

His scalp hung halfway down over his face, obscuring his eyes.

Long, deep, bloody gouges marked where the great horned's talons had ripped his head open.

Houston launched himself again, eyeing the disturber of his territory. The winged tiger swooped once more, knocking Beau to his knees and slicing his head open like a razor blade. Then he escaped to freedom through the open door.

Behind him, the winds sent leaves swirling across the flight cage.

Blood flowed over the *vampiro*'s head, obscuring his features almost completely, and he waved his arms wildly. *"Yixrib beetak!"* he cursed, trying vainly to put his scalp back into place.

Grania pressed her fingers over her jugular to slow the flow. As a doctor, she knew damn well it was a mortal wound by normal standards and it was amazing that she was still conscious at all. Perhaps drinking Rafael's blood last night was helping her.

Rafael, she whispered.

Just a few more minutes, mi alma, he promised.

Emilio's eyes were anguished, his movements clumsy and ineffectual as he tried to stand up. Any recourse would be up to her but how? She tried to rise but fell over.

"Give me your clothing, *sharmuuT*," Beau ordered Emilio angrily.

Emilio rose clumsily and staggered directly toward Grania, stripping off his weapons. She glanced back at Beau but he was trying to wipe the blood out of his eyes.

Was mind control extremely literal, like a game of Simon Says? Maybe Emilio could walk in her direction because Beau hadn't explicitly forbidden it.

"I don't care what you do with the rest of your things. Just get the clothes to me fast!" Beau screamed in frustration.

Emilio rapidly dropped his sawed-off shotgun and pistol, with their ammunition, behind Grania. Their eyes met for a moment, his agonized. She nodded understanding. Then he stumbled toward Beau, unbuttoning his shirt.

Three minutes, Grania . . .

Beau efficiently bandaged his head with Emilio's shirt, his once glamorous countenance and clothes now covered in congealing blood.

He stood up cautiously, his blue eyes a hideous contrast to his ravaged beauty.

"At least you've had *El Abrazo*." He chuckled, the sound both husky and blood chilling. "Should you survive it, I'll enjoy fucking you on Rafael's bed after he's dead."

He started staggering away as he hummed a jaunty pop tune. Lightning cracked in the distance, followed by a low roll of thunder.

She was not going to let the bastard get away so easily.

Grania swung Emilio's sawed-off shotgun out, thankful for the pistol grip. Pressing a standard stock against her right shoulder would have been very awkward, given the blood still running down from her jugular.

All she had to do was point and shoot, as if she was aiming down her finger. That was easier said than done, especially when her vision was so very gray around the edges. If she was lucky and the shotgun was loaded with slugs, a single shot to either the head or heart would kill the bastard. A heart shot would be better; if she missed, there was the rest of the torso close by to bleed.

Strength surged into her suddenly from Rafael. Her lips drew back in an approximation of a grin. *Thank you,* mi cónyuge.

You can do it, mi vida. He sounded as if he was speaking through gritted teeth.

Just point and shoot, she told herself again. Just point and shoot.

BAM! went the shotgun.

Beau went down on his face, blood pouring from his left side.

The shot's vibration slammed through her, momentarily blocking *El Abrazo*'s tearing agony. It deafened her and sent her sprawling in the dirt, as loose limbed as a broken doll, blood pumping faster than before from her jugular.

She fought the ringing in her head to open one eye, just one, to see her enemy. Overhead, helicopters were coming in fast and low.

Beau was running out the door, his face contorted in pain and anger, as he pressed Emilio's T-shirt and trousers against his shoulder. Shots rang out from below, followed by men's voices, "He's getting away!"

That bastard was somebody else's problem now.

Thunder boomed overhead.

Madre de Dios, Grania, hold to a single thought. It will help when you awaken. Another minute and I will be with you, I swear.

Grania allowed her head to settle onto the ground. Emilio was safe now. He'd be able to talk and move again, once Rafael arrived. Please, God, let none of the birds have been hurt . . .

Sluggishly, she brought her hand back up and covered her jugular again. Blood leaked out, dripping over her collarbone and into the dirt.

She had only one thought left.

Carefully, each fragment a temporary victory against insanity, she began to picture Rafael's beloved face as he'd made love to her last night, pledging himself to her for centuries to come.

Rafael raced up the hillside, leaving his bodyguards—even Luis and Caleb—far behind. He'd left Compostela fully armed, but he'd crumbled his MP5 submachine gun into fragments, while linked to Grania. Luis had sat next to him, the only man brave enough to come within arm's length of Rafael as he was now.

Lightning sparked and sizzled across the sky. The winds howled in his face, as if reproving him for delay. *Dios me salve,* if Grania dies during *El Abrazo* . . .

At the top of the path, the big flight cage's door whipped back and forth. Rafael burst through it and saw the scene he'd watched unfold, while he'd sat helplessly aboard the mechanical bird.

He stood in a great, roofed cage, hundreds of feet long, with the storm's shadows dancing through it. Emilio was stiffly seated in the center, tears streaming down his frozen face. Grania was lying in a crumpled heap, where she alone had been able to fight.

He dropped to his knees beside her. "Grania, *mi cónyuge,*" he whispered, lifting her hand to his lips. *Madre de Dios,* she was pale. He would not think, not now, of how everything in this cage reeked of Beau. Her heartbeat was the faintest whisper through his veins.

"Rafael," she breathed. Her eyelids fluttered. He gathered her against him and willed strength into her through the *conyugal* bond. He knew bitterly it couldn't last, not when her body was being ravaged by the beginning of *El Abrazo*.

Behind him, Luis helped his foster son rise, with a quick word of rough encouragement. Then he and Emilio left them alone.

Grania's dark blue eyes slowly focused on him. "Rafael, my love. Thank God you came." Her long fingers tightened on his. "Bob?"

He'd guessed she'd ask that. "He's safe at home. His wife called, wondering what had happened. I'll talk to them later and smooth their memories. But enough of that. *Por Dios*, Grania, how can you look at me? If it hadn't been for me and my enemies, you wouldn't have been attacked."

"I'm sorry I didn't kill the son of a bitch when I had the chance," she murmured.

"You did the next best thing. It will take weeks for Beau to recover the amount of blood he lost."

"You should let me die. That would be better than worrying about me following that bastard's orders, now that he's my *creador*."

Everything in him revolted against the thought. It fitted the ruthless logic he'd followed since founding his *esfera*, that of taking no chances lest he become a slave of Diego again. But to lose her . . . "No!"

She stared at him, wide-eyed.

He sought a quick way to convince her, knowing she should have already lost consciousness. "You are different, Grania. You are my *cónyuge*."

"You finally accept it." She smiled like an angel, her eyes soft and reminiscent. For a moment, her expression was exactly that of Blanche's effigy. And for the first time, his heart didn't ache when he remembered that echoing crypt.

"*Sí.*" He kissed her hand. "Your memories are mine and mine yours, both in mind and body. They will help guide you through what is to come. Also, you drank my blood last night, which is protecting you now. Not halting *El Abrazo* . . ." ¡*Maldita sea*, if only it could! "But it will help you fight off Beau's commands."

Dios mediante, this would come true.

"Two different bonds of blood, and mine came first," he finished.

She was silent, her head against his shoulder, her soft braid tickling his chin.

"Grania?"

She didn't move.

"Grania!"

FIFTEEN

The nightclub's elevator doors whooshed open, revealing a furious Madame Celeste. Her evening gown, a splendid example of Milan's most cutting-edge evening wear, had clearly been donned in a hurry. "You fools! You lazy, incompetent asses, who don't even know enough to hide your traces from *prosaicos*! I should have sent a pair of mules from the French Quarter instead: They'd at least have more fashion sense than you two do."

She disdainfully surveyed the two bedraggled *vampiros* in front of her.

When Beau had raced out of that hell-born birdcage, Devol had been responsible for piloting the helicopter to take them both back to New Orleans. However, Rafael and his men had arrived so quickly that Devol and the helicopter had been badly shot up. Devol had lost enough blood that he'd nearly died, which would have stranded Beau in Texas.

They'd managed to land in Galveston just long enough to feed for their escape from Texas; they'd killed the women, of course. They hadn't lingered to clean up either themselves or the corpses, simply jumped back into the helicopter and flown on, desperate to reach Louisiana and safety.

Beau's shoulder burned like the fires of hell, where his arm was trying to grow back but couldn't, due to his blood loss. He was so hungry that dizziness was repeatedly sweeping over him. A growl built behind his teeth, in rhythm with her shoe's impatient tattoo. It would take so very, very little to crush that white throat between his fingers and silence her vituperative tongue forever.

Devol dropped to his knees in a well-practiced move, landing within inches of her Versace evening gown. Patience worn thin by exhaustion and pain, Beau sneered privately at the man's blatant worship of his mistress. It was honorable for a man to follow another man, but to take orders from a woman?

"Madame, please forgive us," Devol begged, his tone genuinely plaintive. "This trip to Texas was a mistake but we'll do better next time."

"Bah!" she spat, twitching her satin skirts away from him. Devol flinched.

"Are you refusing to provide us with shelter? And food? That we may recover from wounds we took in your service?" Beau asked carefully, grasping at his fraying temper.

She swung to face him, black eyes flashing. "Both of you fools are badly injured and will require a great deal of blood. Providing enough to do so will draw attention, even here in New Orleans. It's not Mardi Gras now, when the streets are packed with *prosaicos* eager to be bled like cattle, in exchange for a few minutes' seduction."

"Are you refusing?" Beau repeated, sharpening every syllable.

"Why should I feed you? Is Don Rafael dead? *Non!* So I owe you nothing."

"Would you prefer that I tell your sister where you *live?*" Beau asked, softly but perfectly clear.

She turned white. "I have no sister," she asserted. But her hand gave her away, as it closed around her throat, the most instinctively protective gesture of all *vampiros*. Her unease was further confirmed when Devol, her most trusted confederate, staggered to his feet to take up a guardian's position beside her.

Beau raised an eyebrow at her, ignoring his shoulder's agony. "Did you truly think I wouldn't investigate you thoroughly before I came here?"

She tensed, her fingers curving into claws.

"I know exactly who you are," Beau went on, well satisfied by her reaction, "who your sister is—and what she believes happened to you. Do you want me to tell her where you are? Then the two of you could enjoy that family reunion you've been avoiding for the past two centuries."

Her breasts rose and fell rapidly under the fragile silk. *"Salopard!"* she hissed.

He shrugged, smelling victory. He wished he could brace himself against the anteroom's walls, until the current bout of vertigo passed. "Or you could occupy yourself by making sure we heal quickly and quietly. Don Rafael is now waiting for the woman he loves to wake to *La Lujuria*. Do you believe he'll survive her death?"

Her expression promptly turned greedy and triumphant. *"Magnifique!* He'll have no thought for anything except grief. Then we can destroy him and claim Texas, and I will dance on his grave."

And my father will finally be avenged. Beau's fangs ached with the need to bury themselves in Rafael's neck.

She drew herself up, trying to reassert her dominance over him. He lowered his eyes, plotting exactly how he'd tear her head off, after he'd killed Rafael.

"Both of you may stay here and heal," she announced with false graciousness. "It's easier to conceal you in a big city than a small one, at any rate. We'll have to work quickly, so we can move while Rafael is still overwhelmed."

Beau bowed and murmured thank you, a satirical curve to his mouth. He'd definitely kill her, slowly and oh, so very painfully as soon as he'd disposed of Rafael.

"Now, come along, both of you. Let's see who's in the nightclub tonight for you to snack on, just for enough energy to wash up. You're both entirely too filthy for my bed."

Rafael strode into his office, feeling haggard despite his freshly washed demeanor. His *vampiros* and *compañeros* came to immediate attention, standing straight and tall, their eyes fixed anxiously on his face. Jean-Marie, who'd just flown back from New Orleans, looked unfamiliar in a workman's rough clothing. His expression was icily controlled, as befitted a *heraldo*. Later, Rafael would have to ask about that slight limp.

Earlier, Rafael had heard him invoke his eldest *hijo*'s privilege and insist that the others remain silent on the mind-to-mind link, something for which Rafael was devoutly thankful.

Ethan was standing by the shutters, one of his revolvers ready in his hand, looking exactly as he had when they'd cleaned out those nests of bank robbers after the Civil War, his eyes green and murderously bright. Only one of Grania's *compañeros* had died so far, but the others were barely clinging to life. Ethan hadn't lost as many men in one battle since Prohibition.

Gray Wolf and Caleb were streaked with mud and clad in cavers' heavy clothing and equipment. Gray Wolf's arm rested around Caleb's shoulder, although Rafael suspected that Caleb was actually steadying Gray Wolf, who looked ready to hit the warpath. He hadn't seen Gray Wolf look so close to losing control since the last of the Indian Wars.

Emilio was now well scrubbed, dressed entirely in black, and wearing his warrior's face, something Rafael still wasn't quite accustomed to seeing. He was also even more well armed than Ethan.

Luis, on the other hand, wore the same classic western wear as Rafael did, although he too was as well armed as Ethan. His weary eyes searched Rafael's and relaxed.

Rafael smiled slightly. *You read me so well, old friend. The battle*

*is over for the moment. Like an old fox, you'll take advantage of this
time to rest and rearm for the coming battles.*

He waved a hand peremptorily at them, instinctively taking his
own station at the fireplace, next to his sword. "As you were, *mis
amigos. We have much to discuss.*"

They settled back down, scarcely relaxed. Jean-Marie was playing
with a wicked stiletto, while Ethan toyed with his revolver. Emilio
had all the focused attention of a torpedo being programmed to destroy a warship. Gray Wolf and Caleb settled onto the big leather sofa
in their usually outwardly stolid manner, although their brains were
often the sharpest ones present.

Luis brought Rafael an ice-cold glass of Hidalgo's La Gitana
Manzanilla. The single best wine to start off an evening, according to
Seville's *tapas* bars. But at this moment, he needed the comfort of its
complex, faintly salty taste, to remind him of the Atlantic Ocean and
Grania's deep blue eyes. He sipped the pale gold wine, letting its chilly
dryness awaken his throat.

Luis watched him, not quite hovering. No doubt another glass
was waiting in the freezer to be filled—and no doubt Luis would very
accurately judge his mood by how quickly he finished this finest of all
aperitif wines.

He'd sworn he'd never tend a *vampira*, yet here he was, planning
to do exactly that. *El hombre propone y Dios dispone.*

"If I may be so bold, how is Doña Grania faring?" Jean-Marie
asked quietly, the stiletto momentarily lying still across his palm. A
beautiful weapon, it had come from Florence over three centuries
ago.

Rafael's mouth tightened but he answered politely. These men
were his family and Jean-Marie was his son in every way that mattered. They deserved the truth. "Still asleep. I do not believe she will
awaken until tomorrow night."

Shock flashed across Jean-Marie's face. "Asleep so long? Have you
ever seen this before?"

"No." He drained his glass of sherry. "I once heard that if a *cachorro* sleeps more than a day and a night before awakening the first time, *La Lujuria* will be either very, very long—or very, very short."

There was an appalled silence. No one there wanted to contemplate the chances of a woman surviving *La Lujuria*, if it was much longer than usual.

Gray Wolf hummed something under his breath and beat his thigh, as if drumming. Caleb, who was perched beside him, closed his eyes for a moment, apparently in prayer.

Rafael set his empty glass down on the mantel, bringing their attention back to him. "We need to make plans. I will challenge Beau to a duel, saying he's such a coward that he attacked a *prosaica* instead of me."

"Madame Celeste's assassin?" Ethan's face shone with enthusiasm.

Rafael smiled in agreement with his *hijo*'s certainty, flashing his fangs. He'd worked like the damned to learn dueling tricks during the past five centuries, from as many schools as possible, in order to destroy Beau.

Besides, he had to do it: He was the only living *vampiro* duelist with a chance of defeating that seven hundred-year-old *pendejo*. It was the only way to protect Grania from being enslaved by Beau, when his foul blood demanded her as his *hija*. For her, Rafael would risk anything, even his life and his *esfera*.

He would not, of course, involve her in the duel. For one thing, Beau needed to be defeated as quickly as possible, while he was still weak from his wounds. For another, Rafael couldn't risk either her body or her sanity by bringing her too deeply into the duel, especially now that she had a chance at eternity.

"Can you carry the gauntlet, Jean-Marie, as *heraldo* of Texas? Or do you think you were noticed in New Orleans during the last trip?"

Jean-Marie shook his head immediately, casually flipping his stiletto. "Not by anyone who would carry tales to Madame Celeste or Beau. Of course, I'll carry the gauntlet."

"As the challenged, Beau can choose either the time or the place,"

Emilio said slowly, lifting his head from the knife he was honing. "Which do you think it will be?"

Rafael shrugged. "If he chooses the time, it will be because Grania wounded him more deeply than we know. If he chooses the locale, it's because he can't afford to let me specify New Orleans."

"And wants to have Madame Celeste here so she can seize Texas when he wins. Or so he thinks!" Ethan barked with laughter.

The others joined in, except Gray Wolf. Rafael's heir's black eyes saw all too much as they studied him.

"How long do you think it will take Beau to heal?"

Rafael glanced sideways at the former medicine man, as he accepted another glass of La Gitana. He should have known Gray Wolf would cut to the core. "One month is typical for that kind of injury."

The others fell silent, listening.

"When do you wish the duel to occur?" Gray Wolf probed further.

"A week from today, at most two weeks."

"Thereby forcing Madame Celeste to choose between healing Beau—and hoping to take over Texas if he defeats you—or the risk of discovery by the *prosaico* authorities through the trail of dead bodies. Excellent."

Rafael bowed his thanks for the compliment. "Ethan, as *alferez mayor*, you will be in charge of the field of honor, should it be held in Texas."

"Of course, sir."

"We'll hold it at the Santiago Military School."

Ethan nodded thoughtfully. He holstered his Super Redhawk and pulled his smartphone out. "That will work. They're closed now, to prepare for Hell Week when the new freshman class arrives. Do you want the football stadium or the soccer field?"

"Football stadium. The fixed seats there will restrict Madame Celeste's minions to where we can see them."

"Anything else, sir?" Luis asked, his black eyes filled with steady confidence. It was exactly the same question he always ended planning meetings with during peacetime, and the others responded to the signal. They rose, ready to begin work.

Rafael shrugged, falling back on his lifetime hunting habits. "Not for now. I'll rest before going out—"

"You're overlooking something," Gray Wolf interjected dryly.

Rafael raised a quizzical eyebrow. "Which is?"

"You're Doña Grania's sole support. You need to remain strong for the trials ahead and to nourish her."

"So we've made arrangements to keep you well supplied," Ethan continued, "for as long as necessary."

"More than enough," Jean-Marie drawled, "for you to lead the most ravenous *cachorro* through *La Lujuria*, as we always do when there's a new member in our *familia*."

"You will not need to leave Compostela," Luis finished, drawing himself up, "for any reason whatsoever."

Rafael started to speak.

Emilio's mouth curved, the first softness he'd shown since being forced to watch Beau attack Grania. "It's no use arguing with *Papá* Luis, Don Rafael. Nobody ever wins against him."

Faced with the solid wall of protective opposition, Rafael threw up his hands and acquiesced. He comforted himself he was letting others provide food for him, just to let Emilio feel better. It was a more dignified thought than admitting that he'd fallen into another of Luis's traps for protecting his well-being.

"One other suggestion, *mon père*," Jean-Marie said softly, putting his hand on Rafael's arm. "It's whispered that Gorshkov has kept his *cachorras* alive through *La Lujuria* by . . ."

"Only for a few days," Rafael growled.

"Longer than anyone else makes a practice of!" Jean-Marie retorted.

The room fell silent. Rafael gestured Jean-Marie to continue.

"It's whispered that he does so by speaking continuously of his love for her, and her alone."

Ethan looked extremely thoughtful, his hands finally lying motionless on his guns. Luis glanced sideways at him.

"I would have done that anyway," Rafael protested. "She is *la luz de mi corazón*."

"May I suggest that you do so with extra frequency then, *mon père?*"

Rafael spread his hands. "*Con mucho gusto, mi hijo.*"

Rafael paced his pitch-black bedroom, scrutinizing the arrangements one more time. No *cachorro* had ever awoken here before; he'd always taken them to a specially prepared suite. Now his carefully tended quarters were radically rearranged, yet he still wasn't sure everything was safe enough for her.

Steel shutters, originally installed for protection against an attack, covered every window against the July night. Everyone—*vampiros, compañeros,* and *prosaicos*—had been banished from the wing. Three layers of carpets covered the floors. Even the fountains had been silenced in the garden, lest their gentle music alarm his lady.

Grania tossed her head fretfully, scattering her red hair across the fine Egyptian cotton sheets. Rafael was at her side in a moment.

She'd finished rejecting the last traces of her *prosaica* body a quarter-hour ago, almost two hours after sunset. Her eyes had remained closed throughout, of course, while she screamed and sobbed. All entirely typical for a *cachorra* about to awaken—and no predictor whatsoever of whether the *cachorra* would live.

Every one of his *hijos* had survived *La Lujuria*, a record only he could boast of as *creador*. One of the most important factors was that he'd never forced anyone into *El Abrazo*. But Grania had been brutally compelled—and the odds of survival after that were very poor, even for a woman who wished to become a *vampira*.

A fine sweat gleamed on her brow. She was about to awaken.

He glanced up at the Madonna on the wall and said one last, quick prayer. Then he crossed himself, slipped into the bed with his beloved for one more time, and bit down hard on his lip. Blood welled up instantly, running down his face and scenting the room. He'd also filled it with lust earlier by masturbating. The more there was of both in the air for her to smell, the easier she'd gather herself and the more satisfying her all-important first meal would be. The meal that taught her to feed, for the rest of her life as a *vampira*, on blood and sexual pleasure.

Not death and terror, as Beau preferred.

"Grania, *mi vida*," he whispered. "Grania, you are my life," he repeated, calling her in English, in case *La Lujuria* had stolen her skills in Spanish. He slid his legs between hers, caressing her silky skin with the rougher touch of his hair-prickled legs. Bringing her feminine folds close to his masculine organs for the gentlest awakening possible. Earlier, he'd fantasized of coming home to her but not like this.

"*Te adoro*, Grania." He nuzzled her face, little kisses that teased her with the scent of blood. She moaned softly. Her body stirred against his, her leg rubbed over his. *Bien.*

"*Calor de mi corazón*, Grania."

Her eyelids fluttered open and she opened her mouth to scream. The *conyugal* bond tore at his heart, ripping him open with the same knife shards tearing apart her soul. Grania, *mi vida!*

He captured her head in his hands and pulled her close, back to where she could smell his blood. Por favor, *Grania, find the path out of the abyss . . .*

"Grania, *querida*."

Her head turned to follow his, as her hands stroked him restlessly. The knives carved them both more slowly.

He fondled her gently, keeping her close. Always careful of her fragile skin, but rubbing every possible inch of himself against her. Scent and touch were so very helpful in awakening a *cachorro. I am here, Grania. There is a way out of the chaos. Just hold onto me and we will walk it together.*

She sniffed delicately. Hope leapt through his heart.

"*Te adoro*, Grania!"

She growled softly at the back of her throat and kissed him hard, her tongue lapping eagerly over his lips. She tasted every inch of his mouth, their tongues tangling together as she explored him. She pressed hard into the bond, her consciousness less agonized but still incoherent. She was more forceful, more demanding, more aggressive than he'd known her before.

He threaded more words together for her to follow. "*Te llevo en el alma*, Grania."

Her blue eyes were glazed with desire. Her fingers rose over his shoulders, clawed his back, drew blood. She groaned, moved closer, rubbing herself against him more boldly.

Ah, the heat of her cream between her legs as it poured through the *conyugal* bond! *Mine*, she questioned, *mine?*

To his surprise, his hips began to rock against her. He'd never before lost command of himself at times like this.

"Rafael," she sighed, so softly even he could barely hear.

He froze. His name. She'd recognized him, despite *La Lujuria's* madness.

"*Te adoro*, Grania." He shuddered, small suns going nova under his skin now wherever they touched. His pulse speeded, as his blood raced to satisfy her. His chest tightened and his balls swelled, aching to pour his come into her. His life, his soul, his *cónyuge*.

Grania grew frantic with lust and his passion rose with hers. They tangled together, rolling across the sheets, sweat and blood and lust scenting the room. He tasted her breasts, suckling her like a madman. Stabs of lust rocketed through her nipples down her spine into his bones simultaneously. She raked her nails over his back as she fought to pull him closer and he laughed in triumph, before switching to the other breast.

Pressure built, hotter and harder, at the base of his spine. His cock was ready to burst from desperation. Yet he fought to delay and excite her further, as sensations raced between them, until he knew not who started which delight. Filling the air with the scents of blood and sex, the passion that would soon pour into her throat and core, to start rebuilding her.

She yanked at his hair, pulling him up. She kissed him fiercely, her hips rocking against him in a primal demand for completion. *Rafael . . .*

He groaned into her mouth, lying on her, arms around her. Her legs locked around the small of his back and her folds caressed him, blatantly pouring her hot cream over his cock, steaming him with the heat in her veins. His balls tucked themselves high and hard against his cock.

Grania . . .

He rubbed against her, quickly falling into a steady rhythm. He teased her clit. She bucked against him, her nails sinking deep into him, spurring him on and increasing her passion.

He growled deep in his throat, gone far beyond words. Lifted her hips and impaled her on his cock. She cried out in shock and pleasure, clinging to him.

A practiced flick of his index finger opened his jugular slightly. He thrust—and gasped at the desperate thrill of her scalding channel closing around him.

Her head dropped, her hair rippling over his shoulder and arm. She nuzzled his throat, following the trail of blood. Found his jugular, licked. Hummed in pleasure. Began to drink it in earnest, faster and faster.

Por Dios, the taste of himself on her lips, like the finest cognac! Her determination to drink more weakened his knees.

Her mouth suckling at him sent an echoing jolt down through his spine to his cock. He thrust in unison, which traveled back up to her mouth, and into his neck. A cycle quickly formed between them, building both their ecstasy. The faster and harder he thrust, the faster and harder she drank, the faster and harder rapture spiraled higher for both of them.

Rafael could not have said who was deeper in *La Lujuria*, himself or Grania. Only that he was desperate for more of his *cónyuge*.

And still they fought for sanity as they shared blood.

Grania muttered something. She worried at his neck, backed off. Tried again—with small, sharp fangs, and then drank with a grunt of satisfaction as his blood flowed hot and fast. Orgasm's waves rose in her, wrapping around his cock.

Rafael roared in delight.

All leashes on his self-control shattered. Her ecstasy triggered his, sending him over the edge into a series of bone-shattering contractions. Stars burst inside his skull as his come erupted into her.

He cuddled her afterward, savoring the few minutes' respite before she'd need to be fed again. *Por Dios*, she'd made it. She'd come through *La Lujuria* sane enough to create fangs and feed herself.

After the duel, they'd live as *cónyuges*.

Dios mediante.

SIXTEEN

Rodrigo and Diego circled each other in the arena, while The Syrian watched silently from above. After almost two centuries, The Syrian didn't need to tell them when to start fighting. But they fought now in the latest European armor, heavy suits of plate mail, not animal forms. They'd both grown so fast and vicious that a shapeshifter's duel caused too many injuries and thus happened too rarely for The Syrian's taste.

Diego charged and Rodrigo countered in a complicated flurry of blows that even other vampiros would have been hard put to follow. Coño, it was the same old pattern: No matter what he did, Diego was always there, waiting for him to strike—and getting in the first blow! When they separated, both vampiros lacked their shields and Rodrigo's left arm ached.

Barely pausing, Diego charged again. Rodrigo parried automatically and knew immediately that he had done exactly what his enemy wanted. An instant later, after a series of moves whose final outcome was preordained given that beginning, he lay on his back in the sand, *cursing his luck. Next time, dammit, next time. Next time, he'd find a way somehow to break this training and kill the* pendejo.

Singing in triumph, Diego raised his sword high over Rodrigo's head, ready to give the coup de grâce.

Rodrigo cleared his mind, saying his final prayers. After more than two hundred years of torment, he'd be glad to finally rejoin his wife—but he'd hate to leave this world without ridding it of these two devils.

The Syrian's voice snapped across the arena. "Do not kill the unbeliever. We have not broken him yet."

"What!" Diego spun to face his adopted father, pulling off his helmet with one hand. "But what more can we do to him? He's a boring opponent because he always loses to me, no matter how we fight."

"He has never begged." The Syrian dismissed all opposition with a brisk wave. "Finish this quickly so we can have dinner. There are some new Armenian slaves to play with."

Diego's expression was filled with frustration as he turned back to Rodrigo. He raised his sword, twirling it. An evil thought danced into his eyes.

Rodrigo started to lift himself up on his right elbow.

Diego giggled, nastily. He swung his sword up and brought it down hard and fast. It smashed through Rodrigo's left arm at the shoulder joint.

Rodrigo screamed as his life's blood spurted across the arena.

Grania sat bolt upright in Rafael's bed, her heart pounding.

Dear God in heaven, she hadn't had a nightmare like that in years, not since she was a child. She crossed herself slowly, as she'd done in the orphanage.

A big, strong, warm arm wrapped around her waist. "*Querida?* Are you well?" He propped himself up to look at her, dark eyes soft with concern.

She smiled at him. "Very well, darling. How could I be anything else, when I'm with you?"

She lay back down and he promptly cuddled her close.

She hid her face against his chest and prayed the dream was only one of the nightmares from *La Lujuria*. Because if it was one of his memories, then what did he truly face in the coming duel?

Grania frowned at Rafael from the other side of the Mercedes's back-seat. Agonizing as *La Lujuria* had been, at least it had passed uncommonly quickly for her. Apparently the damn thing normally took two to three months.

She shuddered. Two weeks of waking up only to find the first available being to fuck and drink blood from as often as possible before crashing back into sleep. Thank God, Rafael had been there to provide for her. If left to her own devices, she could have cared less who'd seen them or what they did, as long as it had included blood and sex.

If *La Lujuria* had taken months instead of weeks and she'd had to find enough blood and emotion to survive on, while not thinking any better than a newly hatched eaglet . . . No wonder so many *cachorros* went insane or died.

Now it was Friday night, almost two weeks after that dreadful Sunday, and she could form complete thoughts, enough to know Rafael was a pigheaded fool.

A fine pair they made for the world's oddest Friday night date, if you could call it that. He'd provided a long cream silk chiffon dress for her, made by a brilliant coutourier named Carolina Herrera, echoing his all-white attire. Hers had long sleeves and skirt and was almost medieval looking, with its embroidery and fine hand-sewing. She wore low-heeled, fragile sandals and delicate pearl earrings. Her hair was pulled back simply, with curls on both sides of her face.

"Dammit, Rafael, you have to let me help you tonight!" She went straight back to the same fight they'd been having all evening, ever since she found out he planned to duel Beau. They were both so angry that the *conyugal* bond no longer existed between them.

The full moon illuminated his stubborn expression. "No, I will not risk using our *conyugal* bond. You are too precious to me and must be protected at all costs."

"There's all sorts of things I can do. For one thing, you've sated me so much that I can be a reservoir of strength for you."

He cast a knowing glance at her. She blushed but went on determinedly. "I can watch your back, let you know what he's up to."

"You're too young a *cachorra*, Grania. You could lose your sanity very easily, if you're inside my head when I shapeshift."

She glared at him, clinging to her temper. "I'm also a vet. I can give you more animal shapes than you can dream of. Not just from today but from millions of years back in time! How about a T. rex or a velociraptor? Or a terror bird that ruled a continent for twenty-six million years? Or something simple like a sabre-toothed tiger?"

"I have a dozen shapes of my own. They will be enough."

The car turned off the road, rumbling over a different pavement. They were almost at the stadium.

There was so little time left for them. Tears welled up, unbidden. "Doesn't it mean anything to you that I'm Blanche reborn? I have all her memories of your children and grandchildren. We'd have a better chance of sharing them together, if you let me help you."

His hand closed over hers and his throat worked. "Grania, don't you see that's why I can't risk you? I know you're Blanche; I touched the edges of those memories during *La Lujuria*. I will do everything in my power to protect you—and that means keeping you off the dueling field, even if you'd only see it through the *conyugal* bond."

"Rafael, you're treating me just as you did her, as if I'm made of glass. But I'm not."

"I've had five hundred years to learn how to defeat Beau. Trust me—and pray for me, *mi alma*."

She sniffled and yielded. "With all my heart, Rafael."

"All will be well, Grania. You can watch from the penthouse, where Gray Wolf and Caleb will guard you."

The car slowed and stopped on a broad stone plaza. The door swung silently open, outlining Ethan and a pair of his *mesnaderos*, garbed in heavy black body armor. Ethan's hazel eyes were deadly calm, as if he was prepared for Hell.

Behind them rose a high steel grate, twice Rafael's height, glowing under streetlights. Humid air streamed in, laden with the scent of fresh-cut grass.

Grania's lips tightened before she put on her best expressionless mask. Damned if any of Madame Celeste's pals were going to see that she was scared.

Rafael handed her out of the Mercedes and wrapped his arm around her waist affectionately. Heads high, they moved rapidly across the plaza, Ethan in the lead, while his men fell in behind them. A *mesnadero* opened a narrow gate for them and Grania gaped in astonishment at the building beyond.

The immense, curving brick edifice was emblazoned SANTIAGO STADIUM, and a lion snarled defiance at all its enemies. Five arches supported its base, allowing ample room for people to pass under. Two enormously tall poles climbed toward the sky beside it, topped by platters of glimmering lights. *Vampiros* and *compañeros*, most dressed in full body armor, guarded the plaza.

The visitors wore brilliant evening clothes, fragile and gaudy, as they too hastened into the compound. They were both men and women, of all races, all adult, very fit, and mentally tough—and all *vampiros*. They were hardly the remarkably beautiful people of fiction; in fact, some were scarred or even ugly. But all of their clothing was too flimsy and minimal to hide the smallest weapon. They studied her curiously but most gave Rafael genuine smiles.

A few minutes later, Rafael and Grania entered a narrow passage, guarded by hard-faced *mesnaderos*. A luxurious elevator, complete with high-tech television screens and operated by a ferociously armed Emilio, carried them upward.

Grania moved closer to Rafael, grasping at one last chance to be near to him. He kissed her brow and she remained quiet, memorizing every detail of him.

The door opened silently on an opulent room with rows of windows spanning one wall. Light shimmered beyond the glass, while rows of massive leather chairs faced the expansive view. Tables stood ready by the chairs, ready for visitors to take notes on whatever occurred. Rows of monitors high above showed a dim view of a superb natural grass football field. On the other side, big comfortable sofas and armchairs offered conversation centers, outlined by soft lights. Beautiful murals showed warriors in battle and in camp, from the Civil War through World Wars I and II, Vietnam, to the present. A beautiful clock chimed the hour—11 p.m.

More comforting to her than those martial displays were her friends. Caleb came forward, followed by Gray Wolf, and kissed her on the cheek. "Good evening, Doña Grania."

She smiled back and returned the salute, without leaving the shelter of Rafael's arm.

"*Luz de mi corazón.*" Rafael turned to her, his dark eyes agonized in the soft lighting. The others stepped away and pretended to study the murals.

He opened his mouth but nothing came out immediately. He closed it again and swallowed.

His distress cut her to the bone. She couldn't keep fighting him. Tears sprang to her eyes and she touched her fingers to his lips. "*Te adoro*, Rafael."

"*Te adoro*, Grania." He swept her up and kissed her, crushing the breath out of her. She tightened her arms around his neck and kissed him back, giving him everything she had.

Then he set her down and strode to the elevator, Ethan at his heels. She waggled her fingers at him, the smallest of movements, her body hiding it from Caleb and Gray Wolf.

His eyes blazed and he returned it in kind, as the metal doors cut him off from her. She was left gazing at the image of a charging cavalryman.

Rafael stared at the elevator doors, as he commended Grania once again to the protection of San Rafael Arcángel. He'd have preferred to have left her at Compostela Ranch or the Austin Commandery, his strongest fortress. But he didn't have enough men to guard both the stadium and either ranch. So he'd brought her here, to the penthouse suite in this fortress called the Santiago Stadium, where Gray Wolf and Caleb would protect her.

He'd been shriven by a priest earlier, safeguarding his soul. His men would protect Texas's peace to their dying breath.

He had no more worries. The only thing left to do was fight. His old prebattle calmness swept into him as he turned his full attention to the coming duel.

"Who did you finally obtain as judges for the duel?"

Ethan turned to face him, white teeth flashing in his hard grin. "O'Malley of San Francisco, Alioto of Chicago's South Side—and Gorshkov of Trenton. Three *patrones*, one accompanied by his *cónyuge*, with ninety-five *mesnaderos* between them."

Rafael clapped him on the back. "Added to ours, it's a match for Madame Celeste's army. Plus, it's the three *patrones* least likely to ally themselves with her."

"She'd be a fool to try anything during the duel." Ethan was obviously hoping she would.

"Although Alioto and Gorshkov could change sides."

"Not while you live," Ethan said flatly. "So there's nothing to worry about."

The elevator came to a stop before Rafael could find an answer to that.

Grania wrapped her arms around her knees, rocking the big leather armchair, and tried not to think about the odds against Rafael. She wished there was some way she could sneak some help through the *conyugal* bond to him. But she just didn't know enough about how the damned thing worked to do anything with it.

She was at the top of a five-story tower, in the penthouse suite. The grandstands below were full of gaudily dressed people. Close to the field, an excellent mariachi band was playing bullfight music.

"Place is almost full," Caleb observed from behind Grania.

"*Vampiros* have come from all over North America, as well as Europe. It's not often you see two *vampiros mayores* fight a duel." Gray Wolf thumped Caleb's shoulder. "It'll be different from any duel we've fought. In our case, we've got the advantage that it doesn't matter how old *cónyuges* are, as long as one is a mature *vampiro*. The *conyugal* bond usually makes them a match for anyone, even a *vampiro mayor*."

"Seen that work for us before," Caleb admitted.

Ethan's *mesnaderos* ringed the track oval, dressed in black, all carrying carbines and looking fierce. A few cars and trucks were hidden in the darkness at the short ends of the oval. The moon shimmered on the hills but there were no signs of people living anywhere nearby.

The clock began to chime midnight—one . . .

Instantly, with the roar and hiss of great power unleashed, the massive lights above Santiago Stadium came to life, turning night into day on the football field below. Friday night lights in Texas.

A moment later, trumpets sounded, calling across the field and echoing back from the hills beyond, their martial cry underlain by drums. They sang an ancient music that rang in the blood, a song that a gladiator or a bullfighter would have understood.

Gray Wolf and Caleb immediately came to frozen attention, on either side of Grania. The crowd quickly rose to their feet on both sides of the field.

Grania sprang up and slammed the two great, sliding glass doors open, desperate to see as much as she could. Every monitor showed the same image: Ethan, his expression deadly calm and carrying a rifle, marched onto the field and took up position on the center of the fifty-yard line. A tall, broad-shouldered *mesnadero*, his face hidden by his helmet, strode beside him, ready to use an even bigger rifle.

A single trumpet sounded, as soon as Ethan and his second were established, summoning the challenger to do battle.

Rafael entered the field from the tunnel, his right arm raised in salute to the crowd. The crowd under the great lion, so like the Castilian banner he'd once fought under, roared its approval.

He wore white linen from head to toe, beautifully embroidered and tailored. An impressive outfit, it was also an easy one to shift out of to start a duel. He was, of course, barefoot, for the same reason. The ultimate insult, one rarely achieved, would be to kill one's opponent while dressed as a human.

"Who are you?" Ethan demanded as soon as Rafael came close, the traditional challenge given by a duel's marshal. The words echoed around the stadium, borne by the public address system.

"I am Don Rafael Perez of Texas, who comes here to fight Beau of New Orleans, a sniveling coward." He bowed formally to Ethan and retired to the forty-yard line.

A very long five minutes later—six minutes and the challenged would forfeit the duel—a single trumpet sounded a flourish. Beau appeared on the opposite side of the field, with Madame Celeste hanging on his arm and Devol following close behind.

Beau wore a brilliantly colored silk shirt and trousers, the latest resort wear from Europe and a startling contrast to Madame Celeste's black leather bustier and trousers, topped by her gaudy ruby and diamond jewelry. He appeared perfectly healthy, of course, as the reports from New Orleans had told. They'd also spoken of unease and fear over the strange killings, as the *prosaicos* began to band together and whisper about *vampiros*.

When the deadly trio reached the fifty-yard line, they paused to exchange a passionate embrace. Rafael wondered if Madame Celeste truly cared for the *pendejo*—or was she simply reminding him what side his bread was buttered on?

Then she broke free and ascended the stands on Devol's arm, her head high, and accepted a cushioned seat.

Beau stood erect on the sidelines until he'd regained the throng's full attention. Holding his chin a little higher and with a pleased curve to his mouth, he marched onto the field as the trumpet sang again.

Upon hearing the marshal's challenge, he reared up in aristocratic hauteur, as if he ruled everyone and everything in sight. "I am Beau of New Orleans, who comes here to destroy my *creador*'s murderer."

Madame Celeste's coterie screamed approval. The other side yawned. Anyone called a coward usually came up with the most blood-curdling countercharge possible, whether or not it was true. Usually it wasn't.

Beau's mouth tightened slightly before he bowed to Madame Celeste and retired to the opposite forty-yard line. He flexed slightly, eyeing the setting and his opponent, then assumed the supple posture of the ready duelist.

Their eyes met across twenty yards of living grass.

Breathe the night air for the last time, yaa ibn sharmuuTa, Beau snarled. *You murdered my beloved father and for that you will die.*

Rafael curled his lip. *You will die before you touch Grania or Texas,* apóstata.

A low rumble sounded in Beau's throat, his eyes promising slow death.

Jean-Marie's clear tenor rang out through the loudspeakers. "All present are reminded that no one, for any reason whatsoever, may enter the field of combat, upon pain of death. Should anyone cross the center of the track surrounding the field and survive, the marshal shall exact the appropriate penalties, after conferring with the judges."

Ethan and his second took their seats in the grandstand, centered under the great lion. Rafael spared a quick glance at the top of the tower where Grania waited. Safe, *plegue a Dios*, although he couldn't see her.

"As is customary," Jean-Marie continued imperturbably, "the duel will continue until one *vampiro* dies or a half hour before sunrise. Should both *vampiros* still be alive at that time, the duel will be considered a draw and will begin again an hour after sunset, on the same day."

It was hardly likely that he and Beau would both be alive at dawn. No *vampiro* duel had ever lasted six and a half hours. One, yes. Three, in the last known duel between *vampiros mayores*. More to the point,

Rafael should have enough energy for three or four different shapes, assuming long bouts in each form.

He crossed himself and waited, ready to do battle.

"When the gong sounds, the duel will begin. Are you ready, combatants?"

Rafael raised his hand, never taking his eyes off Beau. He gathered his will, holding his first shape clearly in his mind.

His enemy also lifted his hand, hatred hot and bright in his glance.

The gong rang, shaking the heavy air. Rafael sprang, his body's molecules reshaping themselves as soon as they escaped his clothes. The cloth fell to the grass, immediately forgotten.

His face lengthened as his teeth grew. Cinnamon fur appeared, tipped with silver. His hands gained weight and deadly claws. He gained mass from the moisture in the air. A hump grew above his shoulders, to add power to his strikes.

Rafael, the grizzly bear, roared as he charged his enemy, the gray wolf.

High above the field, grizzly and wolf raced at each other in monitor after monitor. Grania tensed and crossed herself.

Beau leaped, jaws opening to bite, great teeth eager to rend flesh.

Rafael's heavy right front paw slammed into him. Six-inch claws sliced down Beau's shoulder and flank, knocking the wolf aside.

Gray Wolf . . . Caleb whispered.

What is it? His *cónyuge* glared at him for breaking his concentration. *I'm supposed to watch Don Rafael. You're supposed to watch Doña Grania.*

Caleb jerked his head toward Don Rafael's lady.

Gray Wolf shot an impatient glance sideways and his jaw dropped.

Eyes fixed on the field below, Grania's right hand slammed her wineglass over—using exactly the same arc, at exactly the same speed, at exactly the same time Don Rafael ripped into Beau's shoulder. Her silk-clad arm had perfectly matched the furred paw shown, again and again, on the monitors above. Champagne dripped unheeded to the carpet.

Their eyes met above her head.

"*Cónyuge?*" Caleb mouthed.

Gray Wolf shrugged. "Don't know," he answered, equally silent. "*He* never said. But he gets close-mouthed, when he's being protective."

But his assessment of Grania this time was speculative.

Blood spurted, fur shredded. White bone gleamed as the wolf rolled, howling. A dark patch blossomed under him on the green grass.

The crowd under the tower roared its approval.

The grizzly circled, looking for his next strike.

Grania's breathing steadied, matching Rafael's.

A grizzly had been a good starting shape for her lover: fast, smart, tough, a good fighter, and unexpected to a European. But Beau would never let Rafael retain such an advantage.

What else could be useful? Leopard, the predator who'd conquered every land ecosystem? Hyena, who held their own against lions, after all, no matter how ignoble their reputation? Wolverine, the vicious little bear who made far larger predators back down?

Or an older shape? Velociraptor, smart and fast with knife-edged claws? Or a terror bird, nine feet tall and fast as a horse, whose cruel beak had ruled South America for twenty-six million years? Or *Smilodon fatalis*, that legendary ambush predator, otherwise known as a sabre-toothed tiger?

*   *   *

Beau shifted into a goshawk, Persia's beloved King Hawk, and launched himself into the sky.

Rafael immediately shifted into a peregrine and went after him, beating his wings rapidly as he fought for altitude. *Mierda*, where had Beau learned such a large, excellent fighting bird? Defeating him would not be easy.

The sluggishness of the second shape change told on him, but he grimly ignored it. Beau had to be worse off, especially since he'd needed to heal his wound when he shifted.

Still, going to this much smaller form was worrisome. The penalty paid for blood loss was proportionate to the overall size of the shape. Lose half of your blood in any form and it didn't matter if you'd lost a thimbleful or a gallon; you were still in trouble. And trouble meant that a much larger shape, such as a grizzly, would be beyond his power to control if he wanted to fight for any length of time.

He finally reached the level of the light standards, a welcome thermal lifting him higher as he watched for his enemy.

A dark shape caught the corner of his eye, diving on him from the other side—Beau.

Rafael shrieked defiance as he tried to dodge and gain more room to fight. But Beau anticipated his move, as he'd learned to do in all those bouts, for so many years, at The Syrian's fortress.

The heavier bird struck Rafael, talons piercing his back. He skidded sideways, knocking the talons loose. His back muscles screamed in pain.

They fell out of the sky tangled together, wings thrashing, beaks and talons stabbing and slashing at each other's head and chest and back. Screaming at each other when they could.

Grania's shoulders twisted, her elbows bent. Sometimes she punched the air, sometimes her head came back in a silent cry. She watched the monitors desperately, working hard to see Rafael in the swirling feathers.

Words sifted into her ears.

"Relax and be with him completely. Focus on what he feels. The flex of his muscles," Caleb whispered. "The air beneath him."

"The taste of his enemy's blood," Gray Wolf added. "Salty. Satisfying."

Her mouth worked. Blood? It was almost on the tip of her tongue.

The two birds landed on the ground together, bounced, and sprang apart. Rafael and Beau paced the grass, settling their feathers, glaring at each other as they took stock of their wounds.

Rafael flexed his back and cursed when he realized he couldn't move his shoulders well. His right wing was growing numb.

The crowd's roar was a distant buzz, while Ethan's *mesnaderos* seemed little more than fence posts as they faced down Madame Celeste's troops. For the honor of Texas, they would not intervene in the duel itself.

He'd lost too much blood in that round. He could change shape once more and fight. But twice?

If only he could see Grania face to face. He'd thought he'd felt her once through the *conyugal* bond during that wild fight in the sky. Surely that was a fantasy, occasioned by her being a student of the fighting birds.

Beau shifted. A gray wolf again?

¡Mierda, *he couldn't become a grizzly again!*

Rafael shifted into a puma. Roughly the same size, weight, and quality of fighter as the gray wolf.

They circled each other, looking for an opening. Both were limping, Rafael definitely more so. He breathed deep, fighting to pull air back into his lungs. He hadn't been able to heal all of the injuries suffered as a peregrine.

You will be dead within the hour and my beloved father will finally be avenged, Beau snarled.

Save your breath for your death rattle, Rafael snapped back.

They circled again, the requisite insults out of the way. Suddenly Beau charged, Rafael wheeled, and raked his claws across the other's nose. They tumbled across the field, spitting and clawing, tearing the other apart.

Beau bit Rafael's shoulder. Agony flared in the half-healed wound. He struck out and slashed into Beau's front leg.

Clumps of grass, clods of dirt, and streaks of crimson marked their path.

Up above, Grania brought the binoculars Caleb handed her into sharp focus, a skill she'd learned so long ago that it was pure reflex. Cougar and wolf sprang into sight, crystal clear against the white line markers.

They bit and clawed at each other. She flinched when the wolf's teeth sank into Rafael's flank, ripping the great muscles. Agonizing pain flooded her body. Instinctively, she willed strength into him, even as she clapped her hand over her own thigh.

She saw an opening in the wolf's guard, created by his attack on Rafael. She fought to tell Rafael, strained so hard she half stood up.

"Easy there, easy," Gray Wolf murmured, so soft it was like a gentle river. "He's focused on the duel, not on listening to you. He can only hear his *cónyuge* when he relaxes."

"He could die!"

"I know."

Rafael attacked a different place than the one she'd seen—and the wolf twisted himself into an impossible curve, bit Rafael's hind leg, and sprang away.

Beau barked triumphantly, as Madame Celeste and her minions screamed their approval.

Dammit, that bastard should be smacked down by something

bigger and furrier than himself, with even larger teeth to rip out his throat. If he thought he was hot stuff now, she'd like to see him take on some of Mother Nature's better efforts from the past!

Grania clenched her hands, her nails drawing blood from her palms. *Rafael, darling, I am with you.*

Rafael licked his teeth clean, dragging his hind leg as he paced. He blinked hard to clear his right eye but it was still filmed with blood from that fight in the sky. His breath wheezed in and out, as he considered his next move.

He faced the truth reluctantly. Five hundred years of dueling had taught him damned little about how to defeat Beau. The *pendejo* still knew exactly what move Rafael would do next. It was, after all, still very much like fighting his fencing master.

He might have one more shift left in him, if he was lucky—and if he lasted that long.

Beau jumped at him again, snapping at his leg. *Dammit, he just wants to exhaust me.*

Rafael gauged the attack carefully, more by smell than sight, and lashed out with his claws when Beau was very close. *Gracias a Dios*, puma reflexes were good, good enough to make Beau back off a little.

He panted, every breath burning through his throat, as he circled to keep Beau in sight. Where would the *pendejo* attack next? How long could he keep fighting him off?

Grania barely breathed as she watched. The damp grass seemed to prickle then give under her feet, as if she was pacing on the football field rather than standing in a tower. Every bone in her body ached, while her muscles burned more than when she'd finished a marathon. If she'd tried to run, her leg would have given out under her. And every square inch of her skin felt as if blood was running out of it.

Beau charged, Rafael answered as he had before. But this time,

Beau blocked Rafael's move—and tore a chunk out of his neck. Blood spurted across the grass.

Agony screamed through Grania's neck. Instinctively, she clapped a hand to her throat.

Rafael staggered, shaking his head, clearly unable to effectively counterattack.

Beau danced back and forth, barking insults. He came within a yard of his enemy.

Rafael wavered then sank down as his bad leg collapsed under him. A half-dead cougar was no match for a nearly functional *vampiro*.

Blackness swept across Grania's eyes, as her heart went out to him. Her own leg ached and wavered.

Beau shifted back into a man and turned to the New Orleans crowd, raising his arms triumphantly. They shouted happily, while the home team sat in stunned silence.

Grania's throat was tight, her body cut from within by needles of ice. *Rafael, Rafael!*

Then she could hear him inside her head, his voice a weak thread. *Grania,* mi corazón, *forgive me for not listening to your wisdom. Please help me and give me your strength.*

Rafael, my life and my love, I would do anything for you. She relaxed utterly, remembering her love, softening her breathing until she lived only through him.

Then she could feel him throughout her, slowly at first like water flowing into a new home until it became complete. His skin, battered and bleeding. His broken bones. His heart, beating through her veins. His thoughts, of regret and loss, for losing her. His love, faithful for all time.

His voice was the merest whisper. *Grania,* mi alma y mi vida, te adoro.

Instinctively, she worked to heal him. She gave him everything she had, taken from the rich stores he'd gifted her with. She considered his wounds with a vet's eyes and poured healing energy into them. Strength flooded back into him. His heart began to beat strongly again, as his wounds stopped bleeding. His broken bones healed and every leg longed to run again.

Rafael's mind began to work with its old speed and ruthlessness. He danced through her mind and found the image she'd been harboring, of the ancient California cat.

Ah, Grania, what a gift you are to a warrior, he purred, recognizing its potential immediately. He shifted immediately into a sabre-toothed tiger with a grunt of satisfaction.

Grania's mouth quirked. Her knight had come back to life.

Down on the field, Rafael planted all four very healthy paws on the grass and bugled his challenge to the skies. It was a deep and throaty roar, the like of which had not echoed through these hills for thousands of years.

Shocked, the crowd fell silent and Beau spun around.

Rafael charged across the football field at his enemy. Grania came to her feet, screaming, her limbs throbbing as they too pushed him forward.

Devol pulled a gun—and *mesnaderos* immediately leveled their rifles at him.

Beau blanched and threw up his hands.

Rafael leaped—and pinned his enemy to the ground with twice a lion's weight.

Beau stared up at Rafael, doom written across his face.

Rafael's long sabre teeth ripped out his throat, decapitating his ancient adversary.

The lifeless body collapsed into the grass, slowly turning into ash. Beau's head rolled away, blue eyes wide and staring, before it collapsed into a heap. Its white dust settled on a hash mark, looking like little more than smudges left over from a particularly hard-fought first down.

Rafael came to his feet as a man, swaying slightly. His people and friends roared approval, as the trumpets sang in triumph.

Grania ran for the elevator. Gray Wolf and Caleb crowded into it with her. A grinning Emilio took them down, as quickly as he could, fast as falcons diving on their prey.

They burst out from under the grandstands and onto the track. Grania lengthened her stride, racing toward the football field and Rafael, caring nothing for the helmeted *mesnaderos* with their automatic rifles. Gray Wolf shouted something beside her but it was drowned out by the crowd, chanting and stomping rhythmically on the bleachers, "Texas, Texas!"

Just before she reached them, the *mesnaderos* stepped sideways, opening a path for her as smoothly as any guard at Buckingham Palace. She hurtled past, her red hair and white silk skirts floating behind her as she ran, intent only on reaching her man. Hers at last, with the past shadows vanquished.

Rafael turned to face her, as he finished tugging his shirt down. He was pale under his golden skin but he was standing. She flung herself into his arms and they clung together, hearts and minds united.

A shadow touched them and they stirred, looking for the source. Jean-Marie and Ethan stood beside them, watching the New Orleans visitors sullenly depart.

Madame Celeste shook her fist at them, her eyes malevolent before she passed from sight. Jean-Marie stirred angrily. "That female needs to either learn the limits of her power or die."

Grania glanced at him, surprised at such harshness from someone she'd only seen as smooth-tongued.

"Devol just wants killing," Ethan drawled. "Like a rattler."

"But like a rattler, *mi hijo*, he can kill," Rafael said gently.

Grania sighed to herself. They were already planning for the next round of fighting. It was undoubtedly necessary but didn't anybody ever give Rafael a few minutes away from all that responsibility?

Much of the way back to the ranch in the car, Rafael was on the phone planning for the next phase of the war. One man after another called him about a different desperate question. At least they'd fed him—and he'd fed her—before they'd started back.

Grania muttered to herself and laid her head against his shoulder, totally ignoring any traffic laws encouraging the use of seat belts in the backseat. Rafael wrapped his arm around her and cuddled her, which at least allowed him to relax a little.

At Compostela, the *prosaicos* and *compañeros* lined the driveway, cheering, "Texas, Texas!"

Grania smiled and nodded and waved, wishing that some of her less charitable fellow orphans could have been there to see her. But she'd have traded the big house and the ranch any day just to have Rafael next to her.

He swept her up into his arms and carried her over the threshold. Thrilled, she wrapped her arm around his neck and kissed him tenderly.

Her eyes widened when he didn't put her down immediately. Instead, he carried her all the way down the hall to his bedchamber.

He set her down near the bed, letting her glide down over his body. Grania shivered, enjoying every contrast in shape and texture between them, which gave her an idea. She stroked his dear face tenderly. "Your color is so good. Did they feed you in the locker room?"

He kissed her fingers and began to play with them. "You know they did, *querida*."

"I'm trying to learn how to give you privacy," Grania defended herself. "Aren't there times when I shouldn't read you through the *conyugal* bond? I know there are times when I don't want you to know what I'm doing." She choked, as a particularly strong tingle ran up to her throat.

He raised an eyebrow, still nibbling gently on her hand. "Such as when?"

"Christmas shopping," she suggested, a bit desperately, closing her eyes against a toe-curling surge of pleasure. "Planning your birthday."

He folded her filmy sleeve back and started to work his way up the inside of her wrist.

"*Por favor,* continue, *mi corazón*. You have my fullest attention."

She sighed as her knees weakened but forced them to stiffen. "Can you orgasm without ejaculating?"

His dark eyes flashed up at her. "Certainly, *querida*. Why?"

She'd caught his attention. "How many times can you do so before you must ejaculate?"

He hesitated. "Grania, *mi vida* . . ."

"You see, you do not want me reading you through the bond right now!" she declared triumphantly.

He drew himself erect, every inch the haughty *grandee*. "I can orgasm more than once, *querida*, without ejaculating."

"Exactly how many times? *Siete?*"

His jaw dropped. "Seven times? Are you trying to torture me?"

She grinned, very pleased with herself. "Can you think of a better way?"

He shook his head. "Not at all, *luz de mi corazón.*"

"If I fail," she added, "you must torture me."

"Grania, I would never—never!—do—"

"In your dungeon in the basement. You know, the place with all the toys, like the feathers, the dildos, the vibrators . . ."

He caught her up and kissed her, a salute she returned with enthusiasm.

"You are a marvel, *mi vida*," he murmured against her cheek.

"As are you, darling. But you're the one who's dressed."

He moved away and peeled his shirt over his head. Grania slid her hand up his chest, exploring the springiness and prickles of his chest. She caught the nubs of his nipples between two of her fingers and stopped. "Nice."

He froze. Through the *conyugal* bond, she felt him shudder down to his bones.

She very delicately squeezed her fingers together around his nipples. The jolt that ran through him made both of them gasp.

"Yummy," she breathed. She leaned forward and pressed an openmouthed kiss to the top of his chest, just below his collarbone. Slowly, very slowly, she began to kiss him with lips and tongue and teeth, along the great sweep of muscle. His chest ached but so did hers. Her breath rasped in her throat at his taste.

"*Por Dios*, Grania, have mercy!" His voice was ragged.

"Mmmmm." Her answer was muffled as she moved to his other nipple. "Trousers?" she reminded, more intelligibly.

He somehow managed to remove them without losing a button.

"Good man." She dragged her teeth very gently over his nipple, quivered as his gasp reverberated through her lungs, and repeated the gesture.

He sucked in his breath, then began to strip the pins out of her hair with ferocious speed. An instant later, he combed it out with his fingers, spread it over her shoulders, and caressed her head. His strong fingers felt like heaven as they kneaded her scalp. She purred, nuzzling him. It seemed the easiest thing to do to open her mouth further and draw him in with deep, hard pulls.

He groaned, shuddering, and rose up on his toes against her. She moaned, locked her arms around his waist to pull him in, and dropped her hand to his cock. She caressed it with long, slow pulls, fondling the fat mushroom cap and the thick shaft that had brought her so much pleasure. Her hands slid lower and cupped his balls. Every move of her hands was gentle and slow, a steady show of appreciation, while her mouth worked his chest and he crooned his encouragement in soft Spanish.

Her pussy heated approvingly and her clit pulsed. Her breasts throbbed with every pull of her lips on his chest.

He growled softly—and orgasm rippled through him, traveling upwards from his hips. He groaned again but didn't ejaculate, both of them savoring the waves of pleasure washing through his body like a gentle tide.

The same gentle tide caught Grania into an orgasm. She laid her head against him, moaning, and enjoyed herself.

Rafael panted softly until he caught his breath. He rested his cheek on her soft hair, triumph running through his veins at her soft warmth against his heart. His at last, in his arms forever, sharing their every breath.

"Grania, *mi vida*, did you seduce me deliberately?"

She didn't move. "Whazzat?"

He chuckled softly. ¡*Ay de mi*, how her curls tickled his arm as easily as they fell down her back! He slid his hand into the silken strands and played with them. He needed to be strong for both of them. She was such a young *cachorra* that she'd be sure to follow his lead.

She snorted. *Do you really think so?*

I thought you were trying to stay out of my mind, he observed mildly.

Oh, that's right. Sorry.

She snuggled closer. His arms tightened around her and their breathing matched again.

If she fed from him again, it would increase his emotion, of course. He'd very nearly lost control in the penthouse when she'd drunk from him so hard and so long after the duel. It was a miracle he hadn't told Ethan they'd stay there for another day while he rode her.

She kissed his shoulder and wrapped her arms around his waist.

He really shouldn't make love to her again. She was a very young *cachorra* and must be desperate for a long sleep, at least fifteen hours. Maybe eighteen or twenty, given last night's exertions.

Grania began to gently rub the small of his back.

He personally needed only two or three hours of sleep. He'd have plenty of time to talk to his men and make plans.

She stroked his ass.

¡*Ay, mierda*, they could wait a little longer to rest!

"Grania, *mi alma*." He kissed her, teasing her mouth with promises of more until she was moaning and twisting impatiently against him. He dropped little kisses along her jaw and down her throat. She trembled, arching her neck and silently begging for more.

He bunched her fragile, exquisite silk skirts up in his hands, stroking her legs and hips. She moved closer still, pressing herself against him. She arched her head back for another kiss and he pulled her dress over her head, then smoothly kissed further down her throat.

She moaned, pressing his head closer. Her fingers sank into his hair, tousling it and kneading his scalp. Spine-tingling delight leapt down to his toes. He groaned her name and nuzzled her breast.

She sobbed, pulling him closer, as he enjoyed her breasts. They were so perfectly formed for his mouth, with their rosy buds that furled so quickly under his tongue, and the blue veins for him to trace, while she shivered. His pulse raced, as his mouth dried. His balls grew heavier and fatter.

¡*Por Dios* but he needed her to drink from him!

He lifted her up in two strong, callused hands, braced her against the wall, and ripped her thong off.

He paused, fighting to slow down. He could not simply take her like a rutting beast. Surely they had time for some pretty words, a few kisses, some long caresses . . .

Grania ran her finger down his spine. His breath stopped. His cock throbbed wildly against her soft belly.

Her blue eyes opened, blazing with lust. She slid one leg over his hip, opening herself to him. His balls tucked themselves up tightly against his cock, desperate for release.

He gritted his teeth. Slowly, making the most of every moment, he slid into her. She groaned with pleasure, fluttering her sheath around him. Sanity fled and he howled, hot, wet delight bouncing back and forth between them through the *conyugal* bond. Cock deep in pussy, pussy kissing cock. Even their breath was in harmony when he began to move.

Rafael growled in pleasure, unable to say where either of their bodies started or stopped, only that all was ecstasy. She fitted him perfectly as she always had but now there was no fear of harming her. He was free to enjoy her without holding back, without keeping part of himself aside to keep watch lest he hurt her.

He roared in delight when he felt her womb grip his cock, then change shape as he stroked in and out of her. When her strong internal muscles gripped his cock and she sobbed her encouragement, he chanted in Galician as he hadn't done since he was a teenager. Nothing existed but the ecstasy passing back and forth between them, as the pulses built higher and higher in their blood and bones.

He slammed her again and again against the wall, their bodies locked together as they strained together for climax. It came closer and closer, the pulses faster and stronger, until Rafael sliced his jugular, growling.

Instantly, Grania bit down hard and drank.

He threw back his head and howled like a wolf as orgasm racked him to the bone. He shot jet after jet of come into her, as she simultaneously gulped his blood.

Linked at three physical points and through the *conyugal* bond, they were entirely one, so perfectly united the world beyond ceased to exist.

She roused when he slipped into bed with her afterward, snuggling against her back and wrapping his arms around her. "Any more councils of war tonight? Or should I say today?"

"No, *querida*, not today. Jean-Marie has returned to New Orleans and everything here is quiet." For now.

Grania kissed his hand, in unspoken acknowledgment of his worry. She summoned a question from her long list, trying to stay awake with him. Being a *cachorra* and having to hibernate fifteen hours a day was hell, when you had a lover like him. "Why did you change your name to Rafael? Is it because I prayed to San Rafael Arcángel for you?"

He began to tuck the sheet around them. "Will you ever run out of questions, *mi corazón*?" His voice held only amused acceptance.

"No, never," she answered simply, hiding a jaw-breaking yawn. "And how did you wind up in Texas?"

"Those stories, *querida*, will have to be told another day. You, like all *cachorros*, need your sleep."

He kissed her hair. *Amarte para siempre, no sería suficiente*, he added, a catch in his voice.

Even forever doesn't seem long enough, she agreed, nestling closer. *But we have it now*, Dios mediante.

ACKNOWLEDGMENTS

"During 2005, the Wildlife Center of Virginia admitted 2,369 animals for treatment—injured, ailing, and orphaned wildlife from all across Virginia. As expected, the 2005 total included many common species—Eastern Cottontail rabbits, Virginia opossums, and Eastern Gray squirrels—but also admitted for treatment were a number of threatened species or species of special concern, including twenty bald eagles, eleven barn owls, a peregrine falcon, and two long-eared owls.

"In April 2006, the Wildlife Center admitted its 45 thousandth patient—an orphaned Virginia opossum."

They also warmly and patiently answered endless questions from at least this author.

Thank you.

The Wildlife Center of Virginia
P.O. Box 1557
Waynesboro, VA 22980
(540) 942–9453
www.wildlifecenter.org

Jean-Marie's story will be told in

Bond of Fire

coming Fall 2007 from Berkley Sensation

Hélène d'Agelet strolled into the private club in Mayfair just after sunset, very pleased with her new Stella McCartney outfit. Its crisp jauntiness, from the ridiculous hat to the miniscule purse and the high-heeled shoes, had proven to be exactly what she needed to take her mind off yet another rainy English day. After two centuries of living on this island (except for duties overseas during wars), she'd once expected to grow accustomed to the weather, but that had never come to pass.

She'd originally diverted herself from the weather by trying to outspend her pension from the British *vampiros* on clothes. She hadn't succeeded. In fact, she'd become so irritated at the stodgy Britons for continuing to fund her extravagance that she'd learned to make a great deal of money. But she still enjoyed fashion more than anything else in Great Britain, except their men. And none of those had kept her attention for more than a few months. Oaths kept her here, bonds of duty, not affection.

In the main clubroom, a centuries-old hymn to carved wood, old books, and leather chairs, a dozen *vampiros* were gathered around a table, talking excitedly and peering over something with what looked like a magnifying glass, or perhaps a jeweler's loupe.

"Good evening, gentlemen," she said sweetly.

A glass crashed to the floor. A tall decanter swayed wildly, its golden contents tumbling like an earthquake's barometer. *Vampiros* tried to pretend they'd been behaving like adults, not schoolchildren caught by their teacher. Their leader rose to face Hélène.

"Madame d'Agelet." Lord Simon, the current West End *patrón*, bowed profoundly and gracefully, as befitted a duke's son and former colonel. He glanced back at his men, raising a supercilious brow. They rushed to stand up, looking more like abashed schoolboys than deadly *mesnaderos*. Chairs pushed back rapidly. One fell over.

He lifted her hand and kissed it. "Hélène."

The white scar slashing his cheek, courtesy of a Prussian general in the dying days of World War I, puckered as he smiled at her. She'd heard the Prussian general hadn't lived long enough after the meeting to count his scars.

"*Mon cher* Simon." She smiled back at him, letting her genuine affection show.

"You look remarkably beautiful tonight. Stella McCartney, I would hazard a guess?"

Senses trained by two centuries in the deadliest profession came fully alert. Why the devil had Lord Simon, who had no fashion sense, tried to butter her up by mentioning her couturier?

She nodded confirmation, tossing her head so the silly hat's finer points could be seen.

"Please, join us for a cognac. Delamain Très Venerable, *s'il tu veux?*"

A polite invitation and she'd bet a million pounds he was hoping she wouldn't accept it.

One of the men—a fit-looking fellow, probably one of Lord Simon's SAS recruits—tried to slide the paper off the table and into a leather portfolio.

Hélène promptly lit the ornamental candelabra at his elbow. He froze, obviously aware that she could have torched him as easily—or the entire house.

"Sounds good," she answered. She enjoyed using Americanisms, just to remind the British she wasn't one of theirs. "Can I have the loupe too?" She held out her hand and smiled sweetly at Lord Simon.

His eyes narrowed slightly before he gave a resigned shrug and nodded at his underling. He was eighty years old, the oldest of London's current set of *patrones*, while most of his men were the typical ten- to thirty-year-old *vampiros*. He had a good, tough set of *mesnaderos* that no other *patrón* sought a fight with, even if none of his men could stand up to her.

They'd worked together briefly in Occupied France and she still remembered his delight in the more outlandish masquerade costumes. She'd been a firestarter on his team of saboteurs, since she could kill any *vampiro* before a duel started or a weapon was fired.

But he'd known her long enough to be certain that she wouldn't fly off the handle. So why was he afraid?

She examined the photo carefully under the light, setting aside her eternal French bemusement at using Spanish terminology. After all, they had lived with Arabs for centuries on that peninsula and translated the great Arab encyclopedias and travelogues, thus creating the vocabulary that all *vampiros* now used.

The photo's creator had shot from an elevated vantage point at an awkward angle, making the print less than straightforward. Still, some things could be gleaned. Late 1920s America, somewhere that understood high fashion—New Orleans, perhaps? A festive street scene, probably Mardi Gras, given the masks and costumes. Most of the faces in the crowd were turned away from the camera or out of focus, making them unreadable.

She moved the lens methodically over the print, as she'd been taught. Somebody swallowed hard behind her and was admonished with an elbow.

A face sprang out at her. She froze, her hand clenching on the loupe until her knuckles turned white. A woman, the image of her mother.

Impossible! Maman had died during the Reign of Terror, while her little sister, the image of *Maman*, had been killed by French spies. If *la petite* was actually alive, how much of that time had been truth or lies? How many of those deaths had truly been necessary?

Lord Simon set a snifter down beside her. She gulped the fine cognac with scant regard for its quality or high cost. *Nom de Dieu,* if *la petite* was alive, answers must be demanded.

She shifted the loupe slightly to give herself time to think. A man's face appeared beside her sister. Jean-Marie St. Just? She almost knocked the loupe off the table before she could control herself.

Her mouth tightened when a second man came into focus. Don Rodrigo Perez, Jean-Marie's *beau-frère*. A most polite and intimidating fellow when she'd met him at Versailles two centuries ago. In this picture, he was alert and menacing, as if ready to kill the unseen photographer.

She tapped the photo and stared at Lord Simon. "Who is the woman?"

A muscle ticked in his jaw. "Madame Celeste, now the *patrona* of New Orleans, who holds most of the southeastern United States."

Hélène gaped. *La petite* was a *vampira patrona*? Why on earth would she do that? She'd always preferred to work through the men she slept with.

And living in New Orleans? Probably to avoid her older sister. A righteous anger curled in Hélène's gut, as she considered all the deaths she had to ask her sister about. Other questions first, though.

"And the two men?"

"One is Jean-Marie St. Just, the *heraldo* of Texas, who I've met before. I assume that the other is Don Rafael Perez, the *patrón* of Texas."

Well, now, what were they most afraid of—Don Rafael's reaction or her own? Proof of *vampiro* immortality could spark a *prosaico* outcry and lead to a mob, the one thing all *vampiros* feared. Possessing a picture of a *vampiro* was therefore very unhealthy. But a photo of two *patrones*, especially when one of them was a *vampiro mayor* and notoriously thorough about protecting himself? Even one of London's *patrones* could fear for his life under those circumstances.

As for her own reaction, it was entirely possible that Whitehall had warned the *patrones* to keep her from learning *la petite* was alive, lest she ignore her oaths to Britain. Rage stirred deep within.

She raised her eyes to Lord Simon. "How long have they known?"

"Two years. I warned them you'd be furious."

She smiled wryly, caught despite herself by an old friend's understanding. "Bastards. They should have told me immediately."

"They were probably afraid of your reaction."

"Or Don Rafael's."

"Agreed. All of these lads have come up against his Santiago Trust before and have the bruises to show for it."

A thought flashed through her head.

"Whitehall doesn't want me to leave, do they?"

He shrugged.

"But I'll just bet they don't want Don Rafael to know about this picture either—or that they've been hiding it from him for two years."

Gasps ran around the room. Someone muttered a soft, vicious curse.

A gleam of appreciation for the situation's irony lit Lord Simon's eyes. "Do you plan to ring him up?"

"No, I'll take it to him, since he obviously knew it was being taken," Hélène announced briskly. "He's known for his courtesy to women so I can do it in safety, which none of you can. I can tell him it recently came into your hands through a rare prints dealer, offered solely because of your interest in pictures of Mardi Gras celebrations."

Lord Simon started to chuckle. "Whitehall will hate it but I don't see they have any other choice."

They smiled at each other in perfect understanding.

Hélène began to tuck the photo briskly into the folio. "I'd better be going now, so I can leave for Texas as soon as possible."

"Would you care for some company on the drive home?" Lord Simon offered graciously. "I'm sure one, or more, of the lads would be glad to give you an excellent time."

The lads froze, like Cornish game hens in a butcher's window.

Hélène scrutinized them thoughtfully. Lord Simon really did have a fine lot, mostly ex-military, on the whole much stronger and more mature than her usual selection of Oxford college students. They'd all provide an excellent meal. It was even possible one or two could string a sentence together.

Somebody choked. Several others turned pale as they watched her, as if they expected to be barbecued at any moment.

But she greatly disliked taking the unwilling.

"Thank you, but I've already fed. Perhaps when I return." She kissed him on the cheek and went out, humming a childhood tune, "The World Turned Upside Down."

GLOSSARY

The Texas Vampire universe is founded on a science-based theory, which was vetted with top animal metabolism and behavioral experts. Every attempt has been made to stay consistent with that theory.

Terminology used in the Texas Vampire universe is taken whenever possible from medieval Spanish, supplemented by modern Spanish. The only exception is that *patrones* are given an honorific appropriate to their *esfera*'s ethnicity, e.g., don in Texas, madame in New Orleans, lord in England, etc.

Adelantado mayor. Governor. The head of an *esfera*'s civilian hierarchy.
Adoro. Adore, as in "te adoro." (The statement, using the second person, informal form of address.)
Alferez mayor. al-FEH-reth. Military commander-in-chief, overseeing all warriors in an *esfera*.
Alma. Soul.
Amante. Lover.

Amigo/Amigos. Friend.

Amor. Love. (Spanish)

Amour. Love. (French)

Arcángel. Archangel.

Bandolerismo. Banditry. *Vampiros* owing allegiance to no *patron* and living outside the *esfera*'s laws.

Bel/belle. Beautiful. (French)

Bête. Beast. (French)

Bien. Good. (French and Spanish)

Bisnieto/bisnietos. Great-grandchild.

Caballero. Knight.

Cachorro/cachorra/cachorros/cachorras. cah-CHO-rroh. "Cub." Immature *vampiro,* who is unable to shape-shift except to feed.

Casamentero/casamentera. Matchmaker.

Certainement. Certainly.

Cher/chéri/chérie. Dear. (French)

Chou. Cabbage.

Cinco. Five.

Comitiva. "Retinue." Assemblage of *prosaicos* attached to a single *esfera, patrón,* or *vampiro.*

Commandery/commanderies. Garrison of *vampiro* warriors. A large, stable *esfera* has a commandery in every major city (e.g., Dallas, Houston, Austin, etc.) and also at every major strategic point, such as border crossings. They are rarely staffed by *mesnaderos,* since those are always concentrated near the *patrón.* Usage primarily taken from medieval Spanish military orders.

Compañero/compañera/compañeros. "Companion." Someone who drinks *vampiro* blood regularly but has not become a *vampiro.* A *compañero* always has greater strength, speed, senses, and healing powers than a *prosaico.* The anticipated lifespan is a century, while surviving two centuries is extremely rare.

Compañías. com-pah-NYEE-ahs. A company or team of *vampiro* warriors. *Mesnadero compañías* are named for their commander, while *compañías* from a commandery are usually named for their city. A *compañía*'s size can vary considerably, from a dozen *vampiros* up to a hundred or more.

¿*Comprendes?* Do you understand? (The question, using the second personal, informal form of address.)

Concubino compañero. A *compañero* whose duties are confined to those of sex slave.

Cónyuge. CON-yuh-heh. "Spouse" or "partner." Life mate, to whom a *vampiro* is linked by a psychic bond of total trust. The creation of this bond cannot be forced in any way.

Corazón. Heart.

Creador. "Creator." Sire of a *vampiro*.

Cumbia. A flirtatious *Tejano* dance in which couples circle the dance floor.

Dame. Lady. (French)

Dieu. God. (French)

Dios. God.

Dios mediante. God willing.

Doctor/Doctora. Doctor.

Dulce. Sweet.

El Abrazo. "The Embrace." The entire process of becoming a *vampiro*.

Encantado. Enchanted or charmed.

Enchanté. Enchanted. (French)

Escudero. "Shield bearer." Squire.

Esfera/esferas. "Sphere," as in "sphere of influence." A *vampiro* territory, which does not necessarily exactly coincide with a present-day geophysical territory. *Esferas'* boundaries are fluid and frequently fought over. The basic concept is adapted from gangster territories in Prohibition Chicago and New York.

Espada. Sword.

Étalon. Stallion. (French)

Exactement. Exactly.

Excelente. Excellent.

Extase. Ecstasy. (French)

Frère. Brother. (French)

Gracias. Thanks.

Gran. Big.

Heraldo. "Herald." Herald, who is also a diplomat and a spy. Usage is taken from medieval and Renaissance Europe.

Hijo/hija/hijos. E-hoh. "Son/daughter/sons." A *vampiro* sired by a specific *creador.*

Infante/infanta/infantes. Prince/princess/princes.

Juguete. Toy.

La Lujuria. "Lechery." The Rut. Upon awakening as a *vampiro,* every *cachorro* will undergo weeks or months of insanity during which their only goal is to obtain blood and emotion.

Luz. Light.

M'sieu. Sir.

Madre. Mother.

Magnifique. Magnificent. (French)

Mais. But. (French)

Maldita sea. Dammit.

Maman. Mother. (French)

Mano/manos. Hand.

Merci. Thank you. (French)

Merde. Shit. (French)

Mesnadero/mesnaderos. A *vampiro* warrior and a member of a *patrón*'s personal guard. Taken from medieval Spanish, for a member of the royal household guard.

Mierda. Shit.

Mon. My. (French)

Mort. Death. (French)

Nieto/nieta/nietos. Grandchild, grandchildren.

Niña. Daughter.

Nom. Name. (French)

Non. No. (French)

Notre. Our. (French)

Nuestro Señor. "Our liege-lord." The formal form of address for a *patrón,* used by his dependents. Taken from Spanish.

Nunca. Never.

Oui. Yes. (French)

Patrón/patrona/patrones. pah-TRON, pah-TROH-nes. The ruler, who is an absolute monarch, of an *esfera*. He is also usually the *creador* of all the *esfera*'s *vampiros*.

Pequeña. Little lady.

Père. Father. (French)

Perfecto. Perfect.

Pésimo. Dreadful.

Petit/petite. Little. (French)

Pobrecito/pobrecita. Poor little one.

Precisamente. Precisely.

Princesse. Princess. (French)

Prosaico/prosaica/prosaicos. "Prosaic" or "mundane," similar to the Society for Creative Anachronism's usage. A mortal human, neither *vampiro* nor *compañero*. If he has drunk *vampiro* blood, it happened so rarely and in such small quantities that it has not affected his everyday life in any noticeable manner.

Puta. Whore.

Querida. Dear.

Relajate. Relax. (Instruction in Spanish to do so, using a second person, informal form of address.)

S'il vous plaît. If you please, or please. (French)

Sabe Dios. God knows.

Salopard. Bastard or swine.

Santiaguista. san-tyah-GIS-tah. A member of the Order of Santiago, formally known as Saint James of the Sword, one of the three great Spanish military orders and the richest. Santiago based its rule on St. Augustine's but remarkably incorporated married knights, not as *confrères* but as full members. Like other military orders, it had convents of nuns but some sisters were married. The term is used both as a noun and as an adjective.

Santísima. Most holy.

Seguro. Sure (if an adjective), certainty or permission (if a noun).

Seis. Six.

Señorita. Miss. Traditionally, young (or little) lady; the equivalent *"señorito"* means young lord. (Spanish)

SharmuuT. Bastard. (Arabic)

SharmuuTa. Prostitute. (Arabic)

Sí. Yes.

Siete. Seven.

Silencio. Silence. (Instruction in Spanish to do so.)

Siniscal. Seneschal. Responsible for the *patrón*'s entire household and its accounts. The *siniscal* can also call out the *esfera*'s warriors. Taken from fourteenth-century Spanish, but rooted in ninth-century Visigothic.

Sobrino/sobrina. Nephew/niece.

Tío/tía. Uncle/Aunt.

Vampiro/vampira/vampiros. Vampire. Someone who survives on emotional energy carried through human blood. Mature *vampiros* can shapeshift to at least one other form (if only mist) and are resistant to telepathic suggestions.

Vampiro mayor/vampira mayor/vampiros mayores. "Elder vampire." A *vampiro* who has lived for at least three hundred years, can walk in full daylight, and drinks less than a quarter cup of blood per day (except in times of great physical need). He also becomes more and more difficult to detect, even with the heightened senses of other *vampiros mayores*.

Vampiro primero/vampira primera. "Primary vampire." The *vampiro* that a *compañero* is principally interested in drinking blood from. The *compañero* becomes utterly loyal to that *vampiro*, when fed from him long enough. The amount of time needed to form this bond is extremely varied.

Vaquero. "Cowherd." Cowboy.

Verdaderamente. Truly.

Vida. Life.

Virgen. Virgin.

Y. And.

Yaa 'ammo. "Hey, uncle." A term of respect for an older man who does not merit some higher title, such as professor, doctor, king. (Arabic)

Yaa 'abi l-'aziiz. "My dear father." (Arabic)

Yaa ghabi. "Hey, idiot." Not friendly. (Arabic)

Yaa Himaar. "Hey, donkey." Said to someone lacking all subtlety and/or mental powers. (Arabic)

Yaa ibn kalb. "Hey, son of a dog." Very harsh. (Arabic)

Yaa ibn sharmuuTa. "Hey, whoreson." Very harsh. (Arabic)

Yaa ibnii. "My son." (Arabic)

Yaa ibni l-'aziiz. "My dear son." (Arabic)

Yaa kaafir. "Hey, unbeliever." Actually just a statement of fact. (Arabic)

Yixrib beetak. "May God destroy your lineage," as in the family honor, name and line. (Arabic)

A Quick Guide to Pronouncing Spanish

Pronounce almost every vowel and almost every consonant.

If there's an accent over a vowel, emphasize that syllable.

Spanish words are usually pronounced with the stress on the second to the last syllable unless an accent indicates otherwise. Therefore *patrón* is pronounced pah-TRON, not PA-tron; and *patrones* is pah-TROH-nes (which is why it doesn't need an accent over the "O").

Unlike English, each vowel has basically only one sound.

A as in "father."

E as in "ten."

I as in "he." (If found before a vowel, it's almost like the Y in "you.")

O as in "hot." At the end of a syllable, "O" has a soft sound like the O in "note" but without the glide; when it's followed by a consonant in the same syllable, it has a harder sound, like the O in "organ." [See the examples below with *patrones* (soft O) and *patrón* (hard O).]

U as the "oo" in "fool."

The biggest exceptions to the pronouncing of every vowel are: (1) *U* when it follows a *G* or *Q and* precedes an *E* or *I*: The *U* in this case is silent; with *G* it indicates that the *G* has a hard sound (pronounced like "go"), and not the usual soft sound (which is like "home"); and (2) two vowels side by side are pronounced with one sound ("elided") *unless* one of the vowels has an accent. This means that *Santiagu-ista* is pronounced san-tyah-GIS-tah, not san-tee-yah-guh-IS-tah; and *compañía* is pronounced com-pah-NYEE-ah, not com-pah-NYAH.

When followed by an *E* or *I*, *C* is pronounced like "th" (as in "think") in Castilian Spanish but has an "s" sound (like "cent") in American Spanish. When it's followed by an *A*, *O*, *U*, or a consonant, it's pronounced like "c" in "come."

When followed by an *E* or *I*, *G* is pronounced like the *H* in "home"; when it follows an *A*, *O*, *U*, or a consonant, *G* sounds like "go." Therefore *cónyuge* is pronounced CON-yuh-heh, but Rodrigo is roh-DREE-ghoh.

H is silent in Spanish; thus *hijo* is pronounced E-hoh.

J is pronounced like a soft *H*, similar to the "ch" in the Scottish "loch." In Spanish, Mexico and Texas are spelled *Méjico* and *Te-jas* (hence *Tejano* for its native culture).

Double *L* is considered a separate letter in the Spanish language. It's pronounced somewhat like "lli" in "William" in Castilian Spanish, but like "y" in American Spanish. Don Rafael pronounces *caballero* as cah-bah-LLYEH-roh, not cah-bah-YEH-roh, nor cah-bal-LEH-roh.

Ñ sounds like the "ny" in "onion."

Double *R* is pronounced with a trill or rolled like a Scottish *R* (and is treated as a separate letter in Spanish). Thus, *cachorro* is pronounced cah-CHO-rroh, not cah-Chor-roh.

X is pronounced like "ks" in "axis," never like "gz" in "exult."

Y is pronounced like *I* in "bit"; but when preceding a vowel, it's pronounced like *Y* in "yes."

Z is pronounced as "th" (as in "think") in Castilian Spanish but has an "s" sound (like "cent") in American Spanish. Therefore Don Rafael pronounces *"alferez"* as al-FEH-reth, not al-FEH-res.